THE WATCHERS
IN EXILE
BOOK TWO OF
THE WATCHERS OF MONIAH

Barbara V. Evers

New Mythology Press
Coinjock, NC

Chris Kennedy/New Mythology Press
1097 Waterlily Rd.
Coinjock, NC 27923
http://chriskennedypublishing.com/

Publisher's Note: This is a work of fiction. Names, characters, places, and incidents are a product of the author's imagination. Locales and public names are sometimes used for atmospheric purposes. Any resemblance to actual people, living or dead, or to businesses, companies, events, institutions, or locales is completely coincidental.

Cover Design by J Caleb Design.

Ordering Information:
Quantity sales. Special discounts are available on quantity purchases by corporations, associations, and others. For details, contact the "Special Sales Department" at the address above.

The Watchers in Exile/Barbara V. Evers -- 1st ed.
ISBN: 978-1648551161

To my husband, Bruce, and our children and grandchildren. I love each and every one of you.

Acknowledgments

Writing a book is exciting, fulfilling, and often a bit scary. Thank you so much to each person who gave a debut author a chance and read "The Watchers of Moniah." Thank you for picking up the second book in this trilogy, too!

Many people helped with the writing of this series. I will forget someone—I already realized that with the first book—but to anyone who ever gave me encouragement or feedback, thank you. This includes my high school English teacher, Mary Seamon. You were the first adult who told me I could write. Although we only reconnected on social media in the last few years, your encouragement carried me over many barriers and bumps on the road to publication.

As always, I must thank my husband, Bruce, whose support, especially during the editing stages of this book, was so helpful. You accepted my constant disappearances as I waded through changes and struggled to get this one just right. I love you.

My beta readers, Tina, Linda, Sarah, Christina, Roiselyn, and Chris, continue to give me encouragement. Thank you for all you've done to help me write these books and for telling others about them. And I can't forget my writing tribe, the members of the Greenville chapter of SCWA including Marcia, John, Bob, David, Susan, Phil, Adrienne, Valerie, Jim, Roiselyn, Larry, Irena, and Jim. You saw these books in their roughest forms and helped me improve my writing and the stories.

A heartfelt thank you to my editor, Rowe, for embracing this story and characters long before publication became a reality. A special thanks to Beth who helped find typos and any last-minute confusions still in the story.

A special thanks to Jake Clark at J Caleb Designs for creating an amazing cover and making Adana and her world so beautiful.

And, last, but definitely not least, thank you to my publisher, Chris Kennedy, who continues to push me to write and build new worlds.

Map of the Four Kingdoms

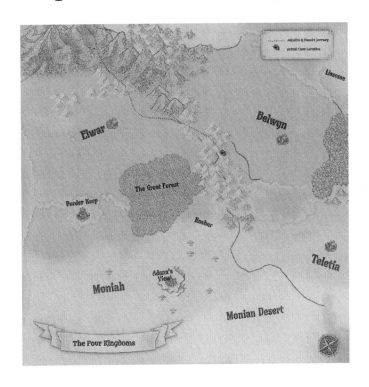

* * * * *

Chapter One

The battle raged behind Adana, heir to the throne of Moniah, as she skirted the huge trees of the forest, keeping a close watch on Lady Elayne. At least, the lady managed to keep pace. The noblewoman still looked dazed. Probably still shocked over the soldier she'd killed moments before.

Adana grabbed the lady's arm and dragged her along, following the telepathic call from Am'brosia. The link with the giraffe faded in and out as she wound her way around the camp. *What could that mean?* She paused. The sounds of pounding feet and strangled shouts approached from the left. She veered right, suppressing the urge to stop and fight. Am'brosia's call resounded in her head. A warning to flee. She headed away from the battle.

At last, visible only from the flickering fires behind them, Adana spotted Joannu, a member of her honor guard.

The Watcher paced beside three saddled horses. "Thank the Creator," Joannu exclaimed as they rushed toward her. The three mounted the horses, but before Adana could spur hers into a run, Joannu grabbed the bridle. "We must move quietly so as not to draw attention."

With a quick nod of acknowledgment, Adana reached out to Am'brosia, feeling the rise and fall of the giraffe's loping stride through their link. "You released Am'brosia and Bai'dish?"

In the gloom, she saw the Watcher nod. "It seemed best. Before the soldiers came for them. Can you sense her? We should find them."

Adana closed her eyes and fought to hold the link, feeling the bond tighten with the stretched tension of distance. "The connection is fading. We must hurry if I'm not to lose her." She pointed to the east. "That way."

Joannu nodded. "Slowly, we're still close to the battle."

It made sense, but Adana glanced back at the skirmish, shame heating her face over fleeing. Elayne had pulled her from sleep and dragged her from the fray, repeating orders from Montee, the First Vision. As heir, she must leave. She knew the truth, while she despised the act. Across the bond, Am'brosia agreed with Montee's directive.

They ducked under low branches and followed Joannu through the dense forest, cries and the clash of swords fading behind them. Joannu kicked her horse into a gallop as they came across a path. The other two followed suit.

Anger shrouded Adana as she fled east. Why had her soldiers attacked each other? Flashes of the battle replayed in her mind. Shouts, the flash of swords in firelight, the crackle of fires eating away her encampment's tents, the smell of burning wood and canvas. Who had attacked them and how? She didn't need to ask why. Too many people objected to her betrothal to Prince Kiffen of Elwar and the joining of the two kingdoms.

Increasing her guard during the trip back to Moniah hadn't prevented an attack. Once again, she wondered if she should have declined the betrothal to Kiffen. Of course, she'd tried, heart breaking at the idea of wedding someone else. Their counselors refused to listen to her or Kiffen, insisting their combined forces would strengthen the kingdoms for the inevitable war.

When the horses emerged from the forest, the three women pushed them into a hard gallop. Joannu rode on Adana's left flank, Elayne on her right, the thuds of hooves the only sound in the night. They reached the top of a slight rise, and Adana slowed her horse and twisted in the saddle to check behind them. A half-moon shone across the landscape. A slight breeze lifted the hair pulled free from her braid and stung scratches on her arms from the struggle with the soldier.

No one in sight. No smoke in the air.

The forest trees lined the horizon as far as she could see. Would the fires set by her attackers burn out or destroy the forest?

"Ballene's fire!" She huffed the expletive, her concerns jumping from alarm over the night's events to concern over a large-scale fire. At least, it appeared they hadn't been followed.

She kicked her horse into a gallop again.

How far had they ridden? Rolling hills rose to meet the horses' hooves as they put distance between them and the forest. Her mind flew along her connection to Am'brosia, trying to determine the location of the giraffe she had been bound to for six years. Am'brosia led the way, along with Bai'dish, the giraffe bonded to Kiffen. The two beasts held a large lead on her small band. Adana recognized the rocking sway as Am'brosia raced across the land without hesitation. The clarity of the image conveyed confidence in their direction. Through Am'brosia's eyes, the landscape resembled the same plains Adana now crossed, the hills dwindling into the flat grasslands of her kingdom, an occasional small herd of animals grazing in the distance.

The giraffe's assurance spilled through the link, a calm awareness of a plan.

Their route continued many leagues east, away from Adana's View, her royal fortress and original destination. Chills ran down her back over how far off track they might be. Her mother always told her to trust the giraffes' instincts. *No other choice at the moment.*

There were greater concerns for now. Where might Maligon's soldiers lurk in the distance? Nothing disturbed the scenery, seen through her eyes or through the giraffe's, but after last night's attack, she didn't trust her sight as much. An odd thought for a Watcher, blessed with the gift of vision, much less the rising heir to Moniah's Seat of Authority.

As the sun peeked above the horizon, warmth crept over her body, a welcome relief to the horrific night. Joannu and Elayne slowed their horses, murmuring sighs of thanks in response to the light of day. None of the three had spoken since the first hurried words as they fled. The sun might provide comfort, but the trio remained silent and vigilant in their flight.

The ground flattened, with an occasional rolling hill interrupting the landscape, and Adana's heart gave a double beat of hope. This was home. Moniah, at last. She glanced over her shoulder. No signs of pursuit.

A blanket of tranquility flooded through the connection from Am'brosia. Adana embraced the peace and paused to let it settle over her. Warmth and gentleness eased the tension in her shoulders, and she got a glimpse of a valley from the giraffe. A stream flowed through the quiet setting. Am'brosia beckoned Adana to hurry. Safety waited there.

How far? A distance, still.

Their horses crested a squat hill. A shallow creek twisted among the rocks and bends below. Their mounts hurried to reach the cool water, not waiting for the women to slide from their backs. The three women slid free of their rides and stretched. Adana checked her horse's saddle and bridle, then moved upstream to fill her water cask. Elayne dropped down on the bank, scooping water into her mouth.

The young woman's dress spread out around her, and Elayne hiked the skirts up to her knees, pulled off her shoes and stockings, and plunged her feet into the water. She turned and grimaced at Adana. "Your leathers make better riding clothes, I believe."

Adana looked down at her sand-brown leather tunic and leggings. On her feet, she wore soft leather boots. What a relief, after three years of living in Elwar, to wear the uniform that fit like a second skin. She nodded to Elayne. "Much better than your dresses. Maybe we can find you something more suitable once we've reached the giraffes."

The sensation of being observed crept over Adana, and she turned to find Joannu's gaze upon her. The Watcher nodded once, then turned to maintain a careful guard over their surroundings. How strange to go from an entire unit of Watchers to protect her to only one. Had the others escaped the battle, or did their bodies lie on the forest floor, returning to the ground?

The thought made her hands shake. And what of her father? Had he escaped? She could ask Am'brosia. The giraffe would know if Va'lent, the regent king's giraffe, had died in response to the ultimate loss, death of the royal bond. She didn't ask, though. And Am'brosia, ever aware of her moods, didn't reveal a thing.

Drying her hands on her tunic, Adana approached Joannu. "I'll watch while you tend to your needs."

Joannu joined Elayne by the water. Laughter between the two women rang in the quiet of the still morning. What could they have to share between them? Adana barely knew Elayne and still hadn't determined whether to trust her or not. She turned her back on them, keeping watch on the horizon.

When Joannu appeared at Adana's side, she turned to the soldier. "What happened? How were we attacked?"

Joannu scanned the horizon, then turned back to Adana. "It wasn't my watch. I was asleep. Montee woke me and Lady Elayne and told us to get you and the giraffes out of the camp."

Montee, her First Vision, the woman marked by the Creator to stand at Adana's side as she ruled. Where was she?

Adana thought about those first confusing moments after Elayne woke her. They had come upon a clearing where two men fought each other. Both men wore Elwarian uniforms. She had drawn an arrow but hesitated, unsure who was the ally and who was not. "Who attacked us?"

Joannu's face remained in a Watcher's stoic mask as she answered. "They attacked from several points around and within the camp. Elwarian soldiers, mostly. I recognized several from one of our right flanking troops."

When Adana left Elwar to return to Moniah, everyone knew of Maligon's attacks against the neighboring kingdoms of Belwyn and Teletia. The traitor, once exiled by her mother, was still alive and renewing his attempts to overtake the four kingdoms. Or it might be his supporters, rebelling now that Adana would take the Seat of Authority.

For this reason, she had ridden out of Elwar in the center of a vast force of Monian Watchers and First Soldiers as well as Elwarian military. Prince Kiffen led one of the left rear flanks, but when they reached the dense forest, the surrounding troops could not stay as close as before. It made sense to strike her there.

Adana swallowed and looked back up the hill. Had Kiffen's own men joined the traitor's forces? Bile rose in her throat, the taste bitter and hot. She leaned toward Joannu, fighting down anger, and asked the one question plaguing her. "Why would Elwarian troops attack us?"

Maligon had struck at her in the forest before. Three years earlier, when she had traveled to Elwar after her mother's death. That day, he used a solitary archer. This time, he struck from within, using her ally's soldiers in his treachery. Who could she trust?

Joannu glanced behind Adana, and she turned to see Elayne approaching them, looking disheveled in her proper lady's dress.

"My lady," Elayne said, "they kept shouting, 'Long live Queen Quilla.'"

Adana shivered at the words. *If Quilla claimed the throne, where was Kiffen's father?* "King Donel?"

Joannu took a deep breath, glanced down for a moment, and then met Adana's gaze. "Killed."

Kiffen, her betrothed, fatherless. Adana swallowed. That made him, officially, King of Elwar despite Quilla's actions. His stepmother, never endearing herself to Adana, seized the power that was rightfully Kiffen's. Was she part of Maligon's supporters or had she chosen this time of unrest to serve her own desires?

At least, she wouldn't have to pretend to like the woman anymore.

"You're sure of this?"

Joannu snorted. "The attackers kept shouting it as they fought. 'Donel is dead. Long live Queen Quilla!'" She swallowed, then added, "'Death to Kiffen.'"

Adana rushed toward her horse. "I need to find Kiffen."

"Adana. No."

She halted at the words. How long had it been since Joannu had called her by her first name? She turned and found the Watcher had moved forward and braced to stop her.

Elayne glanced between them. She laid a gentle hand on Adana's arm. "My lady, your Watcher is correct. You cannot go after Kiffen."

Of course, they were right. She must move on. Moniah needed her to return. Going back could endanger all of them, but going forward would take her farther from Kiffen, wherever he was. Had his camp survived the night, or did they suffer the same fate?

She took several focused breaths to fight the emotions tearing up her insides.

Am'brosia's mind nudged Adana's shoulder in the precise spot where Montee had pricked her skin during the recognition ceremony on her eighteenth birthday. Just days ago, but it felt like years. Strength radiated from the spot. A puncture, now healed, destined to help her know right from wrong, good from evil. Ever since the ceremony in Elwar's court, the strange concoction infused in the pin provided warning or strength to her soul when she needed it, and it reinforced her connection to Am'brosia.

Through her tie to Am'brosia, she saw the two giraffes together, and beyond them, an image of Kiffen. The image was hazy. Kiffen was not with them, but the message was clear. He lived.

She sighed with thanks for the news and the enhanced gift of the potion that helped her understand Am'brosia better.

A tiny voice in her head reminded her the potion also served to strengthen her awareness of the Creator's wishes, to make her aware of his plans for her in leading Moniah. The ceremony claimed her to be the Creator's chosen, the person who stood to protect the people. The Creator must be laughing at her for daring to ask for what she wanted, betrothal to Kiffen. Quick to show her failings, the Creator destroyed the only peace of her world. How would the Teachers of the Faith explain that?

Tentatively, she pushed on the link with Am'brosia and pictured a distinct image of Kiffen and Bai'dish. She held her breath. Could she sense his condition through Am'brosia or had her overuse of drunkenberry stunted that ability? If not, would Am'brosia recognize her mistress' need to know more of how Kiffen fared?

Seconds ticked by.

In a rush, a clear image came to her. Bai'dish stood beside Am'brosia as they watched the horizon. No weakness showed in the animal's stance.

Tension seeped out of her shoulders. Kiffen was strong and safe. She looked up to find Joannu and Elayne staring at her. She smiled, blinking back tears of relief.

"Am'brosia showed you something," Joannu said.

She nodded and chuckled at the confused look on Elayne's face.

"I thought you were having a fit," Elayne said. "Your body froze. Your eyes...they didn't roll back but...it looked strange."

The smile on Joannu's face was friendly. "Elayne, you have much to learn about our world." She turned to Adana. "What did you see, my lady?"

"Bai'dish standing strong beside Am'brosia."

"That is good news."

Elayne glanced between them, her frown deepening. "Bai'dish? The giraffe? What does that mean?"

Could the woman have missed so many details over the last week? Adana tried to fit this into the puzzle of Elayne, the companion she never wanted, but out of respect, accepted from an old friend.

"Kiffen is bonded to Bai'dish, as I am bonded to Am'brosia. If Kiffen were unwell, Bai'dish would be, too." She started toward their horses. "We must go. The giraffes are ahead of us and impatient."

"You learned that from the giraffe, too?" Elayne stared into the distance as if she might spot the giraffes.

"Yes. They are not far, but we still have a ride ahead of us. Both stood alert, watching the horizon. Their location is safe for the moment."

As they remounted their horses, Elayne turned toward her. "I heard, when Prince Serrin died, Bai'dish should have died too. Because of the bond. But the giraffe lived."

"That is true." This news, old for three years, perplexed many. Her first betrothed, Serrin, had died the same day as her mother.

Serrin and Bai'dish had begun the bonding process, but Bai'dish had survived Serrin's death. Only after Montee received a prophetic vision from the Creator had they begun to understand. Bai'dish held the bond at a distance with Adana's first betrothed, Prince Serrin of Elwar. Somehow, he had managed to bond with Kiffen, Serrin's elder brother. And the Creator's games continued to plague her.

"Then how do you know Kiffen is alive?" Elayne interrupted Adana's thoughts. "If Bai'dish lived while Serrin died, couldn't the same be true, now?"

Adana sagged in the saddle, the question frightening her for a moment.

Joannu answered for her. "When Serrin fell ill, Bai'dish did too. We expected Bai'dish to die. There was no reason not to, but somehow, he broke the bond or ignored it. After Serrin's death, he returned to health."

Elayne looked thoughtful as their horses plodded up the hill and onto the flatter plains. "I didn't think that was possible."

Adana paused her horse and turned to face the woman. "No one did."

"But the bond should have killed him?"

"Elayne, we can discuss this later." Adana spoke in a sharp tone. "For now, we must ride."

As they crossed the creek and continued south, Elayne ventured one more question. "If Am'brosia dies, will you?"

Adana slowed the horse but didn't stop. Would the woman's questions never cease?

Elayne drew up beside her, a concerned frown deepening between her eyes.

Unsure whether to trust the woman's visible worry, Adana considered Elayne. After the announcement of her betrothal to Kiffen, the Earl of Brom's son, Pultarch, attacked the prince in a jealous rage. Pultarch, among many others, thought he would become her betrothed. Now this young woman, a gift in apology for the nobleman's rash actions, rode by her side as a companion. One of only two companions still with her. As a spy determined to follow her or just coincidence?

With a sigh of frustration, she said, "No. The bond doesn't affect me the same way."

A chill ran through her bones as she recalled the reasons why Maligon had turned on her mother twenty-five years earlier. He had pursued the queen's hand in marriage, and she had rejected him.

Had Pultarch chosen the same path?

Did Elayne serve Pultarch or Adana?

She spurred her horse forward, not looking at Lady Elayne. She didn't mention the overwhelming despair she would experience for the rest of her life if Am'brosia did die.

* * * * *

Chapter Two

Pultarch struggled behind a soldier's horse, his wrists bound and tied to the saddle. The soldier chuckled and yanked on the rope, throwing Pultarch off balance. A long, disorderly line of rough-looking soldiers led the way. Behind them, wagons trundled over the grasslands, threatening to roll over Pultarch if he lost his footing.

The night had been a long and confusing one. He had awoken at the first cries of men in their camp. The soldier watching over him shot a warning look at Pultarch and ordered, "Stay here." Then he had rushed from the tent.

The cries of men and the clash of battle had drawn closer as Pultarch struggled into his gear. Outside the tent, he heard a grunt and thud, then two Elwarian soldiers jerked open the flap of the tent.

At first, he thought they were Kiffen's men taking the opportunity to harass him while the prince was away from camp. Most of Elwar's soldiers despised Pultarch and had witnessed his jealous attack on the prince the day after the announcement of the prince's betrothal to Adana.

The first soldier grabbed his arm and dragged him through the opening. The second soldier followed. At the sight of a body sprawled on the ground, Pultarch halted. The second soldier shoved him forward, and he fought to keep his balance as he stumbled over the body. The prone soldier's eyes stared at the sky, unblinking. Blood spilled from his mouth.

Around them, shadows rose and fell in flickering firelight. Men cried out in alarm and pain. Two men fell to the ground in a heated struggle in front of Pultarch.

He jumped back in shock. The reality of what he saw hit him like a blow to the stomach. Elwarian fought Elwarian.

Pultarch struggled against his captors, eager to fight, to join the battle and discover why his countrymen fought each other, but they pulled him away from the fighting.

"What's happening?" he said, struggling to turn back toward the conflict.

"Justice." The second soldier shoved him in the other direction with as much force as he used to spit out the word.

"Whose?" Pultarch struggled to turn back. His size was enough to overcome one of these men, but the two combined proved more than his match.

"The queen's." The second soldier continued to push him forward. "Now stop your questions before I make you."

Pultarch bit back the name of the only queen he cared for, Adana. Hope settled in his shoulders, and he submitted to the rough treatment without complaint. If Adana sent the attack on Kiffen's camp, it meant only one thing. She despised Kiffen and refused his betrothal.

His captors dragged him to the rear of the camp where a few soldiers stood guard over the horses. Neither the soldiers nor horses had been part of Kiffen's original unit.

They handed him off to one of the guards. "Tie him up. We found him in the prince's tent. We will take him back to camp and let him answer to the Lord."

The sounds of battle died away as a distant glow in the east announced the approach of morning. His two captors returned and took Pultarch's ropes. They dragged him back through the carnage of battle pausing at different bodies. "Which one is Prince Kiffen?"

Injured and dead soldiers littered the ground amidst the nauseating smell of blood, sweat, and released bowels. Pultarch choked back a surge of vomit burning his throat.

He had scanned the ground for any sign of Kiffen's body, shying away from one man's bloody hand groping for help. With Elwarian soldiers as attackers and defenders, he had no way of knowing which of the fallen were Adana's supporters and which were loyal to Kiffen. Would he feel relief or despair if he spotted Kiffen dead or injured? He never learned the answer to that question. The prince's body wasn't there.

Now, as the sun broke over the horizon, Pultarch trudged behind the soldiers and listened to them mutter about the prince's cowardice. Kiffen a coward? If only they were right, but he knew the truth. The prince had left camp to ride to Adana's aid.

If Adana attacked this camp, how had she responded when her betrothed ran to her rescue? Did she embrace him, then drive a knife in his back? Was he bound like Pultarch?

Shame followed the pleasure he felt over the thought. Kiffen was once his best friend, but Adana's loveliness ended that.

His captor yanked the rope and laughed at Pultarch's attempts to stay upright, but the young lord smiled. Adana would punish these men later for mistreating her love.

Around midday, the soldiers climbed over a rise, and Pultarch lurched to a halt at the sight before him. Thousands of soldiers milled around tents that reached far into the distance.

How had their troops missed the evidence of such a large force? The answer came faster than he expected. A woman dressed in a Watcher's uniform approached them. He studied her for a moment before he realized why she looked odd to him. Her long, reddish-brown hair flowed over her shoulders, glinting in the bright sunlight. The only Watcher he had ever seen without the mandatory braided hair was Adana, and only when she wore Elwarian clothes.

Two other Watchers jogged past him, their hair bound in battle braids. The three Watchers conferred, casting glances in his direction. With a nod, the first dismissed them and then sauntered toward Pultarch.

She scrutinized him, her lip curling in displeasure. Then she turned to his captors. "I understand you allowed Kiffen to escape. I told Father he should have sent me."

The two soldiers stared straight ahead, voices silent. Pultarch grinned at their discomfort under the woman's scrutiny.

"Nothing? No defense?" She strutted back and forth, glaring down on them like filth. "Imbeciles. That fiercely loyal Rolanna was part of his Watcher detail, and she's missing, too. Someone probably gave him advance warning." The woman turned her angry gaze on Pultarch. "Who are you?"

His grin faded.

A Watcher would know him by name if not by his face. Did she act by Adana's command? Hope swelled in his chest at the idea, but he knew he must proceed with care until he discovered whether this Watcher served Adana or not. Pride straightening his back, he attempted to speak in a strong voice. "I am Pultarch, the son of—"

"Ah, our heir to the Earl of Brom. How interesting to find you in the prince's bed." She smirked at him. "Did he abandon you, too?"

The words stung, and he wanted to punch the smugness from her face.

She waited, her head cocked to the side, but Pultarch stared straight ahead, not saying any more. Behind him, Horace and his soldiers chuckled at his discomfort.

"So, you're not talking? Well, the Lord will see about that, won't he? Bring him." She turned and walked toward the center of the camp without looking back.

Horace laughed as he dragged Pultarch along. "Smart to keep your mouth shut, boy. The Lord doesn't appreciate mistreatment of his daughter, the Lady Kalara."

"Aww, Lorent," said the other soldier, "why warn him? We could have had a bit of fun at his mistakes, ya know."

"Who is the Lord?" Pultarch found himself asking before he thought better of it. Why had they called that Watcher the Lady Kalara? Watchers rejected noble titles once they were accepted into service.

"You'll see." They stopped in front of a large tent flying four banners—the lion of Elwar, the giraffe of Moniah, the eagle of Belwyn, and the war horse of Teletia. Pultarch only had a moment to ponder the meaning behind all four flags flying in one place.

Lady Watcher Kalara waited at the tent's entrance, flanked by two heavily armed guards. "He is most interested in meeting you." She grabbed Pultarch by the arm and shoved him into the tent.

He stumbled and fell face first into the dirt. As he struggled to regain his footing in the darkened enclosure, he heard a deep grumble of displeasure. A pair of purple velvet slippers appeared just inches in front of his nose. Twisting his face out of the dirt, Pultarch looked up.

A man swathed in a cape made from the same cloth as his slippers peered down at him. Struggling to right himself, Pultarch rolled to his side and met the intrigued gaze of the older man, gray-haired, but still with strength in his posture. With the toe of his slipper, the man poked Pultarch's shoulder, rocking him onto his back.

"For Ballene's sake, someone help him up." The man returned to a large chair and dropped into it. "And unbind him."

Large hands lifted Pultarch and set him on his feet. With a quick slash of a knife, the ropes fell to the floor.

Blood flow prickled back into his hands, and Pultarch rubbed them, encouraging the circulation, while he studied the man.

The purple-robed man stared at him over a pair of templed hands, one disfigured beyond any use.

Pultarch blinked in surprise at the deformity, his mind forming the name of a traitor. Maligon, the man sentenced to death by exile into the deep desert. Could Maligon truly be alive and seated before him, a mere two steps away?

Maligon had destroyed many and created havoc for the kingdoms in his father's time. He should be alarmed, but for some inexplicable reason, he felt peace under the man's gaze.

He glanced around for Adana just to be sure she wasn't there. His hopes of her presence drained from him as fast as the blood rushed into his numb hands. The pain of her absence felt the same.

"You are Pultarch, Sarx's hope for success?" The man still studied him, but his face held a curious smile.

Sarx's hope?

A kind laugh burst forth from the man. "Sit down, my boy. Have some wine."

Dumbfounded, Pultarch dropped into the nearest chair and seized the cup a servant offered him. He gulped the wine, the lush flavors lost in his haste. Wine trickled down his chin.

Maligon offered him a towel. "Slow down. There's plenty."

Pultarch wiped his chin, looked up into the smiling brown eyes of the man, and felt a sense of belonging. Was it truly Maligon? "I am sorry, but you have the advantage. I do not know—"

"My name? No, of course you do not. Sarx would not have mentioned me, would he?"

"Why do you keep mentioning Sarx? What does he have to do with…" He paused. With what? Sarx commiserated with him when Adana chose Kiffen over Pultarch. Did Sarx work for Adana? Or was some other plan unfolding before him?

"You will come to understand very soon. But first, introductions must be made. I am known as the Lord."

"Lord of what?"

"Why everything, of course. I have been gone for many years, but I'm back, and this time, they won't send me away." Anger sparked in the man's eyes for a moment, then he smiled, and the fury faded. He leaned toward Pultarch. "We have much to do, Pultarch. With me, you will gain your dream."

"My dream?"

"Come now. You haven't forgotten your heart's desire so soon have you?"

Pultarch's heart pounded in his chest. Adana. "But how?"

The man smiled and settled back in the chair. "The how will come soon enough. Just know, Adana will be yours."

Elation pumped through Pultarch's veins. He would have her, and Kiffen…

"What about Kiffen?"

The deformed hand waved the concern away. "Just a gnat in the drinking water. He will be dealt with."

Pultarch smiled. "Will I get to deal with him?"

The Lord laughed. "Yes, I believe Sarx chose correctly in you. By all means, son, if the opportunity presents itself, you may deal with the mighty Kiffen."

A broad smile stretched across Pultarch's face. He settled back in the chair and took another glass of wine. After a moment, he said, "Lord, I am pleased to meet you."

* * * * *

Chapter Three

By late afternoon, Adana and her companions found the secluded valley where Am'brosia and Bai'dish waited. A river flowed southwest through the area, the shallows clear, with silver flashes of fish. A few trees lined the banks, providing shade without blocking the view. The surrounding hills were low and abundant with flowers, their perfumes wafting on the air. Flutterbys danced among the blossoms, their fragile wings redirected by a slight breeze that lifted the hair that had pulled loose from Adana's braid.

Am'brosia and Bai'dish stood sentry on a mound rising from the center of the small valley, their long necks and keen sight adding to their ability to warn of anyone's approach.

Adana extended her mind into the link with Am'brosia and saw beyond the valley, empty of pursuers, the grasslands extending to the horizon. The sky remained clear, no churned-up dust from an encampment or army on the move clouding the view.

Joannu took the first watch with the giraffes while Elayne tended to the horses.

Adana wandered along the river, gathering firewood, as she focused on the events of the night. Who survived? A deep sense of loss tightened her chest at the thought of kind-hearted King Donel. Unlike his second wife, he had provided a calm in the storms Quilla rained on Adana during her exile in Elwar. If the rumors were true, Kiffen was an orphan.

She longed to wrap her arms around him. If Kiffen knew about his father, he would prefer she didn't give solace. The man she knew preferred to hide his feelings. Maybe, when they finally found each other, she could convince him to soften his stiff demeanor. At times, he appeared more stoic than her Watchers, a feat hard to imagine if she hadn't witnessed it.

Wood laid for a fire, Adana worked at coaxing a small flame to life, glad to see three years in Elwar hadn't diminished her skill. She settled beside the fire, staring into the flames. Images of burning tents danced in the small blaze.

Unease forced her to her feet. She studied her surroundings again, seeking to look through Am'brosia's eyes. The sun setting in the distance hid most of the landscape, but to a Watcher's eyes, details could still be seen. Nothing stirred. All remained quiet.

With a sigh, she sat down and searched through her pack for something to eat, finding little. A short while later, Elayne wandered up with a string of fish.

"There's plenty of food for us here." She reached into a pocket in her dress and pulled out a handful of large, red berries. "There's a large patch of sweet berries on the hill. I don't think the rabbits will mind if we take a few."

Adana accepted a handful and bit into the largest one. She moaned as the sweet juice rippled across her tongue.

Elayne smiled. "I haven't baked fish with berries over an open fire in a long time." She squatted by the fire and began to clean the fish.

The comment surprised Adana, and she sat back studying the lady. "You've cooked over an open fire?"

Elayne glanced up, her eyes wide for a brief moment. Then she smiled. "As a child. With my brothers. I insisted on going on their campouts with Father. They allowed it but made me do all the cooking."

Adana returned her smile and added this to the tiny bits of information she had learned about the lady.

The three ate and lingered by the fire until well after nightfall. Standing to dust off her clothing, Joannu said, "I'll take the first watch of the night. The giraffes need sleep, too. We'll let them rest until morning. I'll wake you in a few hours to take over."

* * *

Adana dreamed of fires shooting high in the night sky and of people fighting. She ran through the trees searching, searching, but always ended up where she started.

A nudge from Am'brosia pulled her from the dream. The sun peeked above the horizon. Joannu hadn't wakened her. She sought the link to ensure all was safe and saw Montee approaching. The First Vision, the highest-ranking Watcher and main advisor to Adana, greeted Joannu who stood on the rim of the valley.

The soldier strode down the slope and knelt before Adana. Her shoulders heaved once before she spoke. "My lady, forgive me."

For the second time in Adana's life, she found herself staring down at the perfect seam dividing Montee's hair into a braid. Even as the heir to the Seat of Authority, this was one Watcher she never felt comfortable looking down upon. Montee's role in Adana's life had shifted from her teacher to First Vision, and now, when she needed the advisor most, the soldier had dropped into the role of supplicant.

"Forgive you? For what? I am safe, thanks to your quick actions. Am'brosia tells me Prince Kiffen is safe." Adana's gaze returned to Montee's perfect braid, not a strand out of place. She hesitated, wondering at the woman's humility. A cold fist formed in her belly. "Rise and report."

Montee lifted her eyes to meet Adana's. She didn't rise but spoke in a voice just above a whisper. "They attacked from several directions at once. I moved to protect you, not your father."

Adana stiffened. Montee gazed up at her with deep green eyes, but Adana saw her father's blue ones staring back at her instead.

"One of the soldiers guarding his tent betrayed you. Your father is…" Montee took a deep breath. "Your father did not survive."

Adana's throat closed with tears. She struggled to swallow the rising pain. Focused breathing, the first skill a Watcher learned, provided little comfort. This she remembered from her mother's death.

Still, she tried. Holding out her hand to pause Montee's report, Adana inhaled through her nose, then exhaled through her lips in a quiet hiss, one slow breath at a time.

After several breaths, several, but not enough, Adana refocused her gaze on Montee. "What else?"

"Elwarian soldiers attacked. Joined by many from within our units."

Adana recalled the two men she witnessed fighting as they fled camp in the night. Both wore Elwarian uniforms, and one had been part of the troops chosen to escort her safely to Moniah. An Elwarian soldier provided by King Donel. She had hesitated, her arrow nocked and bow drawn. She hadn't known which one to shoot.

Anger over this treachery and the strange twist of fate flooded her body. Her shoulder burned deep inside the puncture wound. It ached as if the pin still stuck in her shoulder. She fought to keep her breathing controlled. At least, the rising frustration cleared the tears from her throat, but she fought the urge to scream insults at the Creator.

Turning her back on Montee, Adana marched up the rise toward Am'brosia.

King Donel dead.

Her father dead.

Quilla on Elwar's throne.

Kiffen alive.

Kiffen alive? The attack came from Elwar. Was Kiffen involved?

Horror burned in her chest, making each breath a painful drag of inhalation. Did he seek power through their betrothal? The night of their betrothal, rioters outside Elwar's castle had claimed that. She thought over her last few days in Elwar. Their happiness was real, based on true feelings. Wasn't it?

Expanding her link with Am'brosia, she formed an image, foreign and painful to consider, of Kiffen standing over her, sword in hand, ready to strike her down. She saw herself cringe and sink beneath his attack.

Am'brosia's head swung toward her. "No!"

Adana stopped mid-stride. Had Am'brosia just spoken to her through the link? The golden beast tramped down the slope and stopped a few steps away, towering over her. She recognized the giraffe's intent but couldn't move fast enough. Am'brosia's great head butted her shoulder, hitting the spot of the pinprick. The giraffe's single word resounded in Adana's brain again as she toppled to the ground. "No."

Her shoulder burned with intense heat.

"My lady?" Elayne rushed up the slope toward her.

Adana took a cleansing breath before pushing up from the ground, her back to Elayne. She eyed Am'brosia with caution and brushed the grass off her tunic. The answer echoed in her mind once more, overwhelming her with a mix of confusing emotions. The sting in her shoulder brought tears to her eyes as she confronted the truth. Her father, separated from her three years ago, was gone forever. Never again would she hear his voice or look into his kind eyes.

He wouldn't stand by her side as she took Moniah's Seat of Authority. Her father, gone.

Yet, Kiffen, the man she desired even when she knew the impossibility of such a match, had been given to her. He lived and was hers forever. Did the fulfillment of her desires steal the lives of her father and King Donel? She shook with the effort to regain her composure. Nothing could hold back the strange combination of relief and sorrow.

The reassuring bulk of Am'brosia stood before her, and she moved toward the giraffe, but this time, the animal stepped sideways, away from her. The great head swung toward her again, but this time, with a gentle sweep, Am'brosia nudged her toward Elayne. The woman took one look at Adana's face and wrapped her arms around her.

Adana fell into Elayne's arms and cried out her pain and anger and guilt, unable to hold back, even though Elayne might be her enemy. The woman stroked her back and murmured sounds of comfort, none registering in Adana's mind beyond their intended purpose.

After a few moments, Adana straightened and stepped out of Elayne's embrace. She wiped her eyes before glancing toward her Watchers. Montee stood at the bottom of the hill, wary and tense. Joannu stood at the center of the top of the rise with Bai'dish. Both scanned the horizon, sentries over their small band.

When Adana again swiped at her eyes with the palms of her hands, Elayne pushed a frilly handkerchief into her grasp. The tatted lace rendered it an accessory rather than useful, but she appreciated the woman's kindness. The contrast between this handkerchief, given in compassion, and the knife the woman wielded in Adana's protection two nights earlier struck Adana.

"You saved my life," she said, recalling the soldier who attacked her during their escape. She had struggled under his weight as he held her pinned to the ground. One moment, she felt true fear, and the next, the soldier's body went limp. "You killed that soldier who attacked me. He would have killed me."

Elayne swallowed and licked her lips. "I didn't think about it. I just did it."

"Thank you." Adana squeezed the woman's hands then turned and descended the hill, seeking strength with each step. When she reached Montee, she motioned for her to sit and waved Joannu over to join them. She turned toward Am'brosia and Bai'dish, sending a request for them to maintain lookout. A brief flash of indignation flew down the link from Am'brosia. Even briefer, she sensed a flicker of amusement from Bai'dish.

The giraffes' reactions spoke volumes about the complications of her three-year separation from Am'brosia while exiled in Elwar. She wondered if Bai'dish's amusement stemmed from his recent bonding with Kiffen. It felt like him.

Under normal circumstances, she would have taught Kiffen how to communicate with Bai'dish years ago, but now they both must learn. Her mother's decision to remove her from Moniah at such a crucial point in her training still baffled her. It hadn't stopped Maligon. As far as she could tell, it hadn't protected her from anything, either. It only served to complicate her training and keep her from her kingdom.

Aware her companions waited, uncertain of her thoughts, she turned toward them. Joannu came toward her and dropped to the ground, her eyes downcast. Montee, alert as always, scanned the valley, tension in her shoulders the only sign she still shouldered the responsibility for Adana's loss.

"Montee," Adana said, "your apology is unnecessary. We knew the risks when we departed Elwar. My father…" Adana swallowed at the sudden catch in her voice. "My father knew the risks."

She turned toward Joannu, surprised when the Watcher's eyes remained downcast. She could not recall a time when Joannu had not met her gaze.

"Joannu?"

The Watcher raised her head, but she bowed it again before she spoke. "My Queen?"

Adana's knees weakened. In a few weeks, the title would be hers, but with her father's death, coronation or not, she was Queen of Moniah, the Seat of Authority.

Oh Mammetta, how I wish you were here.

As if summoned, she heard her mother's voice. "Adana, when you are queen, you must stand firm. No matter how unprepared you may feel, don't show it to your Watchers or your people. They must see your confidence in all that happens. Never show doubt or weakness to them."

At least her Watcher's training had prepared her for this. She knew how to hide her thoughts behind a calm façade. Envisioning her mother's royal demeanor, she squared her shoulders and assumed a straight and commanding posture. Then, in the same tone her mother used time and again, she said, "Joannu, look to me."

The Watcher looked up. Eyes wide with sorrow, she had chosen to reveal her emotions rather than mask them, a gesture of great honor from a Watcher.

Adana breathed in deeply and inhaled the smells of the wood fire, the action drawing her back to her own training, a time focused on her obligations, her future as queen. "Joannu, I am your queen and your Seat of Authority. Thank you for reminding me of that." She broke eye contact and glanced toward Montee, noting the woman's nod of approval. "I'm counting on you and Montee to ensure I stay your queen and live to sit on the Seat of Authority."

The fire Adana had built crackled and popped as she waited, allowing those words to resonate within them. Finally, she asked, "Do you have any plans? How we move forward?"

"Yes." Joannu's voice rang in the firm confidence of her rank, a Strategist Leader of the Watchers.

"Good." Adana turned to Montee. "What do the two of you suggest?"

With a stick, Montee sketched a rough map in the dirt, pointing first to a spot to the west. "We are two to three days from the Border Keep. Four from Adana's View." She marked a point to their south. "That's if we encounter no trouble."

Adana pondered the map. The keep sat on the border between the two kingdoms, the original seat of royalty before Yarada's ruler divided his kingdom in half for his two daughters, Elwar and Moniah. Adana's View, her home, beckoned to her, but four days without knowledge of the enemy's whereabouts would make the journey treacherous.

"Our plans were to head for whichever was closer if we encountered trouble." Montee squinted up at her. "The giraffes took us in a different direction."

Adana studied the map and reached out to Am'brosia, scanning the area through the giraffe's watchful gaze. Still nothing of concern stirred within sight. Why had they sent her east instead of west?

"Where is the nearest village?"

"A half-day's journey in that direction." Montee jabbed the stick at a point to the southeast.

An excited tingle whizzed in her shoulder. Approval?

"What of our troops? You followed us. Did you encounter anyone? People you trust?"

Montee shook her head. "I ordered Sinti and Veana to scout a larger area along your escape route while I followed your path." She glanced up the hill. "Am'brosia and Bai'dish led you to an obscure location. They did well. I've never crossed this valley, and its features are not on any of our maps."

The tingle in her shoulder hummed with energy when she turned her attention to Elayne. The woman squatted beside them as best she could in her Elwarian dress, but she didn't seem to mind or exhibit any discomfort. A notion about this new companion had plagued Adana since their entry into the forest.

At first, she had thought Elayne showed latent signs of a Watcher's abilities, but when she and Montee tested the lady, she didn't exhibit any enhanced visual skills. Still, Elayne noticed things others didn't.

She'd had plenty of time to contemplate the woman's comments about the sounds in the forest. Distant bird songs Adana could not hear without straining to pick them out. Then, Elayne had led Adana toward safety as the battle raged around them, veering the right way every time, except for when the soldier jumped her. And there had been the storm that rolled in on the night before the caravan entered the forest. Elayne knew of it without seeing the lightning in the far distance. She'd heard the thunder long before most people could see or hear the storm.

Adana scratched her shoulder, the energy vibrating from the puncture creating an aggravating itch. Might as well pursue her suspicions.

"Elayne? Do you hear horses in the distance?"

"Horses?" A frown crossed Elayne's face.

"Yes, are there any approaching riders?"

A furrow divided Elayne's brow, causing her to squint. She tilted her head and closed her eyes.

Adana watched carefully, looking for signs of when or if Elayne dropped into pure concentration. The woman inhaled as she settled her mind and relaxed her body. A subtle clue to potential gifts, but she'd take it. Her actions resembled a Watcher's focused breathing.

Elayne released each breath through her mouth, then tilted her head to the left, paused, and then tilted it to the right. Her breathing became slower.

Confidence radiated warmth deep within Adana's shoulder as she strained to listen for what Elayne might hear. A log on the fire popped. A fish splashed in the stream. Their horses stomped and snorted. Those were the only sounds she heard, but what about Elayne? The thunder. The faint bird songs. Did she possess a different gift?

A look of wonder and surprise spread over Elayne's face as her eyes popped opened. She scanned the sky with excitement.

"No one approaches, but I heard—" She pointed upward. A hawk, with a small animal clutched in its claws, flew overhead.

She jumped to her feet and turned to watch the bird soar away, then she spun back to look at them, a grin spreading over her face. "I heard it." The words tumbled out of her. "There was a whistle of wind, a thud, and a squeak, then wings beating so loud they drowned out the mouse's struggles." She took a step in the direction the hawk had flown.

Montee's eyebrows shot up. Joannu twisted to look after the hawk.

Adana smiled. "Montee?"

Silence settled over the First Vision as she scanned the sky. "She's a Listener," Montee whispered.

"A what?" Elayne asked.

"A Listener?" Joannu leaned forward. "I thought Listeners were bedtime stories."

"They disappeared centuries ago." Montee turned toward Adana. "How long have you suspected?"

"A few days. Ever since the—"

"The storm," Montee said.

Fighting back a self-satisfied grin, Adana nodded.

Elayne crossed her arms. "What are you talking about?" She paused, a look of loss and fear settling over her face. "Please don't talk over me. What is a Listener?"

Adana smiled at her and patted the ground, inviting her to sit back down. Did the woman know and hide the truth or was she truly ignorant of her gifts? It would be useful to have a Listener working for her, though. If she could trust her.

"I've never met one. Tradition says they died out centuries ago, but Listeners possess keen hearing. They specialize in eavesdropping."

* * * * *

Chapter Four

Adana felt a surge of triumph when Elayne blushed at the mention of eavesdropping. Her mother's deathbed decree may have taken Adana from Moniah and intensive Watcher training, but the strange environment in the mountains of Elwar taught her different observation skills. Maybe the time in Elwar hadn't been a waste.

Joannu leaned forward, excitement spreading a smile across her face. "You have, haven't you? You've eavesdropped on people."

Elayne shrugged. Her hands fidgeted in the lap of her skirt. She didn't make eye contact. "It made life easier."

They sat in stunned silence.

"Can you sing? On tune?" Montee asked.

Elayne nodded.

"Imitate sounds?"

"Imitate sounds?" Elayne spoke in an exact imitation of Montee's voice and inflection.

Joannu clapped her hand over her mouth.

"Amazing." Montee tilted her head to the side as she examined the younger woman. "A Listener."

Adana reached into her belt and touched the lacey edges of the useless handkerchief Elayne had given her. The gesture, small and simple, spoke of a woman who cared for others. She had killed the soldier attacking Adana, and even Am'brosia had pushed Adana into the lady's embrace. The urge to trust Elayne came at a price if the woman's loyalties fell with the wrong people, but to have a Listener in her midst, helping her? She could not resist this gift.

Eyes still on the ground, the confidence Elayne exhibited when she heard the hawk appeared to have flown away as fast as the bird with its meal.

"Do you know the story of the Gifted Ones?" Adana leaned down and tried to peer into Elayne's downturned face.

Eyes round with fear, she said, "My mam, uh, mother used to speak of them, but Father made her stop telling the story. I was quite young. I don't remember much."

Mam was not the word of a noble, but of a farmer. Adana glanced at Montee. The First Vision had caught the slip, too, and she inspected the woman with a hawk-eyed stare.

Despite Elayne's slip, Adana decided to extend some acceptance to the woman. Maybe her nobility sprang from a more rural area. Besides, she needed a Listener.

"I will tell you the story." She turned toward Montee, afraid the woman would discourage her, but the First Vision sat back and waited.

Seeking the correct words, yet knowing a Memory Keeper would provide a better delivery, Adana leaned her elbows on her knees and studied the fire before she spoke.

In the early years of Yarada, the kingdom was a safe place. All people within a season's journey from the castle were loyal subjects of the crown. Beyond the borders of Yarada lay an empty, barren land. No one ventured there, and no visitors ever crossed the mountains or deserts into Yarada. Yaradanes believed they represented all the Creator's people.

One day, an injured farmer rode into the castle, warning of an army from the north, killing and burning everything in their path as they marched south.

The king and queen rushed to the Temple to seek guidance from the Creator. The whole village joined them, kneeling before the altar, begging for assistance. Close to one hundred people gathered there, and the Creator called on his Teachers of the Faith to divide them into four specific groups.

Adana glanced at Montee and Joannu, gracing them with a smile of fondness. This was their story, too. The origin of the Watchers.

To the first group, the Teacher spoke of special gifts from the Creator. "You will be known as Watchers," he said to this group, all women, young and old alike. "As Watchers, you will prophesy through your dreams and provide advanced warning of events to come. The Creator will enhance the clarity of your vision so you will always see what is coming and be able to strike a target even at a great distance. Your weapons of choice will be the archer's bow and knife. From now on, you will observe and recall minute details of your surroundings and be able to discern changes around you that most will miss. Danger often arrives through subtle clues, and you will note and report on those."

Adana paused and studied Elayne before continuing. "You notice small things, little details that hint at more. That's why I first thought you might be a Watcher. But I suspect you descend from the second group."

The young woman swallowed, her throat bobbing.

The second group called forth was a mixed group of men and women. The Teacher told them, "The Creator calls you Listeners, gifted with the ability to hear, recognize, and understand the tiniest sounds over extreme distances. Your weapon of choice will be eavesdropping for safety and imitating voices when it will help your kingdom survive an attack, whether physical, spiritual, or mental. You will also use the gift of song and melody to soothe your enemies and maintain a history of Yarada's people."

Elayne glanced at the three Watchers. "Does that mean I will be like you? Able to protect?"

"If you choose," Montee said.

Elayne leaned toward Adana, a look of faint hope on her face. "You told me being a Watcher meant freedom. What about a Listener?"

Adana looked to Montee for assistance.

"In times of war, that depends," Montee said. "But yes, it provides you with different avenues for your life."

The tension in Elayne's body dissipated as confidence settled in her shoulders, and her chin lifted a little higher. "What of the other two groups?"

Adana nodded and resumed the story.

The third group, all men, received the gift of touch. "You are Empaths," the Teacher said. "You can imitate any action with perfection. Your weapon of choice is your body because it will allow you to perform great feats of strength. To keep you from using your strength for selfish reasons, the Creator has given you the ability to identify with and sense the emotions of any living thing, human or animal. You will always think twice before causing harm to anyone."

And the fourth group, made up of men and women, he called Seers. "The Creator gives you the gift of intuition. You will know if someone speaks the truth. Your weapon of choice is your mind. Using your knowledge of truth, you will aid others in seeking the right path. This is a dangerous gift because believing some-thing is true does not mean it is."

The Creator tasked these four groups with protection of their kingdom and monarchy. Through their combined strengths, they saved Yarada from the invad-ing army, but the knowledge of their fertile lands spread, and others sought to conquer them.

The people of Yarada, assisted by the gifted ones, fought off every attacker until one wise invader requested a covenant between his people and theirs. From then on, Yarada accepted the outsiders and, within a few generations, began to marry into their families. Only the gifted ones did not. They remained separate from the others, reproducing offspring with multiple gifts.

Elayne said, "What happened to them? Why are there only Watchers, now?"

"Horrible things. This is probably why your father wouldn't allow this story to be told to you," Adana said.

The memory of the kingdom's need for the gifted ones faded, and people began to fear what they did not understand. Villagers burned the homes of those who would protect them and killed gifted ones on sight, seeking to annihilate all of them.

A remnant of gifted ones fled into the desert where people never traveled. Their history became a myth told around the fires at night for many generations, until the Princess Moniah found an injured baby giraffe and sought to save it. While trying to find the animal's herd, she stumbled upon a small group of Watchers. The women, amazed the princess had formed a telepathic connection with the great animal, recognized the seeds of their gift in the princess. Because of her unusual bond with the giraffe, Moniah grew to be more powerful in her gifts than all other Watchers.

Once again, the Watchers entered the court of a monarch, pledging to protect the Princess Moniah and her heirs with their lives.

"I remember that part of the story," Elayne whispered as Adana finished. "And you are Princess Moniah's heir." The lady thought for a moment, staring into the fire. "Why do you think my father kept my gift from me?"

"I suspect you come from a hidden line of Listeners," Montee said. "Do you think either of your parents or siblings have the gift?"

"No." Elayne spoke with conviction. "But my mother's sister knew things. I remember a big argument. My father forced her to leave that day. We never saw her again."

"Your mother's family, then. He probably feared you would expose them, and people would fear you."

"And for now, we must keep your secret." Adana made firm eye contact with Elayne. "Not for fear of discovery, but because I need every weapon at my disposal. No one has seen a Listener in generations." She smiled at Elayne. "It's a great gift."

Adana stood and faced southeast. "Once Sinti and Veana join us, we will go to the village. I need information only you can hear."

* * * * *

Chapter Five

Kiffen's makeshift troop traveled all day and into the night. They paused for a few hours' rest, then pushed on toward the Border Keep. The keep, and its surrounding lake, came into view early the next morning. The gates bulged with the arrival of soldiers and refugees, a surprising number for the early hour of the day. The air stank of sweat and tightly packed bodies. In the cool air, steam rose above the crowded mass.

Kiffen's heart sank at the sight of so many, especially when he recognized several from the troops who had led Adana's caravan out of Elwar. He had hoped those troops had escaped the fighting and were headed to Adana's View in Moniah.

With a glance toward Simeon, he said, "It doesn't look like any of our troops made it to Moniah." This evidence added weight to the concerns already settling on his shoulders. "What other problems will we encounter?"

Simeon didn't answer, but Kiffen recognized the look of concern on the man's features as he slid from his saddle and summoned a stable hand. The young boy, eyes bright with excitement, rushed to take their horses. "Don't worry, sirs," he said in a voice not yet changed to manhood, "I'll take good care of these fine steeds. Whose name should I give the stable master?"

Simeon handed his reins to the boy. "King Kiffen and his companions."

The boy dropped the reins and gawked for a moment before re-membering his duty and bowing to Kiffen, then he grabbed the reins, a flush of red climbing his neck. "Yes, Your Majesty. Don't you worry about a thing. No other horses will get better care. I will give them the best stalls and feed."

He clucked to the horses and led them away, peeking back over his shoulder, his eyes bright with curiosity.

In spite of his exhaustion and worries, Kiffen couldn't hold back a smile at the young boy's behavior. The Border Keep rarely had visitors. So many at once, and most of them soldiers with the stories of a battle fought in the darkness of the frightening forest, would thrill any young boy.

Kiffen searched the jumble of people for someone of rank. Sim-eon touched his sleeve and nodded toward a Monian First Soldier headed toward them.

The man stood taller than most of the Elwarian soldiers, just like his female counterparts, the Watchers. His brushed golden armor and horned helmet gleamed in the sunlight, and his leather leggings showed no sign of battle wear. This man had been at the keep long enough to clean up.

As he paused before them, Kiffen recognized the soldier as the one who had carried Moniah's banner on the day King Micah arrived in Elwar to celebrate Adana's birthday. *Was that only a week ago?* So much had happened in that time.

The soldier bowed to Kiffen. "Your Highness, a high council has formed."

Kiffen noted the title of a prince in the man's address. Word of his father's death had not reached the keep. Another piece of infor-mation he must share, along with their missing heir and the death of

Moniah's regent king. If only he knew how to reach Bai'dish, he might know more about Adana's whereabouts.

The soldier gestured toward the inner walls. "They meet in the Central Tower. The First Vision sent me to escort you."

Kiffen's gaze locked on the older man. He swallowed once to ensure his voice would hold. "The First Vision? Montee is here?" He was painfully aware the man had not mentioned Adana.

The soldier dropped his gaze for a moment, then looked up, an apologetic smile on his face. "Forgive me. I refer to Kassa."

"Kassa? Here?"

"Yes."

Kiffen glanced at the soldier's armbands, red to signify a commander in the First Soldiers. Kassa was First Vision to Adana's mother. She held that position for over thirty years, and the man's rank and age indicated he had spent many years following her lead. But her position had changed the moment Adana's mother died three years ago. Montee had become Adana's First Vision then, and Kassa accompanied Adana to Elwar to continue her Watcher training.

"Kassa has no rank," Kiffen said. "She's no longer First Vision."

The man grimaced, and his shoulders lifted slightly in an apologetic shrug. "It's what she does."

Kiffen considered the statement. His observations of Kassa as she chaperoned and trained Adana in Elwar supported the soldier's comment. Fighting exhaustion and disappointment over Adana's absence, he strode with purpose toward the Central Tower. He needed a bath, rest, and food, but a high council required his presence. "Take me to her."

The castle of the Border Keep was the original stronghold for the kingdom of Yarada before it was divided between the twin sisters, Elwar and Moniah. Thoughts of the two ancient queens and their legacies surfaced in Kiffen's mind as he passed under each wall. Twins born mere minutes apart, each princess possessed important skills and strengths for rulership. Their father determined neither should rule the other and divided the kingdom in two, giving half to Elwar to rule and half to Moniah to rule. Kiffen was Elwar's direct descendant, while Adana was Moniah's.

The Keep sat on an island in the center of a lake, a strong defensive position. The lake's shoreline teemed with soldiers awaiting a boat to carry them to the safety of the keep. The fortress consisted of three towers. Arrivals entered through the East Tower, which faced the direction from which the majority of soldiers and refugees approached. A high wall extended around the keep and included this tower. Within this wall, a small village of people lived. Because the fortress sat on the border between Elwar and Moniah, neither kingdom claimed ownership, and for centuries, the occupants of the Border Keep lived in homage to both.

A second wall rose inside the first one. The West Tower, as part of this wall, overlooked a spread of land that, at times, flooded from the melting snows in Elwar. This inner section housed the army and the castle staff.

The third wall encircled the castle in the depths of the keep. The Central Tower, rising from this wall, provided a panoramic view of the land. To the north, the edge of the forest spread out toward the rugged mountains of Elwar. To the south, a lookout could watch huge herds of animals roam the plains of Moniah. Additional lookouts faced west and east.

Kiffen and Simeon followed the commander into the map room. There was a rustle as the gathered soldiers bowed in Kiffen's presence.

Kassa stood at the huge table in the center of the room, studying a map. She did not bow. At the sound of movement, her Watcher's gaze flicked toward him, and then returned to the parchment. "Have you connected with Bai'dish, Prince Kiffen?" she asked.

He paused. Was it that easy? He concentrated on the giraffe and felt a spark of awareness flicker within his mind. The hint of a link taunted him, but he had no idea how to use it.

"I have had more pressing duties."

Kassa didn't look back up but continued to study the maps. She placed a lion marker at the Border Keep. He glanced at a point to the north, marking Elwar's castle. His father's larger marker, the king of lions, stood there. Inaccurate, but that information could wait. He turned toward Kassa, wondering at her role within this gathering. She obviously had reassumed her former position as First Vision. Had Montee not made it to Adana? The only reason a former First Vision might step back into authority would be the death of the current one. No one in the room, all of them high-ranking officials, seemed to question her place, either.

He picked up his marker from the map and rolled it between his fingers. "I hoped you were with Adana."

She blinked at him like a hawk considering its next meal. "I was too far from her camp to aid her. I came here with the first wave of troops." She turned back to the table. "We have a war to fight."

Kiffen fought the frustration welling within him while reminding himself that Kassa thought strategically. He needed her intelligence and skill, but he knew he needed her respect and compliance, too.

"Kassa, why didn't you head for Moniah to prepare the fortress for Adana's arrival?"

The woman straightened and swiveled her steel gray eyes toward him. "Maligon attacked from the south. His troops blocked that route. It seemed wiser to muster here."

New information. Since soldiers from Elwar had alerted Kiffen of the possible attack, he had assumed it had originated in the north. He hadn't known about the attack from the south.

Had Maligon surrounded them? Come at them from all sides? That could mean Adana rode into the traitor's army to the east, the direction he knew she'd taken when fleeing the attack.

He studied the map table. None of the markers on the board provided a clear picture of their enemy's position.

Disturbing, but at the moment, he needed to assume his position within this gathering. Kassa held the lowest rank in the room, yet she appeared ready to lead their armies. He couldn't fathom why no one challenged her authority. The Watcher did command respect through her presence, so he needed to tread with care. He needed her.

Replacing his marker on the board, he asked, "Why have you taken command?"

Kassa paused and looked around the room. Kiffen's gaze followed hers, taking in the presence of three officers from Elwar, two more from Moniah, and three high command Watchers, including Samantha, Kassa's daughter. This quick study of the officers present reminded Kiffen that most of them had fought side by side with Kassa during Maligon's uprising over twenty years ago. Following Kassa's authority was a habit for them. None of them questioned it. Had he overstepped his bounds in his youth?

Then Kiffen's gaze fell on the soldier who had escorted them to the room, and he frowned. A smile twitched on the soldier's face. He glanced back at Kassa. Her mouth twitched once before she quickly hid her amusement.

Kiffen scowled. "You find the situation humorous?"

"If I may, Your Highness," the soldier said, "I believe my wife has just realized her presumption in leading. I believe I told you, it's what she does."

"Your wife?" Kiffen stepped back and glanced between the two. He had never considered the idea that Kassa might be married, even though Samantha obviously had a father.

Kassa ignored his question. "Your Highness, Commander Halar makes excuses for me. Forgive us both. Please, I meant no disrespect."

"None taken, Kassa."

Kassa stepped back and gestured toward the large map in the center of the room. "May I share my intelligence with you?"

He nodded and approached the chart. "What can you tell me?"

"Many of your soldiers are in the keep. The news they bring …" She hesitated. "Is it true? Your father?"

He swallowed back a rush of emotion. "You've heard of my father's murder and Quilla's treachery?"

The others in the room bowed their heads and murmured their sorrow. Their condolences renewed the ache he'd managed to ignore for two days.

Kassa nodded. "I'm truly sorry. Your father was a great warrior." Kassa moved the marker for the king of Elwar to the Border Keep on the map.

Kiffen fought to straighten his shoulders and remain focused on what needed to be done. Strategize. Gather information. Plan. Locate Adana.

"Thank you for your words of comfort." He stepped back up to the table. "We must stop this before it becomes worse. What have you learned?"

"Of course, Your Majesty." Kassa bobbed her head. "We know the princess' camp was attacked internally, as were most of our camps. Those who survived have gathered here."

Kiffen realized she did not mention Micah's or Adana's fates. As if in answer to his unspoken thoughts, Kassa asked, "Have you news of the regent king or the lady Adana?"

Kassa would appreciate a straightforward answer, but he hesitated. On the heels of the news of his loss, how could he share Micah's fate with the woman who had been there when Queen Chiora first met Micah?

The woman was steel, but the news was cold iron. "I received word from Elwar of the murder of my father and warning of an attack. When I reached Adana's camp, she was gone. Montee sent her out with the giraffes."

At the mention of the giraffes, Kiffen felt another short, but firm, flicker of awareness from Bai'dish. "Before Montee followed the princess, she told us about the regent king. He was killed. Early in the battle."

A gasp ran through the council. Kassa's shoulders twitched once, and Kiffen noted her slow, deliberate breaths as she inhaled and exhaled twice, much like Adana would do when trying to maintain composure.

"I brought his body with us. For proper rites."

When Kassa looked at him again, she said, "Moniah thanks you. And Adana? She is safe?"

"Last we heard. We met Montee on the edge of their encampment. Joannu and Lady Elayne evacuated the princess. They followed the giraffes in a southeasterly direction."

"And you have not connected with Bai'dish?" Kassa stepped closer as if she could read the answer in his eyes.

He reddened and dropped his voice to a whisper. "How? I'm not sure—"

"Sire." The Watcher Samantha stepped forward and placed her hand on his arm. "It's easier when you can see across the distance." She turned toward an archway. "There's an eastern-facing window in the room through here."

Kassa nodded. "It would be best if you do this now. We need to learn of Adana's welfare."

Uneasy over the responsibility and unsure of what to expect, Kiffen followed Samantha. Sunlight streamed into the adjoining room. The walls were rough river stone; a bench sat before the window.

Samantha gestured for Kiffen to sit. Through the window, he saw the river flowing east from the lake.

Samantha crossed her arms and leaned against the wall to his left, a slight uplift to her lips. "You've never done this?"

He shook his head.

"It's not difficult." She shrugged. "So I've been told. If Montee were here…she could guide you." Two wrinkles creased her forehead, pointing toward the bridge of her nose. "I can attempt to talk you through it."

Kiffen regarded Samantha. Adana rarely spoke of this Watcher, and he had sensed unease between the two of them at times. As Kassa's daughter, he imagined Samantha might have been a tough trainer for Adana. She'd only arrived in Elwar a week ago. Except for attending the Kingdoms Council three years earlier, she had remained in Moniah. Her offer to assist him with this foreign act of connecting his mind with a giraffe touched him. The only other person who had offered to help him through his first link had been Adana, but there hadn't been time to do so before they left Elwar.

"What do I need to do?"

Samantha walked behind him and placed her fingers on his temples. "Relax. Close your eyes." She gently massaged his head with her fingertips. Until then, he hadn't realized how much his head ached with the weight of the changes thrust into his life.

The tension began to ease. His eyelids drooped, and calm seeped through him, creeping down his temples through his face and neck muscles. After a few moments, the exhaustion of the last few days flooded over him, and his shoulders slumped forward, giving into the burden he held there.

"Good. Breathe slowly." She slid her long fingers down to his shoulders and began to knead them. "Breathe."

Kiffen relaxed into her hands and released a little more of his burden with each breath. The first breaths stung his nose, but soon his muscles loosened, and he dropped his head further forward, his chin falling against his chest.

Her long fingers slid under his chin and cupped it. With a slow, gentle motion, she pulled his head upright, straightening his neck and back until it aligned against her firm frame. Cool hands glided to the broad expanse of his chest.

Surprise sizzled through him, and he jumped forward.

"Shh." Her hand massaged his chest, then slithered under his chin, an insistent, but gentle, pressure compelling him back against her warm body. "You're safe. Concentrate. Keep breathing."

Exhausted, Kiffen yielded to her soothing voice. He inhaled and exhaled two, three, four more times.

"Slower and deeper."

Trance-like, Kiffen complied.

"Good. Notice where you're breathing." She pressed against his chest. "Here." She snaked her hands down to his abdomen, her body molding into his as she leaned over him.

He gasped as her musky scent drifted up his nostrils.

"You need to breathe here."

His muscles protested at the closeness of her body, her hands just above where he longed for Adana's touch. He sucked in his breath, pulling his abdomen away from her touch.

"Breathe. You must breathe here to find Adana. Relax. Focus." Her voice carried a soothing tone and consoled him with the importance of their task. He relaxed into it and ignored the strangeness of her proximity. Looseness spread through him.

His abdomen rose and fell with each inhalation and exhalation.

"That's right. Relax.

Breathe.

Relax.

Breathe."

His acute awareness of Samantha's body diminished. The remaining tension in his back and shoulders dissipated as the exercise drew him deeper and deeper.

"Good." Her voice sounded far away.

His mind registered the distance, but he still felt the closeness of her body pressed behind him. Breathing was all that mattered. Seconds rose and swelled with each inhalation, and Kiffen's body flowed with the pulse of blood beneath his skin.

"Good. You are ready. Call to Bai'dish."

As he exhaled, he thought the giraffe's name. He continued breathing. In. Out. In. Out.

He thought the name again, releasing each breath slowly. Joy from the beast spilled across the link. Kiffen's fingertips tingled in response to the giraffe's welcome. Sight came to him, a hazy image of Bai'dish looking at him.

Bai'dish gazed back at Kiffen until the image became more distinct, then the giraffe turned away and showed him a view of a stream flowing southeast into the flat lands of Moniah. Kiffen sensed, and then saw, Am'brosia walking along the stream, her head held high and alert. The image grew hazy and disappeared.

With one last deep inhalation, Kiffen opened his eyes.

And looked into Samantha's green ones. She leaned against the wall in front of him.

In confusion, he glanced behind him where he still felt the warmth of her body pressed against his.

"You saw her?" Samantha asked.

He turned back to her, aware of a splendid peacefulness still flooding his soul. "I saw Bai'dish."

"Was Am'brosia with him?"

"Yes. She was following a stream. Does that tell us anything about Adana?"

"If Am'brosia looked well, then Adana is, too."

He recalled the image, brief as it was, and noted the angle of the giraffe's shadow. "I believe they traveled southeast."

Samantha straightened. A frown transformed her gentle bearing into one of surprise. "Southeast?"

Kiffen stretched. "Yes. I'm sure." He looked out over the lake toward the river, and the Watcher's gaze followed his. "I believe it was this river."

Samantha crossed her arms and squinted eastward.

Kiffen followed her gaze, but his thoughts returned to the breathing technique. "That was focused breathing, right?"

She arched an eyebrow at him. "Yes. It will come easier with time."

"You were behind me." Kiffen hesitated. "I didn't feel you move away."

"Focused breathing used in that manner blocks the rest of your senses. Doing it alone can be dangerous. You'll never see or hear an attack."

"But Watchers use it during battle and while scouting?"

She shrugged, her attention still focused in the direction Adana traveled. "A different method. It takes much more practice and control. We use it to fine tune our senses." She cocked her head to the side and smiled at him. "Just focus on your link with Bai'dish. That will take enough work." Turning toward the map room, she said, "Kassa can help you develop it more."

Kiffen watched her walk out of the room, her dark braid twisting down her back. Her tunic, swaying as it outlined her hips, drew his attention to her cat-like grace. He had never noticed her beauty before.

* * * * *

Chapter Six

By evening, Kiffen knew the Border Keep housed close to seven hundred soldiers, some fleeing from Quilla, some survivors of Maligon's attacks on Adana's caravan, and a few from Moniah's border patrols, alerted to the attacks by messenger or Watcher scouts. Of these soldiers, one hundred were Watchers, four hundred were Elwarian, and just under two hundred were First Soldiers.

In addition, the keep housed seventy-three villagers and refugees and forty-nine of the keep's regular staff. Prior to Kiffen's arrival, Kassa had dispatched birds and runners to Linus, the commander who remained in Moniah to protect Adana's View and the kingdom.

Kiffen stared at the map, realizing how successfully Maligon had divided them before striking. Create chaos, one of the first rules of strategic warfare. His ability to strike their caravan from the north and south, as well as from within their own ranks, concerned Kiffen, but he had to acknowledge the brilliance behind Maligon's approach. Somewhere on the map lay the secret to Maligon's weakness. Kiffen just needed to find it.

He had suspicions about the location of Maligon's camp, but not enough to confirm the man's whereabouts. He feared Maligon held several positions.

Thankfully, his connection to Bai'dish gave him a stronger idea of Adana's position. Since Samantha had helped him establish his link, he had continued to feel more than the random flicker of awareness. In the back of his mind, the connection remained intact. On Kassa's advice, he stopped to focus on it several times during the day. Each time, the bond became easier to hold.

Through Bai'dish, he learned Adana's small band was tense, but he noticed a tingle of excitement from them, too, as if something pleased them.

"Your Majesty?"

Kiffen turned as Samantha and Simeon joined him. The sight of Samantha gave him pause. Since she had awoken his bond with Bai'dish, the Watcher had remained nearby, interrupting his concentration just by being in the same room with him. Her presence throughout the day confused and embarrassed him, and he hoped those thoughts did not translate through his tie to Bai'dish.

"The funeral pyre for the regent king is ready," she said.

Kiffen gave a quick nod of acceptance. He could not properly send his father back to the Creator, but he could send his future father-in-law. As he followed the two from the tower, he concentrated on the bond with Bai'dish. Kassa had instructed him to focus on what he saw and imagine sharing it with the giraffe. If he succeeded, Bai'dish could share the ceremony with Am'brosia which meant Adana could attend her father's funeral through sight, as well.

* * *

Adana and Montee sat by the fire in the deepening twilight while Joannu and Elayne hunted for food. The other members of her honor guard, Veana and Sinti, had not arrived yet.

"Should we continue to wait on them?" Adana asked. "What if they've been captured or killed?"

Montee tilted her head and studied Adana. "Do you sense something in your shoulder or did you receive that impression from Am'brosia?"

Adana shook her head. Her shoulder had remained calm since her decision to go to the village. No pain, tickle, energy, or heat resonated from the puncture wound. She had forgotten about it as the day wore on. "It's quiet."

"Good," Montee said.

For a moment, Adana watched Montee's gaze follow Elayne and Joannu, her eyes lingering on Elayne. For safety, and to keep the woman from slowing them down, Adana had given Elayne a Watcher's uniform to wear. The young woman moved more freely and didn't exhibit any modesty toward the more revealing clothing.

"It was wise to dress her in uniform, Your Majesty. She looks much like you."

Adana nodded. "As much as I hate to admit it, she does look enough like me to fool someone."

"Is that the plan? To fool someone into believing she is you?"

War came quickly. She must consider every potential weapon at her disposal. That's what her mother had taught her. "It's crossed my thoughts."

Adana stared into the surrounding darkness. After years of living in Elwar's ruling city, the quiet calmed her. It allowed her to focus on her thoughts and concerns.

"Do you trust her?"

Joannu and Elayne had disappeared into the darkness. Except for the outline of various plants and the flash of a night animal's eyes, Adana saw nothing else. The moon had yet to rise, and clouds threatened to keep them in the dark. "I don't extend trust easily."

She preferred to keep Elayne nearby. That way, she could trust Joannu to alert her to any danger.

Montee nodded. "It would be unwise to do so."

The fire popped and crackled, and Adana got up to feed it more wood. Sparks flew as the logs clunked against each other. The fire drew her back to the night before. "I can't believe he's gone."

Montee's brow wrinkled. "Your Majesty?"

"Montee, it's just you and me. Please drop the formalities." She dropped down next to the fire again. "I need that from you."

"Of course, Adana. It will be my honor."

"Huh. Honor. It's not about honor. It's about trust. I need you to always remember that. Now more than ever."

"Of course." Montee skewered Adana with her gaze. "Under the best of circumstances, your father's death would be difficult. This. I never saw it coming."

"I wonder if Mammetta did." Adana propped her cheek in her palm. "In reality, I lost them both the same day I lost Mammetta." She picked up a stick and poked at the fire, readjusting the fresh logs. "I saw so little of him over the last three years. Just days ago, he told me several secrets were kept from me. He planned to discuss them with me once we reached the Border Keep." She tossed the stick aside. "I guess I'll never know. I fear, without that information, I'm going into this war blind."

Montee shook her head. "You're not blind. I know the secrets he needed to tell you."

A tide of relief washed over Adana's soul. So many problems, so many deaths. Her mind struggled to keep up with everything. Sudden worries crept into her mind at odd times throughout the day, just like the mention of these secrets. She'd forgotten until a moment ago.

Elayne's laughter drifted on the night air in stark contrast to Adana's mood. In the shadows, she noticed Joannu and Elayne returning.

Before the women reached the fire, Montee leaned toward Adana and whispered, "We need to scout this village. Send the two of them to do so tonight. You and I can remain here and discuss these secrets."

Adana nodded, wondering if the village offered a place of rest or housed a nest of Maligon's supporters. Until they checked it out, she could only hope for sanctuary. Her shoulder remained quiet.

"You won't believe this!" Joannu dropped several fish on the ground by the fire. "She could hear the fish under the water. It's a crime how easy it was."

Elayne laughed, her eyes dancing with a delight Adana had never seen from this woman. "I never tried to listen for fish before. If I'd only known as a child, I could have—" She bit her lip and became preoccupied with cleaning the fish.

Adana met Montee's cautious look. What secrets lay behind that half-sentence? She needed to trust Elayne if she wanted to use her abilities. Like it or not, she had to take the chance.

After Joannu and Elayne cleaned and cooked the fish, the four sat around the fire. They ate in quiet, devouring their first meal since the night before. The meat fell into juicy morsels in Adana's mouth. She paused and licked tiny bits from her fingers. "I'm licking my fingers, Elayne," she said, laughter shaking her shoulders.

The woman paused, her thumb thrust in her own mouth. Eyes widening, she yanked out the offending thumb. "I'm sorry, m'lady. I didn't mean to forget my table manners."

Joannu's laughter trilled around them. "Elayne, the best meat sticks to your fingers. Every Watcher knows that."

The woman glanced between the three Watchers, a look of confusion on her face.

"Forgive me, Elayne," Adana said. "I meant to say I'm starting to feel like me, not the dressed-up figure Quilla forced me to become while in Elwar."

Still, the woman stared at her, a wrinkle on her forehead. "So, it's not a bad thing to lick your fingers?"

"Of course not." Joannu giggled. "We're not as prim in Moniah. Looks like putting on that uniform has rubbed off on you. I saw your thumb in your mouth."

"And that's a good thing?" Still the woman looked doubtful.

The usually stoic Watchers answered her in unison. "Yes."

Adana leaned toward Elayne. "Some of my best memories are of training expeditions into the wilderness. No one saw me as a princess or royalty. I was just a Watcher in training. I had no idea how wonderful it was at the time, to sit around the fire with my sisters, enjoy a simple meal, stare into the flames, and watch the stars above. It's home."

She leaned back on the grass and licked each finger, making loud sucking noises.

Joannu flung herself backward and followed suit.

Elayne shook her head. "I don't understand. What manners should I ignore?"

"Don't mind them," Montee said. "In Moniah's court, you will be fine. Watcher trainees may relax and forget the rules of rank at the end of a tough, but successful, day. Not all of them come from noble upbringing, so many don't know proper behavior, anyway. These two seem to have forgotten they aren't trainees." At that point, Montee stretched her arms above her head and fell backward onto the grass, too.

Adana laughed, and Joannu broke into a fit of giggles. Elayne only followed suit after Joannu jumped up and tickled her. "Come on. Don't you know it's bad manners not to misbehave if the queen allows it?"

Adana listened to the others talk and laugh for a few moments, but her thoughts soon returned to her problems. She rose and left Joannu and Elayne pointing out various stars and making up silly stories about each constellation. By the stream, she rinsed her hands. She couldn't wait any longer for Sinti and Veana. When she returned, she stood over the three women. "Joannu, I would like you to take Elayne and scout this village."

Both women sat up, and Joannu nodded, exchanging a quick smile with Elayne. Was this an indication that Joannu found the woman trustworthy? Joannu maintained an amiable relationship with most of the Watchers. Was this her way or did she see more?

Still conflicted about this uninvited member of her group, Adana sat back down by the fire and assumed a tone of command. "Whatever you do, don't enter the village. I don't want to alert anyone to our presence. Yet. Report back to me on everything."

Satisfied the two understood her needs, Adana stretched her legs toward the fire and leaned back on her hands.

The image from Am'brosia hit her suddenly. A courtyard with a large funeral pyre swam in her vision.

Adana jerked forward, her gaze turned to the west.

"What is it?" Montee spun toward the giraffes.

Without looking behind her, Adana knew the two giraffes had descended the hill and approached her in a solemn, single file.

"Oh!" Elayne jumped as Am'brosia's head bobbed down next to Adana's. Both giraffes stood behind Adana, forming a protective arch over her.

Montee turned to Adana. "What are they showing you, Your Majesty?"

Adana's hand groped for and found Montee's, her grip hard. "Papa's funeral."

* * * * *

Chapter Seven

Kiffen stood in the courtyard with the rest of the keep's inhabitants, awaiting Regent King Micah's funeral. He had practiced the bond the way Kassa told him to throughout the day, but those connections felt like tiny glimpses into Adana's world compared to the clarity flooding through the connection now. He recognized Adana's grief as it overwhelmed him. Was the emotion only hers or did the giraffes add their sorrow for the lost regent king? His chest ached with sorrow, and tears pricked his eyes. His or hers? He didn't know. He yearned to stand with Adana, his arms holding her close, her soft hair tickling his chin, her grieving heart next to his.

Quiet reigned over the mourners in the keep as ten Watchers and ten Soldiers of the First Sight carried Micah's body strapped to a pallet into the courtyard. Ahead of them walked four Watchers including Kassa and Samantha. Each of the four carried a torch, providing the only light to the gathering.

Samantha was positioned between her mother and another Watcher, her unbound hair gleaming like silk in the firelight. Briefly, Kiffen felt drawn to the bounce of dark curls flowing over her shoulders. He took a step closer and then Bai'dish reared his head in the link, and Kiffen felt the connection snap. He turned his gaze away from Samantha, forced by an unseen pressure, gentle but firm, on his cheek as the connection returned. The giraffe pushed him to look toward the funeral pyre.

The procession stopped in front of the high, wooden platform. Two ladders leaned against the front and provided access to the raised stand. A Teacher of the Faith waited to receive Micah's body on this platform, but the torches didn't cast the light high enough for the teacher to be seen yet.

Kassa and Samantha stepped away from the other Watchers and approached the platform. They ascended the ladders. Four Soldiers of the First Sight followed them, two climbing to the midway point, and two stationed a few rungs above the ground.

When Kassa and Samantha reached the top rungs, they held their torches aloft and touched them to a trough along the front of the platform. Liquid fire raced around the edges of the stand, illuminating the Teacher of the Faith standing in the center. He stood motionless, his hands folded at his waist, while flames billowed from the troughs.

The mourners in the courtyard stepped back from the radiant heat, and Kiffen held his hand above his eyes to shield them from the glare. The blazing element, glimmer fire, burned hotter and brighter than any other fuel within the kingdoms. Its secret was closely guarded by Moniah. The same substance, when woven into cloth, became iridescent and fireproof, creating the coveted glimmer cloth his stepmother and sister loved so much. These two items represented a large portion of Moniah's wealth.

The First Soldiers carrying Regent King Micah's pallet droned a low note as they passed the board holding King Micah's body to the soldiers near the base of the ladders. The soldier on the left ladder supported the head of the board while the soldier on the right supported the foot.

The wordless drone sung by the soldiers rose in pitch and volume as the first set of soldiers passed the body upward to the next two. The pitch shifted higher as the second set of soldiers received the body.

The unearthly song permeated the courtyard with an element of eeriness as it echoed off the stone walls and shrouded the mourners in its tone. For some reason, Kiffen found it comforting.

When the regent king's body was passed upward to Kassa and Samantha, the Watchers in the crowd combined their higher voices with the soldiers' requiem, vocalizing a note two octaves higher than the men.

Icy tendrils raced down Kiffen's arms as the dirge hung in the air and blanketed the crowd like a haunting spirit. He glanced upward, expecting to see a haze or gathering fog. Instead, stars twinkled in the clear, night sky.

Kassa and Samantha carried the pallet to the Teacher of the Faith. The song rose to a crescendo as the three turned the pallet upright, so King Micah's body faced the crowd. A fire-conjured wind lifted the regent king's cape like a flag. It snapped in the breeze, its loud cracking adding an odd tempo to the song of mourning. The cape flirted with the fire as the teacher raised his hands and clapped them together, the sound deafening as it echoed throughout the courtyard.

At once, the song ended.

An expectant silence hovered over the gathered mourners. The crackle of glimmer fire and the snap of Micah's cape the only sounds in the night.

Kiffen held his breath and stared into the intense heat on the platform. Would the Creator demand three more lives? As far as he knew, no one on the stand had ever burned with the departed loved one, but Kassa's, Samantha's, and the teacher's proximity to the fire and the dance of the regent king's cape made him uneasy. How could they stand being so close to the heat? None of them flinched.

He should have stood on his father's pyre. Could he have shown such immobile devotion?

No one touched him, but arms embraced his shoulders. Within the bond, his sight shifted inward. Adana smiled at him, tears sparkling in her eyes. She nodded once and mouthed the word yes.

Amazement over Adana's ability to know and respond to his thoughts caused Kiffen to lose focus. When the teacher spoke, Kiffen concentrated hard on the bond so he could continue to share the scene with Adana. She wouldn't hear the words, but she would see and experience Kiffen's responses.

"Micah, Regent King of Moniah, cast your eyes one more time on this land." The teacher's voice rang throughout the night. With Samantha's and Kassa's assistance, the three turned the body to face each compass direction.

"Look west, where the waters flow," said Samantha.

"Look north, where your strongest allies live," said the Teacher of the Faith.

"Look east, where your origins lie," said Samantha.

"Look south, where your heart and soul have thrived," said Kassa. "Look south to home and hearth and land."

The mourners turned in each direction as Micah received his last look at the land and Moniah.

Kassa and Samantha laid the pallet against a stand beside the teacher, then bowed low before the body. Heads still bowed, they backed toward the ladders and descended.

Once they reached the ground, the teacher pushed a wooden lever beside the stand and lowered the body to a reclining position. He raised his hands to the night sky. "Creator, receive this servant in peace and charity. Bestow his wisdom and great knowledge on his daughter, Adana, Queen of Moniah."

Kiffen felt a shock and thrill wash over him at the pronouncement of Adana's title. How much had been his reaction, and how much hers, as she watched through his eyes the last moments of her father's earthly body?

The teacher bowed three times before King Micah, then backed away, descending the ladder in the same posture used by Kassa and Samantha. On the ground, he stepped below the platform and pulled a large handle, the strain of the task evident in the bulge of his neck muscles, glistening in the bright light of the fire. Glimmer fire flowed from the torches atop the pyre and raced into channels surrounding the regent's body. As the two channels of fire converged, the flames roared across the funeral pyre, engulfing Micah's body.

A devastating surge of loss rose through the link, and Kiffen fought to keep his stance under the rush of so much grief. He closed his eyes for a moment and sent the image of him standing with Adana in his arms, bathing the thought in a promise to help her destroy Maligon.

A spark surged back toward him, fired with a force of will he'd only witnessed when Adana tangled with his stepmother. It flared for just a moment, then subsided in exhausted grief.

When he opened his eyes, the teacher stood in front of the flaming pyre, arms raised to the sky. "Go in peace," he shouted over the fire's roar.

"Go in peace," the crowd intoned.

Heat swarmed the courtyard, and the inferno blazed into the night sky. Despite the discomfort, the people drew closer to the platform, sweat intermingling with the tears pouring down their faces. Each person remained, tethered to the cobblestone yard, until the wood cracked and crashed in upon itself.

Then, the gathered people turned and silently departed, except for Kiffen. He stood under the night sky, watching the flames burn down until no one else remained. When he felt Adana's mind retreat in the link, he turned and walked inside.

* * * * *

Chapter Eight

Montee sat in silent contemplation until the giraffes lifted their long necks from their protective position over Adana and returned to their guard posts at the top of the hill. The funeral must have ended, but Adana's gaze remained distant, staring deep into the fire.

Elayne and Joannu stood by the fire, mesmerized by the stillness of Adana.

Montee turned toward them. "You should follow the queen's orders and go to the village. Report back to us by dawn."

The two women, one a true and valued Watcher, the other a questionable ally, walked off into the darkness. Montee sat down by the fire and waited.

As the night descended into the darkest hours, the valley's nocturnal creatures woke, rustling in the grass. An occasional hoot of an owl echoed through the valley. Peace reigned in this secluded vale, and Montee offered a plea to the Creator to shower this peace on Adana's grieving heart.

Complying with the decree established by Queen Chiora for her death, Adana hadn't stood by the funeral pyre of her mother. The young queen had never witnessed the ritual.

Unbidden, Montee felt again the overwhelming heat of Queen Chiora's pyre three years earlier. She'd stood on the pyre that night, and even in the chill of this evening three years later, she still felt the sweat trickling down her face, the fire searing her soul, stamping her with the truth of her own destiny.

"Kassa and Samantha are at the Border Keep."

Montee looked up in response to Adana's quiet words. She looked peaceful, not troubled. Sometimes, the finality of the event helped those left behind, gave them a way to move forward. The relief Montee felt over her queen's composure caused her to take longer to absorb the words Adana had spoken. Samantha and Kassa being at the keep meant things were worse than expected.

Montee leaned forward. "You saw them? You are positive?"

Adana sighed and stretched her arms out before her.

"They delivered Papa to the Corners of the Land." Her voice sounded subdued, exhaustion radiating in her words. "When did you last see Samantha?"

"Before the attack."

As one of the honor guard, Samantha should have sought out Adana during the attack on their camp. After they cleared the battle scene, Montee had sent the other two members of the guard, Veana and Sinti, to scout a larger area rather than coming directly to this valley. If they had found no problems, they should reach the camp soon. She had hoped Samantha would find and join them.

"Could you pick up anything from your connection? Any clue as to why she's not following us?"

"No. Nothing. The link wavered at times. It felt difficult for Kiffen to maintain." Adana paused, a distant look returning to her face. "There was a point of pure clarity when they brought out Father's body. Kiffen looked right at Samantha. She looked so beautiful. I've never seen her look that way before with her hair curling down over her shoulders. Then the connection collapsed. When it returned, Kiffen was looking at the platform."

Montee swallowed. Samantha was not beautiful. Harsh like her mother, few ever looked on her with adoration. Did Adana know how emotions could alter sight through the link? Unsure of how to respond and confused as to why Kiffen would see a lovely woman rather than a soldier, Montee said nothing.

"Where are Joannu and Elayne?" A look of uncertainty crossed Adana's young face as she glanced around the fire.

"I sent them to the village."

"Good." A small smile. "I believe we will be joined by Sinti and Veana soon. And if I see correctly through Am'brosia's eyes, Glume is with them."

Montee considered this last piece of information, not surprised that the giraffe keeper sought to catch up to his four-legged charges. The man might be portly, but nothing stood between him and his duties to the royal giraffes of Moniah.

Adana's eyelids drooped low, and Montee heard her take deep, restoring breaths. With the ebb and flow of each breath, her body showed signs of the releasing tension, and Adana regained her regal bearing.

Moments later, a more alert woman raised her eyelids and nailed Montee with a royal gaze. She sat straighter, and color returned to her face. "Queens don't have the luxury of proper mourning, do they?" Adana stretched her legs out in front of her and grasped her toes, arching her back like a trail cat. She sat upright again, and attentiveness shone in her blue eyes. "I believe you have information to share with me?"

Montee stood and circled the fire, extending her senses to the edge of the basin. Am'brosia and Bai'dish stood at the top of the hill in the center of the dell, alert and solid against the quiet night. Although she was not a Listener, Montee strained to hear anything beyond the hoot of an owl or the breeze in the trees. Nothing human lurked within her hearing. Satisfied no one eavesdropped, she returned and sat beside Adana.

"There are parchments hidden in key places: your chest at the estate, a hidden room in the Border Keep, and a cache in the cave. I believe your father planned to share the information stored on them with you once you arrived at the keep."

Adana shook her head in objection to Montee's revelation. "Kassa taught me how to open my mother's chest. There was no secret parchment."

"There's a hidden compartment. Kassa wouldn't have shown it to you."

"Why?"

"You left the next day for Elwar. It wasn't a safe time."

Adana scowled. "She did not trust me?"

"Of course, we trusted you," Montee said, thankful she was holding this conversation without any others present. If she'd learned one thing about this older Adana, it was that the woman hated to be left out of any discussions or details significant to her position. She couldn't blame her. She was a queen, returning to rule a kingdom after a three-year absence. She was young and vulnerable when she left Moniah. No one knew what might happen while she was gone, so secrets remained secrets.

"Three years is a long time to hold onto confidential information."

Adana's eyes narrowed. "No one in Elwar had knowledge of this information?"

Montee expected the question but was still surprised at the speed Adana fired it at her. Moniah's returning queen had left her kingdom as an impulsive girl, but somewhere along the way, she'd learned to think through things with a critical eye for gaps in logic and truth. Her reluctant use of Elayne's skills demonstrated this.

"Of course. King Donel and his advisor, Simeon."

"Not Kiffen? Not Quilla?"

Good questions.

"Kiffen might know now, but at the time, he did not."

Montee leaned back on her hands and stared into the night sky. The clouds had disappeared, and the moon cast its crescent glow across the land. The stars seemed brighter in this little valley. She wished they could return to that moment of gaiety after dinner and enjoy the night, the peace, without worrying about the future. From the day she became First Vision, those days of harmony dwindled until she couldn't recall a moment when worries and responsibilities didn't plague her. She glanced at Adana, aware the young queen's life had taken a similar turn on that same day.

"Who, in Moniah, knows of these parchments?" Adana's body seemed to be pulled forward toward Montee, the urgency of gaining knowledge stiffening her shoulders.

"Kassa, myself, and Linus."

"Do you miss Linus?"

Montee sat back in surprise. Did Adana know of their attraction? They had never admitted it to each other until it was too late. She became First Vision, forbidden to have anything beyond a military relationship with the royal commander. Their paths lay side by side now, never intertwined.

Montee leaned forward, brushing dirt from her hands. "Why do you ask?" She kept her face closed, wearing the mask of the First Vision to hide her thoughts.

Adana squinted across the fire, her gaze like tiny daggers penetrating Montee's skin.

The mask hid everything, and Montee held it, unwilling to let a short romance distract Adana from the importance of their discussion.

Finally, the queen dropped her study of Montee.

"What about Belwyn and Teletia? Do they know of these parchments?"

"Yes. Empress Gabriella and King Ariff are aware of their existence." Montee sat up straighter, her shoulders inclined toward the queen. "They have copies, too, but I do not know where they keep them." She paused to see if there were any more questions, hopeful the subject of Linus was finished.

Tension continued to build in Adana's shoulders while she thought about the parchments. Montee waited, aware Adana hadn't asked what information the parchments held.

A log collapsed in the center of the fire, sending sparks into the air. Adana stared at them a moment. "What do the parchments say?"

"We compiled the information after Maligon's exile. It seemed prudent for only rulers and their closest advisors to know of their existence. When Queen Roassa declared Donel her legal successor, she feared others would seek her throne, and the secrets would fall into the wrong hands, so she had Simeon place Elwar's copy in the cave."

"Quilla." Adana whispered the name. "Did she know about Quilla's ambitions?"

"No. They did not know who to suspect, but Maligon left unrest everywhere he went. We feared many of his supporters were still among us."

"But why the cave?"

"Its location. It's not where most believe it to be."

Adana stared at Montee. "The cave is not close to the Monian border?"

"It's in Teletia near the border with Belwyn."

The girl sketched a crude map in the dirt, glancing back and forth between the disclosed location of the cave and the true one. "Why keep its location secret?"

The rapid succession of questions frustrated Montee. She had planned to share this information with Adana in a controlled manner, preferably in the Border Keep, with the parchments at hand. Their circumstances made that plan impossible, and she struggled with how much to share in the short time they had before the others arrived.

Adana knew none of this except what she'd heard from the Memory Keeper's story about her parents' first meeting at the cave. The story of King Micah's and King Donel's entry into their lives as two bedraggled foreigners was a popular one. Just a week ago, Adana requested it be told to a gathering.

Resuming her explanations, Montee said, "In danger, the cave offers a safe haven. That's why your mother's squad camped there the day she met your father. Its underground channels are extensive and well-stocked with supplies."

"Ballene's Fire." Adana jumped up. "Someone could be there. Seeking protection."

The thought had occurred to Montee, as well as King Micah. "Your father sent Ostreia and Karyah with a small unit of Watchers to check after we received the news that Maligon holds Belwyn and Teletia."

"So, others do know of its location."

"Only a few, all sworn to secrecy. Ostreia and Karyah were with your mother as Trackers when your father stumbled upon the cave."

"I thought they were involved in war maneuvers at the time."

"They were."

Confusion echoed in Adana's voice. "But Trackers are still in training. They haven't learned how to cover their tracks yet or shoot an arrow into a crowd and hit their mark."

Montee shook her head at Adana's lack of warfare knowledge. Had Kassa omitted the facts about troop shortages created by war? How much of the queen's education would she learn while on the run? "Your Majesty, war does not wait for candidates to become fully trained." She leaned forward. "Some of your best Watchers earned their promotions on the battlefield."

Adana gazed beyond the fire. After a while, she spoke. "We will most likely face that issue again."

"With our forces spread wide? Yes."

"What is on this parchment?"

As much as she wanted to return to the purpose of this discussion, Montee knew she must lead Adana into the next revelation. The young queen would not appreciate the next question. "Have you had your dream recently?"

A glimpse of the girl Adana used to be squirmed under Montee's gaze.

In this dream, Adana struggled to survive river rapids, pulled under and pushed about by the current. Her crown floated ahead of her, just out of reach, and at the moment she might reach it, she banged her head on a large rock. The dream then shifted to an underground tunnel. In the tunnel, Adana followed a path through the darkness until she saw a light in the distance ahead of her. Elwar's crown. Adana awoke, every time, before she reached it.

For some reason, Adana showed reluctance to discuss the dream. It was rare for a Watcher of her age to have prophetic dreams, but not unheard of. The fact that Kassa and Montee had had the same dream, but with less regularity and detail, marked it as significant.

"What does my dream have to do with the parchment?"

Montee smiled. "Maybe nothing. But I believe I know what the underground represents."

"I already know," Adana said, her tone taut with misery. "King Donel is dead. It's his tomb."

"Possibly." The thought had occurred to Montee, but she felt a strong conviction that it meant something else. "King Kiffen is at the Border Keep. There are extensive tunnels under the keep. They extend below the surrounding lake into both kingdoms."

"I assume this is one of the secrets of the parchment?"

Montee nodded. "Your mother used the tunnels in the war against Maligon. No one knew they existed until our forces were driven back to the keep. Your father found them."

Adana sat forward. "No one in the kingdoms knew until then? They must be well-hidden."

"His discovery helped turn the war in our favor. Otherwise—"

"The keep was under siege, wasn't it?"

"Yes." Montee stopped and tilted her ear toward the north, toward a distant high-pitched whistle. An alert used by approaching Watchers. "Do the giraffes sense anyone?"

Adana straightened, and her eyes took on a distant look. She smiled after a moment. "Sinti and Veana approach."

Montee nodded. "Are they far enough away for me to share one more piece of information with you?"

Adana paused for a moment, then nodded.

"Good," Montee said. "There is much more, but it will have to wait." She dropped her voice to just above a whisper. "Considering the current circumstances in Belwyn, what I'm about to say is dangerous in the wrong hands. Do not repeat it to anyone."

The familiar frown of displeasure crossed Adana's forehead. "I'm sure I can judge accurately how to deal with secrets, Montee."

Montee opened her mouth to speak but closed it and bowed her head. When she looked back up, she made sure Adana felt the heat of her stare. "I am aware you are queen, and that my request sounds presumptuous, but important lives are at stake."

"All lives are important." Adana spouted the response immediately, but a moment later, bowed her head. "Forgive me, Montee. I'm unaccustomed to seeking your council. So much has been withheld from me these last three years. It chafes."

Montee gentled her tone. "You must understand, we had to make decisions and protect Moniah without your presence. Often, we couldn't risk sharing information with you. Not with you so far away. As for my warning, all lives are important, but some lives have more power than others. You know this. You might not like it, but I beg of you, do not take offense at my request."

She received a brief nod from the young ruler, almost the same nod her mother had used when she decided to acknowledge someone's request. "Of course. Please continue."

The news held a lot of weight, but time to tell Adana was running out. "Empress Gabriella has an heir. Of legitimate age."

Bewilderment flashed over Adana's face, and she bit her lip in thought for a moment. "How?"

"How is a discussion for another time. Sir Jerold is her son. A prince of Belwyn in his own right."

"Jerold." Adana grinned. "Leera knew something was different between them. They appeared much too close for a knight and empress when we met them during the Kingdoms Council."

Montee thought back to the council. It had provided the opportunity she needed to pull King Micah out of his depressed state after Chiora's passing and the revelation of the plan for Adana's extended stay in Elwar. Although he had been reluctant, she managed to convince him to attend. A better man and regent returned afterward.

"Jerold was born some time during the last war with Maligon," Adana said, disbelief evident on her face. "Surely people know."

"Adana." Montee knelt before her and grasped her hands. "I'm sorry I cannot tell you more now. I hear Sinti and Veana approaching."

They both turned toward the flicker of movement on the edge of the firelight. Sinti, a sinewy brunette, and Veana, a brown-eyed woman with light brown skin, entered the camp. On their heels, gasping for air, stumbled Glume, the giraffe keeper, red-faced with exertion.

"Your Majesty." The Watchers knelt before her, fatigued, but alert. "We have news of a possible encampment south of here."

"South?" Adana looked dazed. "But you came from the north."

"In a circuitous route. We narrowly avoided the advance of Maligon's troops after they attacked our camp." Sinti extended her hand toward the queen. "I am relieved you avoided them."

"Are we in danger of discovery?" Adana asked.

"No, Your Majesty," Veana said. "They don't travel this way. They appear to be headed south."

"South? Toward Adana's View?"

"It would appear so," Veana said.

Montee turned toward Adana. "My queen, this is distressing news, but these Watchers are tired and hungry. Since Maligon's forces do not threaten us here, shall we allow them a few moments before we question them further?"

Adana nodded. "Of course. Forgive me." She arched a brow at Glume. "And Glume? How come you by this company?"

The man was bent over, hands on his knees, wheezing and gasping for air. "My duty is to the royal giraffes. Am'brosia and Bai'dish need me." He straightened and peered in the direction of the two long-necked creatures, his chest visibly rising and falling as he struggled to calm his breathing.

"Glume, we are pleased by your loyalty." Adana gestured toward the stream. "There is fresh water, and we still have fish by the fire. Help yourself."

The man nodded, took a deep breath, and trudged up the hill toward the giraffes.

A smile twitched on Adana's lips as she watched the man clamber up the incline. Then she turned back toward the Watchers. "Before you attend to your needs, I must know what you can tell me of Samantha."

Veana frowned. "She disappeared during the attack. The last I heard, she went in search of Kassa's unit. She claimed she needed to ensure your route south was clear."

"Why would she do that, Montee?" Adana asked. "I can't imagine Kassa supporting that decision."

Montee did not speak at first. She didn't know how to interpret the information, especially since she suspected Kiffen saw Samantha in a different light. "I don't know. I would like to think about this." She turned and walked away from the fire, Sinti and Veana following her at a distance.

When she glanced back, she saw Adana walking up the hill where the giraffes stood. When she reached the top, the young queen leaned close to Am'brosia's flank. The giraffe sidestepped closer to her until Montee could see the animal bearing some of the woman's weight.

The largest animals known to Monians towered over Adana, making her appear small and uncertain, exactly how Montee suspected she felt after so many upheavals in her life.

* * * * *

Chapter Nine

Sir Jerold of Belwyn paced his cell in the barracks. Three steps to the wall, three steps back. The guard outside the door watched him, doing little to hide his yawn of boredom.

What had happened to Maligon?

Ever since the traitor had usurped the throne and imprisoned the empress, soldiers had kept Jerold locked in this cell except to parade him out for the populace to see. Soldiers surrounded him as he walked along the parapets of Belwyn's castle behind Maligon. After the first time, he kept his eyes averted from the macabre spectacle of heads spiked along the wall. Rebels, according to Maligon. He knew if anyone suspected his true birthright, his head would join them.

Images of his mother's bedraggled appearance during the one visit Maligon had allowed him with her in the dungeon kept Jerold quiet. They had stripped her of her fine gown and left her in her underclothes. Her hair, usually a glorious tumble of dark curls, hung in a tangled mass. Dirt smudged her face, but her eyes glittered with clarity. Did she maintain that clarity still? Six days later?

He remembered his reaction at the shocking sight. "Blazes, Maligon! Have you no honor? Keeping her caged like a rat in this filth?" Jerold had reached through the bars to comfort her. "My lady, what do you require?" Even as he had asked the question, Jerold recognized how ludicrous it sounded.

He hadn't spoken to her of his own treatment, aware her quarters made his look magnificent.

Empress Gabriella had ignored Jerold's question and glared at Maligon. "Are you pleased with your coup? Do you really believe you can rule? You, the illegitimate spawn of my cousin's rape?" She had spat at him then, the glob of spittle landing on Maligon's forehead.

A smile twitched on Jerold's lips at the memory. He never had suspected his elegant, ladylike mother's talents included hurling spit at someone.

After exchanging a few more insolent comments with the empress, Maligon had allowed Jerold a moment alone with her.

Her first words haunted him each night when he closed his eyes. "He has Watchers imprisoned here. The guards say a Watcher set the trap for them."

The traitor's ability to infiltrate the military of the four kingdoms included the esteemed soldiers of their ally, Moniah.

At her words, he had tried not to stagger or react, wondering who would turn on a Watcher. Then she had told him the worst of it. Maligon had a secret daughter in the ranks of the Watchers. Jerold had shivered while recognizing the irony. His mother's efforts to hide her own son might be mirrored by Maligon.

Before he had had enough time to gather more information, the guard had told him he must leave. He had held tight to his mother's hand, and she had given him an order the guard wouldn't understand.

"You must go." She had released her hold on him but held his gaze. The words and the action echoed a lesson taught him at an early age when they lived in fear of discovery. She had never needed to use it before that day.

Jerold dropped down on the cot in his cell and rubbed his forehead while staring at the soot smudges on the ceiling. How to leave? His mother expected him to get out of Belwyn. She wanted safety for him, but he wanted to save her, too. There had to be something he could do.

He sat back up, his hands on his knees, and looked through the barred door at the morning sunlight streaming across the grounds. Where had Maligon gone? Three days had passed since the traitor had yanked him from the cell to follow him as he strutted back and forth in front of the people. That night, Jerold heard the shouts of men and the sounds of many horses, soldiers, and wagons departing. Did Teletia still stand? Elwar? Moniah? Where was the fool man?

The guard who stood outside his door, today, was a new one. Maybe he could persuade him to answer a few questions. Jerold rose from the cot and wandered over to the door and leaned against the frame. He nodded at the guard, who glanced at him. "Hello."

The guard grunted.

"What happened to Moret?" The previous soldier hadn't shared his name, but Jerold had overheard the soldiers joke and call him that.

No response.

"Moret? You don't know him? He was my guard until today."

The man shrugged.

Jerold shifted to the other side of the door so he could see the soldier better. "Surely you know where he is. I wanted to ask about his son. The one with the bad leg."

All false, but Jerold hoped this man didn't know Moret.

The guard turned. "A bad leg? I wouldn't know."

"Could you ask him for me? We talked about it all night a few days ago. He truly worried about his son's ability to work when he comes of age."

"Afraid I can't do that." The soldier turned away.

Slumping against the doorway in feigned disappointment, Jerold said, "That's too bad. After sitting in here so long, I recalled a remedy that might help him."

The guard turned and came closer to the bars, looking in at Jerold. "Look, I can't say where he is. The army left three days ago. If he's still alive, maybe you'll see him again."

"Still alive? So, they went into battle?" Jerold's heart pounded at the news. "Where?"

The guard backed away from the door and repositioned himself as sentry. He said no more.

The morning trickled by, slow and monotonous. Jerold lay back down on his cot and drifted to sleep in the warmth of the tight space.

He woke to the jangle of keys. "You have a visitor."

The door opened, and a Teacher of the Faith peered in at him, his green robes brushing the ground. The man, his face hidden under a hood, turned and thanked the jailer. "I'll see if I can bring him to see the truth of things. Maligon wants him as a willing figure of the faith."

The guard rubbed a hand over his chin, his beady eyes looking over Jerold. "I don't know why. He's just a soldier."

"Yes," the teacher's deep voice rumbled, "but he's not just any soldier. This man was the Empress' favored knight. His presence with the army will quell many doubters."

The guard took a step into the cell and peered at Jerold. In a heartbeat, the teacher grabbed him by the back of the neck and slammed his face into the wall. The soldier's body slumped to the ground.

"Hurry, we haven't much time." The teacher dragged the guard's body fully into the cell and struggled to yank the shirt off the man.

Jerold stared, unable to process the events.

"Put this on." The teacher thrust the shirt at him.

Sitting back on his heels, the teacher slid his hood back. He had a bushy, brown beard and friendly, dark eyes. "Would you prefer to remain here?" He shoved the shirt at Jerold again. "Or will you help me get this man into your clothes? We have scarce time to make the switch and get you out of here."

Jerold jumped into action, yanking his shirt off and dragging on the soldier's sweat-soaked one. He hopped on one foot and pulled one pants legs off, then switched and pulled off the other. The teacher, meanwhile, yanked the pants off the guard. "Here."

Within moments, the two had stuffed the guard into Jerold's clothes and laid him out on the cot.

"How did you find me?" Jerold asked.

The bearded man turned to him and met his gaze. "Father Tonch sent me a message, requesting me to try. We can discuss more later. We must go."

He hurried out the door, Jerold quick on his heels, thankful for word from the Keeper of the Faith. Could they actually escape?

They turned away and peered in at the soldier as three men walked toward them.

"That should keep the idiot quiet," Jerold said, taking the keys from the teacher and locking the door. He held his breath, waiting for the men to pass by.

"It's a shame I couldn't persuade him differently," the teacher said. "Thank you for getting me safely out of there."

One of the men stopped and glanced into the cell. "Is everything alright?"

Jerold hesitated while the teacher turned a magnificent smile toward the soldier. "Of course. I tried, per orders, to convince this young man to join our fight, but he tried to attack me." He slapped a hand on Jerold's shoulder. "This fine soldier took care of him."

The man peered into the cell again. "Can't see why we haven't put his head on a spike, too."

A slight kick from under the teacher's robes hit Jerold's ankle. He spun toward the soldier, thinking fast. "Maybe you should report this to the commander. Give this traitor what's coming to him."

"A good idea." The man nodded. "Carry on." The trio turned and continued on their way.

Once they turned the corner, the teacher grabbed the keys from Jerold. "Quick thinking, but the keys shall go with us. Let's give this man a chance at life."

They rushed down the side of the barracks through crowds of soldiers. Jerold struggled to keep up with the man in the green robe. The only reasons he didn't stop to study the layout of Maligon's encampment were the man's hurried pace and his desperate desire to escape.

When they reached the edge of the tents, a wagon waited with a younger man in teacher green sitting on the seat, reins in hand.

They climbed into the bed of the wagon, and the younger man slapped the reins. The horse started off at a steady *clip-clop*.

Jerold ran his hand through his hair and looked back toward the camp. Maybe fifty tents separated him from the walls of the castle and his mother's prison. Maligon had left a bare minimum as guard. That information could prove useful.

He turned back to the teacher. "And whom should I thank?"

The bearded man bobbed his head. "Brother Honest. But don't thank me yet. We have much territory to cover before nightfall. Then we switch to horses. You have a long day and night ahead of you, I'm afraid."

* * * * *

Chapter Ten

Night creatures scurried in the low-lying shrubs and grasses of the plains as Elayne followed Joannu toward the village. Even though it would take most of the night to get there, the Watcher chose to stay off the roads, a wise decision in Elayne's opinion. For the most part, they trotted through knee-high grass. Traveling in the Watcher's uniform loaned to her by the queen made the journey much easier. Elayne chuckled at the idea of any of her fellow tavern maids seeing her like this, or her family, or the real lady of Glenhaven.

Joannu paused and glanced back at Elayne, her eyes glinting in the moonlight. "Was that a laugh?"

Had she broken some rule of scouting? Elayne shook her head. "I'm sorry Joannu. I'm used to my own thoughts. I forgot we needed to be quiet."

Turning to face her, Joannu grinned. "Here? We're fine. When we get closer, I'll warn you. Until then, we can talk." She relaxed her stance. "So, do I get to share in your humor or am I to be left in the dark?" Joannu swung her arms out to her sides, including the surrounding night in her meaning. Her teeth flashed white in the faint glow of the moon.

"You want to know what I was thinking?" The idea shocked Elayne. No one cared what a tavern maid thought. In fact, no one cared what a lady's maid or lady's companion thought, either. Of course, Joannu didn't know she was all those things. She saw a lady of breeding before her. Nothing more.

Joannu nodded. "It's a long night. We have no reason to travel in silence. I want to know more about you. The first Listener I've ever met. You're amazing."

"I find that hard to believe." How much did Joannu expect to learn? She hadn't even known she was a Listener until a few hours ago.

"But you are the first one I've met. I'd guess most people would say the same thing."

"I still don't know what it all means or how to act."

"Is that what made you laugh?" Joannu tilted her head in thought. "I remember my mother laughing at the notion that I might be trained as a Watcher."

Elayne felt a short pang of empathy for Joannu before she realized the Watcher's voice held no enmity toward her mother's laughter. "No. I was enjoying wearing the uniform rather than dresses, and it struck me how others might react if they saw me."

Joannu nodded and gestured for them to resume walking. She slowed her pace until Elayne drew abreast of her. "I remember my first uniform. It felt so foreign. I felt a bit exposed, to be honest. If you put me in a dress, now, I might expose more of me than you want just to be rid of it."

Elayne giggled. "You wouldn't strip in front of others, would you? I'd love to see the queen and Montee react to that."

"Probably not. But I'd be tempted. It's best I don't test my impulses on this point. Don't you think?"

"Agreed."

They walked along in silence for a few moments, but the Watcher's suggestion stuck in Elayne's mind. She imagined herself in the middle of her first employer's grand estate, refusing to wear the plain skirt and blouse delegated to her. She imagined how the puffed-up matriarch of the manor would pause and stare at her as she ripped off the clothes and flung them in the lady's face. The skin around her mistress' eyes would tighten and then her face would turn purple, just as it had done the day she accused Elayne of seducing her husband, the honorable Lord of Glenhaven. A shiver ran down Elayne's spine at the memory.

Joannu peered at her sideways. "Are you cold?"

"No, just a memory turned upside down by your suggestion."

A cluster of large rocks rested at the foot of a tree to their left, and the Watcher crossed to them and sat down. She patted the boulder next to her. "We can rest for a moment."

"I'm fine. Really. We don't need to stop."

"I know that, but I think we should. You've been through a lot lately."

Another chill ran down Elayne's back at the woman's words. She tried to ignore the haphazard turns of her life. That ability had made the last few years easier to bear, but no one ever noticed her troubles. She shrugged. "A lot has happened to all of us, Joannu."

Watchers were known for reading a person's actions and knowing more about them than others could see. Had Joannu discovered her secret? She didn't want Joannu to see her as an imposter or weak. Not after the kindness the Watcher had shown her so far.

"That's true." Joannu leaned forward, her elbows on her knees. "But I'm trained to adapt to changes, as are the other Watchers and the queen. You have been thrust into our midst. From what you've told us, you aren't accustomed to these upheavals. Except for caring for your grandmother, your life has been protected."

Elayne held her breath, waiting to see if Joannu would say more. When the Watcher remained silent, she relaxed and sat down next to her on the rocks. "I guess my life has changed a lot in the last few weeks."

The coarse surface of the rock would ruin the fabric of a dress. Even though she squirmed a bit to find a comfortable position, she found the uniform leathers stood up to the rough stone texture. She couldn't hide a grin over that discovery.

"Were you close to your grandmother? You must miss her after so many years of caring for her."

Her grandmother might be a safe topic; she just needed to imagine the events had occurred recently to fit the story Sarx had concocted about her. "I know it was just weeks ago, but it feels longer, and then, suddenly, something happens, like the attack on our camp, and it feels like it was yesterday."

She did miss her grandmother, but she hadn't spent the last few years caring for her as Sarx had told everyone. She had died many years ago. Still, Elayne remembered how her grandmother had always noticed her as a young girl. Most people had seen a slew of brothers and never noticed the young girl in their midst. Only her grandmother had. She wiped at a tear that slipped from her eye. She didn't cry. How could this soldier's simple questions elicit such emotion?

"You haven't had time to grieve for her, have you?" Joannu rested her hand over Elayne's but turned away, looking out over the plains stretching toward the dark horizon.

This was the Watcher's traditional way of providing privacy, choosing to not look at the person. Elayne had learned that in her short time among them. Joannu wouldn't try to read the signs her body gave away at this time. Touched by the simple act of kindness and the gentle, warm pressure of Joannu's hand over hers, Elayne stared across the plains and allowed a few tears to escape down her cheeks. The night swallowed her ability to see the point where ground met sky, and she wondered if Joannu's gifted sight allowed her a clearer view.

After a moment, Joannu withdrew her hand and stood up. "We should move on. But if you ever want a moment to talk or sit beside someone, I'll be here for you. I remember what it's like to be thrust into a vastly different world. Believe it or not, I was a companion for a noble's child before I came to the Watchers. I lived a life like a lady's, but I never had the right to claim the nobility that went with the way I lived."

Stunned at this simple revelation and the closeness to her own story, Elayne followed Joannu into the fields.

They reached the outskirts of the village a few hours before dawn. The first signs of habitation were the farmers' fields. Harvest should be soon, but the ground lay fallow and dry. As they crossed the ground-up turf, Elayne heard the wheels of a cart and the plodding *clip-clop* of a horse coming from the east. She tapped Joannu's shoulder, and when the Watcher turned toward her, she pointed to her ears and nodded in the direction of the sounds.

"You hear something?" Joannu turned and scanned the distance, then turned back toward Elayne with a frown. "I can't see anything."

"It's beyond those buildings. A cart with one horse. Wait." She listened longer. The timber of three voices came to her on the night air. One sounded rushed and worried, another tired, and the last carried a hint of relief in his few words. Two men and the worried voice of a woman.

"Someone has arrived. The person who met them doesn't sound happy about it, but the other two are glad to make it to the village."

Joannu grinned in delight. "You could hear that much?" She turned and studied the distance for a few moments. "I still don't hear a thing and can't see anything. Do you think you can get us closer without being seen?"

Elayne hesitated. "The queen said not to enter the village."

"Just get us a little closer."

Elayne crept forward, letting her ears guide her. As they drew near to the buildings, she could distinguish the voices a little better. A few words reached her. The woman's voice had risen a bit in anger, maybe, as she objected to something. The word "here" sounded clear in the night, but nothing else. The tired man's voice never got louder, but Elayne did hear him say "long night" and "safe." She had given up on the third person speaking again, but as the woman's voice began to soften, he said, "Thank you for your hospitality." The voice rang clear on the night air, the tone proper, cultured, and too close to where she and Joannu stood.

She motioned Joannu away. When they reached a safe distance, Elayne said, "I think a traveler has arrived, but the innkeeper isn't happy about it. He's staying though. I don't think we'll find out anything else unless we go into the village."

Joannu nodded. "Let's scout along the edge of town. Keep listening."

* * *

The next evening, Adana and her Watchers sat around the fire in the coolness of the day's end, enjoying freshly caught fish. Elayne sat by the stream, mending a hole in the skirt she'd worn on the night their camp was attacked.

"The village is called Roshar, Your Majesty," Joannu said. "It's small and on the Monian side of the border. These are your subjects."

Adana nodded, turning the phrase, "your subjects," over in her head. It never meant much before, but, with the threat of Maligon lurking around the next bend in the road, she felt fiercely protective of them. "How large is the village?"

"Maybe ten farms, a tiny inn. There's not much, but there is a small gathering of the Teachers of the Faith on a hill beyond the village."

Adana nodded, but her heart thudded at the mention of the Teachers. Since her mother's death, she had found little comfort from them except when dealing with Father Tonch and Mother Sariah. Those relationships were based on a lifetime of guidance and friendship.

Guilt flooded her heart as she realized she had not thought about the safety of the Protector or the Keeper of the Faith. Tonch left Elwar the night before she did. He had gone to prepare for her coronation. Sariah remained in Elwar. Adana shied away from considering their possible fates. Instead, she allowed a spark of hope to fill her; maybe she would find Father Tonch in Roshar.

"And you didn't enter the village?"

Joannu shook her head. "Elayne was able to get us a bit closer, but she feared we'd be discovered if we went any farther into the town."

"Did you see anything of concern?"

The Watcher squinted into the distance. "I saw nothing to suggest a problem, but Elayne overheard voices. Travelers, she said."

Adana looked over her shoulder at Elayne and gestured for her to join them. Elayne hurried over and settled beside Joannu in front of the small fire.

"What did you hear?"

"I listened for as long as I felt it was safe, Your Majesty. I heard three people talking. Unusual for the time of night."

"What were they talking about?"

"A cart arrived in the middle of the night. A woman, possibly the innkeeper, was not happy about its arrival. I think one of the travelers knew the innkeeper. He sounded tired. They might have traveled a long distance."

"Are you positive the traveler was a man?" Adana wrinkled her brow and turned toward Joannu. "Did you see these people?"

"We stayed in the fields, so we didn't get close enough. There were a few lights in the distance. But Lady Elayne heard their voices. She interpreted a lot from what she could hear. She said one of the travelers sounded like a noble."

Elayne nodded in agreement. "One of them had a deep voice, and he spoke in proper tones."

Adana contemplated this information, unable to accept that a Listener might detect something a high-ranking Watcher couldn't. "How could you have heard so much when Joannu didn't?"

Elayne's cheeks flushed under Adana's scrutiny, but she smiled. "From what you've told me, I'm aware of sounds, just like you're aware of what you see. You hear the sounds but don't interpret them as I do."

Adana stared at her. She wanted to ask Montee her opinion but suspected the woman would agree with Elayne. "I wish I knew more about Listeners and how they work."

"I can only go by what I've done and heard in the past." Elayne tilted her head to the right as she looked at Adana. "When your father or mother returned from an outing or trip, did you know they were home before you were told?"

"Of course. Any child knows their parents' return."

"If I had to guess, I'd say you heard certain sounds or clues. You just didn't realize it."

Adana stared at the lady as she recalled a time when her mother had stayed away for half a season. She had been in her rooms at the estate when a maid bustled in to straighten the chamber and check Adana's attire.

"I saw people reacting."

Elayne tilted her head to the side, a gentle smile on her face. "What did you hear? Horses? Footfalls? You must have heard something."

Adana placed herself in the room again, focusing on everything but her sight.

Horses' hooves clopped on the stone inside the gates, gear jangled, voices called out commands. Servants' feet pounded as they scurried around. Logs were plunked down on fires to build them up.

"I never noticed before. Watchers spend so much time focused on what they see. I believe we might have much to learn from you, Elayne."

Elayne's smile broadened, and her eyes sparkled with moisture.

Adana wondered at Lady Elayne's transparent joy. Her whole demeanor had changed once they discovered her skill. Could she trust her? Was her information accurate or meant to set a trap?

Kassa's, and even Quilla's, voices floated through her mind:

Do not trust anyone until you have several reasons to do so.
You must be able to explain your trust.
Once trust is given, it is hard to protect yourself from that person.

Still, the woman had saved her life when Maligon's traitors attacked their camp. What else could she do? She needed a Listener.

"Do you think it could be Maligon's forces?" Adana turned to Montee.

"From Sinti and Veana's scouting, it would be doubtful. They are further south than this."

"As far as we know," Adana said. She turned back to Elayne. "Were you able to detect if others arrived with them? Could it be a large party?"

Glancing at Joannu, Elayne said, "I believe Joannu would have heard something if there had been several. Two arrived on the cart. One person met them."

Adana stared at the Listener, astounded at this gift so casually added to her company. In childhood, she had dreamed she might be one of those rare people who appeared in bedtime stories, the ones blessed with dual gifts. Some nights, she imagined the Seer's truth telling. That would help tonight. Most nights, she dreamed of joining the Listeners even though she could not fathom what it would be like to possess a fine-tuned sense of hearing.

"Do you have anything else to report?" Adana turned back to Joannu, still feeling the need to confirm Elayne's report.

"I did notice one oddity as we neared the village. The fields were bare, as if they harvested everything early."

Why would the village clear their fields early? Adana turned to Montee. "Does harvest come sooner here than in Adana's View?"

"No, my lady."

After pondering this bit of puzzling news, Adana said, "Two travelers shouldn't be a problem. I think we need to go into the village. Rest a few hours, then we'll head out. I want to get there by early morning."

* * * * *

Chapter Eleven

Just outside the Monian village of Roshar, Adana's group stopped in a small clearing hidden from the road. Tall trees separated them from travelers and disguised the giraffes' presence. The village was only a short walk up the road. Glume, Sinti, and Veana settled down to wait with the giraffes and horses.

Adana, accompanied by Montee, Joannu, and Elayne, entered the village on foot, just as a small squad of Watchers would do. Each one, except Elayne, had their bow and quiver slung on their back. Since trainees often did not carry a bow without the approval of the squad leader, they knew Elayne's lack would not give her away. In order to conceal Adana's identity, Montee walked in front as the leader. For the hour of the day, few people traveled the main road.

They walked past a few homes, and the nearly barren fields stretched in the distance behind them. In Moniah, most farmers shared the arid land, the only way to yield sufficient crops. These fields should be heavy with produce waiting for harvest.

A man wearing dusty pants and a fringed, dirty blue coat, sat on the steps in front of the inn. The structure was simple—earthen walls on the first floor, with a wooden porch and second floor above. It appeared tidy, if not large. The farmer stopped chewing on a twig, his eyes bugging out when he spotted the four Watchers walking toward him.

He pulled the twig out of his mouth and jumped to his feet.

"Esteemed Watchers!" He made an awkward bow, never taking his gaze off them. "How can our village serve you?"

Montee regarded him with a commander's stare. "We seek food and information. Where is your village guard?"

The man swallowed. "Our guard is gone, Watcher. He responded to the call from Adana's View."

Adana fought the urge to step forward at his words but remained in place. Had someone alerted Linus to their troubles? Hope beat in her chest that her home remained safe from Maligon.

"We come from Belwyn and are not aware of this call," Montee said. "Who is in charge here?"

"That would be me." A plump woman stepped out on the inn's porch. Her billowing green pants and white shirt identified her as the innkeeper.

From her vantage point behind Elayne, Adana saw her companion stiffen in recognition. *Was this the woman's voice overheard in the night?*

Adana studied the innkeeper more closely, noting how her sharp eyes swept over them. Adana was positive she had caught every detail of their weaponry in one glance.

"Come in. We have little news to share, but maybe you have news to swap?" The innkeeper turned and walked through the doorway without checking to see if they followed.

Montee hesitated, but nodded, and they entered the inn.

The main room was small with just a few tables and chairs. A fire burned on the hearth, and the delicious smell of fresh baked bread permeated the air, causing Adana's mouth to water. The fish the night before was good, but she'd become accustomed to eating heavier meals indoors and prepared by others. She glanced around. Where were the inn's customers? She had never entered the common room of an inn without at least a few old ones gathered for a smoke and gossip.

The innkeeper stood by the fire, arms crossed in defiance. Adana examined their surroundings, unease creeping up her back. Why would a Monian exhibit disrespect toward a Watcher? She reached out to Am'brosia, sharing the view of the empty common room with the giraffe. In return, she saw the clearing where the giraffes waited. All was quiet and peaceful there. Her shoulder responded with a faint tingle.

The man wearing the dirty, blue coat shuffled in behind them.

The innkeeper nodded in his direction. "Did you bring horses with you? Clart can go retrieve them if you like."

Montee turned toward the woman. "We travel faster without them."

The man stopped shuffling from one foot to the other and skirted past them. The door to what must be the kitchen squeaked as he shoved through it. "I'll tell Cook to bring you some food."

"Please, sit," the innkeeper said.

Elayne slumped into the first available chair but jumped up when no one else sat. She blanched under the reproachful look Montee cast her way.

Adana stopped studying the room to consider her new companion. No lady would plop into a chair. They sat, the entire effort an elegant act.

"You've come from Belwyn?" the innkeeper said.

"Yes." Montee walked around the small room, peering up the stairs and pushing the door to the kitchen open. "Where did the man go? There is no one in the kitchen."

"I imagine out back to the barn. Where Cook spends his free time. We don't get many visitors lately, much less Watchers. It's as if we're not part of the kingdom." The woman whipped out a cloth and swiped it over a table, scratching at an invisible spot.

Most villages welcomed Watchers with excitement. People thronged to see them and brought them gifts of food and water. Was this odd behavior typical of a village on the border or was something else happening? Elayne's report about the traveler rang a warning in Adana's mind. He had arrived two nights ago and spent the night in this inn. Was he still here?

The faint tingle in her shoulder pulsed stronger.

She laid her hand on her knife and backed toward the stairs, giving her a broader view of the outdoors and access to the rooms above. She caught Montee's attention and tilted her head toward the stairs. The First Vision nodded, and Adana ascended a few steps, still watching the upstairs and both doors in the main room.

Joannu moved to position herself by the one small window.

The innkeeper became silent and still as the Watchers surveyed their surroundings.

In the silence, Elayne whispered, "Men." She rushed toward the door to the street.

Joannu stood to the side of the window and peered out. She nodded in agreement. "Our arrival has been marked. Several men are gathering down the street. They don't appear to be welcoming us."

Their host paused and put her hands on her hips, exposing a long knife tucked in her belt. She glared at Montee. "We won't let you steal our crops and supplies again. We may be a small village, but we protect what's ours."

Adana turned toward the woman, shocked at the suggestion they might steal from these people. She hovered on the stairs, fighting the urge to take over while Montee edged closer to the innkeeper.

"Why would you think that? Do you not serve the queen?" Montee said.

"The queen?"

"Yes, Queen Adana."

The woman looked askance at Montee. "You do not know? Or are you conspiring against us again? We know she's dead. The poor child never lived to become queen."

Adana bit her lip and choked back revealing words.

A movement at the top of the stairs distracted her from the lies the woman spoke.

"Montee." She nodded in the direction of the stairs. No one was in sight, but a shadow had crossed in front of the dim light filtering through a small, round window at the top of the stairs.

Montee advanced on the innkeeper. She grabbed the woman's pudgy arm, the one closest to the knife at her belt. "Who is up there?"

Eyes bulging, the innkeeper sputtered. "It's no one. My son. He isn't right in the head."

Adana crept up the steps, trying to peer into the dark hallway above. Slow, focused breaths did nothing for her pounding heart. Her shoulder pulsed in time with the beats, but not in alarm.

All five women jumped as a man appeared at the top of the stairs, his deep voice resonating with excitement. "Adana."

Adana leapt down to the foot of the stairs and turned, tensed into a fighting stance. Joannu and Elayne rushed to her, Joannu blocking the man from reaching Adana.

The man bounded down the steps toward them, his steps clumping in the quiet room, his thick brown hair falling over his forehead. Days-old stubble could not mask the broad smile shining in his brown eyes. He wore peasants' clothes, but Adana knew Belwyn's young knight at once. She corrected herself, remembering the secrets disclosed by Montee two nights ago. Standing before her was Prince Jerold of Belwyn, not a knight.

"Sir Jerold?" Montee maintained a hold on the innkeeper while scrutinizing the man.

The man stopped on the last step and turned to Montee. "Montee. It's a relief to find the two of you alive.

He frowned as he noted the tension in the room and Montee's hold on the innkeeper. "Talia, is everything OK?"

"Do you trust this woman?" Adana said, pushing past Joannu to face Jerold.

"Of course." He turned to Montee. "Whatever Talia has done to raise your suspicions, I assure you, she is loyal to the Seat of Authority."

Montee let go of the older woman's arm and glanced between the innkeeper and Jerold. She pointed toward the street and the sounds of the gathering crowd. Her voice held no warmth. "Then, why do men gather?"

"Forgive me, my lady Adana." The plump woman bowed as best she could while rubbing her arm. "We thought you were part of the Watchers who attacked us the other day."

"Attacked you?" Adana stormed over to the woman. "Why would Monian Watchers attack a Monian village?"

The plump woman shook her head. "We wondered the same thing."

"Let me alert those in the street to our safety. I'll explain everything, Your Majesty." Jerold rushed out the door. They heard his voice, tapering off as he walked down the road toward the group. "No worries. We are safe. They are known to me."

Joannu stood in the doorway, watching. "They are dispersing."

Jerold returned. "I think it's best we don't alert them to the presence of their queen yet, my lady."

She nodded and watched as this young knight—prince, she reminded herself—took charge. In little time, the innkeeper, Talia, produced food and drink and bustled around apologizing to everyone. "The queen, alive and here in my simple inn. I can't believe it!"

Jerold winked at Adana but turned to the woman and said, "Yes, but Talia, we must keep this to ourselves. Let the others believe she is dead for now."

Dead! Adana shivered. After all that had happened, it never crossed her mind that Maligon would announce her death.

In short detail, Jerold apprised them of Empress Gabriella's imprisonment in Belwyn.

"I tried to save her, but she bade me escape and seek assistance." His relaxed composure had shifted to sorrow and anger. Before, Adana would have considered him a very loyal servant to his empress. Maybe a bit too zealous. But now, aware this man was Gabriella's son, hidden in front of everyone for his entire life, she ached for him.

Noting her gaze on him, he turned and shared more news. "I'm sorry to tell you, my lady, but Maligon holds Watchers in those cells. The empress told me she overheard the guards talking about it. He keeps them blindfolded in the dungeons of Belwyn."

Stomach threatening to reject the food she'd just enjoyed, Adana rose from her seat and walked toward the window, strengthening her connection with Am'brosia. In her mind, she saw pure darkness, then one giraffe kicked and shattered the darkness, let in the light. She nodded. She must find a way to save her Watchers and the empress.

"My lady," Jerold interrupted her thoughts. "I know this news is troubling, but there's more. According to what the Empress overheard, a Watcher turned them in. One of your own." He whispered the last words.

Adana stiffened. Her shoulder spasmed in alarm. She spun on her heel to face the group. "Not one of mine, Jerold. Maybe one who wears the uniform, but not one of mine. No Monian Watcher harms her sisters in this way. Or steals from my people."

She fumed as she paced the small room. How could her Watchers turn on each other? Images of Elwarian soldiers fighting each other flashed in her mind. Somehow, Maligon had infiltrated the Watchers. Cold dread stilled her pacing. How could any of her Watchers turn to him?

In the silence, Elayne spoke. "Sir Jerold, how did you manage to leave Belwyn?"

Adana swung around and gaped at Elayne. She posed the one question none of them had thought to ask.

Jerold shook his head. "I would prefer to discuss that somewhere more secure." He turned to Montee and Adana. "I've only arrived a day ago. Talia is known to me, so we can trust her. The others in this village are hurt and outraged. They fear any strangers, especially those dressed as Watchers. I think it's best we sort out the details with my rescuer, Brother Honest."

* * * * *

Chapter Twelve

Montee sipped her drink. Talia still bustled around with platters of bread and cheese and tankards of warm cider. It tasted watered down.

"My apologies for not providing better food. The Watchers who attacked us...forgive me, Your Majesty...took most of my food stores."

Adana turned to the woman, but her face stiffened, and she bolted from her seat. Talia dropped a tankard as Adana rushed across the room, a wild look in her eyes. "Am'brosia."

Montee exchanged an alarmed look with Joannu, and the two jumped up to follow the queen.

Adana reared her head back when Joannu blocked her from running out into the street. Her voice sparked with fury. "Allow me through."

Montee took hold of Adana's arm and drew her back toward the center of the room. Adana battled each step. She fought like a wild animal.

Montee blocked Adana from the door. Whatever was happening with the giraffes, the queen was there, not here. She needed to break into her vision. If she used force to stop this sudden outburst, she might hurt the queen. She sidestepped as Adana sought an exit. "You can't rush out there."

A quick glance toward the door showed Montee nothing. She nodded to Joannu. "Check the street."

Joannu slid past Adana and stood just inside the doorway. She peered into the street, checking the surroundings before stepping out onto the porch. Jerold followed her.

Montee grasped Adana's shoulders. She peered into her eyes. "What is it? What is wrong?"

The girl's nose flared in determination. Her feet pawed the ground like a raging bull's, forcing Montee to tighten her hold.

"I must stop them. Danger. Wrong." Adana twisted in Montee's grasp. "Let me go."

Joannu returned. She shook her head. "There's nothing out there."

Adana still struggled against Montee. What was happening with the giraffes? She considered sending Joannu to check on them, but the earlier gathering of angry villagers stayed her decision.

Montee took hold of Adana's arms, holding them close to her sides. "Does Am'brosia need help? What do you see?"

Adana froze, her mouth turned down. She blinked at Montee, but her sight remained distant.

Behind Montee, Talia's voice rose in command. "Fire's breath. What new trouble have you brought? I agreed with the villagers not to trust another Watcher. I break that agreement, and reap this catastrophe."

Montee turned to reprimand the innkeeper, but Elayne reached the woman first.

"Her Majesty is experiencing a communication with the royal giraffe." Elayne's soothing tones dropped to a whisper as she pulled Talia away. "Feel honored you are here to witness it."

Montee still held Adana. The queen stood before her, body rigid and eyes focused elsewhere. The rank smell of fear rose from her.

"Help Am'brosia from here," she said. "Tell us what you see."

Adana swung her head and choked out in alarm. "Armed men."

"Soldiers?" Joannu hurried to the door and scanned the street again. "No one is there."

"No one?" Talia yanked her arm out of Elayne's grasp and stormed toward Montee and Adana.

Whip-fast, Elayne grabbed Talia's arm. Her fingers turned white at the knuckles as she held tight to the woman's arm.

The innkeeper struggled against her. "Unhand me!"

"When you are calm." Joannu approached the two. Arms crossed, she stood in front of Talia. "I'll watch her." She jutted her chin toward the street. "See if you hear anything."

Elayne hurried to the queen's side, ignoring the innkeeper's confused response. "Of course, she hears this outburst. We all do."

Joannu advanced a step closer to the innkeeper. Montee focused her attention back on Adana. "You see soldiers? Where, Your Majesty? How many?"

In reply, Adana started to pitch her head around wildly, again.

Elayne stepped from Adana's side. Her head tilted one way and then the other. She shot a menacing look at the innkeeper, who kept up a stream of grumbling comments. Jerold remained at the door, watching the street.

With careful, measured steps, the Listener approached the doorway as if dragged by her right ear. Montee watched out of the corner of her eye while keeping an eye on Adana, who still swung her head around in confusion and alarm. She shot an occasional glance toward Joannu and Talia. The innkeeper must know something. Montee bit her tongue and prayed for Elayne to hurry. If she ever found the Watchers responsible for this reaction to their presence, stripping them of their rank and throwing them in a dungeon of darkness would be lenient.

After a few more breaths, Elayne returned to Montee and whispered, "It sounds like an angry gang. More than before."

"How far? What about metal?" Montee thought for a moment. "Clanging?"

Elayne shook her head. "Not far. No metal."

Montee sought Adana's wild gaze again. "Adana, please." She gave her arm a slight squeeze. "What do you see?"

Adana slumped against Montee. "Surrounded. Angry."

"Will she be all right?" Elayne dropped her voice lower as she spoke to Montee, an obvious attempt to prevent the innkeeper from hearing.

Jerold had followed Elayne to Montee's side. "Am'brosia must have panicked. The bond must be strong and close." He cocked an eyebrow at Montee. "Am'brosia's emotions have overwhelmed the queen."

Montee understood Jerold's confusion. At her age, Adana should dominate the connection and not let the giraffe's emotions overcome her. One more problem combined with impending war for her to correct. Her attention returned to the queen as the fight seeped from her. She fell against Montee, who settled her into a chair. Despair poured from the young queen's eyes.

"Watch her," Montee said to Elayne and Jerold.

Withdrawing, she turned an angry glare on the innkeeper. "What have you done?"

Head shaking back and forth, Talia backed away from Montee.

"Unless I miss my hunch, those are your villagers out there." Montee took a step closer.

The innkeeper's back straightened. "We have to protect ourselves."

Grabbing Talia's arm, Montee shoved her toward the door. "In the name of your queen, call them off. Now."

"But—"

"Now." Montee glared at her. "And beware," she shoved her face up close to Talia's, "no harm better come to the giraffes. None."

* * *

Adana watched Joannu escort Talia to talk to the mob. The moment they reached Am'brosia, the image of the two women filtered along the bond. Talia, looking much plumper than she actually was, walked beside Joannu, who looked twice as tall as normal, and the crowd surrounding the giraffes backed away in deference to the innkeeper.

She breathed a sigh of relief. "They're there."

The chair beside Adana scraped the floor as Montee sat beside her. "What do you see?"

"The villagers stepped back for Talia. She spoke to them, and no one appears to object. They hold her in high regard."

"Are you sure?" Montee leaned forward.

Fighting a desire to lay her head down on the table and rest, Adana sent the image of looking around through the link. In moments, Am'brosia was showing her the people surrounding them.

"That man. Clart is frowning, his arms crossed." She scanned the rest. "The others show no tension in their faces or shoulders. Some are staring at the giraffes like trainees do." Adana smiled at that image. As much as Moniah honored the giraffe, every year, several of the Watcher candidates greeted a giraffe up close for the first time. The awe on the villagers' faces resembled the trainees' reactions.

The image from Am'brosia flickered with amusement, and Adana perked up. "Ah. It appears Talia has noticed Clart's anger. She's shouting in his face just like Kassa used to do in training exercises. He's backing down."

The air stirred as Montee rose from her chair. "Good. How many are there?"

"Close to thirty. Then, of course, Veana and Sinti and Glume."

The information appeared to satisfy Montee who left Adana's side and wandered toward the door. Quiet settled over the inn.

The scraping of chairs on the floor drew Adana's attention to Elayne. She wandered through the common room, righting the few chairs knocked out of position. Most ladies wouldn't think to straighten chairs, especially in an inn. Odd.

Her curiosity evaporated as the presence of Am'brosia drew closer. With a glad cry, Adana ran to the window.

The royal giraffes, Am'brosia and Bai'dish, ambled into the village of Roshar. Neither appeared any worse for their mistreatment. Glume walked between them, his head bent in consternation. To either side of the giraffes walked Sinti and Veana. Talia led the villagers, and Joannu followed them, her posture tense and alert.

Montee came to stand beside Adana but turned back to address Elayne and Jerold. "Remember, no one must know about Adana. These are not Bai'dish and Am'brosia; these are extra giraffes from Moniah's herds."

"What if someone already said something?" Elayne whispered.

Adana glanced her way. "They won't. It's part of Watcher training."

"What about Glume?"

Montee shook her head. "He rarely talks. I guarantee you he has not said anything to these people, except to chastise them for harassing the giraffes."

She turned toward Adana. "Have you communicated your wishes to Am'brosia?"

"Yes."

In public, Am'brosia was trained to spread her forelegs and lower her head toward the ground whenever she greeted Adana. Today, she must not. Adana noticed a twitch in the giraffe's jaw muscle, a distant tremor from Am'brosia's scowl of disapproval over the command.

Despite her displeasure, the giraffe would comply, but she had been quick to relay her own order to Adana. Bai'dish must be taken to Kiffen. Glume had agreed to accompany him.

Shock raced through Adana's mind at the implication of the vision. How did Am'brosia know what Glume would do? Could this be another gap in her knowledge of the bond?

Maternal superiority flowed from Am'brosia. Although Adana could not describe how she knew it, Am'brosia was trying to tell her she had a lot to learn about their connection.

Montee led the way into the street. Am'brosia played the role well, never even looking at Adana. Instead, with a hint of amusement skipping down the link, she butted her head against one of the villagers who had attempted to draw close.

Beside Am'brosia, Bai'dish stood tall, his neck extended its full length as he looked over the crowd, his stare so intent, the entire throng of people turned to see what had captured the giraffe's interest.

A cluster of Teachers of the Faith approached from the other direction, a man of about thirty years in the lead. As they stopped before the Watchers and Sir Jerold, the townspeople stepped back, deference reflected on their faces. Even Talia gave way to these representatives of the Creator.

The teacher in the forefront was a muscular, tall man. His sandy-brown hair hung to his shoulders and covered his face in a bushy beard. He regarded the group with serious, brown eyes until his gaze fell on Adana and Elayne. It flicked between the two and then settled on Jerold. When he spoke, his deep voice carried a friendly tone. "The Temple welcomes these Watchers to our small home. Would you join us there?"

Jerold turned to Montee. "What is your preference?"

Both glanced back at Talia, who appeared to agree with the teacher. Maybe she'd had enough excitement for the day.

Montee inclined her head in thanks. "We accept your offer."

"Excellent." The teacher smiled and nodded toward them, but Adana felt his gaze settle on her, again. She noted a flicker of awareness lighting his eyes, and her stomach, unsettled as it was, lurched. "I'm Brother Honest. The Teachers of the Faith in Roshar are honored to host you. Our temple rarely receives visitors."

Adana held back before following the man and the others. This teacher, a man unknown to her before, lived in her dream. He was the teacher who held the branch out to her as the river carried her away.

* * *

The temple was small, but, to Adana's surprise, the grounds surrounding it encompassed a small estate, with a high stone wall encircling it. She followed her companions as the teachers led them down a wide corridor through the living quarters. The walls of this building reminded her of home, the sandstone reflecting the light shining through numerous openings cut into the walls. The teachers who greeted them broke off from their assemblage as they passed various corridors, until Brother Honest and a young boy were the only ones accompanying them. Brother Honest entered a room near the center of the building.

"Our solarium provides a peaceful place to rest and relax, especially during the heat of midday."

Potted trees and plants scattered around the room created a garden-like atmosphere, and the sweet perfume of late-blooming flowers permeated the air. In the center of the room, several cushioned chairs sat around a circular table with an unlit brazier in the center. Adana glanced up and noted a covered hole in the ceiling. She glanced at Elayne. What would a Listener notice in this room?

The lady's head tilted to her left, a smile spreading across her face. She glanced toward a corner. Adana followed Elayne's gaze and spotted a tiny fountain. Its gurgle sounded hushed in the large room.

As they settled into soft chairs, Brother Honest sent the boy to ensure the giraffes were provided shade, feed, and water. After the boy trotted away, Brother Honest turned to the group and smiled. "We've had a giraffe paddock for many years. I'm glad giraffes will finally inhabit it, even if for a short time."

He walked back to the large, wooden doors and shut them, closing out the sounds of the servants and teachers going about their daily duties. His gaze drifted back over to Adana and Elayne. Her skin prickled as he studied them intensely. After a few seconds, he approached and knelt before Adana.

Adana swallowed at the man's recognition, and a ripple of surprise ran through their group.

"Your Majesty, I am relieved to find you alive and in my humble order. The Teachers and I will assist you in any way necessary."

Adana struggled to remember if she had ever met this man, but her only memory came from the prophetic dream. Every time she woke from the dream, she wondered who he was. Now, he knelt before her. Should she trust him? Even if she only knew him through her dream, she doubted a man who tried to save her would cause her harm. She laid a gentle hand on his shoulder. "Arise, Brother Honest, and tell us how you come to know me on sight?"

The man smiled before standing. "Mother Sariah describes you well. I've seen your likeness in her painting."

"Sariah!" Adana sat forward. "Is she here? Is she well?"

"No, Your Majesty." His shoulders sagged. "We have heard nothing of Mother Sariah."

"Oh." Adana sank back into the seat. Disappointment, mixed with overwhelming fatigue, enveloped her.

"I had hoped you might bring news of the Protector." Brother Honest glanced around the group. "And I'm hoping your being alive means the rumor of your father's death isn't true, either."

Fighting the despair his words wrought, Adana said, "No, I'm sad to confirm the news of my father's death."

"And King Donel?"

She nodded.

Honest backed up to a chair and sat. The pleasant expression his face had worn moments earlier turned tortured. "I am sorry for your losses, my queen. If I can offer any comfort, I am at your disposal."

As much as she desired comfort, Adana denied herself that, especially from one of the Creator's teachers. Too much stood at stake for her to find time to mourn more than she'd already done. She glanced around the room, noting the pallor of sorrow settling on each person. As queen, she must move them forward.

With a deep inhalation, she sought energy. Am'brosia complied with a jolt through the link. First, she must learn more about how he recognized her.

"You said Sariah paints? You have seen my face in her paintings?" She shared a look with Montee. It might prove difficult to keep her presence a secret if many had seen the paintings. "Who else might recognize me due to these paintings?"

"No one, save me. There's only one painting. The Mother told me she painted it for my eyes only. She assured me I would need to know your face some day. I thought she meant because you would be queen." He regarded her, wonder in his gaze. "It seems Sariah knew more than she told me."

"They usually do," Adana said under her breath. A painting of her resided in this sanctuary for the teachers. Adana couldn't recall ever seeing her likeness in a painting. "I would like to see it."

"Of course."

"We both would like to see it, but for now, I must ask you," the First Vision nodded toward Elayne and Adana, "how you knew which one was Queen Adana?"

Honest smiled. "I hesitated for a moment. No offense to you." He nodded toward Elayne. "The queen has a royal demeanor. She holds her head like a queen. Anyone familiar with Watchers couldn't miss her stance, either. You," he hesitated as he turned toward Elayne, again, "must still be in training."

Adana thought about her mother's bearing. Did she really carry herself with such confidence? Did her stance give away her Watcher training? She glanced at Elayne who had opened her mouth to speak.

Montee interrupted. "You have keen eyes, Brother. Were you raised among Watchers by any chance?"

"Yes." His mouth stretched into a sad smile. "My mother died fighting Maligon. She was young, not fully trained." He settled into a seat. "War sends them into battle, no matter the experience."

The mention of war crowded other thoughts from Adana's head. She faced some of the same obstacles her mother had, but with less training or capability. And Honest's words caused her to recall Montee's warning that Watchers earned their promotions on the battlefield. Could she prevent this from happening, again? The pain of losing her parents too early created a hole in her core. One she doubted would ever heal. She didn't even know which of her Watchers had young children. "What rank was your mother?"

"My mother was an Archer when the war started. She moved quickly up the ranks and earned her Watcher rank when she died." His gaze softened. "Queen Chiora visited me, along with Father Tonch, soon after. Your mother was a gracious and great queen, Your Majesty. I'm sure you will be just as she."

Decisiveness straightened Adana's back. She must live up to this man's expectations, for him and for all the other children of her kingdom. The weight of her responsibilities pressed down on her, but she welcomed it. She would live up to her mother's legacy.

"Brother Honest, I regret the pain Maligon's Rebellion caused you." She folded her hands in her lap and focused her attention on the man. "Unfortunately, he still threatens us. I would like to know more about the women who claimed to be Watchers who robbed your village of its stores." She looked around at the gathered people in the room—Montee, Joannu, Elayne, Jerold, Sinti, Veana—her heart thankful for each person's presence. "But first, we should introduce ourselves." She turned toward Sir Jerold, unsure if his identity was known to the teacher or not. "Would you do the honors?"

* * *

Around midday, Adana wandered out to the giraffe paddock. The story of Jerold's escape from Maligon amazed her. The teacher in her dream saved royalty as a habit, it would seem. The news that the Keeper of the Faith, Father Tonch, had alerted Honest to Jerold's need provided a short moment of peace. And Honest had confirmed that Tonch was safe in Adana's View.

She entered the large, wooden barn-like structure, amazed that it looked brand new. Honest assured them it had been built over ten years earlier at a suggestion from Mother Sariah. The wood gleamed from polish. Fresh hay, scattered over the floor, provided soft bedding for the giraffes. Two feeding trays and water troughs hung from the walls at the height of the giraffes' heads. Glume fussed over his charges, checking the water troughs and testing the quality of the vegetation provided for their meals.

He smiled in satisfaction. The Roshar teachers had taken great care in preparing for this long-awaited day.

The information gleaned from their meeting with Brother Honest still shocked her. She regretted the message she must try to send to Kiffen through Am'brosia and Bai'dish. How would Kassa respond? The Watchers who had ransacked the village of Roshar a few days ago referred to Samantha as the rightful First Vision.

Kassa's daughter, Samantha, guilty of treachery. She had never enjoyed the Watcher's presence, but she never suspected any disloyalty from her either. The other name Honest had mentioned was Kalara. Adana recalled her from the Kingdoms Council held in Elwar soon after her mother's death. Kalara's startled reaction to some of the information shared, and her quick excuse to depart once the council ended, now held a different meaning.

For a brief moment, Montee had dropped her Watcher's stoic visage, looking shocked and sickened over the revelation of both names. Most knew Samantha and Montee began their training together and had formed a quick bond of friendship. That bond hadn't survived Montee's promotion to First Vision.

It was ironic. Adana's main disadvantage, her absence from Moniah and her troops, had become an advantage in learning of these traitors. The knowledge of Samantha's treachery gave Adana a sense of relief, though. She had worried over why she disliked someone so high in the ranks and so closely related to the last two First Visions. The news would pain Kassa though, and she worried for the older woman.

As for Kalara, the news made sense. Adana had only had a few short encounters with her, and she had no personal feelings for the Watcher, only anger over the woman's stupidity in aligning with a monster like Maligon. What did trouble her was Kalara's part in the capture and imprisonment of loyal Watchers in Belwyn. It was one thing to go against Adana's crown, but another to strike out at the sisters she'd trained with from her first days as a Watcher.

The news of Maligon's mistreatment of Empress Gabriella, giving her care unfit for the lowliest animals, sickened Adana, and she tried to imagine how Jerold must feel. She had studied revenge and its effect on people, especially in the history of the four kingdoms. History kept the information sterile and impersonal. No longer distant information, the reality of revenge cut deep and painful.

Maligon had been exiled to die in the desert. Even though Gabriella hadn't passed the sentence, did his treatment of his cousin stem from his sentence or did it stem from something deeper, rooted in the jealousy of her noble birth contrasted with his illegitimate one?

For the first time, she was thankful neither of her parents had lived to see the mess their world had become.

Unaware Am'brosia had been eavesdropping on her thoughts, Adana jumped when an image of her mother interrupted her reverie. Am'brosia showed her Queen Chiora overlooking the scattered troops of Moniah, Elwar, Belwyn, and Teletia. Although hazy, she could tell the troops were shattered and confused with not enough soldiers in any position.

A vision of her mother's? Had this, coupled with Montee's vision of Chiora's death, caused her mother to make the questionable decision to send Adana away when the kingdom might be most vulnerable? Try as she might, Adana could not fathom why sending her to live under the tutelage of Queen Quilla would help her in this war.

Some things could not be answered, but she could seek the answer to one question. "Glume?"

The man turned from brushing Bai'dish, an expectant look on his face. He bobbed his head. "Yes, mistress?"

She walked up and laid a hand on the short, soft fur of Am'brosia's flank. The giraffe peered down at her with the intelligent, liquid-brown eyes that set them apart from so many animals. In times of trouble, those eyes provided precious, link-building tears, something that set giraffes even further apart from other plains animals. "Am'brosia told me you agreed to accompany Bai'dish to the Border Keep and Kiffen."

The man's eyes widened. He glanced up at Am'brosia. "She told you?"

"Yes. Is it true?"

"Yes, mistress. I promised her." He tilted his head up to look at the giraffe. "She's the first giraffe to ever tell."

"Tell what? I need to understand how this happened." She stared at this simple man who had always been more at home with Moniah's giraffes rather than its people. Her shoulder, which ached earlier, quieted as she contemplated her next question. "Have you always talked with the giraffes?"

Although a large, burly man, Glume appeared to squirm like a little boy caught eating a fine dinner with filthy hands. He shoved those hands into his deep pockets, causing the animals' heads to turn to him in anticipation. His pockets carried treats. Realizing their expectations, he extended crispy pieces of flat bread to each of them before he answered Adana.

"The first giraffe who spoke to me was your grandmother's. I was just a small boy, and my father was the keeper at the time."

Unflinching, his gaze met Adana's. "She told me her daughter's daughter would need me. I never was sure if she meant you or Am'brosia. I think she meant both of you."

The revelation hit Adana in the gut. How many more secrets lurked around her? How many would she discover, and how many would never be known to her?

Glume ran a shaky hand through his hair. "I've never told anyone."

He stroked his hand down Am'brosia's nose when her head dropped closer to his. Adana recognized the gesture. Am'brosia did the same thing with her when offering comfort.

"She must believe you need to know." Glume sighed and turned to face Adana, wonder widening his eyes and softening his voice. "From that point on, I could hear their thoughts and talk to them. All of them."

"The whole herd?" Adana swallowed at the implication. She could only speak to Bai'dish through Am'brosia.

"Yes, mistress. Every giraffe since then has spoken to me, but Am'brosia and Bai'dish do it more than any of the others. They are the strongest giraffes in the herd. They all are connected somehow."

"So, the way I communicate with her, you do the same?"

"Maybe. I'm not positive. It's images, not words. And feelings." He ran his hand along Am'brosia's flank. "She never let go of you while you were gone. It kept us both awake at night as she sought to hang on to your connection from so far away. They all love you, you know."

Guilt flushed over Adana. She had spent so much energy during her first few months in Elwar searching for the plant that allowed her to shove the link into the background, avoiding the frantic need for connection Glume described. Did he know she had done that?

"Yes. I knew. I gave Am'brosia the image of the plant to share with you."

Her head shot up. She hadn't spoken out loud, yet he answered her. Did he know she had ignored his warning that it should be used sparingly?

Glume nodded at Am'brosia, a deep sadness in his eyes, so similar to the depth of a giraffe's eyes when it cries. Adana stepped back from the man, shame and concern plaguing her.

"Don't be alarmed, my lady. Your secret is safe with me."

"You've told no one about my use of drunkenberry?" Another secret. But Kassa and Veana knew.

"I don't tell anyone what I learn from the giraffes." He giggled, a sound so incongruous with his large form and the seriousness of the conversation. "Who would believe me?"

Ashamed, she said, "I realize how wrong I was to drink the elixir made from the berries, but the headaches caused by our separation made it impossible to cope."

Am'brosia swung her head in Adana's direction, the link fading to quiet and peaceful.

"She knows, mistress, and understands. We agreed you needed the drunkenberries to eliminate your suffering. She insisted."

Adana pondered this new piece of information. How much did Glume know? She shot a look at Am'brosia, a warning in her eye, the order to not share her current thoughts blazing across the link. The gentle beast lowered her ears, an indication of submission. A deeper calm floated through the connection. Am'brosia trusted Glume.

"Please forgive me if I've alarmed you," Glume said.

Adana tilted her chin up toward the man. "We will discuss this further, but right now, I need to try to communicate with Kiffen.

He bobbed his head. "You need to warn the young king."

Adana raised an eyebrow. "Is there anything you do not know concerning our link?"

The flush that spread up his cheeks caused Adana to shiver in realization.

"In your absence, the little king and queen have been more talkative than their ancestors. I assure you, though, they don't tell me everything. Bai'dish just told me you needed to warn the king of something. I know not what."

Adana held back a grin at Glume's reference to the giraffes as little. "It's alright. I had planned to share the information with you, in case the king misunderstands the message. As you already know," she glared at the two giraffes, and shook her head when both straightened enough to avoid eye contact, "you and Bai'dish will be leaving for the Border Keep quite soon."

"Yes, mistress."

"And I will share the knowledge of your special skills with Montee and Kiffen. And Kassa."

The man paled but nodded.

* * * * *

Chapter Thirteen

Princess Leera's tears had dried up days ago. After mourning her father's death and the absence of everyone important to her, she didn't have another tear to weep. She wandered the gardens around Elwar's castle, numb and exhausted, pausing at her favorite haunts to recall pleasanter times with Adana. The servants watched her from a distance. No one interrupted her or spoke beyond a quick bob of the head and a formal greeting.

Her mind still echoed with the cries in the night, soldiers running in the halls, and her mother sweeping into her room to deliver the news. Her father, the king, murdered.

She had been awake at the time, wishing she hadn't been so cruel to Adana after the betrothal, wishing she could have traveled with her to Moniah. Each time the memory of that night washed over her, she shivered from an internal chill. Five long days stretched behind her since the world had shriveled up and died.

Today, she awoke to a dull world and realized this was her future. First, she roamed the halls of the castle. It no longer looked or felt like her home. Where were the friendly faces of the guards who normally stood outside her quarters? Everywhere she looked, she saw guards, more than usual, wearing the royal blue and gold of Elwar, but all of them were strangers to her. None of them exhibited the polished look of the castle guards she remembered. More than once, she caught one of them eying her in a most inappropriate manner. Their stares made her stomach churn with uneasiness so she fled to the gardens.

What had happened? Was this truly Elwar?

Somewhere in the midst of her grief, she had overheard chambermaids whispering about treason. As these thoughts plagued her, she disturbed a flock of birds in an arbor. They flew into the sky, squawking in protest. As she watched them flee, she wished she could join them and soar high above these gardens.

Settling on a bench, she glanced around. No one had trimmed the bushes in the past few days. Leaves and debris from a storm two nights ago still littered the paths. She bent and picked up a dried, brown leaf; it crumbled into tiny flakes in her hand. Just like her life, brittle and falling apart.

Leera stared at the pieces as they drifted to the ground. The gardens were her mother's pride and joy. Had the duties of running the kingdom kept her mother from ensuring the gardeners remained devoted to their work?

"I must speak to her of this," she said out loud. "She will be furious."

Or will she?

Her brief interludes with her mother had not been pleasant. Lord Sarx had been present each time, and the two of them had appeared satisfied at the arrival of more bad news, the death of Adana's father and the disappearances of Kiffen and Adana.

Taking a deep breath, Leera studied her surroundings. Maybe she would find peace in caring for her mother's gardens. She stood among the withering flora, taking breath after breath, feeling it awaken her soul. The sun beat down, warming her in this unshaded spot, but she knew its warmth was fleeting. Cold weather approached, and the warm days would be few. She took deeper breaths. In. Out. In. Out. Each breath filled her with the scents of dying flowers, but the fresh air awakened something within her.

I must remember that breathing exercise next time I feel fatigued, she thought, and then halted on the stone walkway. Adana did a similar breathing exercise whenever she sought calm. Was it a Watcher skill? Leera shook her head and pushed that question away. It demanded exploring, but her mother and righting whatever was wrong in Elwar's castle were her first priorities.

She started toward the castle and her mother.

Just outside the door to the castle's audience chamber, Leera paused. The guards weren't standing attendance in the corridor, and the doors stood wide open. From habit, she slid between the door and the wall to peer through the crack into the large receiving room.

Queen Quilla sat on the throne, holding court. Few people attended, but she preened and acted as if the chamber was full. She wore mourning black, but the crown on her head and the heavy golden chains around her neck negated the effect. A man, dressed in drab-colored pants and overshirt, knelt before her. When the queen bade him to stand, his bald head reflected the sun shining through the windows. He mopped his brow with a red kerchief and shuffled his feet.

"What do you request of the queen?" Lord Sarx stood to Quilla's right and addressed the supplicant

The man quivered. "If it pleases the queen, my store's stock is almost gone. I've been ordered to supply the queen's troops as they arrive, but I've received no payment."

"Payment." Quilla sat forward in her chair, a flush spreading across her cheeks. She laughed harshly. "You expect payment for serving your queen?"

The man took a hesitant step backward. "I beg your pardon, Your Majesty, but how am I to restock if I'm not paid for my goods?"

"What of your other patrons? Raise your prices for them."

He mopped his brow again. "I have no other patrons. My shop is overrun with soldiers."

"I see." Quilla leaned back in her chair, a benevolent smile spreading over her face. The merchant's shoulders relaxed.

"I see we have relieved you of stock you could not sell anyway," Quilla said in an imperious tone. "You have no patrons, so, as I see it, we did you a favor. Of course, you are no good to us without stock. I will need to seek another supplier, one more adept at business."

The merchant's shoulders sagged as if a weight fell upon them and, even from her hiding place, Leera saw tiny tremors run down his back. She'd seen servants tremble like that before, after her mother's scolding.

She clenched her hands and fought the desire to step into the room to defend the man.

The queen waved her hand in dismissal. "Escort this man out. He has no need I can address."

Horrified, Leera watched as two burly guards grabbed the merchant by his arms and dragged him out of the room. She pressed her body against the rough, stone wall as they passed. The merchant, pedaling his short legs to keep up with the guard's pace, looked fragile in their hands.

Why did this one man's plight draw pity from her? Leera followed the guards.

They dropped the man on the floor in a heap. She balled her fists tighter as the guards barked with harsh laughter at the defeated man huddled on the floor. They dusted their hands and turned back toward the audience chamber. The larger of the two, a swarthy man with gaps in his teeth and hard black eyes, stopped in front of her. "What have we here? Has the lamb finally emerged from her slumber?"

Leera straightened her spine and stared at him with contempt. She waited for him to look away from her in discomfort.

The soldier guffawed and jabbed his partner. "Look at her. She thinks she's the queen now, I s'pose." Laughing, the two men brushed past her, the larger one so close, he almost bumped her into the wall.

Leera maintained her footing and opened her mouth to reprimand them, but she heard shuffling from where the guards had dropped the merchant. She turned back to him instead. "Wait," she ordered his retreating back.

The man hesitated in the doorway and twisted to peer at her over his shoulder.

"Please wait," she said, surprised at the fervor in her voice.

His eyes widened as he recognized her and knelt. "Princess Leera. I apologize. I did not see you there."

Leera smiled. At least someone knew how to respond to a princess. "Rise, sir, and tell me your name."

The man frowned, but he struggled to his feet. "I am Gerguld."

"Is it true my mother has commandeered your store's supplies?"

"Yes, Princess." The man fidgeted and stared at the floor.

"How much?"

"Begging your pardon, mistress, but all of it."

Leera tapped her foot and thought. The man looked honest to her, and he treated her with respect, unlike anyone else she had dealt with in the last few days. "Are you without any funds to resupply?"

The man wrung his kerchief in his hands. "They've taken everything."

Leera noted his obvious discomfort. She wanted to help and found the urge a little unsettling. From the looks of his faded and patched clothes, his shop must be in a less than desirable location in the city. He definitely did not wear the fine clothing her favorite merchants wore to the castle. As she considered these thoughts, the man backed away, casting a fearful look toward the audience chamber entrance.

Leera paused and listened. The sounds of the rough guards dismissing another supplicant reached her. She grabbed Gerguld's arm, dragged him down the hallway, and ducked behind a stone pillar before letting go of the man.

He gaped at her, his mouth hanging open.

"Close your mouth!" Frustration and doubt rolled through her. Why this man? Why should she care?

"Where is your shop?"

"In the south quarter. I'm sure nowhere the princess would have visited."

"You're right about that. How close to the city walls are you?"

His eyes bugged in surprise. "The walls?"

"Yes. The walls. How close are you to them?"

The man dropped his gaze to the floor and worried the kerchief in his hands. "My shop is on the outer wall."

Leera smiled. This could be useful. She wasn't sure why yet, or when, but she feared she might need a discreet exit to the outside soon. The wall was a good location to have an ally. "Do you have a door through the wall?"

"Uh, well, we're not supposed to have any entrances, 'cept inside the wall."

"But do you?" She was shorter than the man, but her continued stare worked on him, even if it hadn't worked on the guard.

"Yes." His answer was a bare whisper. He cowered before her.

"He was right." Leera never forgot her brother Serrin's suspicions, voiced so many years ago. He told her stories, mainly to scare her, about secret entrances into the city through the walls. Entrances used by thieves and kidnappers bent on capturing her favorite horse or even a young princess.

Serrin's death may have been the first stone to fall away from her perfect life, but her brother had shared some perceptive insights with her.

"Your Highness?"

Leera turned back to the merchant, her thoughts spinning with ideas. "Who else knows of this entrance?"

"I'll close it up, mistress. The minute I get back." He backed away from her with slow careful steps.

"You will not." Leera advanced on him and grabbed him by the arm. His clothing felt rough and foreign under her delicate fingertips. She sniffed. He didn't reek of onions or any other horrid smell; his scent was plain, like her maid's. At least he was clean. "This is vital to the kingdom's survival."

Was it? She didn't know, but it sounded like something a heroine might say in a story.

"Who else knows of this exit?"

The man licked his lips, white saliva sticking to the edges. Leera quivered at the sight of his obvious distress, thrilled to hold such power over him. She shoved her face closer to his. "Who?"

He half-sobbed the words as they escaped from him in a rush of air. "My wife and children. We work the shop. And one of my suppliers."

She released him and smiled with satisfaction. "See? That wasn't so difficult, was it?"

Gerguld's hands shook as he rubbed his chin, his gaze darting up the hallway.

"Can they be trusted?"

The merchant's frantic hand froze on his face. He turned his head sideways a little and scrutinized Leera.

She wondered what he saw in her, and she forced a smile to her face, not a big one, just enough to set him at ease. Her mother had taught her this trick for enticing suitors, but surely all men responded to a woman's gentle smile.

When his whole posture shifted, shoulders relaxing and chin rising so he met her gaze, she interpreted it to mean yes.

"Good." Leera laid a gentle hand on his arm.

He jerked in surprise.

"Gerguld, I believe we can be of use to each other."

Dragging him behind her, she sought out an empty room. When she pulled him inside and eased the door shut behind them, he glanced around in surprise. "Mistress. My lady. I shouldn't be here like this." His hands worked the kerchief again. "If your mother's guards find us…"

He was right, of course, but she needed to speak with him for only a moment. She stalked across the room and stood where the light cast a beam across the floor. Her hair always glistened like an angel's in such light. At least, that's what her mother said.

Arms crossed, she studied him up and down. "Gerguld. I won't keep you long." She glanced toward the door. "And I'll ensure your safety when you depart."

"Yes, mistress."

"Tell me about your store. What you sell, what other stores border it, where the door to the outside leads."

He was nodding until her last request. Then the fear she'd seen when the guards dragged him from her mother's presence returned to his face.

"Never mind the outside door," she said, amazed at how his shoulders relaxed or tensed based on her words. "Let's start with the store's goods."

"General merchandise, mistress. Food, clothing, weapons, building supplies."

She couldn't have found a more perfect ally if she'd gone in search of one. If she needed a quick departure, he offered the means and the supplies once he restocked.

"Will this help?"

Gerguld's eyes grew huge when she dropped a few gold coins into his hands. He fell to the ground and soaked her slippered feet in kisses and tears.

The coins meant so little to her. She had never thought about the value of her money. It bought her rare glimmer cloth and other beautiful things. The meager amount she gave him would have covered the cost of only one fine outfit.

"Princess. My lady. I can stock my shop two times over with this. You are too kind."

After the man left, Leera marched back to her mother's audience chamber, lightness in her step.

Afraid of her mother's spies discovering his restocking efforts, she had ordered Gerguld to wait at least a week before buying any supplies. "Only buy in small quantities to begin with," she had ordered him.

Her caution gave her pause. Was her mother truly the enemy? She would know soon enough.

She paused, straightened her dress, and walked into the audience chamber.

Leera stood inside the entrance, her spine straight, her shoulders back, and waited to be recognized. To her left, she heard the snickers of the soldiers but ignored them.

Her mother sat in whispered conference with Sarx. A young man of about twenty stood off to the side behind Sarx. He wore the royal blue and gold of Elwar's royalty. She frowned. Who was he, and why did he dress in such a way?

He was attractive, but unlike anyone she had ever seen. His skin had an olive hue, and dark hair curled to his shoulders. Even from this distance, his bright green eyes shined in an unusual contrast to his darker skin. The man spotted her first, and a pleased smile bloomed beneath his full mustache. When he leaned over and spoke to Sarx and her mother, Leera stared at his well-defined muscles, rippling beneath his close-fitting tunic. Although he was of average height, not much taller than Sarx, his muscles tricked the eye into believing him taller. Leera had noticed the same effect with Pultarch's physical appearance. She caught the man staring at her as she waited, his gaze not dropping when she met his, and she gasped at the flutter that erupted in her stomach.

"Ah, Leera, my princess, you have chosen to return to our world." Her mother's musical voice interrupted her thoughts. "Come here and join us." She beckoned to her with smiles and dimples. Leera hesitated, fighting the urge to run into her mother's arms. They reached for her, but were those arms as safe as she once thought? She approached with decorum, but hope flooded her heart.

Queen Quilla rose and grasped Leera's hands within her own. "Are you feeling better? You look refreshed. There's even some color in your face." She stroked her daughter's cheek with a dove-soft hand. "Doesn't the princess look well?" Queen Quilla turned to Lord Sarx, who bestowed a smile on the both of them.

Sarx bowed at the waist and placed a kiss on the back of Leera's hand. "Your Majesty, she is as lovely as you."

Leera recoiled at his words. Normally, she enjoyed fawning praise over her beauty, but Sarx's glittering eyes appraised her in a disturbing way.

The sound of shifting feet reminded the three of them of their surroundings, and Leera noted the few remaining supplicants straining to observe their interaction. "Taren," Quilla addressed the strange, green-eyed young man. "Dismiss them. I will not receive any more today." She turned to Leera. "Come. We have much to discuss."

The princess allowed her mother to lead her into the small, but plush, room behind the audience chamber. Several candelabra burned brightly, flooding the room in a soft glow. Strewn around the room were couches and chaises covered in thick, luxurious, golden velvets and fluffy blue cushions. The carpet sank beneath her feet and cradled her every step. Leera blinked in surprise at the transformation of the room. Her father had kept the room stark and austere. Her mother's touch was evident in the opulent furnishings.

Noting her surprise, Quilla smiled and patted a chair beside her. "Come sit. Isn't this so much more to your liking than the cold, bare room it used to be?"

Leera sat and felt her body sink into the softest, most luxurious cushion she had ever touched. It felt magnificent, and she relaxed into its embrace.

"I believe she approves, dear Frank."

Leera started. Since when did her mother call Lord Sarx by his first name and refer to him as dear? She watched in shock as the man settled in next to her mother and placed a familiar arm behind her.

"Yes, Quilla, I believe our lovely princess will come to enjoy her privileges as heir to the throne."

Leera scrambled to sit forward, but she found the embrace of the cushions difficult to escape. She floundered for a moment, and then Taren, entering the room, rushed to assist her. "Uncle, Your Grace, you mustn't let the princess struggle so against your comforts."

Leera flushed at his touch but noted how he addressed Sarx. She should have known he was related to the one man in Elwar she disliked. As if he knew her thoughts, Taren knelt before her and bowed his head. "Forgive me, Your Highness. We have not been introduced, but I could not bear to see you swallowed by these instruments of softness."

She stifled a giggle and turned expectant eyes to her mother who had been watching this interchange with keen interest.

"Princess Leera." Lord Sarx smiled upon her. "I would like to present my nephew, Taren. His mother, my sister, is a baroness in the kingdom of Lisseme."

Leera extended her hand to the young man and smiled as he took it formally and bowed low over it. His moustache tickled her fingers as he placed a chaste kiss on them. "It is a great pleasure to finally lay eyes upon you, Princess. I have heard rumors of your beauty, but they are all false." He smiled as she straightened and frowned at him. "You are far more beautiful than any words can describe."

The words fell on her ears in a welcome rush, but somewhere in the back of her mind, a warning flashed. Something Lord Sarx had said a moment ago should concern her, but Taren was quite a distraction. Up close, he was exquisite. How could he be related to Lord Sarx? Obviously, he had not inherited his looks from his uncle.

She shook her head and tried to recall what Sarx had said.

"My dear, you look befuddled. Have you had too much excitement for one day?" Quilla smiled down on her.

At the queen's words, Taren jumped up and retrieved a water goblet from a table. He leaned toward Leera. "It's only water, not my father's vintage wine, but a cool drink might refresh you."

Leera took it from his hands. A charge of desire rushed through her arms when his fingers brushed hers. She sipped the water and eyed the three of them over the edge of the goblet. She needed to get her wits about her if she was going to discover what was truly happening in the kingdom. What was it Sarx had said? Something about the heir?

She slammed the goblet onto the table, water sloshing over her hand. Taren jumped back and cast an anxious look at his uncle. Sarx and Quilla straightened, and their kind dispositions evaporated as they watched her struggle to stand. Taren reached out to assist her, and she slapped his hand away.

"Whatever is the matter?" Quilla asked.

"What did dear Frank mean when he called me the heir to the throne? Is Kiffen dead?" A cold fear swept through her.

Quilla's mouth formed a tight smile, and she darted an angry look at Lord Sarx. "No, my dear. We have heard nothing of your brother's plight." She paused and pulled a frilly handkerchief from her belt. Dabbing at her eyes, she said, "One can only hope he is alive." Quilla sobbed into the handkerchief, and Lord Sarx rushed to comfort her.

Leera crossed her arms. "Since when do you weep for my brother? Do you really think I will believe this feigned mourning?" She stalked over to her mother. "Where is your widow's grief? That I might believe. But for Kiffen. No, Mother. The two of you despised each other."

Quilla shoved Lord Sarx away and jumped up in Leera's face. "How dare you speak to me in such a tone! I am queen, not just your mother. I have responsibilities, and if you do not see me mourn, do not assume I don't. If you only knew." She placed the back of her fingers over her mouth but dropped her hand immediately. "No, I will not ruin your cherished memories of your poor, departed father. Just remember, I am the monarchy now, and you are the only heir."

Leera quailed beneath her mother's onslaught. Never in her life had she been on the receiving end of her mother's sharp tongue. Kiffen, Adana, even her father had suffered from these tongue lashings, but not Leera. Suddenly, she felt small and wanted to disappear back into the fog that had been her existence over the last few days.

"Your Majesty, if I may suggest?" Taren took a small step, placing him slightly between the two women. They turned their gazes on him, Quilla's glittering anger, Leera's fighting desperation. "A short walk in the fresh air of the gardens might revive the princess' spirits."

Quilla retreated a step and considered his suggestion.

"My nephew would make a perfect strolling companion for her, Quilla." Sarx laid a familiar hand on Quilla's arm. "Now is not the time to address these pressing issues. Our lovely lady has only just returned to us from her own mourning." For once in his life, Lord Sarx made sense, Leera thought, although she resented his reference to her as "our lovely lady."

Moments ticked by, then Quilla threw her hands up. "Of course. Go enjoy the flowers before they all die."

Leera let Taren lead her from the room, but she frowned at her mother's comment. What an odd way to refer to the gardens. Just before the door closed behind them, she heard Lord Sarx say, "They will make a perfect couple. My nephew, King of all Elwar!"

She looked sideways at the young man, but he showed no sign that he had overheard the statement. Oh, he was beautiful. Marry him? Become Queen of Elwar? She stumbled over her feet at these thoughts, and Kiffen's face loomed in her mind.

* * * * *

Chapter Fourteen

Samantha stood beside the map in the Central Tower. The markers placed on the board represented Kiffen's and Kassa's best guess as to the locations of their allies and enemies. Adana's View looked heavily armed unlike the Border Keep. Her eyes drifted along the line indicating the river flowing east from the keep. Somewhere along the banks of that river, Adana and the giraffes camped. Should she inform Maligon, yet? Or should she wait for more information?

A shadow fell across the map and she jerked upright, surprised to find Kiffen facing her, a pleased smile on his face. Unlike most men, he approached quietly. Where had he learned that?

She batted her lashes a few times, feeling foolish over the flirtatious action, and smiled at him. He nodded back, a blush creeping up his neck to his jawline.

Her smile turned true.

"King Kiffen, have you news of the queen's location?"

He shook his head and leaned over the map and pointed to a spot along the river. "I believe she is in this vicinity."

Samantha slid along the edge of the table until she stood within a breath of him. She leaned her body forward, brushing her arm along his side, placing her hand over his. "Here?"

He jerked upright and took a step back.

It came so easily. Maybe she should have tried this with Linus after Montee dropped him for the title of First Vision. A sour taste washed over her tongue at the memory of her friend's complicity. Instead, she smiled and turned to face Kiffen, leaning her backside against the table. It was so easy to unnerve him. Linus might have been a different story.

"Are you all right, Your Majesty? You seem a bit agitated." She reached out and touched his cheek, marveling at the warmth created by her presence. "You're flushed."

Her mother used to rest her palm on Samantha's forehead to check for a fever. Biting her lip to fight back a chuckle of delight, she stepped forward and did the same. A lock of his hair brushed softly under her fingers.

For a moment, he did nothing but stare into her eyes. She saw the decision in his eyes a half-breath before he ducked back and stepped away.

"I'm fine. Just overheated from running up the steps, I guess."

"Of course." She turned back to the map. "This is the same point you guessed at yesterday. Does this mean you haven't connected with Bai'dish today? You don't know if they have moved?"

Kiffen angled around the table to the opposite side of the map, rubbing his hand along the stubble on his chin. "It's still hard for me to maintain the link long enough to learn anything."

The smile plastered back on her face, Samantha took a step in his direction. "Would you like me to help you? You experienced such great success last time. I believe we are well-matched. Don't you?"

If she hadn't been a Watcher, schooled in controlling her actions, Samantha would have shrieked with laughter. Kiffen's eyes bulged in fear, and his jaw flexed as he clenched his teeth. With a swift glance toward the doorway, he said, "Your offer is kind, Samantha, but I have just recalled a meeting with Simeon."

He hurried from the room.

Arms crossed, and a smile spread over her face, Samantha leaned back against the table and chuckled. Who knew seduction was so much fun?

* * *

Kiffen followed Simeon down the corridor in an old and little-used part of the Border Keep. Their footsteps echoed in the solitude of this part of the keep. Lit torches, spaced infrequently, revealed rough-textured gray stone walls hung with faded wall hangings. The few pieces of furniture appeared clean, but faded, too. A chill in the air added to the dismal atmosphere.

Thankful for Simeon's silence, Kiffen tried to fight down anxiety over his response to Samantha. For many reasons, it made little sense to him. She was harsh to most people, unkind to the rest. He suspected she was playing with him, but why?

He stopped in front of a tapestry, staring at it, but not seeing it. More important matters needed his attention. He needed to find a way to avoid Samantha.

"Your Majesty?"

With a distracted nod, Kiffen trotted up to Simeon's side as his advisor hurried forward, checking around each corner before proceeding farther. "Why so much secrecy, Simeon?"

"In a moment, you will see."

Kiffen's heart pounded. Had Simeon noticed his attraction to Samantha? Was he taking him deep into the keep, away from prying eyes and ears, to reprimand him? Unbidden, Samantha's eyes, lit up by her smile, surfaced in his mind. When she laid her hand over his, sparks of energy raised the hairs on his arm. No matter where he had moved, she prowled after him. She had to be at least ten years older. Why did she affect him like this? He loved Adana and couldn't bear the idea of causing her any pain, yet his body didn't act like he felt.

"Almost there," Simeon said.

Kiffen studied the hallway, shoving Samantha to the back of his wayward mind. The next intersecting corridor created a momentary tug of familiarity. If he was correct, the next hall housed statues of the final king of Yarada and his daughters, Elwar and Moniah.

Simeon turned in that direction.

So, this was where he chose to discipline his king, in front of the statues of the founding mothers, his and Adana's ancestors.

The light pooled in a large, recessed area set off on the right. It reflected on the three statues. The middle one rose taller than the other two, the last king of Yarada.

Kiffen stared up at the stately figure and braced for Simeon's accusations. They didn't come. Instead, the man gazed in silence at the statues.

Relieved, Kiffen studied the king of Yarada's statue, the stone face set in a smile of kindness. Could Kiffen ever be seen that way? A kind, benevolent king? Not if he couldn't keep his desires under control.

The ancient ruler's wide-set eyes, fine nose, and angular chin reminded Kiffen of his younger brother, Serrin, a much kinder and nobler man than himself. The statues of the king's daughters, the first queens of the new kingdoms of Elwar and Moniah, sat to the left and the right of the king's. Twins they had been in birth, but not by appearance or interests. Sculptors often downplayed and softened less attractive features in their reproductions, but in Elwar's gaze,

Kiffen saw his mother's caring eyes. Centuries may have passed since Queen Elwar died, but the family resemblance remained through his mother, Queen Roassa. A flash of his mother's scent, roses, and the recollection of her bending down to help him hold a sword streamed into his mind. He swallowed the sudden surge of misery that threatened to overtake him. His mother long gone. His father recently murdered. Samantha's presence distracting him. So much in a few short days.

In an effort to regain control of his thoughts, Kiffen turned and studied the statue of Moniah, searching her face for similarities to her newest successor, Adana. It wasn't hard to recognize the high forehead and cheekbones as well as the graceful neck shared by the two women. Although Moniah's eyes differed in shape from Adana's, Kiffen realized the sculptor had managed to capture the intensity of a Watcher's gaze in the hard stone.

"Remarkable, aren't they?" Simeon stood next to him, gazing up at Elwar's statue. "You resemble her."

"Do I?" He shifted his gaze back to Elwar's statue and shrugged, unable to see anything but his brother's face. "I don't see it."

"It's really not a physical resemblance, but I have seen the same look on your face. Penetrating focus, but with kindness."

"Is this what you wished to show me?" Although thankful for the reminder, Kiffen saw no true reason for Simeon to bring him here, not when a battle against Maligon loomed before them.

"A moment." Simeon disappeared behind the king's statue. Kiffen followed him in time to see the man lean over and grope below the rim of the statue's pedestal. A pleased smile announced a click and a brief note of stone grating on stone. A portion of the wall behind the statues slid back, revealing a dark stairwell leading down.

The opening beckoned to Kiffen, and for the first time since the attack in the forest, he felt hope. This secret passageway held the key to beating Maligon. He felt it to his core.

Simeon withdrew two torches from within the passageway and lit them from one of the lights illuminating the statues. He held one torch out to Kiffen and tilted his head toward the opening. "Care to explore, Your Majesty?"

Kiffen took the torch but did not enter. Crouching low, he slid his fingers under the pedestal of the king's statue, feeling for the catch. The marble felt smooth and cool, except for an indentation toward the center of the base. He rubbed his finger over the spot, but nothing happened. "How does it work?"

"You've found the trigger?"

Kiffen nodded.

"Place your finger in the hole and then push to the right."

He did, and the entryway closed, a rush of air flickering the torchlight. Kiffen fought back a sneeze.

Simeon's alert eyes glittered with secrets. "Press to the left."

Stone grated again, but quieter than the first time.

"We'll need to get some glimmer oil to lubricate the hinges." Kiffen grinned. "Lead on."

The air smelled stale, and the temperature dropped as they descended. The stairs emptied into a long tunnel. Unlit torches stood in sconces placed along the walls. They passed a tunnel leading to the right, and then another leading to the left. Cobwebs gathered around the sconces and the dust on the floor only revealed Simeon's footprints. No one had been down here in an exceptionally long time.

"I had no idea this was down here." Kiffen paused to peer down a passageway, excitement warming his arms and ideas tumbling through his mind. "How far does it go? Is there another entry?"

Simeon glanced over his shoulder, a grin on his usually somber face. "I will show you."

They followed one of the tunnels to the right and halted before a large, iron-braced door. "There are secrets in this room known only to a few."

Kiffen waited, his pulse pounding in his ears. So far, Simeon had waved off his questions. The man would enlighten him when ready.

The fortified door creaked from disuse and opened to reveal a round room. As Simeon lit the torches along the walls, Kiffen realized the room's layout resembled the map room in the center tower of the keep. An exact replica of the map table stood in the middle of the room, with a large map of the kingdoms spread upon it. A box, dusty with disuse, sat to the side of the map. Kiffen picked it up and blew the dust off it, sneezing three times as the evidence of abandonment scattered in the air. The box held, as he suspected, map markers designating the various kingdoms: lions, giraffes, horses, and eagles.

"You can handle a siege and direct troops from here if necessary. The other passageways have sleeping quarters and storage space for equipment, weapons, and food." Simeon pointed to a spot on the map near the middle of the lake surrounding the Border Keep. "We are here." He indicated a southwestern point beyond the lake. "There is an exit in a cluster of trees behind this knoll. It's a full two day's journey from above, but just hours from below."

Kiffen studied the map, speechless. "How is the trip so much shorter?"

"Above ground, you must travel around or across the lake and then navigate through rocky ground and hills leading down into the plains. Down here, it's almost a straight path."

While Kiffen leaned over the map, Simeon walked over to the slots built into the far wall and withdrew a rolled parchment from the top row, three slots from the left. He presented it to Kiffen. "Your Majesty, before we left Elwar, your father instructed me to share this with you. It's even more imperative now that he's gone. I regret the circumstances, but the knowledge shared here is extremely confidential, known only to the rulers of the four kingdoms and their highest-ranking advisors."

Kiffen reached for the parchment, brushing a fine layer of dust off it. The paper felt thicker than any map or treatise he'd ever held.

Had his father anticipated his death or determined the unrest in their world signified the right time to share this information with him? His hands shook as he untied the cords binding the parchment. These were the secrets he didn't know. His father had alluded to them at times. Now, these secrets were his to keep and use.

The parchment was quite long, with neat, numbered details written down its length. After years of storage, the paper kept curling back on itself, so he spread it out on the table, using lion markers to hold the corners down. Nestled beside one of the numbered points, the author had sketched a small map of Teletia. Before he got caught up in examining it, he pulled up a chair and sat.

The words swam before his eyes. "I want to read all of this, but I think it might serve our purposes today if you go over the most significant points." He glanced around the room and at the walls lined with slots, holding more documents. "I'm a bit overwhelmed."

"Very well." Simeon drew up a chair beside Kiffen. "Let's start with some simple geography. Where is the cave where the Watchers found your father?"

Confused by the question, Kiffen slid a corner of the parchment aside and indicated a point on the map table just inside the border of Moniah where the mountains edged into the plains. It was the only place the cave could be since this small extension of the larger mountains in Elwar was the only place those mountains reached into Moniah.

Simeon shook his head. "That is what we let people believe." He indicated a point northeast, near Teletia's border with Belwyn. "This is the actual location. It, too, is a stronghold like this one, storing food and supplies. This map shows the exact location."

The pounding in Kiffen's heart increased as he considered the possibilities suggested by this new knowledge. He leaned over the parchment, scanning the notes. For the first time since rioters attacked Elwar's castle, Kiffen believed he might succeed in this new role forced upon him. Untested in battle, much less as a leader, he had doubted his abilities to overcome Maligon.

This underground fortress, and the secrets it held, could change that.

* * * * *

Chapter Fifteen

Kassa and Halar sat at the small table in their chambers drinking tea in the early afternoon. The room was sparse compared to Elwar's offerings, but fancier than any rooms they used in Moniah. Kassa didn't mind as long as Halar shared it with her.

"Where is Samantha?" Halar's face drooped with exhaustion.

"Watcher's quarters." Kassa sipped from her cup, enjoying the warmth of the steam rising above the liquid. Was she getting old and susceptible to cold chills? She shuddered at the thought and decided it was the climate.

Halar crossed his arms and leaned back in his chair, a frown on his face. "Have you asked her why she's here? Why she didn't attend to Adana as ordered?"

"Yes, but her answer doesn't make sense." Placing the cup back on the table, Kassa grimaced at the bitter taste and reached for the honey. "She claims she wanted to find me and help me secure the route to Moniah."

"I don't believe her."

"Me either." Their daughter's answer plagued Kassa with doubts. After three years of separation, she didn't feel like she knew her daughter anymore. She took another sip of tea and scowled. "This is awful. I thought the keep stored better supplies than this."

"I thought our daughter was better trained than this."

Was his grimace for the bitter tea or Samantha's attitude? Kassa set down her cup and eyed her husband. "She's spent a lot of time with Kiffen lately. I don't like the way he looks at her."

"You don't think?" Halar sat forward, concern deepening the many wrinkles in his forehead.

"No." Kassa stood up and walked around to her husband. "She's managed to confuse him, but he loves Adana. The question is why she's behaving this way." She massaged his shoulders with a firm touch, fingers finding the familiar knots and kinks she'd learned in a lifetime of marriage. "You were with her these past few years. Did you notice anything? Any changes?"

He shook his head. "Nothing much. She withdrew after the queen's death, but I thought it was due to the changes and your absence." He leaned forward forcing her massaging hands closer to his shoulder blade. "Right there. My shoulder is killing me."

Kassa exerted more pressure, concern shifting her thoughts. "Has your injury been giving you trouble? You should have told me."

Halar dropped his head toward his chest. "No more than in the last three years. Now, I have you." He reached up and patted her hand. "You can keep it in shape."

"Hmph!" She pretended gruffness, but the interaction washed her in warm familiarity. Several minutes passed before either of them spoke.

"Still," Kassa said, "there must be something to her behavior. How was Samantha with Montee after I left?" The two women had shared a strong bond of friendship prior to Montee's elevation to First Vision, but there had been no evidence of their friendship since Samantha and Montee arrived in Elwar a few weeks earlier.

"I didn't notice, at first, because Linus had us patrolling the borders for quite a while in search of Maligon, but when I returned, I heard rumors."

Kassa's grip tightened on Halar' shoulders.

"Ow, woman!"

She dropped her hands from his shoulders and turned him to face her. "What kind of rumors?"

"I don't know the details, but Montee had to pull rank. After that, they didn't associate much."

"Why didn't you alert me to this?"

"I didn't think it was important. You did the same thing with Gilda when you were raised to First Vision."

"Pah! Gilda was jealous of you, not my status."

"Really?" Halar straightened, his eyes bright.

Kassa swatted him. "You're lucky she never had a chance with you." She returned to her seat and sipped on the tea, grimacing again. "Who are Samantha's companions?"

"Primarily Kalara and the ones who follow her around."

"Follow?" Kassa didn't like the sound of that word.

"Her squad. The Watchers she spars with and takes on expeditions, maybe a few others."

"My vision always failed me in reading Kalara. That always concerned me." She stood and went to the door. "I think it's time we find our daughter and have a talk with her."

Halar sighed. "This can't go well." He got up.

Before they opened the door, he drew her into his arms. "Remember, you are her mother, not her commander. That might make this go easier."

Kassa shook her head. "I doubt it."

* * *

They found Samantha in the map room of the center tower. She looked up as her parents entered the room. The smile she cast in their direction gave Kassa hope, but she couldn't fight back the fear that Samantha floundered without direction. Why else would she disobey orders with only the simplest of explanations?

"I was just studying the information we have on Adana's location. There is a village near there." Samantha straightened. "Have you seen Kiffen? I need to ask him more about his connection to Adana."

"You mean the queen." Kassa's voice sliced through the air.

Samantha blinked and cast a confused look at her father before responding to her mother. "Of course, I mean the queen. I'm just not used to calling her that." She looked back at the map, sharpness in her voice. "Where is Kiffen?"

Kassa opened her mouth to speak, but Halar interrupted her. "The King is in a closed meeting. What do you want to ask him? Surely, your mother understands the connection with the giraffes better than anyone here."

Samantha smiled at her mother. "Of course, you do, but I need specific details about what he's learning through the connection."

"What do you want to know?" Kassa approached the map and looked at the area Samantha had marked with a yellow giraffe marker to represent Adana.

"Physical characteristics of the land, the number of people with her, whether they have gone to the village or not." She shrugged. "Basic details."

It all sounded innocent, but something about her daughter's interest disturbed Kassa. Once she learned of Adana's safety and approximate location, she should have left the keep and caught up with the queen. That was her place, not here. Had it been anyone else, she would confront them or give them a less responsible task, but this was her daughter, a high-ranking member of the Watchers who, technically, Kassa no longer commanded.

Halar had suggested treating her as a daughter, not as a Watcher.

She struggled to recall how. "Although those are important details, I'm concerned you're focusing too much of your time on this rather than your regular duties."

"These are my duties." Samantha's voiced carried an edge to it. "Aren't you concerned for Adana?"

Halar interrupted before Kassa could reply. "We are, but the queen is with Montee and the rest of her honor guard. They will protect her."

"Which brings us to our concern," Kassa interrupted before Halar could take a breath. "Why didn't you join them? You know approximately where they are. You should have left once Kiffen found them. What plausible reason do you have for deserting your post?"

Samantha opened her mouth to speak, but Kassa threw up a hand to stop her. "Don't tell me you were concerned about me. That's ludicrous, and you know it." She crossed her arms. "Why are you really here?"

To her surprise, Samantha turned on them, her body quaking. "Mother! When will I ever live up to your standards? I only wanted to be near you. It's been three years."

Kassa stood frozen, unable to equate this quivering child with the woman she raised as a Watcher. The woman most trainees feared for her blunt words and cool demeanor.

While she stood there, Halar took their daughter into his arms and hugged her. His hand caressed her hair the way he used to do when Samantha was a child. She had always run to him instead of her mother. Kassa knew she'd been hard on Samantha, but they had shared a different bond. The Watchers.

Pulling back from his daughter, Halar looked into her eyes. "We know you've been separated a long time, but you are a woman, not a child, Samantha. You can't let your emotions overrule your responsibilities."

"Ballene's Fire! Don't coddle her." Kassa pushed her husband aside. "She's not interested in me, she's interested in Kiffen, and I want to know why."

Samantha whirled toward her mother, her face twisted in anger. "I'm trying to locate the queen, Mother, so I can get as far from you as possible. You should be happy I'm so concerned for Adana's welfare. She's the daughter you always wanted."

"Nonsense, and you know it." Kassa stepped closer to her daughter, the air sparking between them. "You are pursuing Kiffen for some pathetic reason, and I want to know what it is."

The anger in Samantha's face slid away, and her lips quirked up in a gloat. "You're afraid I'll ruin your lovely plans for the perfect kingdom, ruled by the perfect king and queen."

Kassa stepped back in surprise.

"Watch out Mother. One of your plans might go awry."

"Samantha." Halar's face flushed red. "Do you hear yourself? Are you in love with King Kiffen?" His hands fell to his sides. "Or with the idea of power?"

Samantha shrugged. "Neither of you understands how your actions and decisions affect others. You might want to ask yourselves how much power means to you before you dare ask me." She turned on her heel and marched out of the room.

* * *

J
ust before sundown, Kiffen bounded up the stairs of the center tower. His mind swirled with ideas. The chambers below the keep were extensive, reaching beyond the borders of both kingdoms. He could bring forces in and out of the keep without Maligon's knowledge, thanks to some forebear's strategic planning. He thanked the Creator, again, for this wonderful advantage.

His step was light when he entered the map room. Samantha straightened from perusing the charts to greet him. She looked different, a bit more vulnerable, and it took him a moment to realize why. Her hair tumbled over her shoulders instead of being bound into the unruly braid she never quite seemed to control. The setting sun shone through the high windows, glinting red in her curly, dark locks.

She's attractive, he told himself. There's no harm in enjoying her presence. Not as long as I remain true to Adana.

"Your Majesty, there you are. I had begun to think you were never going to return." She walked over to him, the smile on her face lighting up her eyes. "I've been all over the keep looking for you."

"Why would you do that?" Kiffen ignored the burst of pleasure at her words. He moved to study the map, plotting in his mind the tunnel's entrances.

"You look very pleased. Have you received good news?"

"Yes, I have." He turned to her with excitement. "I've learned—
"

Simeon's warning came back to him. "Tell no one about the tunnels, no matter how much you trust them. Only rulers and their closest advisors should know of this until the time is right. This information, leaked to the wrong person, can destroy our plans against Maligon."

"Uh, I've learned that..." He struggled to think of something to say. "That, uh, Adana is well. She is safe."

"So, you connected with Bai'dish? Wonderful. Did Kassa assist you?"

Not sure how to deflect her questions, he shrugged and leaned over the map.

Samantha backed away, the smile fading into a perplexed frown. "Kiffen? Did you connect with the giraffe?"

He took a deep breath and straightened to look at her, choosing a spot above her head rather than admiring the way her hair fanned out from her head and framed her face in curls. "Not really. But each day, it gets easier to sense his presence through the connection."

"Of course." She looked down at the map and traced her finger along the river near the marker for Adana's location. "Well, I'm glad the link grows stronger. We need to discuss some strategies concerning the queen's position." She edged her finger closer to the town of Roshar. "Where is she?"

Kiffen frowned and stared at Samantha. Just as he began to answer her, a sense of urgency and danger flowed through his bond with Bai'dish. His mouth turned dry as he saw an image of him walking quickly away from Samantha. He tried to study the map but could not ignore the giraffe's presence in his mind. "We will discuss this later." He turned to leave the room. "I seem to have forgotten a previous appointment."

Kiffen rushed down the stairs. How many times could he use the same excuse to escape Samantha's company? Another image from Bai'dish showed him in his quarters, speaking to Kassa. The giraffe had shown him the entire room and then focused on the image of Kassa and the image of the door closing out anyone else. The direction was clearer than any other he had received through the link. Bai'dish could sense Samantha's presence in the room, but the giraffe instructed him to seek out Kassa. It felt like an order, ramming into his mind, pounding the blood in his ears, and beading sweat on his brow. He must speak with Kassa, now.

When he reached his chambers, Kiffen sent a page to find Kassa. As the boy scurried away, Kiffen's body stiffened from a pronounced surge through the bond, the onslaught of another image— Samantha, looking evil and threatening.

He swore and wiped his hand over his eyes, shame turning his arms cold. Had Adana sensed his physical attraction to the Watcher?

He loved Adana.

Samantha made him feel competent in this strange, new world. Adana would provide the same comfort if she were here, but she wasn't. Surely, she understood his need for loyal support.

Swift on these thoughts came an image from Bai'dish—Adana leaning in to listen to an attractive man, a smile curling her mouth upward, her eyes sparkling with laughter.

He hated the man on sight, but the humor that trickled along the link told him this was made up to show him how he might feel if Adana relied on someone she found physically exciting. He had come to despise Pultarch, even though Adana was not attracted to him. How much more animosity would he feel for a man who really did charm Adana?

As Kassa entered the room, Kiffen received another image from Bai'dish. A Watcher, tall and slim, with red-brown hair. She wore an insignia on her uniform, a brown giraffe surrounded by bushes. He thought it indicated a Watcher trained as a Strategist. Her face seemed familiar, but he couldn't recall when, or if, he had seen her.

The next image caused Kiffen to stumble and fall back on a chair. This same Watcher locked other Watchers in a dungeon cell. They huddled in the dim light, blindfolded, bruised, and bleeding.

The anger rushing through the link was pure Adana.

Behind this image, came more. He groaned trying to absorb it all. He saw Bai'dish leading Glume out of the village of Roshar, their shadows cast out long before them as they moved west. Then there was a flash of the two walking through the forest and arriving at the Border Keep. Next was the Empress Gabriella, dressed in a shift, her hair tangled and wild. She grabbed the bars of a darkened cell and glared through them at a man. Kiffen stared at the image, wondering who the man might be. Bai'dish returned an image of a face Kiffen only knew from sketches, Maligon.

The image of Maligon faded away, and Sir Jerold stood before Empress Gabriella. Just before everything faded, Sir Jerold turned to look at Kiffen. He wore the crown of Belwyn on his head.

The last image faded slowly, a question in the mood of the image. Did he know Jerold was Gabriella's son? The parchment Simeon showed him in the tunnels included Sir Jerold's true identity. Adana had learned of the secrets, too.

He attempted to send confirmation of his understanding to her through Bai'dish. Thoughts were so much harder than showing her what he saw. He settled on an image of him nodding.

Satisfaction trickled through the bond, and he felt her acceptance of his limited skills. Just before the connection weakened, an outpouring of love surrounded him. He settled back in his chair, comforted by the last message. Even though he couldn't hold the bond any longer, he still felt her presence in that promise of love.

Drained, Kiffen slumped forward but glanced up at the sound of movement in the room.

Kassa stood before him, holding out a goblet. "You had a vision." It was a statement, not a question. "Drink this. It will restore your energy."

He grasped the goblet between both hands.

His body ached as if he'd run to Moniah and back. All he wanted to do was lie down and rest for a few days.

He sipped. The wine sparkled along his tongue with a light touch of berry and something he couldn't identify, a slight sweetness, but not overpowering.

He looked with surprise at Kassa. "What is this?"

"Part of my private stores. I added some honey to revive you and a few other herbs." Kassa sat on a chair facing him. "So, what did Bai'dish show you?"

Kiffen set the goblet on the table and leaned forward. "A Watcher. I've seen her before, but I don't know her name or recall when I might have seen her. She was locking several Watchers into a dark cell."

A crease formed between Kassa's brows.

Watchers kept their emotions hidden when possible, but to maintain control, given this news, proved the strength of Kassa's abilities. He admired her effort.

"They were blindfolded and beaten."

"What did this Watcher look like?" Kassa's voice remained calm and even, but a vein throbbed in her temple.

"She had reddish brown hair and was taller than many of the Watchers I've met. I think she was Strategist rank. Her insignia was a brown giraffe surrounded by bushes."

Kassa nodded. "That would be a Strategist." She thought for a moment. "Could you tell anything else about her or the Watchers she imprisoned?"

Kiffen shook his head.

"Taller than normal Strategist. I'll discuss it with the other Watchers at the keep. Can you recall anything else about her?"

Kiffen shook his head. "She looked capable. But the physical characteristics were hazy."

"Hmm, maybe Adana does not know her well. That might limit the suspects." She sat back, her gaze transformed into a flat stare.

Over the last few years, he'd learned to remain silent when she took this pose, but fear of forgetting everything forced him to interrupt her. "It might indicate my inability to handle the connection well."

She glanced up. "That's true. Or it could be Adana's inability. She's been separated from Am'brosia for a long time. What else did she share with you?"

"I believe Bai'dish and Glume are coming here."

She nodded. "Dangerous, but it makes sense. When?"

He tried to recall the image, seeing the long shadows in front of the two, the rising sun at their backs. "They leave in the morning, I think. Or they left this morning."

The tilt of the woman's head reminded Kiffen of the hawk others likened her to. At least this time it wasn't aimed at him.

"Can you try to contact Bai'dish, again? Get confirmation on the departure? We need to send out a party to escort them."

Kiffen took a deep breath. The link had weakened him, but he understood the need to know.

After a few breaths, he thought Bai'dish's name. The link reverberated with the giraffe's pleased response, followed by concern. A quick image of Kiffen lying down rushed into his mind. He couldn't help but smile at the idea of the giraffe playing nursemaid.

Quickly, before he lost the energy to sustain the link, Kiffen sent the image of Glume and Bai'dish. He didn't know how to visualize what he wanted, so he let the question settle in his mind. When do you leave?

It worked. Bai'dish showed Glume packing, going to bed, and the two rising in the morning to depart. The image of Kiffen resting closed the link.

He slumped further in the chair and accepted another glass of wine from Kassa. "They leave in the morning."

"Four, maybe five days journey, if they don't encounter trouble," Kassa said. "We should send a squad to meet them. We have no idea what they might find along the way."

"Agreed."

"Is there more?"

"She showed me Empress Gabriella imprisoned. The man locking her in looked like Maligon. Then I saw Jerold of Belwyn. He wore a crown on his head."

Kassa nodded. "Simeon showed you the tunnels and the parchment today?"

"Yes."

"Then you know what she's telling you about Jerold."

Kiffen did, thankful to know Adana was learning these secrets, too. As Kassa left him to rest, he felt the connection to Bai'dish shimmer and evaporate. Kiffen sprawled on his bed. The afternoon's invigorating discoveries felt distant and foreign after the drain of holding the link to Bai'dish for such a long period of time. He hoped having Bai'dish closer would help him develop strength in the connection.

The one thing he kept from Kassa bothered him for a moment. Samantha. He had not mentioned Samantha to Kassa. He saw no reason to let her know about his attraction or that Adana sensed something.

* * *

Kassa returned to her quarters, stewing over the news. The knowledge that a Watcher had assisted Maligon burned in her belly.

At least, Adana was aware of the secret parchments. Her image of Jerold verified that. Something in the way Kiffen described the young Belwyn prince led Kassa to believe Jerold was with Adana. She had not shared the impression with Kiffen because she sensed he was withholding information from the link. Learning that could wait. The puzzle of the traitorous Watcher was more important than Kiffen's secrets.

* * *

Samantha stalked along the corridor of the keep, annoyed by her mother's summons. Somehow, she had thought her mother's demotion from First Vision would remove her ability to command, yet here she was, answering her mother's call again. She entered the hall on the first floor of the central tower. Several Watchers and First Soldiers stood before her mother. At least, she hadn't been the only one summoned. Maybe this wasn't another reprimand.

Falling in line beside the Watchers, Samantha faced her mother, arms straight by her side, her face held in an impassive pose.

Kassa glanced up from a parchment and noted Samantha's presence. "The queen is sending Bai'dish to join us here. Glume will be with him. Since she can't afford many soldiers to accompany them, you will meet them and bring them safely here."

Finally, an opening. Samantha could send word to Kalara of this move. Kiffen might not excel at his connection, but if they managed to kill Bai'dish, the giraffe's death would devastate him. It might be the edge Maligon sent her here to discover.

They would depart within the hour, so she had little time to send a message. She rushed to the stables and found the one blue-speckled bird hidden among the pigeons. Maligon had told her to look for this one; it was different enough for her to recognize it, but not enough for anyone else to wonder about its presence. She attached the note, dispatched the bird, then sprinkled a solution over the remaining birds' food. Kalara had given it to her before she left Moniah to join Adana in Elwar. The drunkenberry concoction should confuse the rest of the birds, causing them to flee the keep.

She ran up the stairs to retrieve her pack.

* * * * *

Chapter Sixteen

Pultarch rode in Maligon's procession, amazed at the ground they covered as they traveled south. And without opposition. A week had passed since soldiers had dragged him into the man's presence. He spent most evenings listening to Maligon's stories of how Micah usurped his place next to Chiora as Husband King of Moniah. The Lord's deformed arm and other stories of his suffering at the hands of Micah and Donel created a craving in Pultarch's heart to avenge this mistreated soldier. The Lord's favorite statement rang in his ears, "History is a falsehood written by the victors."

When the army stopped for a midday rest, Pultarch led his horse toward the stream. Kalara joined him. "We are close to the next village. My father wishes you to ride with him."

"With pleasure." Pultarch flushed with joy. So far, he had ridden with the squads who skirted the villages, waiting for Maligon's victorious return. He was anxious to see and meet Adana's subjects.

Kalara granted him a small nod before she walked away.

While his horse drank, Pultarch considered his reflection in the water. He wanted Adana's people to see him in his glory. The dust of the road clung to his clothes. His hair hung in greasy clumps. He ran his hand over the rough, six-day beard growth on his face. He dunked his head in the water and scrubbed as hard as he could, including his beard in his efforts. Moniah was much warmer than Elwar, especially as they traveled farther south. His hair would dry before they reached the village. No time to shave though. He picked a bristly stalk from one of the short bushes scattered along the stream's edge and brushed at the dirt on his clothes. With a sigh, he cast the branch aside. Nothing could be done about his clothes, either.

Excitement pulsed through Pultarch's veins as his horse trotted up to the front of the Lord's army. It was easier to accept the man using this new name instead of Maligon. Based on the past five days, he doubted his early education about Maligon, but his conscience wouldn't let him accept the truth that he followed a known traitor who had survived a death sentence.

Four dark and intimidating men rode beside the Lord. One of them uttered something guttural to the others, and they let their horses fall back, providing an opening for Pultarch. The men closed in around them after he came abreast of Maligon. The four only spoke in this guttural language. No one knew who they were, but they remained close to Maligon at all times while on the road.

The Lord assessed Pultarch's appearance, his brow arching in displeasure. "We should find you better garments, soon. For this village, it won't matter. It's minor."

Pultarch flushed with embarrassment. The Lord's flowing robes of purple shimmered with iridescence in the light, a reminder to Monians that he could afford their expensive glimmer cloth, even if he was an outcast. Not a speck of dirt dared attach to his clothes.

"I apologize for my drabness, Lord." Pultarch bowed his head. "It's difficult to remain clean while riding in the rear of such a large force. Now that I'm to ride into the villages with you, I should be able to rectify that."

The Lord's laugh bellowed. "That you will. That you will." He nodded to a commander, and the line of soldiers fell in behind the Lord and Pultarch.

By mid-afternoon, the sun had sapped the moisture from Pultarch's hair and mouth. He lifted his leather cask to quench his thirst, wondering why the caravan had stopped. Relief spread through him when Kalara trotted her horse up next to her father's. "The advance was successful, Lord. We are ready."

A malicious grin spread over their leader's face, but Pultarch no longer felt troubled by the raw emotions expressed by the man. He preferred this honesty to the closed-off postures of the Watchers.

The Lord spurred his horse forward. "Come, Pultarch, and meet your future."

They rode over the crest of a hill. In the valley below lay the village. Within the walls, several buildings clustered around the center of town where a large crowd waited in the square. Along the roads that stretched into the distance outside the walls, homes spotted the landscape, and fields stretched beyond them.

They rode down into the village, the streets quiet and empty. Their horses' hooves clanged on the cobblestones. The air smelled of sunbaked earth. When they reached the street leading into the square, the crowd parted, eyes downcast, as he and the Lord rode to a platform.

Pultarch started with shock at the sight of a scaffold with a hangman's noose next to the platform. The Lord rode right up to the platform, and a soldier helped him dismount and step straight onto the stand.

For a moment, Pultarch considered getting down from his horse and climbing up on the platform, but he didn't see any stairs. With a shrug, he leaped from his horse and landed with a thud next to the Lord. Straightening with a smile, he grinned with joy at the crowd. Their faces stared back at him, angry, disgruntled, and fearful. He swallowed and fought the inclination to step backward.

Ignoring the mood of the people, the Lord spread his arms and addressed them in a jubilant voice. "People of Moniah, citizens of the city of Shamar, I bring you great news."

Murmurs rustled through the crowd, but Maligon ignored them.

"Your queen, Adana, lives!"

A thousand pairs of hopeful eyes lifted toward the Lord's. No one spoke.

"I bring before you, her betrothed, the next Husband King of Moniah, Sir Pultarch of Elwar." He gestured to Pultarch, and all those faces swiveled toward him.

He fought the urge to wave. Did he recognize hope in their scrutiny? He scanned the crowd. Many frowned or refused to look at him when his gaze swept over them.

From the rear of the square a voice called out, "What of King Kiffen? Is he not her betrothed?"

"No." The Lord's voice boomed over the crowd. "A mistake. Neither your queen nor the Watchers support it. Pultarch is the rightful man. A husband who will be her king, not the king."

People turned and talked to their neighbors, their voices murmuring in confusion.

The Lord leaned toward the crowd. "Do you really want to hand over the rule of your land to Elwar?"

Scattered shouts of "no" rang out from the crowd.

The Lord smiled. "Neither does your queen. She desires that this kingdom remain yours, not Elwar's. My soldiers search for her as I stand here, trying to save her from this cruel decision. She does not love Elwar or Kiffen. She loves Moniah. She loves Pultarch."

A small part of the crowd cheered at this pronouncement, but others looked unconvinced. As the crowd shifted their feet and murmured, small tussles broke out between people.

With a nod, Maligon directed his men to break up the skirmishes. Six swarthy soldiers elbowed through the crowd, pulling the troublemakers apart. Two of the men struggled against them until a soldier cuffed one of them across the face, knocking him to the ground.

"Stop this." A well-dressed member of the town's upper class stood at base of the platform, shouting up at Maligon. Beside him stood a Teacher of the Faith. "These men are good citizens. Cease your violence."

The Lord's soldiers seized the two fighting men and dragged them forward. Four other soldiers surrounded the man and teacher at the base of the platform.

"Please," the Lord said, "please join me on the platform so your people can see and hear who speaks."

The men glanced around with the same confusion Pultarch felt earlier. Finally, the teacher lifted her green robes and clambered up. She helped the other three men.

When all stood on the platform, the Lord stared at them with concern. "Do you not support your queen in this decision? You, sir." He faced the wealthy man. "Aren't you the city leader? Do you desire a different fate for Moniah and your queen?"

Pultarch studied the man closer. This was the man Adana entrusted to govern this town. How could he object to the plans of his queen?

The city leader stiffened and glared at the Lord. His voice rang out loud and strong. "You say our queen lives. Where is she? I do not take orders from you. I have not received any information concerning her wishes."

Others in the crowd shouted agreement, and more arguments broke out. The Lord clasped his hands in front of his chest and allowed a smile to bloom over his face.

The leader turned toward the crowd and pointed at the Lord. "Do you not know him? This is Maligon! Surely, you—"

The man gagged. Blood fountained out of his throat.

Pultarch stared in horror as the man's legs collapsed under him, and he fell to the platform. The Lord held a knife in his good hand, blood dripping to the ground. The crowd surged forward, screaming. Maligon held his gaze on them as he slowly wiped his blade on the dead man's coat.

A frightened hush spread through the citizens as he straightened and frowned at the crowd.

* * *

When Pultarch and the Lord left the village of Shamar, the heads of the three men and the teacher were displayed on pikes at the gates of the town. The two men dragged forward by the soldiers and the teacher had been hung on the spot without question. As they kicked their last from the noose, the Lord had scanned the crowd. The villagers huddled closer together, wide-eyed in shock or fear.

The Lord had turned to his soldiers and said in a loud voice, "Cut these traitors down and behead them and the city leader. Place their heads on pikes at the gates as a warning to others."

Pultarch tried to not look into the faces of the people who stood by the roadside as they rode out. Some cheered, calling out his name, but sullen anger like a wet blanket hung over those who remained silent. Was this how the Lord expected him to regain Adana's hand? By killing her people?

"It had to be done." Maligon's voice penetrated his thoughts.

Pultarch looked at the man and saw Maligon, not the Lord.

"If we don't make an example of a few," Maligon continued, "then many will die."

Pultarch did not know what to say.

"Come now, Pultarch. The end result is good. Few will die, and you will sit on the throne."

"I don't want the throne. I want Adana."

Maligon frowned at him. "Of that, I am well aware. But you will have the throne, too. Do you really believe you can marry royalty and never rule?"

"I don't want it." Pultarch shook his head. "And definitely not this way."

"Well, you better get used to it." Maligon kicked his horse forward and shouted over his shoulder, "Adana's View is just four days' ride from here."

Kalara kicked her horse up next to Pultarch's. "The Lord is right. You must set your mind to this. Adana will be here, soon."

His heart leapt at her words. "Adana? How? Are you sure?"

Kalara pulled her horse in closer to Pultarch's and lowered her voice. "Our spies learned much in this village. We know where she is, and we have sent forces to rescue her."

Pultarch gripped his reins tightly. "She is held against her will?"

Kalara scowled at him. "Of course she is. Why else would she be in a small village temple on the outskirts of her kingdom? You know she desires to set foot in her home again. Nothing but imprisonment would stop her."

* * * * *

Chapter Seventeen

Princess Leera, her identity concealed beneath a plain cloak she'd found in the servants' quarters, inched up a side aisle of the temple. She clutched the wrap tight, praying for the worshipers to remain aloof and separate. The sanctuary felt cool, and the spicy smells of incense did little to cover an underlying odor of mustiness. Still, she found the quiet starkness of this temple comforting. In contrast, the sanctuary within the castle gleamed with riches and smelled of wax and expensive fragrances.

She scanned the few parishioners, looking for Gerguld. His message, delivered by a young page while Leera ate her breakfast alone, cautioned her to take care and not be followed. She was early, and he was not, so she took a seat on a pew and slid to her knees in a supplicant's prayer pose.

This was her first meeting with the merchant since their fortuitous encounter a few days ago. The man's entreaty to meet her in secret came as a surprise. She'd imagined the requests, when they occurred, would originate from her.

Intrigued, she knew she must attempt to honor this invitation. In Gerguld, she sensed a kindred spirit, a man anxious for excitement that always seemed to pass him by. The entire morning, she fought to keep her wits, afraid the feeling of adventure burning along her nerves might betray her.

A plump woman knelt beside her, and Leera fought the urge to order her to move away. She took a few deep breaths, touched the tips of her fingers to her forehead, and rose to move to another seat, but the woman's hand gripped her elbow.

"Don't go on my behalf, m'lady," a sweet voice whispered. "I wish to chat with you."

Leera risked a peek into the woman's face and blinked in surprise when greeted by the green eyes of Mother Sariah, Protector of the Faith. The woman smiled at her and patted her arm.

"Don't be alarmed. I'm here to help."

"Why would I need help?" Leera allowed her royal haughtiness to drip into her whispering voice.

"Good, good." Sariah nodded. "You are cautious." She glanced around the sanctuary. "Gerguld told me you are trustworthy."

"You've spoken with him?" She fought the urge to glance around. Had Sariah informed her mother of the money she gave the merchant?

Sariah slipped a piece of parchment into Leera's hand. "Yes, I know him. We can't speak here. Meet us at this location after the temple bells ring."

The woman touched her fingertips to her forehead, rose, and shuffled out of the pew.

"Us?" The question came too late. Sariah was gone.

Curiosity bloomed within Leera. The note held an address from a part of the city she didn't know. It must be Gerguld's shop.

* * *

It was not the merchant's shop. Nice carriages traveled the streets, and the people walking along the storefronts wore the clothing of the upper class, maybe not the nobility, but people of means, anyway.

Disappointed, Leera gazed around the location, checking the address of the shop against the parchment. A dressmaker's shop. Before ducking into the door, she cast discreet glances around to ensure no one followed.

"Good day, my lady," came a woman's bright and jovial tone as she entered.

Leera smirked beneath the shadows of her hood. She knew that voice.

The dressmaker wore a very unflattering style, an unappealing grey skirt paired with a white blouse. This woman had not been so pleasant the last time they had met. She had suggested Leera wear a more conventional color than the pink she had requested for Adana's birthday celebration. Rather than deal with someone who dared question her decisions, Leera had taken hers, and many of her friends', business elsewhere.

"Can I interest you in a flattering shade of rose?" The woman stepped out from behind the counter, tipping her head forward to peer over her glasses at Leera.

She bristled at the irony in the woman's question, but a sparkle of amusement crossed the dressmaker's face, surprising Leera. Everywhere she went, it seemed, people had given up on propriety.

Two could play this game. "I was thinking of something more conventional. Maybe a red...blood red."

The woman sniffed, and Leera overheard smothered laughter behind a curtain in the rear of the shop. The dressmaker gave a sharp nod and pointed toward the sound. "I believe you will find such a color in our newest stock, if the lady does not mind visiting the rear of the store."

Satisfied she had won the interchange, Leera swept past her without response. Before she ducked behind the curtain, a twinge of curiosity overcame her. She had never been in a back room anywhere. What would it be like?

It was not exciting. Stacks of material, shelves with bolts of cloth, wooden bins of buttons, beads, and ribbons overflowed the small room. Daylight glimmered through a partially open door in the rear.

It appeared to exit onto a small patio. She looked around for the person who had been standing behind the curtain moments ago. Her heart thumped an unsteady rhythm when she realized she was alone.

Spinning on her heel, she almost bumped into the dressmaker. The dour woman's mouth twitched, alarming Leera even more.

"Why—?"

"M'lady?" Gerguld's voice sounded from the patio.

She glanced one more time at the shopkeeper and turned to follow the voice, bracing for the knife she feared might slice through her back as she did.

The brightness of day after the dark back room blinded her for a moment, but her hood helped shield her from the worst of the glare. Gerguld executed a proper bow. Beside him, Mother Sariah followed suit and curtsied.

Leera threw the covering off her head and forced her strong regard on the man. "Why have I been summoned in this way?"

"Forgive us, Your Highness," Mother Sariah said. "We had to be careful."

"Of what?" She arched an eyebrow at the woman.

Mother Sariah continued to smile at her. "Child, your intervention with Gerguld's plight was lovely, but we needed to see whether you could slip out of the castle and make it to this point unobserved." Sariah's gaze drifted past Leera's shoulder to the dressmaker who stood in the doorway. "This woman is Helmyra. She says you have met before."

Leera frowned at the woman. "Have we? I meet so many dressmakers in the castle. I suppose it's possible."

To Leera's surprise, this earned a laugh from Helmyra and Sariah.

"She was not followed." The dressmaker's eyes carried a hint of respect. "And we can see she is capable of falsehood, if necessary."

She smiled at the princess. "Although, she does seem to carry a grudge a little far. Don't you think so, Princess?"

Ignoring the last barb, Gerguld gestured for Leera to sit. "Please, mistress. We would like to discuss some things with you."

Glad for the redirection, Leera perched on the proffered chair and waited. The dressmaker unnerved her, but the thrill of intrigue stayed her sharp tongue, and caused her to forgive the woman without much thought.

"I don't quite understand how the three of you know each other." She couldn't imagine an odder assortment of conspirators—a poor merchant, a well-respected dressmaker, and the Protector of the Faith for all the kingdoms.

Sariah settled into another chair and poured tea for each of them. "In difficult times, people seek out those with the ability to help. Be careful, Your Highness, people are never what they seem."

After serving Leera, she sipped her tea, then peered at the princess over the delicate cup. "We have learned of your brother's whereabouts. Have you?"

The suddenness of the statement, combined with Mother Sariah's casual air, left Leera speechless for a moment. News of Kiffen would be wonderful, but she didn't believe it could be so easy. She stirred her tea, trying to determine what they might expect from her. Settling into the role of courtier, the princess set her spoon on the saucer, smoothed her skirts, raised her chin, and said, "Mother Sariah, we are so pleased to hear you have news. Please continue."

Sariah shook her head. "Not yet. What do you know of your brother?"

Impatience flashed through Leera's thoughts, and she fought to squash her response and, instead, returned Sariah's pleasant expression. "He is twenty years old, missing, and, hmm, what else?" She tapped her finger on her chin in thought, then leaned forward, giving her words emphasis. "Oh yes, he should be king, but we have no clue where he is." Leera leaned back into her chair and regarded Sariah with a cool gaze. "So, why don't you share your information with me? Then we will all know what you are about."

Calm radiated from her, but Leera trembled within. She had trained all her life for these kinds of exchanges and had, in fact, used them in flirtatious situations. But she had never felt the need to tread with care during those harmless interactions. This was a different circumstance, and she desired the taste of success more than she ever imagined she could.

Mother Sariah's gaze narrowed on her for a brief moment, but she turned to Gerguld instead. "What do you think?"

He shrugged. "Mother Sariah, she's a princess. I think she is playing with us as her mother would."

Fury flooded Leera's heart. "My mother. After I saved you? How can you compare me to her?"

The man bobbed his chin in deference. "No offense meant. I am new to this." He paused and touched his forehead. "You gave me gracious help, m'lady, and I fear I might need more."

"Is that all this is? A request for more funds for your store?" Leera sat forward and yanked a small purse from her cloak. More money would place the man deeper in her debt. An advantage she liked.

"No, m'lady." Gerguld looked shocked. "Your kindness was more than sufficient."

Perplexed, Leera sat back. She studied the trio and decided to hold her tongue. Make them speak.

Mother Sariah finally did. "My lady, we may have overstepped propriety with you. I should have met with you in private first and learned what I could of your situation, however…certain occurrences have forced us to move more quickly."

At last, they were getting somewhere.

Sariah looked her in the eye. "We would like to share our information with you, but we need to ask you some things. Helmyra needs to touch you while you answer."

Helmyra glided over and sat beside her.

Nausea rolled in Leera's stomach. Her childhood nursemaid had told her stories of people who could discern truth through contact, but she had never met anyone like that. They were only a child's fable, nothing more. "She's a Seer?"

The dressmaker dipped her head in acknowledgement.

Leera felt Mother Sariah's deep interest as they waited for her answer. A Seer changed so many things. If she truly was one, then Leera could use her to discern her mother's true intentions. As soon as the thought crossed her mind, Leera realized its absurdity. This woman would never have an opportunity to touch the queen.

She looked at the trio again. The presence of Mother Sariah comforted her. How could the Protector of the Faith, a woman charged with caring for the people of all lands, cause her harm? For that reason, alone, she trusted them.

She may be selling herself to the wrong camp in her mother's eyes, but she felt sure they sought to help the kingdom, not serve their own private gain. She couldn't claim the same about her mother.

"What kinds of questions?"

"At first, we'll ask simple questions, so I can get a feel for your responses," Helmyra said. "Then we have some questions about the circumstances inside the castle,"

Leera sipped her tea. Her gaze fell on Gerguld, still dressed in the same drab clothes she'd met him in a few days ago. Mother Sariah radiated peace and contentment, her round figure wrapped in a light blue dress rather than the white robes that marked her as the Protector. Helmyra was a thin, angular woman with sharp features and gray hair piled into a voluminous bun on top of her head.

"Why do you need the Seer to ask me these questions?" Leera asked, trying to delay her decision.

Mother Sariah smiled, a gesture Leera recognized, meant to ease her discomfort. "Your Highness, you know things are in chaos in Elwar. It's the same in Moniah, Belwyn, and Teletia. Caution is wise on anyone's part, including yours."

In the castle, Leera learned things from eavesdropping, but she knew little of the conditions outside the castle. The minute she entered a room, the conversation halted or swung in a frivolous direction. Even Taren, beautiful Taren, refused to tell her anything of consequence. Her knowledge was limited, gained from hiding behind doors. She decided to tell them what they wanted in order to find out what they knew.

Leera gave a short bob of her head in assent, but when Helmyra reached out to touch her, she pulled back and shot a warning at the three of them. "If the direction of these questions displeases me, we will stop. To show my willingness to cooperate, you may ask three questions but then you will tell me of my brother. The rest of your questions will be answered once I'm satisfied you tell the truth."

* * * * *

Chapter Eighteen

It was one thing to accept the presence of a Seer, it was another to submit to her hand on your shoulder as you answered questions. Leera shivered the moment Helmyra's hand touched her. Was the shiver from inside her or did some power cross through the woman's fingers?

Sariah asked the first question. "When did you and Adana become friends?"

The memory brought a smile to her face. Leera could still see Adana trying to navigate between bales of hay and tripping over her skirts. "My mother had been harsh with Adana. She couldn't do anything right when she first came to Elwar. I caught her trying to practice walking in skirts. She was horrible at it, and I laughed at her."

Leera paused, remembering the scene as if it was yesterday. "Mother disliked Adana, and for some reason, I decided it would be fun to befriend her. To see how mother reacted."

She glanced between Sariah and Gerguld, wondering why they asked something she couldn't prove.

Sariah nodded. "That is how Adana explained it to me. Helmyra, why don't you go next?"

The pressure on Leera's shoulder didn't change, but she felt more nervous as Helmyra considered her question.

"That day you left my shop, whose shop did you visit instead?"

Surprise flushed over Leera. At a time when they carried news of her brother, was the dressmaker unable to get past the fact that Leera had cost her some business? The other two didn't seem surprised by the question, so she fought the urge to lick her lips in nervousness as she answered. "I went back to the castle and had mother summon the royal dressmaker." She didn't mention the anger her mother expressed over the delay created by Leera's refusal to work with Helmyra.

"That is true." Helmyra's head bobbed once in confirmation.

Gerguld asked the last question. "Why did you decide to help me?"

The question should not have surprised Leera. She had asked herself the same question. Still, she fought to prevent a peevish answer. "I don't really know why." She played with various phrasings, and then spoke again. "Mother seemed so different, and everything had changed. I may have felt sorry for you." She bobbed her head in Gerguld's direction. "You seemed lost, and I wanted to help." Her last statement carried a hint of wonder in her voice.

"You did not plan to use this later for your own gain?" This question came from Sariah.

"I didn't say that." Leera felt heat rise in her face. "Once I decided to help, I realized Gerguld might be of service to me some day."

"How?"

"I haven't determined, yet. At the time, I was afraid of mother's behavior and wanted to know if there was a way to get out of the city."

"Where would you go?" Sariah said.

"I don't know." She shrugged, then straightened, suddenly aware they had asked more than three questions. "The agreement was three questions. We've surpassed that. Please share with me what you know of my brother."

Sariah glanced at Helmyra. "Are you comfortable with how to read her?"

"Yes."

"Good."

Helmyra pulled a sheet of parchment from her pocket. "We received this from your brother. He is safe at the Border Keep."

Leera accepted the letter from Sariah. Kiffen alive! At the keep.

She fought to stop the tears that sprang to her eyes as she tried to study the missive. It was in some code, most of it indecipherable to her, and therefore, to any of the wrong people whose hands it fell into, but the handwriting was his. When had Kiffen become so clever?

"When did you receive this? What does it say?"

"Yesterday," Helmyra said. "The information is crucial. He directed us to locate and assist you."

"Assist me? In what?"

Helmyra held out her hand for the letter, and reluctantly, Leera gave it back, her gaze following it until the woman tucked it into an inner pocket of her dress.

With a smile, Sariah said, "We can help you, and we will, but first, we must know more of what's happening in the castle."

They knew something wasn't right in the castle. Leera glanced between them, aware that the changes in her world had somehow become known in the city. Maybe not to everyone, but to those who were trying to…to do what? Again, she considered the odd trio.

"You are tense. Have a sip of tea and a biscuit. We only have a few more questions." Helmyra held a plate out to her.

Leera turned toward the woman, again fighting the urge to lick her lips in worry. She had told the truth, so why did this woman say she was tense? "You didn't believe my answers?"

"On the contrary," Helmyra said. "You have been completely truthful with us."

Leera relaxed and bit into a biscuit. It tasted like her father's favorite treat, poflas. Sadness eased into her soul as she caught the inevitable crumbs in her gloved hand. "I've never had poflas outside the castle. Where did you get them?"

"There was a time when your father was just a traveler." Helmyra picked up one of the biscuits and bit into its crispy, brown texture. "My mother learned to bake them for him. Later, she taught me."

The stories about her father didn't include his days as a traveler before he married Queen Roassa. What had he been like? The sadness seeped deeper into her soul. She might never know unless she asked this woman before her.

Before Leera could say anything else, Mother Sariah said, "Let's finish with the questions. Helmyra?"

Helmyra's hand hovered over Leera's shoulder. "May I?"

Leera nodded and sat back. This time the woman's hand was cool and comforting in the heat of the sun.

Sariah said, "You said you were afraid of your mother. Why?"

Leera squirmed. She had anticipated this question once she admitted her concerns. To answer seemed disrespectful to her mother, even if it was becoming second nature to her.

"She seems pleased. Even more. Overjoyed at the loss of my father. The castle is in shambles, and she doesn't seem to care. She only wants—"

"What does she want?" Sariah leaned in, her gaze intent upon Leera.

Leera tugged at her ear. "That's what I've been trying to determine. It's obvious she wants to rule. But I think she wants something else. Glory? Satisfaction? Revenge? I'm not positive. Whatever it is, Lord Sarx is part of it...and his nephew."

"Taren?"

"Yes."

"What do you know of Taren?" Mother Sariah asked.

A blush crept over her skin and heated her to the core. She blinked in surprise when Gerguld swore under his breath.

"Forgive me, m'lady, for using such language," the man said, contrition in his voice.

She ignored him. "He is the son of Sarx's sister, a Lisseme baroness. He is charming and clever, and I believe they want me to marry him."

"Do you want to marry him?"

Oh yes, thought Leera, but caution returned. "I don't know how he fits into their schemes." Leera's voice dropped, and she spoke in slow, painful words, realization of the truth coming to her. "If he wants the same power as my mother, then I will say no. But if mother decides I should marry him, I will have to do so."

Mother Sariah clucked her tongue but continued with the questions. "Have you heard them mention anyone else?"

Leera thought for a moment and shook her head.

"This could be extremely important. The mention of someone may have been generalized to keep others from understanding."

Leera's mind traversed the last few days, looking for half-heard words during her efforts at eavesdropping. One particular incident frustrated her. The conversation sounded critical, but one of her mother's burly guards interrupted her eavesdropping before she could make sense of it. She closed her eyes and tried to picture it again.

The gardens were still overgrown, so the plants provided some coverage. Her mother had been upset over some information she had received, and her voice and Sarx's had carried beyond the arbor where they sat.

"He says he has the boy in his control, but the child is a simpleton," her mother said with a snarl. "Can he keep him focused on our ends?"

"The lord knows what he's doing."

"Hmmph. That name. If it wasn't for us, he would still be stuck—"

"Hallo Mistress! Your latest conquest seeks your company."

Leera had whirled around at the voice and missed whatever else her mother and Sarx said. The guard, in his impudent way, had led her away to meet Taren who seemed quite anxious about not finding Leera in her chambers when he came to call on her.

Sariah, Gerguld, and Helmyra sat back and contemplated this fractured piece of information. With surprise, Leera noticed that Helmyra was seated and had not been touching her during the last question.

"Which lord do you think they mean?" Gerguld asked.

Helmyra shook her head. "I don't think it's meant that way." She retrieved the message from her pocket and studied it again. "According to this, he is calling himself Lord. I believe they were referring to him."

Mother Sariah nodded, worry creasing her forehead. "This confirms it. Which means King Donel's murderer—"

"My father's murderer? Who?" Leera's throat convulsed at the thought of the person who stole her father's life.

A weak smile crossed Sariah's face. "Child, I'm sorry. I was thinking out loud and not considering your presence."

Leera did not know how to react. So many people had failed to behave as they should around her, but this seemed less disrespectful than the others. "You mentioned my father's murderer. You think you know who killed him?"

Sariah sighed and brushed at her skirts before meeting Leera's gaze. "The actual person? No. But I have my suspicions as to who set it in motion."

In shock, Leera recalled her mother's words when she'd asked why she didn't mourn her father: "If you only knew. No, I will not ruin your cherished memories of your poor, departed father."

"You think my mother was involved?"

Sariah gazed sadly at Leera, her voice apologetic. "I suspect she had something to do with it."

Leera thought about the rest of her mother's conversation the day she met Taren. "She says I am the heir to the throne. I believe they want Taren to become king by marrying me."

Gerguld swore again and darted an embarrassed glance at the princess.

Sariah pursed her lips. "Have you ever heard them mention Maligon?"

"Maligon?" Leera popped out of her chair. "What has Maligon to do with any of this?"

Helmyra laid a hand on her arm, the touch much different from the act of a Seer. "Your brother says the Lord is what Maligon calls himself now."

It was as if all the air left the patio. Leera sank into the chair, gasping. Gerguld rushed over with some water and knelt before her. "There, there, Missy. Take it slow." He shot a dark look at Helmyra. "We should have waited to tell you."

Helmyra sniffed. "She had to know. Waiting would not have changed the effect."

Leera found herself taking deep, slow breaths like she'd done in the garden the other day. With each breath, the chaos seemed to fade, and calm settled over her. When she trusted her voice, she smiled and said, "Thank you for your concern, Gerguld, but I'm afraid Helmyra is right." She shot a look at Sariah. "A few more minutes, or even days, would not change the shock of it." She thought about this revelation for a few moments, recognizing how it all seemed to fit together. "So Maligon wants Elwar and Moniah?"

"He's already taken Belwyn and Teletia. It looks like Lisseme is in his sights too."

"And my mother is conspiring with him." Leera shook her head. "No wonder the betrothal between Kiffen and Adana infuriated her. What do we do?"

"Do, Your Highness?" Helmyra was the first to react to the question, a glint of satisfaction in her eyes.

"Yes. We must do something. Surely you have a plan. What is it?"

* * * * *

Chapter Nineteen

Leera slipped back into the castle through the servants' quarters and returned the cloak to the hook she'd taken it from. She breathed a sigh of relief. No one saw her as she entered a corridor through a maid's door.

She took a few steps and paused.

Taren strode toward Leera, his jaw set in determination. "Where have you been?"

He was the last person she wanted to see after meeting with Mother Sariah and Gerguld. She ignored him and turned away, hoping he would leave her alone, but suspecting he would pursue her.

"Leera." He seized her arm.

She yanked it free and turned on him. "How dare you grab me like some tavern maid." She spun on her heel and walked away.

Taren rushed to block her path. "Where have you been?"

She tapped her boot, arms crossed in front of her. "I don't recall granting you permission to know my whereabouts. Move aside."

The young man's gaze flicked to her tapping foot. "You're wearing boots? Why? You've been out? Where?"

Impatience won out, and Leera spun on her heel, intent on taking a different path to her rooms.

"You don't want to go that way. Your mother's soldiers are looking for you."

Her boots squeaked to a halt. Leera stood, uncertain. With a sigh of exasperation, she turned back to the most beautiful man she had ever known. "Taren, what are you trying to do to me?"

"Protect you." The intense look he gave her overcame Leera in a hot flash of fire.

She fought the compelling urge to fall into his arms.

"From what?"

In two short steps, Taren stood before her, reaching for her hands. "Everything."

She tucked her hands behind her, so he brushed a strand of hair off her forehead, instead. "Exquisite," he whispered.

His fingers trailed heat along her skin. It coursed to her core. A brief thought crossed her mind. Kassa was wrong. Desire did not flutter; it thundered. She stepped back from his touch and took a deep breath. And another. And one more.

"Why are you here, Taren?"

"Why?" He blinked at her in confusion. "Don't you know, sweetling?"

She shook her head, more to erase desire than to deny his question. "Why did you come to Elwar?"

Taren stared at her, his hands hanging by his sides. "My uncle invited me to meet the queen."

"Not the king?"

"What?"

"Your invitation must have come prior to my father's death. Did it not include an introduction to him?"

A frown creased Taren's olive-colored brow, and he stroked his mustache with his index finger. "I don't understand why you're so concerned about why I'm here." He reached for her arm. "We're wasting time on these foolish questions. Let's—"

She jerked away and rushed by him. "Foolish questions? Not you, too." Leera sailed down the corridor. After she rounded the corner, she paused. Even Taren was trying to keep her ignorant of the world around her. She listened to see if he followed. He did not.

Passion flushed her body, residue from the trail of Taren's fingers. Leera leaned against the wall and tore at the ties at the neck of her dress, welcoming the cooler air against her skin. Sarx had planned well when he decided to bring his nephew to distract her.

The thought made her recall her answer to Mother Sariah's question about marrying Taren. "If he wants the same power, then I will say no. But if mother decides I should marry him, I will have to do so."

"No, I won't." She pushed away from the wall and started up the flight of stairs. She would leave. Gerguld and Sariah would help her, she felt sure of it. Even Helmyra could be of service. Their plan for her to listen in on her mother and Sarx would have to change. Surely, someone else aligned to their cause lived in the castle.

Caught up in dreams of escape, Leera burst through her chamber door and froze. Queen Quilla sat by the window, a piece of fabric in her hands.

"Do you know what this is?" Her mother held up the pale pink, lace-edged cloth. Eyes half-lidded, she rubbed the cloth along her cheek.

Leera's feet inched backward. Her mother's quiet air never boded well for the recipient. Until now, it had never been hers to deal with.

Quilla crumpled the cloth in her fist, her knuckles turning white. Her chest rose and fell, and then she thrust her hand, palm up, toward Leera. "I said, do you know what this is?"

The cloth unfurled in her mother's hand, revealing a miniature napkin.

Leera winced at her mother's shrill voice. "No, Mother."

Quilla shook her head and stood. "When I made this, it was with high hopes that I carried a future queen of Elwar within me." She smoothed the cloth and proceeded to fold it into a tight square. "I dreamed of the beautiful daughter I would have. Of how happy we would be once she stepped into her destiny. Do you understand?" Her voice rose higher still. "Even then, I knew. Even then, I was chosen for this."

Caution tingled across Leera's skin. "Chosen for what, Mother?"

The queen smiled with pride. "He chose me. He trusted me to be the one to succeed. I cannot fail him."

Leera stepped back as she watched insanity dance in her mother's eyes, giving the woman a renewed vitality.

"Who?" she asked.

Quilla's head jerked up, and she stalked toward her daughter. "I have not failed him, but you are failing me." She threw the cloth at Leera. It wafted to the floor. "Even then you failed me. Look at the stains you left behind!"

Leera studied the tiny cloth as she leaned over to pick it up, noting a small area of discoloration on one corner. Had her mother's determination driven her mad? Who would blame a baby for stains on a wiping cloth?

Quilla stood over her, breath hot on Leera's face. "You will remain in your rooms unless summoned." She pushed past her daughter.

"Mother, why?" Leera followed her. "What are you talking about?"

Whip fast, Quilla turned on her. They stood eye to eye. "You will not ruin my plans. You will not stain sixteen years of suffering. Not when success is within our reach."

She nodded at the baby's napkin in Leera's hands. "Maybe you should spend your time getting that stain out."

And then she was gone, the door closed and locked behind her.

* * * * *

Chapter Twenty

Leera sagged onto the bed, the baby cloth still in her hands. She stared at it while replaying her mother's words in her mind. Chosen. Her mother had claimed to be chosen. By whom? For what? Did this confirm Sariah's suspicions? She pushed the thoughts from her mind and spread the cloth out on her lap, studying the small stain on the corner. If she hadn't been looking for it, she might not have noticed.

Had the laundress been unable to bleach it out? Surely, a stain so small couldn't defeat the castle's staff. Holding it up toward the light, she studied the slightly yellow corner. What had it felt like to need such a small napkin?

Without thought, she mimicked her mother's actions earlier and rubbed the napkin along her cheek. The scents of gardenias tickled her nose. With a gasp, she pulled the cloth close to her face and inhaled, her memory traipsing through the paths of her childhood, a laughing mother doting on her daughter's every accomplishment and reassuring her when she struggled.

A clear image came to her of a day much like this one with the sun shining and cooler air announcing the shifting of the seasons. She had been running along the paths of the garden while her mother strolled behind her, stopping to inspect the flowers and bushes. Occasionally, she had called out, "Leera, don't wander from my sight."

A giggle had escaped Leera's lips as she ducked under a bush to hide. It had only taken moments for her mother to call her name in alarm. Hands pressed over her mouth, Leera fought back the giggles of fooling her mother so easily. Then her mother had rushed past her, an edge of fear in her voice, her eyes large and round in alarm. "Guards! Guards! The princess is missing."

The queen had paused on the path just beyond where Leera hid, spinning around, searching everywhere for her daughter. When she drew her hand to her chest and fought back a cry, Leera's giggles had ceased. She had rushed from under the bush and thrown herself at her mother's skirts. "I'm here, Mama, I'm here. Don't cry."

The strength of her mother's embrace had told her everything she needed to know that day. She was her mother's world. As queen, her mother must spend time with the king and her brothers, Kiffen and Serrin, but in the end, it was Leera who mattered.

A tear splashed on the cloth where it lay in her lap. She wiped her fingers across her eyes, fighting the tears. "I'm here, Mama, I'm here," she said. She wiped away more tears. "Don't cry."

* * *

Dusk was settling in when Leera awoke to someone entering the room.

Her maid bustled about lighting candles and lanterns. A gust of wind caused the flames to flicker, and the maid shivered, rubbing her arms. She rushed toward the window, pulling the shutters closed. "Goodness, m'lady. You mustn't keep these open in the evening. It's way too cool."

Not waiting for an answer, she turned and began to pick up the boots and wrap Leera had let fall in the floor. She picked up the tiny baby cloth beside the bed and stuffed it into the pile of laundry she was collecting.

"No." Leera sat up. "Give me that."

The maid froze in her duties and turned toward Leera, her face bowed toward the floor. "Your Highness?"

The woman stood still, waiting, and Leera took the opportunity to study her. She was young, older than Adana, but not by much. How long had she tended to Leera? She couldn't recall. This young woman kept her rooms clean and tended to her needs, but she couldn't even remember her name. How could that be? Unsure of why this aggravated her, Leera spoke, her voice betraying her agitation. "Look at me."

Eyes wide in fear, the woman lifted her head to look at her. Her tongue traced her bottom lip. Her shoulders quivered.

Shocked at the woman's reaction, Leera stood and walked closer. "Are you afraid of me?"

The maid shook her head, her feet shuffling on the floor as if she wanted to back away. She held out the bundle of clothing. "Please, I was only straightening up. Please take what you need, m'lady."

Instead, Leera circled her, noting how her body shivered as Leera passed behind her. This was how the servants responded to her mother. Had they always reacted like this with her, too?

She stopped at the woman's side. "Why are you afraid?"

The maid turned to face her. "Forgive me, my lady. If I have done something displeasing to you, please tell me so I may correct it."

The baby napkin lay on the top of the bundle the woman held, so Leera plucked it from the stack, noticing how the woman shrank back from her hand. "I do not want this washed."

The fragrance wafted toward her, and she fought the desire to draw it to her face and inhale her mother's sweet scent again.

Still curious about the maid's response to her, she sat back on the bed and studied her. "I've forgotten your name."

The maid blinked at her. "Do you wish to know my true name or the one you decided to call me?"

"I decided?"

"Yes, m'lady. You didn't like my name, so you changed it to one that suited you."

Caressing her cheek with the cloth, Leera pondered this for a moment. "How long ago was this?"

"Three years. I came to serve you when the lady Adana arrived. Your maid was given to her."

Recollection flooded Leera's mind. The theft of her chambermaid was one of the many reasons she had hated Adana at first. She had known her mother made the decision, and eventually realized Adana never would have taken her maid from her. Like the child she was, she had refused to speak to her maid unless she used the same name as the former one. "So, I called you Myra?"

"Yes, m'lady."

"What is your real name?"

"Hanna."

"Hanna." Leera tapped her finger on her lips. "I like it." She glanced up. "Forgive me for renaming you."

The woman nodded, her feet shuffling backward. "Of course, m'lady. Whatever you wish. Do you need anything else?"

Leera stared at the woman's shoes peeking out from under her skirt. Had she really become her mother with the servants? Hanna might be the only person she saw while locked in her bedroom prison. How awful to have her only contact afraid of her. She sighed. "No, Hanna. You may go. Call me when dinner is ready."

Hanna turned to flee, but her shoes squeaked to a halt on the stone floor. It took forever for her to turn around and face Leera, again. "Forgive me, Your Highness, but your dinner is to be delivered here. To your rooms. All of your meals. By the queen's order."

Leera frowned, aware she hadn't thought this imprisonment through. "Yes. I recall. I'm no longer hungry, anyway."

After the maid left the room, Leera continued to stare at the door as the click of the lock sounded. Had her mother ever locked Kiffen or Serrin in their rooms? If so, she didn't know of it. How had she gone from the center of her mother's world to a pawn locked away in a closet until needed?

She didn't try to stop the tears this time.

* * * * *

Chapter Twenty-One

Samantha's band of Watchers and First Soldiers found Bai'dish and Glume in the morning hours three days after leaving the Border Keep. From a distance, the sound of raised voices and the clang of swords warned them of trouble. Samantha nocked an arrow and ordered the Watchers to follow suit. They rushed toward the sounds, slipping in and out of the trees on the edge of the forest. The First Soldiers followed, swords drawn.

At the crest of a slight incline, Samantha backed up to a massive tree trunk and peered around it. In the small glade below, four Elwarian soldiers fought to protect Glume and Bai'dish, who stood at the far end of the clearing. Five of Maligon's men moved in closer, but three of their number lay sprawled on the ground.

Samantha sneered at their lack of battle prowess and drew her bow. She sighted along the arrow at one of Maligon's men. Kalara had told her, sometimes, they must sacrifice their own to keep up their double lives. At least, these men weren't trained and valuable soldiers.

Her shot flew true to the chest. The man fell. As his four comrades spun toward the trees, the Watchers lined up on the rise. The twang of bow strings filled the air. Two of Maligon's men shouted and rushed toward them, their backs turned to the soldiers accompanying Glume. Those men shouted in triumph and pushed forward. Samantha's squad raced down the hill into the clearing, swords and knives drawn.

After a few half-hearted clashes, Maligon's men surrendered. They dropped their swords and knelt before the Watchers, hands on their heads. Shaking her head at their cowardice, Samantha turned to look for Glume and the giraffe. During the short conflict, the two had slipped into the tree line. She glanced at the numbers still alive on both sides. Too many to kill if she struck the giraffe here. Embracing her frustration, Samantha stalked over to the captives and drove her sword into the chest of their commander.

A Watcher gasped, her eyes growing wide.

Samantha turned on her, glancing at the Watcher's uniform insignia—a single giraffe. Watcher status, but her behavior betrayed her as a rookie. "Would you prefer we let this scum live?" Samantha advanced on the woman. "How long have you been raised to Watcher?"

A flush of red blossomed along the girl's neckline. "A season."

"Not long." Samantha nodded. "Don't question my authority again."

"Yes, Watcher." The girl stood straight, her arms by her side, her face impassive in the required stance of a lower rank addressing her superior. Following a battle, the stance wasn't required, but Samantha relished the Watcher's action.

She examined the remaining two prisoners and glanced at the Elwarian soldiers, Watchers, and First Soldiers awaiting her command. "Well fought. Tie them up. I will take these prisoners to Adana's View. She nodded at the Watcher she'd reprimanded. "You will come with me."

The others glanced around at each other, but Samantha outranked them. They accepted her command and pulled ropes from their packs.

She scanned the trees. Glume and Bai'dish had retreated quite a way into the forest. Why hadn't they done that sooner? She could have crept along the tree line during the short battle and killed them without being seen. She turned to one of her Watchers. "Retrieve the giraffe and his keeper and deliver them to King Kiffen at the keep. Do not delay."

Then, Samantha grabbed the rope binding one of the prisoner's wrists and dragged him behind her. The two captives, bound by their wrists and waists to the same rope, stumbled in her wake. The inexperienced Watcher rushed to keep up as Samantha marched south through the trees. At least the rookie was quiet.

Samantha didn't look back but kept marching.

An hour later, they paused by a small creek to refill their canteens. The rookie stood guard over the soldiers, her gaze alert and serious. She still hadn't spoken a word since their departure.

Samantha switched places with her. "Get some water. I'll watch this scum."

With a nod, the girl untied her canteen from her belt and approached the creek.

It would have been a pleasure to kill her, but Samantha decided to keep her hands clean and give her prisoners the opportunity.

"Do you recognize me?" she asked them.

They nodded, and one spoke, his gaze cautious. "The Lord told us to watch for you, Watcher. You are Samantha."

"Good." She sliced through his ropes and handed him his sword. "This Watcher bores me. Deal with her."

An evil grin slid over his face as the man accepted the sword. The girl rose from the creek and turned, her eyes widening when she saw the man looming over her. He drove the sword deep into her belly.

She fell backward, a look of shock in her eyes. Her blood washed the creek in a blush of crimson.

Samantha nodded at the man and cut the bonds of the other one. She handed them their swords and, without a word, set off across the creek. The sooner she put some distance between herself and the others, the sooner she could locate Maligon. The plan to kill Bai'dish hadn't worked, but she wasn't going back to the keep. Maligon had promised her greatness. It was time he delivered.

* * * * *

Chapter Twenty-Two

Adana gasped awake, her heart pounding. The dream, always the dream, almost every night since meeting Brother Honest. The images replayed in her mind as she practiced her focused breathing, seeking calm. Her head broke through the water's surface, mouth gasping for air. The river water washed into her mouth, choking her. Each time she kicked her feet and fought the current, trying to swim to the shore, the undertow pulled her further downstream. She struggled to keep her head above the choppy surface.

"Your Majesty!" a man's voice called from the bank.

She twisted. A Teacher of the Faith ran along the river's edge, his eyes wide in panic. Then another teacher, one she now knew as Brother Honest, pushed him aside and thrust a long branch toward her.

Adana kicked toward the branch. The water sucked her under again, and she fought panic, thrashing in the fast current. All went dark. She flailed her arms, grappling for any handhold. Her lungs burned as she fought toward the surface again, then burst above the water, gulping air. She let her body go limp and drift on the current, hoping to remain afloat. Instead, the water dragged her under again.

Something sparkled on the river's surface above, and she kicked upward. The crown of Moniah's Seat of Authority bobbed on the rapids, just out of reach. An overwhelming desire to grasp it overcame her, but the crown danced in the rapids, slipping from her grasp each time she lunged.

"Can you reach the branch?" Brother Honest called to her. He thrust the large stick toward her, but the crown floated farther away, taunting her.

She plunged after the golden image of her royalty. Roiling water drenched her face, and, as she sputtered, a large, shaggy beast waded into the river and scooped up the symbol of her authority. "No," she cried. A large rock loomed ahead of her, and everything went black.

Gasping, Adana stumbled then froze. Firm ground lay below her feet. She patted her clothes and found them dry, but she still felt chilled to the bone. Darkness enshrouded everything. Even though she knew it was a dream, the overwhelming blackness always terrified her.

She brushed against the cool, stone wall and inched tentative hands forward. Fingers skimmed over slime. No sight, no vision, no sound. "Don't panic," she whispered over and over again while counting each breath, trying to find a way to fight down her terror.

After traversing some distance, a faint glow appeared before her. She cried in relief and stumbled toward it. The light sparkled, blinding in the gloom. The crown of Elwar. She reached for it, and it vanished.

Adana shuddered again, her efforts to calm her pounding heart failing after the nightmare. Montee thought the dark cave represented the tunnels underneath the Border Keep, but no matter how many times Adana dreamed about the river and the darkness, she felt overwhelmed with fear and desperation.

In the back of Adana's mind, Am'brosia pressed anxiously to connect. Adana shrugged the contact away. The giraffe usually provided calm and peace after the dream, but this attempt felt distressed. It didn't matter what Am'brosia wanted to share with her, she refused to learn anything troubling at the moment. She wanted peace.

Despite the early hour, Adana rose from her bed and tiptoed past Elayne's sleeping form.

She crossed the courtyard to the temple and entered its solitude. Why she chose the sanctuary, she did not know, but it seemed the logical place to go after the dream. Since her arrival in Roshar, Brother Honest had held daily services for the many refugees and soldiers flocking to the town, but Adana avoided these events, much to Montee's displeasure.

"Why will you not attend? You are the Creator's chosen Watcher, blessed with his presence," Montee had said. "You visited the temple every day when you lived in Moniah."

"What good did it do?" Adana said, aware of her own failures to please the Creator. Every day he found a new way to punish her.

Bewildered, Montee said, "You always looked happier afterward, like a yoke had been lifted from your shoulders."

Adana's response had been venomous. "Do you not recall the last time I went to the temple? You were witness to it. Mammetta and Serrin died."

The memory of her naive beliefs in the Creator's ability or willingness to save them caused Adana to burn with embarrassment. They both had died, and her life had never been the same. Why should she worship a being like that?

For a moment, her shoulder burned, and she rubbed it without thought.

She hadn't given Montee the opportunity to respond to her outburst that day. Instead, she'd stalked away. If Montee held faith in the Creator's willingness to help their battle against Maligon, then she could do homage for both of them.

Adana had other concerns.

The news from each arriving group of refugees added to her worries. She longed to act, to move forward and stop Maligon before he contaminated Moniah forever. What must her people think? Invaded by a monster who trampled across their kingdom without any regard for the beauty and dignity of the land or the people? Monians should hate her and her inability to stop him, yet refugees continued to stream into the village, the Border Keep, and Adana's View, seeking protection.

Adana wandered up the candlelit aisle and slid into a pew, the smooth surface and coolness of the wood providing relief to the heat of her worries. She closed her eyes and inhaled the tart aroma of polish and the reassuring scent of melting candle wax. Her mind drifted back to a time when places like this gave her great comfort, providing a welcome solace. As she sat in the dim light, she wished she could trust again. Childish fairy tales, like the ones she clung to in her youth, could make the circumstances more tolerable.

Shaking her head, she opened her eyes and chided herself for wishing for old myths. Comfort and ease would not defeat Maligon. Strategy and shrewd decisions would help her, nothing else.

A flicker of movement in the shadows near the altar brought Adana's attention back to the present. A tapestry of the Creator looking over his people as a loving parent rippled as a teacher entered the temple through a side door.

The teacher knelt before the long, wooden altar and bowed his head. The candles illuminated the person, providing Adana with his identity—Brother Honest.

After a moment, he rose, turned, and bowed toward Adana. "Forgive me, Your Majesty, for greeting the Creator prior to acknowledging your presence."

That he knew of her presence annoyed Adana. Montee had been correct to ask if he was the son of a Watcher. Men weren't Watchers. Only women. The thought that he might have inherited latent Watcher skills made her uneasy.

"May I join you?" he asked as he approached.

She inclined her head in acceptance.

Honest settled into the pew beside her and gazed upon the tapestry. "This is my favorite part of the day. So quiet and peaceful. I can feel the Creator's presence well during this hour."

Adana did not reply, she just stared straight ahead at the image hanging before her. This tapestry hung in every temple in the surrounding kingdoms. As a child, it had been her favorite, when she had still felt the Creator's presence as a comfort.

"You have lost your confidence in the Creator," Honest said. It was not a question.

Trained to stillness, her annoyance at his statement remained buried below the surface. Adana responded as the queen. "We are limited in our ability to understand how others rely on him."

"Father Tonch told me you were his greatest pupil, your faith strong beyond your years." Honest turned to face her profile. "He also told me you seemed to have forgotten all that after your mother died."

"Didn't you ever question the truth of it all? Your mother died, too." The naked truth of her words surprised her, but they did not seem to bother Honest.

"No. My belief kept me moving forward at the time. That's when I decided to become a Teacher of the Faith. I saw the pain so many felt, and I knew the Creator provided peace for them."

Adana shifted sideways to look at him. "Does your Creator provide peace for Moniah? For Elwar? For all of us, so this war does not have to happen?"

"It's not that kind of peace."

She snorted. "Of course not. Rationalizations ease our disappointment in him."

Brother Honest looked at her sadly. "Then why are you here?"

His question galled her. She did not know the answer. Was it the dream, the presence of this man in it, or was she seeking some solace from her youth in this room?

He took her lack of response in stride, sighed, and sat back in the pew. When she peered over at him, his eyes were closed. Several minutes passed, and she found herself examining his profile, wondering about his part in her vision.

As if he heard her thoughts, he said, "Do you believe in prophecy? In the visions Watchers receive?"

"Of course." Why did this man ask so many questions?

He smiled. "Tell me about your vision."

"What?" Adana sat forward, her back rigid. Did he somehow know she came here to escape the vision in her dream?

He did not open his eyes. "Your Majesty, I only seek to help. I am gifted at interpreting visions." When he finally did open his eyes, the light of the candles sparkled in his usually serious brown eyes. "I interpreted for your mother once."

Adana sank back on the bench. If Mammetta had lived, she would have begun sharing her past visions with Adana. Instead, Adana knew of none of them.

"What did she see?"

"A young girl facing a divided path in the early years of her reign."

Before Adana could respond, the door in the rear of the temple creaked open, revealing Montee silhouetted in the early morning light. The First Vision closed the door behind her and walked up the aisle, a pleased quirk to her lips. "Your Majesty, I never would have thought to look here, but Joannu insisted she saw you enter the temple."

She looked between the two of them and frowned. "You are here, but I fear not in the capacity I had hoped."

Adana stood and slid past Honest. "I sought some peace and quiet. Too much noise in the village."

Montee shot a questioning look at Honest, who shook his head, further annoying Adana. At the same time, the puncture spot on Adana's shoulder began to tingle. She hadn't noticed that the ache had dissipated while she talked with Honest. She paused in her steps. Was her shoulder agreeing with the sentiments of Montee and Honest? Or maybe it was something else. It didn't hurt. Good news, possibly?

"I assume you sought me out for a purpose?"

Montee nodded. "A pigeon from Adana's View has arrived, and Karyah's and Ostreia's units are here. We await your presence."

"Forgive me, Brother Honest. Our discussion was...diverting, but I must attend to my duties." Adana exited the temple, her thoughts turning toward the cave in Teletia and what her Watchers might have found there.

* * *

When Adana arrived in the solarium, she found Prince Jerold pacing like a trapped hyena. A relieved, but tired-looking, woman sat in one of the chairs, a young boy beside her. Karyah and Ostreia stood at opposite ends of the room, vigilant until relieved of their duties.

Adana stopped and studied the seated woman, noting that she returned the same intense stare. It had been two years since she'd seen Queen Morana of Teletia and her son, Prince Navon.

Montee closed the door behind her as she followed Adana into the room. "My lady, as we hoped, our Watchers found King Ariff's family in the cave."

Every time Adana thought of the cave, now that she knew its true location, she felt a spark of hope. She longed to see it with her own eyes, a desire from her childhood, reawakened with this new slant on its location and purpose.

"Queen Morana, Prince Navon." Adana inclined her head in their direction. "I am pleased to see you well." She looked around the room in confusion. "Where is King Ariff?"

Morana nodded regally at her. "Your Majesty, we, too, are relieved to find you here. Thank you for sending your Watchers to find us. My son and I join you here, but King Ariff—"

"He's gone into Belwyn to save my mother!" Jerold's interruption startled them all. He began pacing again, his head bowed and shoulders tense.

Adana frowned at Jerold's reaction. She sat in a chair, contrasting its padded embrace to the solid benches in the temple. "That is good news, is it not?"

Jerold stopped his pacing and faced her. "Forgive me, my lady. I would prefer to do something. Wouldn't you?"

"Yes," she said. "But my First Vision keeps reminding me to gauge our actions carefully."

"It is true," Montee said. "Perhaps Karyah or Ostreia can provide us more information on King Ariff's plan?"

The two Watchers held equal rank. Ostreia served as a Strategist, trained in espionage and military strategy. Karyah, on the other hand, commanded four units of Watchers. No visible signal passed between them, but Ostreia stepped forward and bowed to Adana. "My queen, I'm pleased to provide information."

"Excellent," Adana said. "I appreciate your steadfast service after such a long journey. I will keep you from food and rest only a moment. What can you tell us?"

"When King Donel of Elwar sent soldiers to aid in Belwyn's fight against Maligon, we did not know Maligon had infiltrated Empress Gabriella's soldiers with his own supporters. We must consider the possibility that they met the same fate as you did in the forest."

Shocked, Adana nodded. Two days before Adana left Elwar to return to Moniah, Kiffen's father had sent troops to Belwyn. It hadn't occurred to her, but knowing how far Maligon's treachery reached, it made sense to suspect the traitor had followers in the troops sent to Belwyn, too. Even if not, Quilla might have recalled Elwar's troops and denied Belwyn aid once she seized the throne. Her actions, so far, indicated an alliance with Maligon.

She glanced at Jerold.

"I agree." He registered no surprise over Ostreia's words. With her thoughts focused on Moniah and Kiffen, Adana failed to recognize the truth he already presumed. They must accept that nothing remained of Elwar's assistance for Empress Gabriella.

Ostreia continued. "King Ariff took two of Karyah's units with him to Belwyn. The other two units remained with us."

"So, King Ariff and ten Watchers?" Adana considered this news. Would a small group fare better than an army?

"He hopes to slip into Belwyn unnoticed and find a way to release Empress Gabriella and the Watchers held captive."

"How many days since he left?" Jerold asked the question Adana had planned to ask, but she understood his need to lead this discussion.

"Four days." Ostreia hesitated, then added, "Your Highness."

How did she know his true rank? Adana glanced between them. He didn't register surprise. Then, Adana recalled his outburst a moment ago when he referred to Gabriella as his mother. A Watcher wouldn't forget such an important disclosure.

"Thank you Ostreia. Karyah. You deserve rest. Please tend to your needs and those of the units who accompanied you."

The women nodded, but before they left, Adana said, "It should be noted, few know of Sir Jerold's identity. Please do not share this knowledge with anyone."

"As the Seat says," the two Watchers responded, then exited the solarium.

Adana looked around the room, her gaze falling last on Navon. Anyone could strike at this one room and wipe out three ruling families in one quick act. The realization hit her like a punch to the stomach, and she breathed deeply to calm her voice before she spoke again. Had Jerold realized their vulnerability?

"We have the future of three kingdoms in this room." Stating the words sent a cold chill down her back. With tentative fingers, she checked the location of the pinprick on her shoulder. After a morning of conflicting signals, no warning resonated from it. She breathed a sigh of relief and sensed a brief contact from Am'brosia, a note of comfort and assurance.

For the moment, all was safe.

"Jerold, Adana is correct." Morana nodded in agreement. "I objected to Ariff going with the Watchers' forces to Belwyn, but we must accept the truth. Ariff is not the future of Teletia, Navon is. Your mother is not the future of Belwyn. You are."

The young man, known for so many years as Empress Gabriella's most dedicated knight, turned away from the women for a moment, his shoulders hunched. When he turned back toward them his eyes revealed the difficulty of the changes in his life. "I've spent so much time protecting the empress and hiding my true self, it's hard for me to think of myself as a prince or future emperor."

The statement startled a harsh laugh from Adana. "I might not have been in disguise, but I assure you, Queen Quilla allowed me little room to feel like the next Seat of Moniah, either. It's as foreign to me as it is to you, I imagine."

Despite her laugh, Adana sat back in her chair and glanced up at Montee in concern. The woman shared the same burdened look. Their presence together was risky. If Maligon learned of it, he could win the battle with one excellent assassin.

Were there traitors in Roshar?

* * * * *

Chapter Twenty-Three

For two days, Leera sat in her room staring out the window, watching the comings and goings of people unknown to her. Her chamber door opened three times each day—breakfast, lunch, and dinner. The maid, Hanna, had startled in fright this morning, almost dropping the tray, when Leera rushed toward her as she entered the room. She welcomed anyone, a maid even, to this enforced sentence of solitude.

It was mid-afternoon, now, and Leera paced back and forth, muttering to herself, aware it would be a few more hours before dinner arrived. With a sigh, she flopped down on the sumptuous cushions of her bed. The small baby cloth lay on a table just in sight when she looked to her left. Yesterday, out of boredom, she had tried to wash out the spot. It persisted on the edges of the cloth, taunting her with her mother's words: "Even then you failed me. Look at the stains you left behind. Maybe you should spend your time getting that stain out."

The shock of her mother's anger still made Leera gasp in pain. Last night, she had lain in bed, crying into her pillow. When her tears dried, a memory of gleefully watching her brothers squirm under the queen's anger disturbed her rest further. When she finally slept, she dreamed of Kiffen and Serrin standing by, satisfied grins on their faces, while her mother screamed at her, veins bulging in her forehead.

A knock on the door startled Leera back to the present. Forcing her thoughts from the offending dream, she sat up, shaking her head.

Hanna entered the room, a tiny smile on her face. "Your Highness, you have visitors."

Jumping from the bed, Leera peered into the glass above her bureau. "Do I look presentable?"

"Of course." Hanna walked around her, straightening her skirts and tucking her curls back in place. Ever since Leera had asked her name, the maid had become a bit more relaxed in her presence, and Leera had begun to realize how much she had ignored the young woman.

"Who is it?"

"Your mother." Hanna paused as she straightened a bow on Leera's skirt.

Leera plopped back on the bed. "Then why do I care how I look?"

"Because the young lord, Taren, is with her."

Taren? Leera jumped up again and surveyed herself in the mirror. Young men didn't usually visit a young lady's chambers. The idea of him just outside her door sent tantalizing thoughts to her mind. If others knew of his admittance to her chamber, what scandalous talk might they spread? Excitement trilled along her limbs at the opportunity of seeing him again. He might be part of her mother's schemes, but, at least, he treated her with respect and was unbelievably handsome.

After a few more moments of primping, Leera bade Hanna to grant her mother and Taren entrance. Her mother would enter without permission, but Leera felt the need to exercise some pretense of control. She stood very still and waited.

Queen Quilla breezed into the room, her dress of green and yellow swishing as she moved toward her daughter, arms held out. "My darling child, we hoped we might find you feeling a bit better, today."

She grasped Leera's shoulders and studied her face. The gesture reminded Leera of the many times her mother had joined her in her rooms for one last inspection before a royal event. With a glance back at Taren, who stood in the doorway, the queen said, "I've told Taren how ill you've been for the last two days, but he insisted on seeing you."

While she registered her mother's lie, Leera studied the change in the queen's eyes. They shifted from concerned when she turned toward Taren to a threat of warning when facing Leera.

The chill of her mother's gaze forced Leera to step back from the embrace.

Taren bowed, and, as he straightened, said, "It is true, Your Highness. I feared your illness might be serious, and I have asked to see you all day. I'm glad to see you looking well."

"It is kind of you to show concern, Taren," Leera said. "I am much better today."

"See?" The queen clapped her hands together in delight. "Taren, we mustn't exhaust the princess, and it's impertinent for you to even be here. I've shown great restraint and trust to allow you this moment. Please close the door as you leave."

"But?" Leera stared at her mother. Yes, it was true Taren shouldn't be in her rooms, but she had seen no one for two days.

"The queen is correct, my lady. I look forward to you rejoining us soon." Taren bowed and backed out of the room.

Once the door closed behind him, her mother grabbed Leera's arm and yanked her close enough for Leera to see the tiny blood vessels in her eyes. "If you would behave as I require, you could spend many hours strolling the gardens in his company." She dropped Leera's arm only to throw her own in the air. "But you know his presence here isn't proper. How dare you object when I sent him away? What would people say if they knew?"

"I'm sure, if I become court gossip, you will be the source, mother."

"You impudent little brat." The slap came with the same vengeance as the queen's words.

Leera flinched and covered her cheek with her hand. Her mother had never struck her. No one had ever struck her.

"Where did you learn to behave like a trollop?"

Leera stared at her mother, fighting back tears. How had her mother's odd visitation become her fault? She kept this thought to herself, aware nothing she said would go over well.

After a moment, the queen said, "There. That's better. You should learn to be silent more often, or you may find yourself locked up in less suitable chambers."

Fear sizzled along Leera's scalp at that suggestion.

"I have brought you something," the queen said. "I'm almost tempted to not give it to you after your behavior."

Leera cast her gaze toward the floor in the same stance of obeisance she had seen so many others assume in her mother's presence. Once, she had known what to anticipate from her mother, but no longer. She waited with apprehension, her heart pounding so loud her mother should hear it.

"Well? Look up, child. You are a princess, not the chambermaid."

The queen held in her hand a gold ring box with the head of a lion engraved in the lid.

The shock of seeing this particular box caused Leera to sit down on the bed. She shook her head, unable to understand. The box belonged to her father. It held the ring of office for the ruler of Elwar. A quick glance at her mother's hands proved the queen didn't wear the ring. Why not? She had taken the throne.

"For Ballene's sake, take it." The queen took Leera's hand and placed the box in it. It felt warm from the recent contact with her mother.

The urge to give it back thrummed in her fingers, followed by the awareness that she couldn't. Not if she wanted her mother to let her out of confinement.

"Open it."

She lifted the lid to reveal a large, gold ring. The engraving of the lion on the box's lid was molded into the ring. Sapphires in the lion's eyes flashed in the light, staring back at her in accusation. The ring was too big for her. Too powerful. Her father wore it on his pinky finger, and even then, it only slid halfway down, then stuck on a knuckle. For that reason, he had secured it in the box whenever it wasn't needed. The ring granted the wearer the rights of rulership in Elwar. With this ring, she could take the throne.

A thrill ran down her spine as she imagined herself holding audience with supplicants instead of her mother. She would be queen instead.

It slid onto her finger and hung there like the anchor of a boat. Her father's fingers might have been too large, but hers were too small. Unbidden, she saw Kiffen's hands as he handed her an apple or brushed the burrs out of his horse's mane. It would fit Kiffen. She knew it would.

It was Kiffen's ring.

The queen picked up Leera's hand and held it in the light, admiring the ring. "You will grow into it, just as you will grow into your monarchy."

A cold fear gripped Leera's stomach. Did her mother truly believe she could take the throne and rule Elwar? She had said so the other day, but Leera had assumed it would never happen. Sariah, Helmyra, and Gerguld would prevent it. They would help Kiffen retake the throne.

"I can't wear this, Mother."

"You will grow into it."

"No, Mother. I can't wear it. It's not mine."

Laughter trilled from her mother's lips, harsh and cruel. She turned her back on Leera and sailed toward the door. "You don't think so, but it is yours. Wear it for a while. You will see."

The door clicked behind the queen.

Hot acid burned in Leera's throat. She fought to keep her lunch from rebelling and stormed toward the door. "Mother." She rattled the locked doorknob and kicked the unrelenting wood when it didn't cooperate.

The ring glared at her when she stared down at her offending hand.

She yanked the ring off and flung it across the room. It clattered on the wood flooring and rolled like a top for several moments before clanging to a stop.

Leera flung the gold box after it and went to bed.

* * * * *

Chapter Twenty-Four

Pultarch rode next to the Lord most days, but today, the Lord rode within a palanquin carried by the four men who always rode by his side. Just before the midday meal, the caravan halted. Pultarch watched as the four bodyguards carrying the chair lowered it to the ground. They stepped back, one of them answering a question from Maligon in his short, guttural tongue. Moments later, Kalara ducked inside the curtains to confer with her father. Were they preparing to force another village into submission?

Pultarch's stomach quailed at the methods used to tame the people. Even after overcoming several more villages, he found himself wishing for a simpler way. The results were hard to argue with. He knew their destination was Adana's View, and he wished more than anything the unit sent to save Adana would return soon. He spent hours in the saddle daydreaming of the day he could ride into the royal fortress with Adana proudly perched on a horse beside him. Sometimes, he imagined her riding in front of him on the same horse. The crowds would roar their approval, and he would be seen as a hero.

"Your smile gives you away." Kalara interrupted his thoughts, smug amusement in her eyes. "What wild daydream are you about?"

Pultarch shook his head. When had she left the Lord's enclosure? He tried to watch for her since she never failed to antagonize him when given the slightest opportunity. Adana would put her in her proper place once she learned of Kalara's cruelty. "Have we heard from the men sent to rescue Adana?"

Kalara frowned. "The numbers guarding her are larger than anticipated. It makes matters difficult."

Pultarch scowled. "Why do they prevent her from joining us? Can't they see we want her on the Seat of Authority as much as they do?"

"Have you not been listening to the Lord?" Kalara slapped the reins on her horse's back. "They don't want her on the Seat. Kiffen is their chosen ruler for both kingdoms."

"Let me go to her. I'll save her." He blurted the words before he realized it.

"Exactly what I suggested." The smirk on Kalara's face gave him pause. "It seems he has decided you have other uses, as well. We're assembling a small squad to travel with you."

Astonished, Pultarch found himself stammering, "Me? Uh, um, really? I will be the one to save her?" Fear, mingled with the excitement of glory, settled into his chest.

Kalara sighed and shook her head. "Come with me. The Lord wishes to speak with you." She guided him toward the clearing where the curtained chair had been lowered to the ground.

Four hefty soldiers, arms crossed over their chests, stood beside the poles they used to carry the chair. The curtains hung loosely, multiple layers of glimmer cloth in varying shades of purple. Pultarch bent over and entered the small enclosure, gasping at the stuffy air. Why would anyone choose to ride in something so stifling?

"Ahh, there you are, my son." The man leaned back on a heap of pillows, each one purple tasseled in gold. His eyes remained half-closed as he turned toward Pultarch. "Has my esteemed daughter filled you in on our predicament?"

"Yes, but…" He faltered. Maligon looked pale. Sweat thickened the locks of his hair and beaded on his upper lip. "My Lord, are you well?"

Maligon groaned and pushed himself upright. "Your concern is appreciated, but unnecessary. Some days my injuries ache. I find heat improves me."

Anger over the atrocities dealt this man flared in Pultarch's chest. He'd seen horrors along the road, but the more he considered how Micah and Chiora maimed Maligon and sent him to die, the more he accepted the Lord's form of brutality.

"Of course. Kalara tells me you wish for me to rescue Adana." Boyish excitement filled Pultarch's voice, and he cringed at his inability to stifle it. "How many will I take to fight my way in to save her?"

"Oh no, my boy." The Lord laid a well-manicured hand on Pultarch's; the other, crippled hand stayed hidden behind his voluminous robes. "Stealth is required. They must not know you are there to save her. You'll take only four men."

"H-how can we do that?"

"Four of my most *capable* men. Surely, you can find a way to gain access with your nobility and their skills." He fell back against the pillows and closed his eyes. "Be aware, they've brainwashed her into believing they support her claim to the Seat of Authority. She believes she and Kiffen will rule together."

"She believes these lies? I thought her Watcher skills would recognize their deceptions." Pultarch's heart ached at her innocence.

"Exactly why she needs you, Pultarch. You must show her the error in her judgment."

* * *

Two days later, Pultarch found himself closing in on Roshar. He pushed the four men, allowing them to rest at small intervals, traveling day and night. During one of their stops, the man called Cap approached him.

"The village is just beyond those hills. I believe we should wait until evening." Cap looked toward the hills, his arms crossed with decision.

Pultarch considered the advice. At their current pace, they could be in Roshar by midday, but he liked Cap's suggestion. "Which direction do the refugees come from?"

"Primarily, just to the west of us."

Pultarch nodded and looked over his band of mercenaries. They planned to join the line of refugees streaming into the village. Darkness improved their chances of mixing in unnoticed.

Earlier scouts had advised them the Watchers pulled all able-bodied men from the refugees to be questioned and outfitted for battle. If no one recognized Pultarch, he might find a way to gain access to Adana and plead his innocence. He was no fool. She would have heard he rode with the Lord's troops and question his loyalty.

That night, the four men and Pultarch slipped into a traveling band of refugees while everyone slept. Pultarch grinned at the ease of it. The inept men selected to guard these people snored at their posts. If these refugees represented the soldiers who made up Adana's guard, his task would be simple.

Late the next morning, they trudged toward Roshar and the refugee camp surrounding the village. Pultarch stared in amazement at the volume of people. The smell hit him first, unwashed bodies and offal. It stunk worse than traveling with the Lord's army.

How could Adana ever believe this was what her people wanted? How could she allow this to happen?

They reached the huddles of structures and tents first. Watchers and soldiers barred the way, checking each person who entered, pulling a few aside. They pulled Cap from the group, then two more, then Pultarch. One more of his men followed him, and soon the five stood waiting for the Watchers to take them to the barracks.

Pultarch studied each of the Watchers and guards. None looked familiar, but all Watchers looked the same to him, except Adana. Dark hair, gray hair, varying skin tones—those were the only differences.

The Watchers marched the men through the refugee camp. Small structures butted up against each other, and the sounds of crying children, as well as chickens, horses, and other livestock enveloped him. He shook his head at the gathered hovels wrought by the actions of Donel and Micah. If the two foreigners had stayed out of Maligon's way twenty years ago, none of this would be here. He pushed back the awareness that without Micah, Adana wouldn't exist, either.

* * * * *

Chapter Twenty-Five

Kiffen stood at an east-facing window in the Central Tower, focused on the connection with Bai'dish. The escort Kassa sent to accompany the giraffe and Glume on the last part of their journey appeared as a hazy image along the link. Three Watchers, six Soldiers of the First Sight, and four of his own men encircled the giraffe, their bodies attentive to any threat.

The party had kept to the Monian side of the border for the largest portion of the trip but hid in the forest, on occasion, to avoid troops moving south to join Maligon.

He'd experienced the skirmish on the day Samantha's escort reached Bai'dish. Observing from the giraffe's height provided a distinct advantage even if the animal had retreated into the trees. When the soldiers and Watchers overcame Maligon's men, he had sagged with relief. Two Watchers marched south with the prisoners. An odd decision, but he didn't know Moniah's terrain as well.

As he scanned the hazy image of the arrival party, he realized Samantha was not with them. She must have taken charge of the prisoners. Relief filled his chest. Ever since the message from Adana about Samantha, he had striven to avoid the Watcher. Kassa's decision to send her on this task had been fortuitous under the circumstances. Her absence felt like a gift from the Creator.

He wandered back over to the map. Giraffe-shaped markers represented Monian troops and Watchers clustered behind the walls of

Adana's View. The Border Keep held a scattering of lion markers for Elwar and four times more giraffe markers. The village of Roshar appeared to be the most vulnerable position. A few lion markers, double as many giraffe markers, but the bulk of their forces were represented by brown markers, refugee volunteers.

The rest of their forces were scattered across the map. First Soldiers guarded the villages and towns from Maligon's troops. Reports indicated Maligon killed every last soldier in his way. He glanced toward Elwar. Quilla killed those who supported him. How many hid within her ranks still loyal to Kiffen?

Kiffen itched to do something. Just to attack the bands of traitors that Bai'dish's escort avoided would relieve some frustration. Yet, their true fight lay south, in Moniah. Preparation for the battle to come aggravated him. Just a few days ago, he had argued with Kassa and Halar about when they should strike.

A week earlier, Kassa had said, "Kiffen, if I learned one thing from Maligon, it's never to strike until you're fully prepared. Yes, he's amassing an army. Yes, he's almost at the threshold of Adana's View. The fortress is well-armed. But you have few soldiers. Adana's forces are farmers and merchants. She has a few Watchers and soldiers but not enough. It takes time to act. Maligon's had years to prepare."

Not shown on the map, but just as important, were the hundreds of refugees fleeing before Maligon's scourge across the kingdom. The keep and the village of Roshar received them, but the majority of them became the responsibility of Linus, the commander guarding Adana's View.

An image from Bai'dish rose in his mind, as if the giraffe were present and talking to Kiffen. Each day, it became easier to maintain the bond. The image was one sent by Adana three days ago. The refugees in Roshar included a trio of royalty—Adana, Jerold, and Navon. Kiffen felt nauseous every time he thought of it. It would be so easy for Maligon to send a force into the makeshift encampment and eliminate three ruling dynasties at once.

Kiffen would rest easier if everyone he cared about were ensconced in the tunnels below the Border Keep, but even he understood the danger of moving them across the territory recently traveled by Glume and Bai'dish.

The time to move was finally near. He'd heeded Kassa and been patient. They would crush Maligon between the three forces as long as the traitor maintained his course. His arrogance had been his downfall before. With the Creator's help, it might be again.

He turned at a knock on the door. A Watcher entered. "Sire, the Monian giraffe is at the gates."

He nodded. "Thank you."

* * * * *

Chapter Twenty-Six

From her official rooms at the temple's holdings, Adana looked out over the sprawling mass of refugees and wondered how far Maligon would push her people. The accommodations Brother Honest and the villagers of Roshar offered were not perfect, but still people came, fear pushing them toward the safety of numbers. She wrinkled her nose as the breeze shifted and brought with it the smells of manure and tightly-packed humanity.

As bad as this looked, her people still flocked to her. It hadn't taken long for word of their queen's presence to leak out. So far, Jerold's identity and the safe arrival of Morana and Navon remained secret.

Am'brosia brushed her mind. Bai'dish and Glume stood in the courtyard of the Border Keep. She sighed with relief as the crowds parted, and Kiffen approached the two, a shy smile on his face. The giraffe spread his forelegs wide and bowed his head toward the ground in the official greeting of a royal giraffe with his bonded partner. A yearning to be with Kiffen ached in her heart, but Bai'dish's satisfaction to be standing in Kiffen's presence, flowed along the link. She noted a difference from Am'brosia's joy at her own presence. Kiffen's and Bai'dish's joy was evident, but quiet, while with Am'brosia, their joy bubbled. A difference in males or because the two still needed to learn each other?

When Kiffen looked up into Bai'dish's eyes, she gasped. She looked straight into his face and saw the surprise of recognition in his expression. They gazed at each other a moment longer, but then Kassa joined Kiffen, and he was forced to look away. She felt his loneliness in the moods of the animals.

Within a few days, they would march toward Adana's View. Maybe then, they would find time to be together and less lonely.

Glancing out over the huts and tents, again, she tried to imagine Adana's View overrun with this many people. The thought of her beloved home's open spaces covered in cramped hovels nauseated her. Such beauty, such a noble people, reduced to this by one man who shouldn't even be alive.

She turned as a knock sounded at the door. "Come."

Montee entered. "Our guards report five strong and able men in today's arrivals. They appear healthy and well-fed. Unlike the others, they carried little but sacks on their backs."

Most of the men able to fight had arrived days ago. Five? Together?

"They were scattered among this last group, but the Watchers suspect they know each other. After we pulled them aside, they stood separately, but each one tried to not make eye contact with one man in particular. Probably, their leader."

"Yet, they didn't enter the gates together?" Adana walked over to the window again and looked out. One more concern to weigh on her. Who to trust?

Montee joined her. "I welcome good soldiers, but…"

"You question why they pretend to not know each other and have arrived today, not sooner?"

Montee nodded. "Only the weakest and most in need of protection have arrived in the last three days. None of the other refugees in this group knew them. They had never seen them before this morning, but they were there when they awoke at dawn."

"Bring them to the solarium. Let them relax awhile. Place Elayne nearby to listen. Maybe she can learn something."

Montee nodded and turned away.

"And Montee, give them some of our best stores of food and drink."

"Our best?"

Adana smiled. "Good food and wine loosen tongues."

* * *

Elayne sat in a small enclosure outside the solarium listening. As the stamp of boots rang in the hallway, she positioned herself in a relaxed position, so she could remain still and silent.

"We have provided some refreshment for you," a Watcher said. "Please wait here until the commander can speak to each one of you separately."

One of them gave a low whistle and then chuckled. "I'd like to separate her from the herd."

"Be quiet." The cultured voice issuing the harsh command caused Elayne's eyes to widen in recognition. "Show some respect. She is a Watcher."

The same man snickered. "She can watch my giraffe."

The men laughed, then there was silence except for shuffling feet, sounds of chewing, and other grotesque noises made by hungry men, awakening memories of the raunchy atmosphere at The Sleeping Dog and her life as Shana. The familiarity of the men's sounds made her stomach clench. Someday a refugee might recognize her.

What would she do then? She wanted to remain a Listener, but if the queen discovered her true identity, would she allow it?

The genteel voice spoke again, and she leaned forward, trying to confirm her suspicions.

"So, Your Highness," a gruff voice said, his voice lilting with heavy sarcasm, "how do you plan to handle this interview?"

Several snickers sounded from the other men.

In clipped, well-enunciated tones, Pultarch's voice responded. "Are you incapable of speaking with respect, Horace? I will have you gagged and turned in as a traitor to the Watchers if you do not show some restraint in your comments."

"Yes, sir."

Elayne could almost see the man's comical salute as his buddies continued to chuckle at the speaker's antics.

The cultured voice belonged to Pultarch. She was sure of it. The question was whether she should alert the queen now or listen longer.

Another man in the group, his voice secure with authority, settled it for her. "You both are fools. Keep your mouths shut. We don't know who listens. Only I will speak from here on."

Silence followed.

Elayne waited to be sure no one violated his command, and, when they remained silent, she hurried to report to Queen Adana and Montee.

* * * * *

Chapter Twenty-Seven

Adana's response startled Elayne.

"Pultarch? You must be wrong." The queen turned away from her and settled in the chair Honest had carved for her use. Arms crossed, Adana glared at Elayne.

Elayne glanced around the queen's quarters, thankful that only Montee attended them at the moment. The room, although not spacious, felt large with only the three of them present, but with the queen unhappy, the walls shrank around her.

The seat Adana took was centered near the rear wall of the room. To its left and right, small potted trees provided some contrast to the stark walls. A rug woven in reds and browns covered the floor, a contribution from the village's innkeeper, Talia.

"I assure you, Your Majesty, I know his voice," Elayne said, keeping her speech firm, but soft. Had Adana forgotten her embarrassing admission of interest in the young earl? So much had passed since then.

"But you only met him briefly. How can you be so sure?" Adana leaned forward, her hands gripping the arms of her temporary Seat of Authority.

Elayne bowed her head. Of course, the queen didn't know she had first met Pultarch when Sarx brought him to The Sleeping Dog where she had worked as Shana, the tavern maid. How could she convince them without causing these two Watchers to doubt her loyalty? She cursed Sarx for placing her in this predicament. Why couldn't she be where she needed to be without the secrets of others weighing on her head?

Adana turned to Montee. "Can she be correct? Identify a voice she heard only a few times? Do Listeners have that ability?"

The First Vision squinted at Elayne, studying her until Elayne fought the urge to squirm. "I do not know. It's possible. I think I should verify if it's him." She turned to leave.

"Wait." Adana stared out the window on the far side of the room, the one facing the solarium. "If it is Pultarch, bring him to me."

Elayne's shoulders relaxed. The queen's tone held resignation, an acceptance of the information she provided. No one need find doubt in her word or be reminded of her infatuation with Pultarch.

Her relief evaporated when Montee motioned for her to leave while she stayed in the room with Adana. "Close the door behind you."

The door clicked shut, and Elayne stood on the other side, trying to calm her pounding heart. At least, she had a moment of privacy here. No one else stood guard outside the chamber at the moment. What if Montee knew of her feelings for Pultarch? Watchers discovered so much from body language. She paused and listened for sounds of approach. Satisfied no one would find her eavesdropping, she eased down the corridor and leaned her ear against the wall. On the other side was the back wall of Adana's chambers where the two women spoke.

Montee's voice had dropped to a quiet, urgent tone, but Elayne could still understand her. "I still don't think you should meet with him." The First Vision's voice held the sharp tang of shock. "He's part of Maligon's army. Surely, he's a spy."

"If it's him," Adana said, her voice ringing with purpose. "He cared for me in Elwar. I believe he will talk to me. From what Elayne said, he is not in charge of this group. I would like an explanation of how the son of an earl has been reduced to answering to a common soldier."

"He could be dangerous. Remember his attack on Kiffen."

Elayne leaned in closer. She'd heard rumors of the young noble's rash actions after the announcement of Adana's and Kiffen's betrothal. It had happened the day after his drunken night at The Sleeping Dog.

She straightened in surprise for a moment. The jealousy she'd felt when first hearing this story didn't rise in her belly. Why? Had witnessing his weakness among these soldiers conquered her emotions?

"I will keep watch for any untoward actions by him." Adana's annoyed tone brought her back to the present, and she leaned in closer to the wall. "I'm perfectly capable of fighting off his advances. I don't believe he will do something that foolish ever again."

In the silence that followed, Elayne pondered the exasperation that seeped into Adana's voice. On the day Sarx presented her to Adana as a companion, gossip about Pultarch and Kiffen's sword fight had swarmed throughout the castle. It never occurred to her that the young noble's actions had impacted Adana. Now that she knew the queen, it made sense. Adana hid any sign of weakness within herself.

When Sarx convinced Pultarch's father to use Elayne as a gift of contrition, he had focused on Pultarch's rashness toward Prince Kiffen, not the lady Adana. The rumors said Adana became a pawn in the fight. Adana was proud and, often, unsure of her ability to command. An error in judgment about Pultarch would have shamed her.

At the time, Elayne had worried about obscuring her own identity as Shana, the tavern maid. There had been some risk Pultarch might recognize her. That was Sarx's first test of her skills, and she had passed, or Pultarch had failed.

She clutched her fist to her chest, willing her heart to calm its rhythm from the memory of those first encounters dressed as a lady with Pultarch. It appeared her heart still felt something for him. He had flirted with her as a lady. Men didn't flirt with ladies the same way they did with tavern maids.

Montee's voice rose to a normal level, drawing Elayne back to the hushed conversation. "Where should his men wait?"

"Tell them we have no room in the barracks today. Send them back to the village but have them followed. It sounds like one of them, maybe this Horace fellow, will eventually let something slip."

Before Montee could discover Elayne taking advantage of her newfound listening gift, she scurried back toward the chamber door and waited at a respectable distance.

* * * * *

Chapter Twenty-Eight

Adana paced from the window to her chair, to the window, again. Should she have Am'brosia alert Kiffen to Pultarch's unexpected appearance in Roshar? Kiffen's animosity toward his former friend burned at a low fire, forgotten amidst the obstacles Maligon placed before them. If he knew the earl's son was in Roshar, he might act on that knowledge rather than think about the battle ahead of them.

"Elayne?" She called out the name, knowing the woman would be nearby.

Within moments, Elayne stepped inside the door. "Yes, Your Majesty?"

"Go alert Brother Honest that I might be sending him a visitor soon."

Adana settled herself back in the chair. Although not the true Seat, it was of polished acacia wood, like the one at Adana's View. The fact that it fit her form perfectly did not escape her notice. Its high back felt smooth and cool to the touch, something the original Seat wouldn't offer her as queen. That Seat of Authority sat in the Great Hall in Adana's View, an expansive room in the center of her fortress, open to the sky and the hot savanna sun, relentless in its warmth.

The Seat burned when the queen first sat in it. She knew. Her mother made her sit in it once a year on her birthday. That was one tradition she hadn't missed while in Elwar.

Before Adana could decide whether to alert Kiffen or not, Montee returned, Pultarch's arm in her firm grip. At a nod from Adana, the First Vision dropped her hold on the man, and he jerked away in the pretense that he had initiated the move.

"Adana." The young man rushed across the room and knelt at her feet.

Montee stalked after him. "Address her properly."

He cowered under the First Vision's shadow but complied. "Forgive me, Your Majesty. I am overjoyed to finally reach you."

Adana studied him for signs of mistreatment. Besides dust from the road, a rank odor of sweat, and the common clothes he wore, he appeared well-fed and in good health.

She straightened in her chair and rested her hand on one of the knives strapped to her thigh. "Our long-lost friend, Pultarch. How surprised we are to find you here. Please, rise, be comfortable, and tell us of your journey."

As he stood, Adana shot a look at Montee. "Leave us."

Back rigid in displeasure, the woman exited the room and shut the door.

Pultarch took a step closer to Adana. "Thank you for seeing me alone. I can't bear to have witnesses to our interludes."

She arched an eyebrow. "Surely, you must realize a queen is never alone. Montee is just outside the door."

"Of course." He blinked and looked around the chamber. "I just was so excited at the prospect of seeing you, of knowing you are alive."

"Come now, Pultarch. Do you mean to tell me you did not know I was alive? After all, your friend, Maligon, has spent the last week assuring my kingdom I'm alive and desiring a marriage to you."

His shoulders stiffened, and the edges of his mouth whitened. "Merely a pretense I've had to hold until I could find a way to reach you."

"A pretense? Oh my." She sat back and studied him. "How did you manage to break away? And with soldiers, no less?"

Pultarch gave her an incredulous look. "Soldiers? You call that riff-raff soldiers?"

Adana studied him. Something was different, more defensive, in his manner. He'd lost some of the boyish charm which caused other women to flock around him.

"Riff-raff, as you call them, are exactly the type of people Maligon attracts." She leaned forward. "Tell me, are these not his men? Are you not in his employ?"

"Me?" A glimmer of steel blazed in his eyes. "Turn to Maligon? I thought you knew better than to believe every piece of gossip delivered to your ears."

Intrigued by his sparring nature, Adana goaded him further. "So, you want me to believe you instead of my own Watchers? You expect me to trust you? Someone who mysteriously disappeared on the same day as the attack on my caravan? On the very day the regent, King Micah, and Elwar's King Donel were murdered?"

Pultarch swallowed, his Adam's apple bobbing in his throat. "Adana—"

"Address me properly."

"Um, forgive me, my la—, er, Your Majesty." He dropped to his knees, his arms outspread, and focused his soft brown eyes on her in the same beseeching expression she knew he employed so well with the ladies of court. It appeared his boyish charm still existed in his tools for attracting women.

"What would you have me do?" he said. "We were surrounded. The next thing I knew Kiffen's soldiers were dragging me from the tent. Elwarian soldiers delivered me to the Lo—uh, to Maligon. I survived by lying to him, knowing I had to stay alive to reach you."

"You've been a willing prisoner, then?"

Pultarch licked his lips and nodded. "Just waiting until I could convince him to send me to you."

Adana shook her head and studied the Earl of Brom's son. Conrad deserved an heir with a backbone, but he had gotten Pultarch instead. She wondered what had changed the young man. She never thought he would stoop to treachery. Either he was a coward or stupid. Neither aided his cause.

"What of my people, Pultarch? The ones you've killed. What about them?"

Alarm crossed his face. "I have not killed anyone."

"Then I'm to call all of the refugees at my gates liars? Monian citizens? I'm to believe a man who has willingly ridden beside Maligon and witnessed torture and killing across my kingdom? A man our spies say has been marching toward my home to claim the Seat of Authority?"

"Your Majesty. Adana. You must know I could not act alone. I had to bide my time until the right moment."

She stood and swept past him. "I'm curious. How did you convince him to let you go?"

Pultarch rose to his feet and followed her. "I'm to rescue you and return you to the Seat of Moniah."

She couldn't hold back the laughter, high-pitched and shrill, at the idea of his success on such an errand.

Montee rushed into the room as Adana spun to face Pultarch, cutting the laugh off with her next question. "Why do I need rescuing Pultarch?"

He eyed Montee's menacing stance before turning back to Adana, for once the confidence gone from his face.

After several silent breaths, Adana nodded. "At least you know when to remain silent." She turned to Montee. "Take him to Brother Honest. He is to be locked in a solitary prayer cell."

Together, Montee and Pultarch objected. "Your Majesty?"

They glared at each other.

Montee stepped closer to Adana, her voice lowered. "Should we not place him under the care of your soldiers?"

"No," Adana said. "I believe a temple cell will do."

Montee frowned but led Pultarch from the room.

* * *

After giving Brother Honest the queen's message, Elayne left the temple but stopped in the middle of the courtyard separating the teachers' living quarters from the temple. As much as she wanted to deny it, Pultarch, after so many weeks of treachery, still triggered some emotions within her. Ones she shouldn't have. Not if she served Queen Adana.

She paused in her thoughts as she heard two people descend the stairs from the wing where the queen received visitors. The tread sounded like Montee's, quick and commanding, while the steps of the other person resounded like an unsure question. Pultarch? Dressed as she was in a Watcher's uniform, would he see the lady Elayne masquerading as a Watcher, or worse yet, would the simpler clothes remind him of the tavern maid, Shana?

Elayne darted into the shadow of a doorway.

Hidden in the cool shadows, she peered past the greenery decorating the walkway in front of the door. Everywhere she looked, the estate sprouted with potted plants. She'd never seen so many plants inside the walls of a building before.

Within moments, the two emerged through an arch. Neither looked happy and neither spoke. With a firm grip on his arm, Montee led Pultarch toward the temple.

Where had the strong and handsome young nobleman from The Sleeping Dog gone? Combined with the evidence of his allegiance to Maligon, his charm seemed distant, if not fictitious. Yet, her heart thumped at the sight of him.

Halfway across the yard, Pultarch froze in his tracks and stared at the doorway where Elayne hid. She held her breath, willing him to move on.

Montee glared at him. "That door will not set you free."

He cast a distracted glance at the First Vision but continued to stare into the shadows. "Who is she?" The command was strong in his voice.

Montee turned an angry glare toward the doorway, and Elayne felt the Watcher's hard gaze penetrate to her bones.

The First Vision grunted and jerked Pultarch's arm. "Watchers are no concern of yours." She dragged him a few steps until his feet complied, but his head stayed turned toward the doorway.

"She looks familiar." His voice drifted to Elayne as Montee pushed him through the temple's entry.

She strained to hear how Montee responded to Pultarch's comment. Relief flooded through her as she realized the Watcher chose to remain silent. She sagged against the wall. Sarx had ordered her to help Maligon when the opportunity arose. He had assured her great wealth if she complied and had hinted at a noble marriage for her, maybe even to an earl. She knew he meant Pultarch. Did Pultarch know he'd been offered in trade?

Her instincts told her to avoid him at all costs. Her heart said other things.

She stepped out from the shadows and rubbed her neck, surprised at the tension building there. Her secret seemed to press down on her more each day. If Pultarch recognized her, she could find herself in a similar cell.

Should she trust the queen with her true identity? Pultarch's presence meant she must choose.

If she remained hidden and did nothing, she defied Sarx, Maligon, and Adana.

If she helped Pultarch, she turned her back on the one person who had recognized her gifts and provided her a new way of life.

If she helped Adana, she faced Maligon's wrath if he won this war.

Shivering despite the heat, she started up the stairs. She'd lied to Adana and the Watchers, allowed Sarx to fabricate her life and place her where he and Maligon needed her. Could the queen forgive her? She preferred a life of freedom, no matter how short it might be, to one chained to Maligon and Sarx.

With slow, heavy steps, Elayne returned to the queen's chamber, determined to confess everything, but she found the room overcrowded with royalty and officials. Queen Morana of Teletia, her son, Prince Navon, and Sir Jerold gathered with the queen. Several Watchers, including Joannu and Veana, stood in attendance beside the queen's chair.

Disappointment and relief flooded through her. She could not confess her secret, not in front of so many.

As she hesitated at the door, Brother Honest came up behind her. "A little overwhelming, isn't it?" His simple smile carried a sweet comfort that Elayne had never felt in her entire life.

At the sound of Honest's voice, Adana looked up from the book she had been studying with Prince Navon. She patted the young boy's hand and said, "Your Highness, I must return to my responsibities. Will you wait for me to finish this with you later?"

He gave a solemn nod and walked over to where his mother sat, leaning his body along her legs.

Queen Adana smiled after the boy for a moment and then turned as Montee entered the room behind Elayne. "Is our prisoner safely ensconced?"

Montee nodded, but Honest stepped forward. "My lady, are you sure of this decision? Unlike your Watchers and First Soldiers, we do not have the security or skills to guard a prisoner."

Alarm beat in Elayne's chest. Imprisoned. If they detained Pultarch for being in the wrong place, what would they do to her? He was the queen's friend, wasn't he? She couldn't claim friendship, just deceit, no matter the reason.

Adana shook her head. "I don't want him in a prison cell. Not yet. I can't tell you why."

Honest turned to Montee. "Can you persuade her any differently?"

Montee's voice betrayed an awareness that her words wouldn't change things, yet she tried. "Your Majesty, your mother made a similar decision with Maligon when she first captured him. It did not go well, as you might recall."

Elayne listened carefully, noting the quick intake of breath among the others in the room. Everyone knew the story of how Queen Chiora let her friendship with Maligon cloud her vision. He seized that opportunity, a moment of kindness, and kidnapped her, endangering her life.

With a regal nod, Adana acknowledged Montee's objection. "You are my First Vision for this very reason, Montee, to guide me and remind me of the history of our struggles, but there's something about my dream…" Her voice faded, and her gaze grew distant for a moment. With a start, Adana sat up straight. "Nevertheless, Pultarch will remain under Honest's roof until I determine how to deal with this new turn of events."

Brother Honest turned a hopeful glance toward Sir Jerold.

"She outranks me." The man held up his hands in a gesture of apology. "I will be glad to assist the teachers with guard duty."

Brother Honest bowed his head. "Thank you. Most of the teachers have never held a knife except to spread butter."

A satisfied smile spread over Queen Adana's face. "Wonderful. Now, I must speak with Elayne, and I require your assistance, Brother Honest."

For a moment, Elayne failed to react. Then she realized what Adana had just said. Had Pultarch learned of her true identity and revealed it in an effort to prove himself? Would Queen Adana confront her in front of everyone, then send her to a cell in Honest's temple?

Glancing around the room, she didn't sense any trouble, but she steeled herself for what may come.

A short while later, Elayne followed Brother Honest into the courtyard, sick dread swamping her stomach. Both were dressed in the plain, dusty clothing of refugees. The queen wanted them to go out into the refugee camp and find the men who had accompanied Pultarch. Honest would attempt to talk to them as a disgruntled farmer. If they didn't rise to his promptings, Elayne was to eavesdrop on their conversations after Honest left. How could she hide her presence from any who might recognize her if she dressed like Shana? Surely, someone in this sprawling camp would.

If only the queen had not issued the command with a room full of royalty behind her.

She sighed and trudged along behind Brother Honest, almost bumping into the man when he stopped. She looked up into his eyes seeing concern in the crease of his forehead.

"We must talk." He guided her toward the temple.

Disheartened, she allowed him to lead her into the building.

The cool, dark interior provided a welcome relief to the heat of the day and the vigilant gazes of so many royals and Watchers. They were alone in the vast room, and the silence enveloped her like a comfortable cloak.

Honest guided her to a bench and then sat beside her. "What troubles you?"

She could not look at him. It made sense to tell him before someone within the village recognized her, but she hesitated, not wanting this gentle man to learn of her past.

He laid a hand on hers and spoke in low, comforting tones. "Whatever troubles you, this is the place to talk about it. I will not judge you. I have seen your devotion to serve the queen in every way, but now you hesitate. Why?"

Elayne began to cry.

* * * * *

Chapter Twenty-Nine

"It's so calm in here." Kiffen stood in the barn beside Bai'dish's stall.

Glume nodded but continued to rake loose hay back into the stall.

Down the length of the building, horses and a few cows stomped, neighed, or mooed, but the place provided peace compared to the hustle of people in the keep.

Kiffen stroked Bai'dish's flank, enjoying the feel of the short, smooth hair under his fingertips. The giraffe had walked up to him the moment he neared the stall. A rumble of pleasure flowed through the bond.

Kiffen regarded the keeper. "How long have you been linked to the giraffes?"

The shy man dropped his head. "Since my childhood, Your Majesty."

Bai'dish butted Kiffen's shoulder and sent an image of Glume as a boy, his face flushed with pleasure, surrounded by the giraffes. Glume touched each one with fond, delicate hands.

Kiffen scrutinized the huge, calloused hands of the man, but Bai'dish countered with a vision of Glume's hand, miniscule beside the giraffe's platter-sized hoof. Kiffen laughed. "Bai'dish tells me you're harmless." He paused and stroked the animal. "At least, I think that's what he's telling me. How did you learn to understand them?"

Glume blushed. "Once they knew I could understand them, the giraffes would not leave me alone. They, um, they are funny animals at times. They pushed so many images on me, I had to learn. It wasn't easy."

Bai'dish bumped his nose into Kiffen's shoulder, again, causing him to stumble before catching his balance.

"He says you're lucky he's not giving you the same treatment." Glume gave Kiffen an apologetic look. "You need to learn faster."

"He's right." Kiffen stared up into the giraffe's liquid-brown eyes, wondering what the bond would feel like if he had spent years developing it. An image of Adana flashed in his mind. She stood at a window looking over Roshar's sprawling mass of humanity. At first, he thought Bai'dish might be trying to answer his thoughts, but then he noticed Adana looked troubled. The image of her shifted, and he caught a brief flash of her drowning in a river. Then the image disappeared. "Did you see that?" Kiffen's heart pounded with alarm.

Glume stood still for a moment. He frowned and looked out of the corner of his eye at Kiffen. "Bai'dish did not share the image with me until you asked. Something troubles her."

Kiffen smacked the wall of the shelter causing Glume to jump and the giraffe to rear his head back. "I understood that. Why was she in a river?"

Glume nodded. "It's part of a dream she's been having for months."

"A vision?"

"Yes."

"What does it mean?"

The man stopped raking and stood the rake on end. He clasped his gloved hands over the end of the handle and rested his chin on his hands. "That's the problem. She doesn't know."

"Do you?"

He shook his head. "She's caught in the rapids. She fights, sinks, fights again. Teachers of the Faith try to help her, but she ignores them because her crown is being washed away."

"She ignores help and goes after her crown?"

"Yes."

"Please tell me she gets it back."

Glume shook his head. "No."

Bai'dish straightened and turned his head toward the barn's entrance. Kiffen followed his alert gaze. Kassa stood there, stoic as always. "There's more to the dream."

The old Watcher entered the barn, and Glume returned to raking, his head bowed in concentration.

Rather than continue to explain the dream to Kiffen, Kassa crossed her arms and watched the keeper. "Glume, your news was helpful. Are you sure the Watcher helping Maligon is Kalara?"

The man stopped and faced her. "Yes."

Kassa nodded then turned toward Kiffen, her eyes softening when she looked up at Bai'dish. "The dream warns of disaster for the crowns of Elwar and Moniah. Her crown washes away. She hits her head on a rock before she can reach it. That's when she ends up in the dark underground. Your crown appears to her there."

"Uhm, begging your pardon," Glume hesitated, "but a bear pulls the queen's crown out of the water and walks away with it."

Kassa's hawk-like gaze fell hard on the man. "Are you sure of this?"

"Yes." He stood straighter and looked her in the eye. "Her dream changed a few nights before I got to Elwar."

Kassa tilted her head and studied Glume like a crow sitting on a fence assessing the danger of a scarecrow. "Your ability troubles me, Glume."

He shrugged.

"But," she looked up at Bai'dish, "if the giraffes trust you, so must I. I just wish I had some way of capturing all the information stored up in your head. There could be some answers in there. Based on Adana's explanation of your ability, I'm guessing you know a lot."

Glume shook his head. "I try to remember only the important facts."

Kassa nodded and turned to leave. "The question is which facts are truly important?" Without waiting for his answer, she left the building.

"She is…" Kiffen hesitated, unsure what to say. Both men grimaced when Bai'dish sent them an image of a large hawk swooping down on a shivering rabbit.

Stillness hummed through the stable for a while, interrupted only when Bai'dish stretched his long neck over the railing and nudged Glume.

Kiffen watched this happen twice, guessing there might be some meaning behind the animal's behavior. "He wants something, doesn't he?"

"Yes, Sire." Glume approached Kiffen. "Bai'dish wants me to explain why he did not die with Prince Serrin."

Stomach plunging, Kiffen ran his hand through his hair, trying to control its sudden shakiness. "You knew why? And didn't say anything?"

"No one knew I could talk to the giraffes. I couldn't risk telling, not while both kingdoms mourned."

Kiffen leaned back against the fenced structure. "But you can tell me now?"

Glume stepped closer, a look of concern in his eyes. "When it happened. To your brother. Were you sick, too? Did you have the same illness?"

Astonishment welled up within Kiffen. He had been sick but kept it a secret. He searched the man's face looking for something, although he didn't know what.

"I hid it. Serrin was so ill. No one realized I was, too. I stayed with him until the end, then went to bed for two days. People thought I was mourning and exhausted from sitting up with him. I got better. To this day, I've never told anyone I had the disease, too."

If he had, would Quilla have found some way to make him worse? He never forgot her refusal to summon the apothecary on Serrin's last day of life.

Glume offered a carrot to Bai'dish who ignored it, his brown eyes intent on Kiffen. When the keeper looked up, his eyes spoke of many memories, long gone. "He says you shouldn't worry about what has passed."

"How do you know what he said? All he sends me are images. I can't always interpret them."

A simple shrug accompanied Glume's answer. "I've been doing this for a long time."

"Something else that will take years to learn. If you haven't noticed, I don't have time."

Bai'dish shifted sideways in the stall, drawing closer to Kiffen.

Glume cleared his throat. "Do you remember the day Am'brosia was born? When I suggested your brother had found his giraffe?" He took a deep breath and let it out slowly between his sun-chapped lips. "While you were laughing at the idea, Bai'dish told me you were the chosen bond, not your brother."

Kiffen stumbled backward and fell over a stack of hay. He managed to right himself, but his insides still tumbled as though he were falling.

Glume looked at him, sadness in his eyes. "During your brother's First Degree bonding, you stayed with him. Do you recall?"

The memory made Kiffen smile. "Serrin was uncomfortable with the idea. Not that he'd admit it. He didn't want to spend a week outside alone with Bai'dish, so I stayed with him."

"And Bai'dish bonded with you instead."

Tears pricked in Kiffen's eyes, and he cleared his throat trying to choke them off. "Did you know then? Did you know Serrin would die?"

A look of compassion settled on the keeper's round face. "No," he whispered. "We did not know."

* * * * *

Chapter Thirty

Tears of rain streamed down the lead-paned windows of the chamber Adana used as her receiving room in Roshar. She stood at the window feeling the weather's commiseration with Kiffen's mood as it leaked along the bond. She felt his grief and sorrow, but Am'brosia only let her experience Kiffen's raw emotion. The giraffes didn't share any images or provide any clues to the source of his suffering. She reached out to him, wishing she could hold him, wishing he could hold her. At the moment, he didn't respond to her efforts, exhaustion washing through the connection. What had happened?

"Your Majesty?" Joannu stood at the door.

She turned from the window. "Yes?"

"Brother Honest and Lady Elayne ask to speak with you."

The announcement caught her by surprise. She had sent them on their assigned task just after the midday meal. "I didn't expect to hear from them until much later." She glanced back out the window before returning to her chair. "Send them in. Maybe they'll have some answers for us."

The pair entered the room, Brother Honest's mouth in a firm line, his eyes intent on her, while Elayne's gaze darted around the corners of the room, never meeting Adana's.

Adana glanced back and forth between them in confusion. "What's wrong?"

Brother Honest took Elayne's hand and whispered something to her. She sat down on a bench along the wall. Even though the woman was soaked to the skin from the rain, anyone could see she had been crying. Joannu hovered by the door, one foot turned toward the young woman on the bench, and the other planted in the proper position to guard the entrance to the room. Adana observed the internal struggle in her Watcher, aware the woman had developed a fondness for Elayne.

"Your Majesty, may we request a private audience?" Brother Honest said.

When Adana nodded to Joannu, the Watcher hesitated a moment before stepping out into the corridor. She would remain just outside the door, although Adana didn't feel the precaution necessary.

Curious about the teacher's information, she turned back toward her visitors.

Lady Elayne's face looked stricken, and when her gaze met Adana's, the lady shivered violently. Adana picked up a blanket from a chest near the window and handed it to Honest, noting with unease the gentle care he took in wrapping it around Elayne's shoulders.

"Has she been harmed?"

"No." Elayne managed a bare whisper and looked up at Adana.

"Well then, you must tell me what's wrong." Adana reached into her pocket and withdrew the handkerchief the woman had given her when she learned of her father's death. "I believe this is yours. You appear to need it."

Honest took the offering and gave it to Elayne who buried her face in it.

A frown creased Adana's brow. "Brother Honest? I hope your information explains this odd behavior."

Honest turned toward Elayne with an eyebrow raised in question. The woman trembled but tilted her head toward the door, listened for a moment, then nodded.

Adana felt her skin grow cold with dread at the obvious check on eavesdroppers. What could they have found out in such a short amount of time?

"What is it?"

"Your Majesty, we need to share some of Lady, er, the lady's background with you. It is important."

"Background?" Adana turned to stare at Elayne, suspicions resurfacing. She had finally decided to trust her, at least enough to employ her listening skills. Since the attack in the forest, she'd begun to like her. Without Leera, she'd missed having a friend. She allowed a sharp edge to come into her voice. "I'm listening."

Honest gestured back toward the chair. "Please sit."

She complied, but the look on Honest's face set her nerves on edge. Her shoulder ached, the pain driving down deep into the bone. She rubbed it, aware the pain wouldn't cease until she learned what Honest had to say.

His explanation was brief, but it turned Adana's blood to ice.

"This explains a few things." She turned a dubious glare on Shana who slipped from the bench to the floor with a cry, her face buried in her hands.

Adana rose and walked to the window, staring at people who trotted through the rain seeking shelter. Moniah rarely had rain this time of year. Laughter rang out below. The people saw it as a sign of good fortune for the upcoming battle against Maligon.

She turned and stared at her latest threat to that victory. "I must say, you fooled me." She shook her head. "Against my better judgment, I had come to trust you."

Shana did not meet her gaze.

"Your Majesty." Brother Honest stepped between them, shielding Shana from Adana's wrath. "You must know she wishes to serve you. Will you hold this against her? Something she had no control over?"

"No control?" The thought was alien to Adana. She was the one who had no control over what happened to her. No. Shana had lived with choices Adana could never support.

The ache in her shoulder spread like fire down her arm. She shook it, trying to break the pressure. When it wouldn't stop, she flung her hand toward Shana, her eyes on Honest. "She chose to leave her position to work for Sarx. A known traitor."

"No." Shana shook her head, her voice thick with tears.

Moments ago, the tears had caused Adana concern, but now, they disgusted her. Why had she failed to maintain her caution around this infiltrator? She returned to her chair, seeking its confirmation of her authority.

"No? Did you not leave The Sleeping Dog in Sarx's employ? Pretend to be someone you are not?"

Shana lifted tear-swollen eyes to Adana, her mouth working without sound.

"Adana, have you no compassion?" Brother Honest glared at her but rushed to Shana's side and took her in his arms.

Adana twitched at his familiar use of her name. "Has she bewitched you, too? Did your Creator not warn you of this?"

Shana's head jerked up. "Your Majesty, Brother Honest is an honorable man. Do not malign him for my sake."

"Malign? An educated word for your sort."

Brother Honest stood up, his arms stiff by his side, tension working in his jaw. "Do you realize what you are saying? This is not the behavior of the queen I've come to admire." He gestured toward Shana. "Would you rather she stayed in the tavern? Serving drinks? Submitting to—" His voice softened. "Submitting to men? Can you blame her for wanting something better?"

Adana leaned back in her chair and pondered the two of them. She had never entered an establishment such as The Sleeping Dog. She envisioned a room filled with energy and excitement, no protocols to follow, just drinking and amusement. Could she be mistaken?

"Why do you trust her?" she asked.

Honest hesitated.

"You do trust her, don't you?"

"Yes." Honest spoke with solid conviction.

"Then why?"

"My mother was a Watcher." He paused.

"I'm aware of that."

"My father was the son of a Watcher," the teacher added in a soft voice.

Adana sat forward. Her childhood stories told of children like him. Could he really claim an ability?

"A child of such a match can be gifted by the Creator," Honest said. "Does the queen remember the legend of the gifted ones?"

Curious, Adana nodded. "I do."

"At your indulgence, I'd like to retell the story."

"So you're a Memory Keeper, now?" Adana pondered his request. Would he claim to be a Seer? Should she believe him?

Others needed to hear this plea, to help her filter out the truth, if there was any. "I'll allow it, but only after you summon the First Vision and my honor guard to join us."

Shana gasped, her face turning a shade paler.

Brother Honest nodded, bent and laid a reassuring hand on the tavern maid's shoulder, then crossed to the door and asked Joannu to summon the others. Moments later Montee, Joannu, Sinti, and Veana joined them.

A wave of relief washed over Adana at the presence of her Watchers. They would know if Honest told the truth or not.

Montee glanced from Adana to Elayne and back again, a stoic look on her face.

Joannu cried out in dismay at the sight of Shana on the floor and moved to comfort her, but Montee stayed the Watcher with a quick motion of her hand. Joannu froze in her tracks, but her concerned gaze never left Shana's form on the floor.

"Brother Honest is going to explain why the legend of the gifted ones will support his claim that we can trust Shana." At the look of confusion on their faces, Adana added, "Oh, my manners have forsaken me. Please let me introduce the tavern wench, Shana."

Three sets of cool Watcher eyes, and Joannu's set of confused ones, turned toward the woman huddled on the floor. Brother Honest stepped between them, his arms folded across his chest.

"May I begin, Your Majesty?" His voice sounded formal and stiff.

"Proceed."

Brother Honest repeated the same story Adana had told Shana upon discovering her Listener talents.

During his retelling, Adana studied Shana, who blinked up at Honest, her face enthralled. When she noticed the queen's gaze on her, she blushed and looked down at the rug.

Brother Honest's stare bored into Adana as he told of the Empaths. "A third group received the gift of touch. Known as Empaths, they could sense the emotions of any living thing, human or animal. They also possessed the ability to imitate any action with perfection and to perform great feats of physical strength.

"And the fourth group, he called Seers." Honest paused and considered Adana for a moment. "He gave them the gift of intuition, able to recognize things not seen or heard, and to know if someone speaks the truth."

Adana expected him to stop there. The expression on his face indicated his point had been made, but Honest continued the story through the rise of The Gifted Ones and the fear and annihilation of these blessed people gifted by the Creator.

Annoyed by his delay tactics, Adana interrupted. "Until the Princess Moniah discovered a hidden matriarchal society of Watchers. Through them, she awakened her own natural gift of watching and learned the talents of the tallest beast in the animal world. Please Brother Honest, we know all of this."

Honest's brown eyes held Adana's attention. "Have you never considered the existence of other gifted ones?"

Adana sat back and tilted her head to the side. "Of course. But there has been no evidence of any for centuries. Until…" She glanced at Shana.

"Yes." Honest took a step closer, excitement radiating from him. "Many gifted ones exist without the knowledge of their special gifts." He gestured toward Shana. "Shana barely remembered the legend. She had no idea her abilities were unusual."

Adana tilted her head. "So, Honest, are you saying you are a Seer?"

He nodded. "And an Empath."

A chill ran over Adana's arms as she gripped the arms of her chair. To discover someone with another gift seemed impossible, but Honest's claim was beyond that. Could a lineage of Watchers produce someone with other gifts? Her shoulder tingled in response.

Montee stepped forward. "You have multiple gifts?"

The teacher met her gaze without flinching. "Yes."

Tearing her gaze from Honest, Adana studied Montee's reaction. "What do you make of this? Is it possible?" She held her breath, something a Watcher never did, but Montee's answer might change everything she knew of her world.

The First Vision approached the chair and whispered, "Adana, do you recall our discussion of the parchments?"

She flashed back to the night Montee had shared with her the secrets about the cave's location, Sir Jerold's identity, and the tunnels beneath the Border Keep. "Yes."

"One parchment contains information about small groups of gifted ones living throughout the kingdoms. They do exist."

"Do people with more than one gift live?"

"Yes. Often the traits skip a few generations, but there are known instances of this."

"And when were you going to share this with me?"

A well-known, grim smile preceded Montee's response. "As time has permitted, I've shared the essential information of the moment. There is still much we have not discussed."

"Much? How much?" She waved the question away as she spoke it. "Do you believe Brother Honest? Is he what he claims to be? Should we trust him and Elayne? Or Shana? Or whoever she is?"

"If we had access to the scroll that lists known gifted ones, we could see if he is listed. Of course, not all are recorded there." Montee glanced at Shana as she said the last part. "Without it...we must use other means of discovery."

"Do you know how?"

"A simple test of his truth-telling should be sufficient for his Seer abilities. I'm inclined to believe he's an Empath. They often gravitate toward the military or the Teachers of the Faith."

Adana rubbed her temples and stared at Honest. "We will have to test you." She glanced toward Shana, now dry-eyed, sitting on the floor. "If he is what he claims to be, you may be the luckiest woman alive."

* * * * *

Chapter Thirty-One

Queen Adana looked up as Honest entered her chambers the next morning. She stared at him for a moment, then returned to the message delivered by pigeon this morning. It came from Commander Linus at Adana's View. Maligon's army drew near.

She sighed and set it aside. "What does Pultarch want?"

Adana didn't expect Honest to know the answer, but she asked anyway. His Seer testing supported his claim. The man demonstrated an incredible ability to recognize when someone lied or told the truth. Six of her Watchers, ordered to tell the truth on some questions and alter the truth slightly on others, submitted to his evaluation. He never missed.

If his Empath abilities were as strong, he might be able to determine Pultarch's motives. She had sent him to Pultarch's chambers the night before with an order to discover what he could about their reluctant guest.

Brother Honest eyed her. "He wants to take you to Maligon."

"I know that. Why? How?"

Honest frowned. "He still hopes to marry you, as Maligon has led the people to believe, and place you on the Seat of Authority."

"Place me." Adana slammed her hand down on the table. "Does he believe I need him in order to accomplish this?"

"Yes. He does."

When would people accept her sovereignty? She forced her thoughts away from that frustration and concentrated on the matter at hand—what to do with Pultarch.

One didn't have to be an Empath or Seer to realize Honest had an idea. A Watcher could read the signs. "What do you propose we do with him?"

"I'm not sure you are ready to hear it," Honest said.

"Ready for what?" Montee stood by the door watching their interchange. She had been quiet all morning. Montee approached the teacher, her gaze studying him, interpreting his stance. "I think Honest does have a plan, but it's risky."

Adana tilted her head to the side, waiting for an answer. In the distance, she felt Am'brosia seeking their bond. She ignored it. Irritation felt good today. Her shoulder began to ache, and she rubbed at it.

Brother Honest said, "Montee has excellent Watcher insight. What I propose does carry some risk."

"Beware Honest," Adana said. "Tomorrow, we march to join King Kiffen's forces on the battleground. I don't have time for half-considered plans."

The man shrugged, his hair falling over his eyes. He pushed it to the side and said, "Let Pultarch escape with Shana."

"What? Why would he do that?"

"Do you believe me when I tell you she wants to aid you, not Maligon?"

Adana and Montee exchanged glances. They had discussed this well into the night. Reluctantly, Adana nodded. "Within limits, we feel we can trust her. This sounds riskier."

Brother Honest shook his head. "It's not. It's bold and perilous, but it could work." He sat forward. "From what Shana overheard yesterday, we know Pultarch has no credibility with these men. If he escapes and manages to capture Shana instead of you, he might claim she is you in order to save his pride. Maligon's men won't know the difference. Most Monians have not seen you for three years."

Adana recalled the first day she met Honest, how he had studied the two of them and used minor differences to determine which one was his queen. "But Shana is not a Watcher or a queen. Can she fool them?"

Montee nodded. "She managed to hide her identity from you for several weeks. She's spent time with us and knows more than most about Watchers. And I don't think Maligon cares if you are a Watcher or not. Many people expect your skills to be diminished since you've been in Elwar."

Adana grimaced at the last statement, but she knew it to be true.

"You support this idea?" She turned toward Montee.

Montee studied Brother Honest for several breaths. Adana counted each inhalation as she waited—one, two, three, four.

"I'm willing to hear him out," the First Vision said. "To see how he proposes we make this happen."

Adana sat back in her chair and stared at Montee. Could she really consider this an option? What was going on in her First Vision's mind? Thanks to their three-year separation, the woman remained a mystery in many ways.

Brother Honest continued. "Maligon is blind to his own desires; he'll see Shana as he wants her to be, not who she is."

"There will be people who know the difference," Adana said.

"True," Montee said, "but if she convinces them for a short while, it may be enough time to protect you from Maligon's men during the battle. If they think you are in their camp, they will not look for you on the battlefield. And if Maligon discovers he holds Shana, he might decide to claim she's you. Why else would Sarx choose a woman who looks like you to infiltrate your companions?"

"Are we sure she doesn't work for Sarx?" Adana voiced the fear that still plagued her. Now that they plotted to aim this imposter at the Seat of Authority, she wished for Kassa's wisdom and guidance about what to do.

The thought shocked Adana like a slap in the face. After complaining that no one trusted her with decisions or information, she wished for just the opposite. Her mother had told her she'd become a queen when she didn't desire the role.

Maybe she was a queen, now.

"She finds Sarx disgusting. She despises the man." Honest got up and poured wine into three cups. He gave one to Adana and another to Montee. "You can trust her to help you return to the Seat of Authority."

Adana set wine aside, distracted by his words. "Once again, we come to someone giving me my Seat. Why does it have to be given to me?"

Montee opened her mouth to answer, but Adana waved her off. "No. I understand. I'm just tired of hearing it. So, if I agree, how do you propose we actually carry out your plan? Is Shana agreeable?"

"I believe she will be. She wants to prove herself to you. She told me she'd never felt any value in her life before she came to you."

Could Sarx's questionable gift of a companion be the answer to her problems? A true gift? There were so many unknown variables.

Would Pultarch take the bait? Would Maligon accept Shana or discard her? Adana surprised herself with a twinge of concern over that thought. What would happen to Shana if they discovered her true identity?

"It's very dangerous for her."

Montee nodded. "Yes, but no more dangerous than going with us into battle."

* * * * *

Chapter Thirty-Two

Maligon's men followed Samantha as best as they could, but they slowed her down. Not only were they poor soldiers, they didn't have the training or stamina to run long distances without stopping. On horseback, they might keep up, but Maligon kept the horses for his calvary.

When Samantha spotted signs of a recent passage of soldiers, she thanked the Creator's providence. If the squad ahead of them planned to join Maligon, she could leave the dead weight of these men with them and go on ahead.

She needed to collect on the promises made by Kalara's father.

As a gentle rain began, they approached the perimeter of a camp. Three men stepped out of the trees and barred her path. They wore common clothes, but their armbands of red, green, and blue stripes indicated their allegiance to Maligon.

"Who's in charge here?" she asked as she approached the men.

At a nod from the one on the left, the middle soldier turned and trotted through the trees toward the camp. The man on the left studied her for a moment before he spoke. "What business does a Watcher have with a small band of families fleeing Maligon?"

"Families?" Samantha walked closer while the two men drew their swords. "You wear Maligon's colors. He's not in the habit of picking up stray families. Strays? Yes, if they serve his purpose, but not families. Too much of a strain on his reserves."

"State your name." The one on the left spoke again, his voice firm with command. The soldier on the right kept an eye on her companions, who stood behind her, quiet for once.

"Samantha."

The soldier sucked air between his crooked teeth. "King Micah is dead."

The phrase required the correct response from her, or she wouldn't gain entrance. "The usurper has fallen."

Both soldiers bowed in respect. "You are welcome here, Watcher Samantha. I hear our commander approaching."

As he spoke, a man in black breeches and a loose, tan shirt strode out of the trees. On his shoulder was a patch of purple glimmer cloth, representing his higher rank in Maligon's army. He stopped in front of her. "So, we meet, Watcher Samantha. I am pleased to find you well. The Lord will be thrilled at the news of your arrival." He glanced at the soldiers who trailed behind her. "Does your presence with this sniper crew indicate success in the giraffe attack?"

She frowned in displeasure as she glanced back at the men. "Unfortunately, no. These men failed in their mission."

Sharp, dark eyes looked past her, and a frown turned the commander's face to stone. "Failures? We will hear their report." He turned back to Samantha. "What service might I offer the new First Vision?"

Ecstasy ran down her spine at his words. True to his word, Maligon had already told his officers of her new rank. She stood tall and addressed the man as her inferior. "I require food and water. These men slow me down so I will leave them with you. I must reach the main force."

Within the hour, she had her supplies and left the camp and men behind. As she ran, her long legs responded to her need, and she covered ground quickly. Based on the commander's information, she would speak with Maligon before nightfall.

* * *

Samantha paused at the crest of a low-lying hill and gazed down onto the teeming mass of soldiers. The camp sprawled across the plains a short distance from Adana's View. Within a day, this force could be camped outside the gates. Her breathing quickened at the thought of striding into the fortress as First Vision, the highest-ranking person in Moniah besides the queen. Would Maligon allow her to lead the charge?

His guards had already spotted her and ran up the hill. She waited, eager to identify herself and receive the homage she deserved.

Moments later, the guards led her to the middle of the camp. She walked with her head held high, her steps strong and confident, enjoying the whispers of recognition as she strode past the men dedicated to aiding her in achieving her birthright. She would be First Vision. She would advise the queen in her rule. All Watchers would follow her lead. If they didn't, they would die. She would reign over all of them.

A wide expanse of ground separated Maligon's tent from those surrounding it. The flags of Moniah, Elwar, Belwyn, and Teletia flapped in the breeze. She had to smile at the display. Kalara had told her he was determined.

As she thought of Maligon's daughter, the tent flap was drawn back, and Kalara stood before her, a smile on her face. "Samantha, you've come. What a joy to see you." She placed her right fist over her left breast and bowed her head. "The Lord is anxious to hear of the death of the giraffe."

Samantha paused mid-stride, suddenly unsure of her reception. The giraffe lived. It wasn't her fault, but he lived.

* * *

Samantha jogged away from Maligon's camp, heading north. Her ears still burned after the violence of the Lord's response to her news. Kalara had remained by her side during the onslaught. When Samantha took a step to approach and strike him for his insolence, Kalara's hand stayed her. Eventually, his tirade shifted to the failures of the men he'd sent instead of her own actions.

Still, Maligon's order jolted her when it came—gain access to the fortress and aid the cause from inside the walls.

She must continue her masquerade as Adana's loyal Watcher. It grated on her nerves as she ran across the grounds of her birth.

The flat lands stretched before her, and she covered ground quickly. Soon, she would look upon Adana's View again. She couldn't enjoy the welcome sight with Maligon's anger fresh on her mind, though.

To avoid suspicion from inside the walls, she took a circuitous route to the fortress, heading out into the plains that stretched below the southern cliffs. If she approached from the southeast, Linus would never suspect her of tangling with Maligon. Anyone wanting to gain access to the sieged fortress would have to convince the First Soldiers to lift them on the rope and pulley system that scaled the cliffs behind the sprawling walls. She had no doubt the commander of the First Soldiers would approve her entrance.

She smiled at the prospect of standing in the Great Hall again, but this time as the First Vision. It was all she'd ever wanted, to hold the position that had been important enough to keep her mother at a distance from her. She became a high-ranked Watcher to seek out her mother's attention and achieved every promotion as soon as she could. Still, her efforts never prompted the acknowledgment she deserved. Soon, the old woman would have no choice. Bow before her daughter or die.

The sheer cliff wall protecting the southern side of the fortress loomed above Samantha as those thoughts assuaged her bruised ego. She waved a yellow strip of glimmer cloth signifying she had news to report. Once the soldiers recognized her, they shouted greetings and lowered the sling down the steep drop. Samantha climbed aboard and looped her foot into the rope as they pulled her up the high walls of stone. The plains spread out before her in a panoramic view. A herd of elephants wandered in the distance, and zebras gathered under some trees to the east.

She breathed in and gave a deep sigh of relief, enjoying the smell of heat, sand, and rock, mingled with the fragrance of flowers drifting on the breeze. Home.

A hearty voice greeted her as she dismounted. "I couldn't believe the reports, so I came to witness your arrival myself."

Linus, the commander of the First Soldiers, stood before her, a huge grin splitting the heavy beard on his face. His eyes sparkled with gladness as he grabbed her in a hug.

She stiffened at first, but relaxed under his embrace, aware this was an intimacy Montee relinquished when she usurped Samantha as First Vision. Foolish woman. She should have forfeited the title and chosen the man instead. When Samantha took charge, she would do away with the stupid rule preventing the First Vision from having a personal relationship with the commander of the First Soldiers. She would take the title and maybe even this man to spite Montee.

"How fares the queen?" Linus stepped back and looked into her face, worry darkening his brown eyes.

"I've been separated from her since the attacks in the forest. The tide of battle pushed me farther west, so I've been in the Border Keep."

Linus' frown deepened. "You didn't feel the need to find her? To go after her?"

"I joined King Kiffen in the keep and aided the queen by providing a Watcher presence for him."

"I don't understand." Linus glanced around at the curious soldiers surrounding them. He turned to walk toward the military wing away from prying ears.

Samantha followed him.

When Linus stopped, he turned to her, a frown creasing his forehead. "You are a member of the Honor Guard. The oaths require you to follow the queen no matter where she goes."

Frustration mounted in her chest. This man's opinion wouldn't count in a few short days. "Were you in the battle? Did you fight off the traitors from Elwar?" Samantha kept her voice low as she stepped closer to Linus. "It wasn't possible to remain with the queen. I did what I could."

Would he accept her explanation? She watched his gaze shift toward the walls as he battled with his expectations. Finally, his brow relaxed, and a shadow of his welcoming smile returned to his face. "Forgive me, Samantha. So much of our current situation defies explanation. I'm frustrated, stuck, waiting for the battle to come. And

Maligon sits less than a day beyond our gates. I am glad to have your help."

"I am glad to be here."

"But?" Linus paused, an apology crossing his face. "I must ask. If you were at the Border Keep, how did you get here? Has Kassa sent you? I haven't received a bird from the keep in days."

"Yes. She sent me when we discovered someone had released all the pigeons. None have returned, so she wanted me to come to you and share the little bit of news I have."

The tension in Linus' shoulders visibly relaxed. "Father Tonch will be pleased to see you. Ever since his arrival, he has worried over the lack of news from the keep."

Samantha paused for a moment, unsure how to respond to the Keeper of the Faith's presence. She took less than a breath before continuing her ruse. With her arm tucked in Linus', an action she and Montee hadn't taken since the three of them had been raised to their official statuses over ten years ago, she smiled up at him. "I am pleased to know he is here, but I would love to eat and bathe first, dear friend. Then we will discuss the coming battle and how we'll deal with the traitor."

She didn't bother to tell him who the traitor was, secure in his belief she meant Maligon.

* * * * *

Chapter Thirty-Three

Clothes lay flung across the bed, the floor—anywhere they landed—while Leera dug through her chests and wardrobe closet. What had happened to the ring? She had crawled around the floor, peering under the large pieces of furniture, but the ring and its box weren't there. She should have noticed where she threw it. Had Hanna found it on the floor and tucked it away in a drawer or chest. Or had the maid stolen it?

In the middle of the night, she'd decided to escape. She might not be granted access to the castle, but from her window, yesterday, she had noticed an increase in soldiers and nobles. Laughter and celebration rang in their voices. They moved with energized steps. Something had happened. Something bad for Kiffen. She needed to find a way out and get to Sariah. If she gave the Protector of the Faith the ring, she could take it to Kiffen.

In the midst of her digging, Leera discovered the green Watcher's uniform Adana had made for her was missing. She chewed her lip, trying to figure out where her mother might hide it. Her plan depended on the ring for Kiffen and the uniform to help her leave. Without the camouflage, her plan to escape out the window to the narrow ledge would never work. Not in a dress, anyway.

Leera sighed and gave up the search for a moment. She stood at the window, pushing damp curls away from her forehead. The plan had felt perfect in the long hours of the night, but in daylight, the distance from the ledge to the first secure footing was farther than she realized. Did she dare risk it? Without the leggings and tunic?

She dropped into a chair.

When Queen Quilla entered the chamber sometime later, Leera didn't care how her mother might interpret the disarray of clothing. She just lifted her gaze to her mother's frowning face and shrugged.

Queen Quilla surveyed the mess for some time, then her gaze settled back on Leera with exaggerated maternal concern. "Are you well, Leera? If I didn't know better, I'd say you'd been attacked."

"Just by these," Leera said, holding up her hands. No one had access to her room, so she saw no reason to deny its condition.

Queen Quilla clucked her tongue and turned back to the door where Hanna stood, her eyes round in amazement. "Well, come on. We have little time if she's going to attend the celebration."

"Yes, Your Majesty." The maid scurried over to a pile of clothes and began gathering them in a heap on the bed. Leera watched, her brain churning. A celebration? Was she allowed to leave her rooms? Maybe she could escape another way.

"We have cause to rejoice tonight," Queen Quilla said. "You will attend a formal dinner and wear a suitable gown. We don't have much time, but I found a dressmaker who is willing to make an outfit for you this afternoon. She will have to alter one of your existing dresses. We don't have time for anything else."

Leera fought the urge to flinch when her mother approached, zealous excitement on her face. Bejeweled fingers stroked a cool line across Leera's damp cheek. A thick rush of her perfume—gardenias—soiled the air.

"You should clean up. The dressmaker will be here soon. I'll send a page with her. If she needs supplies, he will retrieve them."

Leera nodded. A page named Catch had delivered the message from Gerguld a few days ago. The son of a minor noble, the boy had arrived in Elwar just a few days before Adana's birthday. Maybe she could convince him to help her.

Once her mother swished from the room, Leera turned on Hanna. "Where is it? Where is the ring?"

Hanna hesitated, the old look of fear crossing her face.

Leera fought the urge to shake the maid. She settled her face into a relaxed expression and dropped her hands by her side. "Hanna, the queen gave me a special ring the other day when Taren visited. It had a golden box. I—" She hesitated, ashamed to admit her childish behavior. "I threw it across the room."

The maid's face brightened with a smile. She nodded and scurried over to a chest. "I thought it looked important. I hid it in the little chamber in the lid of this chest."

Astounded, Leera watched Hanna slide open a tiny door inside the chest's lid. "How clever of you, Hanna. Do you know where my green Watcher's uniform is?"

The maid shook her head. "Sorry, Your Highness. I've never seen it."

"Never mind," Leera said while she slipped the ring on her finger. This time, she put it on the index finger. It still hung loosely, but she could hold it in place with her thumb.

Staring at the ring, she wondered how it might help her escape.

Leera jumped when Catch and the dressmaker bustled into the room. She blinked in surprise at the tall, stern figure of Helmyra. The dressmaker curtsied, then hurried forward, Catch at her heels.

"Your Highness, let's see how beautiful we can make you in one afternoon. You must be properly attired for this grand occasion."

The woman glanced at Hanna while her hands fluttered around the dress Leera wore, tucking and turning the material. "Could we have some tea? It's going to be an exhausting day."

The maid bobbed once in acknowledgement and headed for the door.

"Make sure it's piping hot," Helmyra called after her. "I can't tolerate cold tea. Brew a new pot. And bring some food too. Something freshly made and warm."

The door closed behind Hanna. Leera opened her mouth to speak, but Helmyra held up a warning finger. "Wait," she whispered.

The key in the lock clicked, then Catch put his ear to the door. After a moment, he straightened and grinned in excitement. "She's gone."

"Good." Helmyra placed her hands on her narrow hips and turned to Leera. "We've got a lot of work to do if we're going to get you out of here before your maid gets back."

Leera squealed, prompting another warning look from Helmyra.

In a loud voice, the woman said, "My apologies, Princess Leera. I didn't mean to tickle you."

At a lower volume, she said, "Although the maid has gone, there's a guard in the corridor. I doubt he'll eavesdrop, but we must be careful."

Leera's heart dropped at the news. "How will I escape if a guard waits to stop us?"

"With the excitement running through the castle today, it shouldn't be hard to create a diversion."

"You knew mother locked me in? How?" Leera said.

"Me." Catch scooted around the piles of clothing and executed a dignified bow.

Leera stared at the young page and the stern woman. In the past, she had given people in their positions no consideration; in fact, she'd cared not whether she offended them. If it wasn't for their loyalty to Kiffen, her selfish actions could have sealed her fate.

"Thank you," she said, feeling humbled by the sentiment. "Both of you."

Helmyra pulled scissors and thread out of her bag. "Which dress do you want to alter? We must appear to do as the queen bids."

The gowns spilled across the bed in glittering disarray. Leera fingered a few with longing, aware she would have to leave them behind. "What are we celebrating?"

Helmyra plucked a deep red one from the batch. "War."

"Maligon's?" Leera said while trying to stop the sudden tremble in her voice.

"Yes. That's what your mother celebrates." Helmyra held the dress up to Leera's body, her head tilted as she studied the cut.

"Where will you take me?" Leera said

Helmyra peered over the rim of her sewing glasses. "That depends on the outcome of the battle. We'll ensure your safety at least for the next few days."

Leera returned to the window, sadness in her heart. "Safe. Is there such a place?"

Helmyra stood and laid a hand on Leera's shoulder, causing her to flinch at the thought of another reading.

"You will be safe."

The woman sniffed and returned to the bed. "Here." She handed a dress to Leera and one to Catch. "Start ripping them into strips. We're going to make it look like the princess climbed out the window."

Catch grinned and tore the beautiful pink gown Leera had worn to Adana's birthday celebration. She watched the gorgeous finery shred under the boy's enthusiastic hands, closed her eyes at the sight, and took a deep breath. With one swift yank, she tore apart the bodice of a blue gown, her breathing ragged to match the uneven scraps.

In a short time, they had created a long rope of torn dresses.

"Now, you must slap me," Helmyra said to Leera.

"What?" The urge to do so surprised Leera, and she hesitated, unsure of the woman's command.

"Slap me as hard as you can. I want your handprint on my face when I tell them you've escaped. And kick Catch."

The page jumped back, his eyes widening.

When Leera still hesitated, Helmyra said, "You will do this. Then we will hide you under this heap of clothes and drop the rope out the window. Catch will run to the door to alert the guard of your escape. When he realizes his one and only charge has disappeared, he will sound an alarm. While they are pursuing you, we will slip you out under their noses."

Leera stared at the woman. Could it really work? Her mother's new guards weren't very intelligent, but they would recognize her.

"How will you keep them from seeing me?"

"We want them to see you, but they won't recognize you in this." Helmyra held up a maid's uniform—plain brown, coarse material with a white bonnet to hide beautiful golden curls.

Leera nodded and drove her foot into Catch's knee before he saw it coming. She spun toward Helmyra, twisted the ring to face outward, and slammed her fist into the woman's sallow cheek.

* * * * *

Chapter Thirty-Four

Mud sucked at the hooves of Shana's horse as she rode out at dawn with Queen Adana's troops assembled behind her. The cool air brushed the young woman's skin, and she scanned the crowds, uncomfortable with their scrutiny. A young child, a bright array of wildflowers clutched in her arms, stood at the forefront of the people lining the street. Shana halted her horse and smiled at the girl as Montee had directed her to do. She handed her reins to Joannu, who held the horse as Shana dismounted.

"For you, Your Majesty," the little girl piped up and dropped into an awkward curtsy.

Shana accepted the bouquet, her gaze never leaving the girl's face. "Thank you." She noted the child's shy glance toward the giraffes. "Do you like giraffes?"

The child nodded, her dark braids bouncing against her shoulders.

Shana turned to the child's mother. "Am'brosia accepts the child's touch, she's told me so. Is it acceptable to you?"

Startled by the direct address, the woman stumbled an awkward curtsy. "Your Majesty, we are most grateful if you will allow it. My daughter speaks of nothing else."

Shana gestured for the girl to approach Am'brosia, who stood among the queen's honor guard, Sinti's hand resting on her flank.

The child laid her small hand along the giraffe's leg and gazed upwards, giggling when Am'brosia dropped her long neck down to gaze at her.

"Are you planning to become a Watcher some day?" Shana asked the girl.

The dark-haired child turned questioning eyes to her mother who bustled over and lifted the girl in her arms. "We truly hope so, Your Majesty. She shows great promise, this one."

Shana arched an eyebrow at the young girl. "You must keep watch until we return."

The girl's green eyes grew wide. "Yes, ma'am."

Shana sniffed the flowers, enjoying their heady fragrance. She remounted her horse and kicked it forward. Sir Jerold and Montee urged their horses to flank her left and right, and the rest of the honor guard followed.

From her position, she heard Joannu's quiet affirmation spoken to Veana and Sinti. "She did well."

Shana glanced back and saw the other two nod in agreement, then all three returned to a vigilant watch over the crowd lining the street. Somewhere within the crowds were Pultarch's men.

Not far behind Shana rode Pultarch, bound and shackled on a horse. He was surrounded by several Watchers. Adana walked much farther back in the caravan with the rest of her Watchers.

Once out of the village, some of the prisoner's guard would drift away from their charge. With fewer to watch him, they hoped Pultarch's men would seize the opportunity to free the young noble.

The question was whether they would grab Shana, too. She licked her lips and smiled at the crowds while her insides shrank in fear. She did this for the queen, to prove her loyalty. Whatever it took.

* * *

The path from the Central Tower to the outer gates of the Border Keep swelled with humanity. Kiffen kept looking into the unfamiliar faces as he rode forth, a mix of Elwar's and Moniah's warriors following him. The people's cheers spoke of hope and confidence, awakening a strong urge within him to protect them at all costs.

On the heels of that awareness, Kiffen wished they could depart in stealth through the tunnels. He had argued the point with Simeon and Kassa a few days earlier. This gathered throng of refugees proved their point. The people needed to see them ride into battle. They needed a hope to cling to. The weight of their faith settled on his shoulders.

"Imagine them cheering your triumphant return," Simeon said as he trotted his horse up next to Kiffen's. "Don't try to carry their expectations with you. We have a long ride ahead of us."

Kiffen quirked his mouth into a wry smile. "How did you know what I was thinking?"

"You are your mother's son in many ways." Simeon looked overhead at the clear, blue sky and inhaled appreciatively. "The Creator has given you a fine day."

"He has." Kiffen nodded. "Adana has already departed."

"Good. We are on schedule. With Linus at the estate and our two armies approaching from opposite directions, we will crush Maligon."

"Do we have any further information on Maligon's location?"

"Since the report from last night?" Simeon shook his head. "It's too soon. I suspect he is still camped north of the estate. He's only been there for a few days. He will want to wait long enough to make things uncomfortable within the walls. We have time."

Kiffen looked back at Bai'dish who ambled behind the first lines of soldiers. An escort of Watchers surrounded the giraffe, but he noticed Glume rode closest, his hand reaching out occasionally to touch the animal's left flank. The caretaker had a faraway look in his eye. He must be communicating with Bai'dish. The thought reminded Kiffen of his most recent vision from Adana.

"Something disturbs me about Queen Adana."

"What?" Simeon shifted on his horse to face him.

"The view I get from Bai'dish. The person leading the troops doesn't look like Adana. I think it's Lady Elayne."

"Lady Elayne?" Simeon's face relaxed. "Maybe it's a precaution. She does resemble Adana. Has the queen communicated any changes to you?"

"No. That's what concerns me. I sensed a lot of concern and anger from her during the last two days, but I don't know what troubles her." Kiffen twisted in the saddle and looked at Bai'dish again. "Bai'dish is not sharing either. I think he's keeping information from me."

Simeon wrinkled his brow. "He knows?" Glancing over his shoulder at the animal, he said, "How can you tell?"

Kiffen shrugged. "It's hard to explain."

He closed his eyes and reached out to Bai'dish. Along the link came the vision of a clear sky and muddy fields, but when he tried to focus on Adana, the view shifted to the left or the right. "It's as if I'm looking through Am'brosia's eyes, but she refuses to look at Adana. If I try, she turns away."

"Turning her head?" Kassa's sharp voice interrupted the two men as she and Halar rode up to join them. "Did I hear you correctly? Am'brosia is turning her head away from Adana?"

"Yes."

Kassa pressed her lips together in a thin line, her wrinkles standing out in stark relief against her tanned skin. She shared a look with her husband.

"What does it mean?" Simeon asked.

"It means," Kassa spoke between clenched teeth, "that something has changed. Something they don't want you to know." She turned and waved forward one of the Watchers marching a few feet behind her. "Send Glume to me."

"What would she want to hide from me?" Kiffen asked, the pain of rejection aching in his heart.

"I intend to find out." The old woman stared down the line at Glume.

The man flinched as he looked up and met Kassa's hawk-like glare. The keeper laid a gentle hand on Bai'dish's flank, patted him once, then rode toward them. Kiffen continued to seek Bai'dish, reaching out to sense his mood. The animal responded with the sounds of a soothing melody and a babbling brook in the background. An image of Adana's favorite hideaway, the pond within the castle grounds, joined the sounds. *Why are you trying to soothe me?* The giraffe intensified the sounds and image.

"Kassa?" Kiffen said. "Why would Bai'dish push peace and quiet on me?"

Halar jerked his chin up and exchanged another look with his wife. He answered instead. "Kiffen, relax into the image. Bai'dish seeks to calm you in case you dislike Glume's message."

The suggestion scared Kiffen. Was something wrong? Had Adana been injured or kidnapped? Bai'dish's image of solace pushed into his thoughts, and one word floated through it: "No."

Kiffen blinked in surprise. "Do giraffes use words?"

"Words, Sire?" Glume rode up next to Halar, the farthest he could be from Kassa and still respond to her summons. "I've sensed simple words once or twice. What did he say?"

"No."

Glume nodded. "Yes, that's a word they all know." He smiled. "Just like children, they learn it early in life." He turned his attention toward Kassa. "You asked for me?"

"What is Queen Adana hiding from us?"

Glume looked from Kassa to Kiffen and back. "I knew this wouldn't work. I tried to tell them King Kiffen's skills were greater than they thought."

"You knew?" Kiffen frowned in dismay at the man's betrayal in keeping more secrets.

Glume dropped his gaze to the ground; his voice fell with it. "I did."

"Why didn't you tell me?"

He shrugged. "My queen commanded me."

At least Glume's loyalty to Adana was firm.

The keeper received a nod of approval from Kassa. "As it should be, but since we are aware of it, so you must tell us. The king will not be able to concentrate on his duties if he's worried about the queen."

Eyes still downcast, Glume said, "I know. Forgive me, m'lord. I meant you no disrespect."

Kiffen smiled at the serious man, surprised at how fond he had become of him in such a short time. Did their connection to the giraffes promote this feeling of companionship?

Glume's gaze locked onto his, and he gave a short nod and pleased smile. No words had passed between them, but Kiffen was sure Bai'dish had shared his thoughts with Glume.

The keeper took a deep breath, squinting at the crowds lining the road, then back toward Kiffen. "I believe this might be better said when we are out of the keep. There are too many people watching, and we don't want them to overhear or see your face while we discuss this."

The sounds of the cheering crowds flooded Kiffen's ears, and he gazed around at the excited men and women. He owed them a departure worthy of the heroics they expected from this combined army. "Glume, you speak sense. But I must insist you tell me if Adana is harmed or missing."

"Oh no, m'lord. She is fine and feeling quite safe and secure. This involves other people. I assure you she is safe."

The tension in Kiffen's shoulders slid away, and, aware of the watching crowds, he fought the urge to relax too much. "Good. I will wait until we pause at mid-morning."

"May I return to Bai'dish?"

"Of course," Kiffen said. As the man turned his horse around, Kiffen linked with Bai'dish and sent his thanks. A brief nod from Glume told him the man had received his message.

* * * * *

Chapter Thirty-Five

Maligon smoothed the edge of the map and brushed away a few specks of sand. He studied the drawn contours of the land surrounding Moniah's fortress. The stronghold stood on the largest precipice within the borders of the kingdom. From the northern approach, it was not high compared to the mountains in Elwar, but the steep incline gave a distinct advantage to those inside the walls. The southern and eastern sides rose above straight cliffs, impossible to scale without being picked off by Moniah's archers. The northern and western sides were protected by large sandstone walls with Watcher towers placed at even intervals.

"Why can't we locate the tributary?" Maligon spoke to himself, his voice a murmur. Below the fortress walls flowed an underground river providing water for the inhabitants. Maligon's spies had failed to find its access point.

Kalara sat beside him, but he knew she could not answer this question. Knowledge and access to that part of the estate were limited to a handful of people. Not even Samantha knew its location.

As if she'd read his mind, Kalara said, "Father, Samantha should be inside the walls by now. Your trap for Linus is set. Why do you wait on that weakling, Pultarch?"

"If he succeeds, we will hold the perfect key to the fortress gates."

"That's a doubtful "if," Father."

He glanced away from the map for a moment, and their gazes locked. "I plan to wait one more day."

"Is that wise? Samantha reported that Kiffen and Adana plan to attack us here."

Maligon barked a short laugh. "I am not concerned with the games played by mere children. We'll swat their armies away like flies. We have the numbers." He tapped at a point on the map. "We'll make our stand tomorrow, at dawn."

Maligon continued to smile as he studied his charts. He had donned his old uniform and felt invigorated by the worn feel of his fighting leathers against his skin. The simple clothes made him forget he was old and maimed. His good hand dropped down to stroke the hilt of his sword laid out on the table. It wasn't an elaborate sword. It had a leather-wrapped hilt, the colors faded from years of sweat from his grip. The smooth metal of the blade sent a chill of power through him. This sword, a gift delivered by his followers once he'd established his habitation in the desert, had remained sharp and lethal after all these years. He had spent hours polishing and sharpening it while in exile, aware someday he would wield it again.

"Lord?" A soldier stood within the tent's entryway. "A scout returns."

A rough-looking soldier entered and bowed from the waist. "My Lord, an army approaches from the east. It must be Adana."

"How far and how many?"

"They'll be here by midday. A mix of Watchers, Elwarian military, and First Soldiers. But mostly, a lot of farmers. Maybe five hundred soldiers and Watchers, but close to six thousand in troops. "

Maligon moved a pin on the map. "See, Kalara? She brings five hundred to fight my twenty thousand." He turned toward the scout.

"Send the east flank to deal with them. Make sure they bring me Adana and that giraffe alive."

The man nodded and backed out of the tent.

"Father, do you think that's wise? Sending troops away from here?" Kalara's voice betrayed her surprise.

"Kalara. They are not a threat. We have the upper hand." He sat down and poured himself some wine.

"What about them?" She nodded toward the four bodyguards who stood awaiting his command. "Why not send them?"

"I have other plans for them." Maligon stared into his goblet, a smile of triumph on his mouth. "Relax, my child, and see how this is done."

Within a short time, they could hear horses galloping away to the east. Chatter among the men in the camp stopped as the troops departed, but it rose to an excited level once the sounds faded away.

Maligon and Kalara opened the flap of the tent and watched the men mill about, a renewed energy in their actions. "Ah, this is what we needed." Maligon smiled. "The promise of battle always invigorates an army."

He frowned as another scout approached and bowed before him. "My Lord, troops approach from the west."

"Numbers?"

"Close to seven thousand. Half a day's journey."

"What sort of soldiers?"

The scout squinted in the sun. "As best as we can tell, they are mainly Watchers and First Soldiers with a few Elwarian soldiers."

Maligon clapped his hands together and smiled. "A perfect recipe for a feast. Send my west flank to stop them."

"Father." Kalara's outburst caused the scout and every soldier in the vicinity to freeze.

Maligon turned a cold stare on his daughter and jerked his head toward the tent. He followed her into the dark interior, slapping the flap closed behind him. "Never question me in front of my men."

Kalara stood her ground. "Father, you would not appreciate my skills if I did not share my opinions and thoughts with you."

Maligon caressed her cheek, ending the stroke with a firm grip on her jaw. "Not in front of my men. Never in front of my men."

Kalara nodded, and he released her, noting with satisfaction that she rubbed her chin where the red mark of his thumbprint remained. His strength had never forsaken him, even though Micah had stolen his body's ability to engage in close battle.

"Now that we are in agreement, call my commanders. We must prepare for battle."

* * *

Linus ran up the steps to the main gate tower. Samantha followed close on his heels. Messenger birds carried little information regarding Queen Adana's and Kiffen's plans. Then, the information had stopped, and no more birds arrived over the last few days. Her arrival two days ago had given him hope.

From the top of the tower, he looked over the flat plains that stretched to the horizon. For three days, Maligon's troops had covered the valley below. Now, he could see gaps near the back of the encampment. Nearly half of the rear troops were gone. Dust to the west and east indicated they had been deployed in both directions.

Linus stroked his beard and turned a ferocious smile on Samantha. "Send the First Soldiers out." He turned back to the landscape and rested his arms on the wall. "Let's see if we can draw Maligon's men into bow range."

* * *

"Lord, First Soldiers. The fortress attacks." The messenger rushed into Maligon's tent without announcement.

Maligon jumped up from his seat. "Excellent. Gather the foot soldiers." Struggling to strap on his sword, he smiled down on Kalara when she pushed his hands away and did it for him.

"It begins." He rushed out of the tent, calling for his horse.

The camp bustled with excitement as men grabbed their swords and saddled horses. Maligon leapt onto his horse and rode through the melee, shouting encouragement to the men. Kalara rode close behind him.

Near the front of the lines, Maligon cantered his horse back and forth. "Today is the day our victory begins."

His men cheered.

"Before the sun sets, we will invade these walls and reclaim the kingdom Micah stole from us over twenty years ago. Our triumph awaits. We have the numbers. We have right on our side. Queen Chiora will look down from heaven, and she and the Creator will grant us this victory!"

The men roared in approval. Kalara and the Watchers inside the camp sang an ululating battle cry.

Maligon raised his hand in the air and dropped it. "Advance."

Swords ready, the men ran toward the line of First Soldiers who marched through Moniah's gates.

The First Soldiers stopped and formed a solid line. Maligon's men, overrun with pent-up anticipation, charged the slope.

Kalara frowned. "They are drawing into range. Pull them back."

Maligon shook his head. "We have to sacrifice some men to draw Linus into battle."

A volley of arrows flew from the walls of the estate, downing Maligon's foot soldiers. The Monian soldiers stood their ranks while the second line of Maligon's men surged forward under a wall of shields.

From the fortress walls, Watchers found the gaps in the shields. Hundreds of arrows soared through the sky, seeking their marks. Men plowed forward, tripping uphill as they tried to avoid fallen comrades. Many fell without the aid of arrows, stumbling over those who fell before them.

The front line of Moniah's soldiers knelt and Watchers, armed with bows, rose behind them, firing into the advancing men.

Maligon laughed in amusement at the chaos they created on the hill, his own men falling over each other. He glanced at Kalara's stricken face and shouted to her, "Never mind them, my child. They are performing their duty. See, they are pulling back. The ones who survive are the true soldiers."

With over half of the first line injured or dead, the Lord's soldiers retreated.

"Watch. We loaded the trap." Maligon nodded toward Kalara, his eyes on the walls. "Let's see if Linus will spring it."

* * * * *

Chapter Thirty-Six

Bai'dish sent the image of dust rising to the southwest, soldiers marching quickstep toward them.

"Halt!" Kiffen raised his hand at the same moment Kassa galloped her horse up to him.

The woman pointed toward a faint discoloration in the distant sky. "The horizon."

Kiffen glanced back at Bai'dish. "The two of you have keen eyes."

The ground they stood on was flat. There were few trees, none of them large. The barren landscape provided no help, but the advance of Maligon's men left him little choice but to fight where they stood. "We muster here until they draw closer. Kassa, gather your archers in the center. Halar, take the left flank. Simeon, take the right."

As the soldiers and Watchers rushed to their positions, Kiffen rode his horse back toward Glume and Bai'dish. He sought sight from Bai'dish's eyes, a much clearer view than his own. Maligon had sent only a few thousand men. Hope surged in his chest. Maybe they could claim victory over the small force.

Assured by the numbers, he followed the link to Adana. She now rode at the front of her army with Elayne and her honor guard flanking her. Pultarch had escaped as planned, but without his intended prisoner. The bond resonated with disappointment. He paused a moment and tried to ease her worry. From memory, he dredged up the image of the Seat of Authority and envisioned her there in royal glory. A lightness came back to him through the bond as if she smiled.

The connection between them grew stronger and vibrated with energy. Kiffen fought the urge to race across the landscape to join her. Glume told him this would happen when they closed the distance between them. Instead, he thought of victory and gave her the vision of Maligon's approaching troops.

Adana's response was quick. The horizon remained clear for her.

Smiling at that news, he turned to Glume. "I need you to monitor both Am'brosia and Bai'dish. I'm still unable to maintain my connection and stand alert in battle. Send a Watcher to me immediately if Bai'dish senses anything I need to know."

He turned his horse away but looked back over his shoulder. "Stay well behind the lines of fighting. I'll send Watchers back to guard you once their bows are no longer of use."

Kiffen galloped to the front of his troops. The advancing army lined the horizon. His heart pounded with excitement. After weeks of waiting, the time to act was upon him. He turned and looked at the array of Watchers, First Soldiers, and Elwarian military. They stood alert, awaiting his command. He felt a surge of indebtedness to their allegiance.

"Fellow soldiers, we stand united today against evil. The approaching army believes they will vanquish us. In his arrogance, Maligon has sent a small force. We will conquer them and join forces with Queen Adana to regain her lands. Together, we will show our kingdoms a united Moniah and Elwar, not only through marriage, but through our belief in a safe and secure land!"

The troops' roar of approval rolled over Kiffen, and the adrenaline of their combined strength flowed into him. He raised a hand in the air and drove it forward. "Advance."

* * *

Adana drew her horse to a stop and stared into the distance, watching through Am'brosia. as Kiffen rode his horse back and forth before his soldiers. She could tell he was shouting encouragement and wished she could hear him. Excitement shot through the link, so she knew his words were powerful.

Turning her attention away from Kiffen, she searched the surroundings. The last small rise blocking the view to her fortress was not far away. She had planned to observe the battle from that vantage point.

She summoned Veana. "Take five Watchers to the rise. Watch for Maligon's men. Even now, they engage King Kiffen's forces."

As she said it, she felt the surge of the distant battle. She could see her Watchers loosing a volley of arrows toward the opposing force. Their aim was true, and many of Maligon's men fell.

"Your Majesty?" Shana guided her horse closer to Adana's and Montee's.

Adana turned to look at the woman, unsure how she felt about Shana's continued presence. Brother Honest swore she would serve her until death, if necessary, but Adana felt betrayed by the woman's failure to be taken. "Yes, *Shana?*"

The woman flinched. Adana made a point of stressing her true name every time she addressed Shana to remind the woman of her precarious position.

"I hear the rumble of approaching men." She pointed toward the southeast. "From there. I don't believe they are far from us."

Adana twisted to look in the direction the woman indicated. She squinted into the sun, trying to see rising dust on the air or any other clues of the army's approach. "Do you see anything, Montee?"

Montee studied the horizon. "Not yet. If King Kiffen is under attack, we must assume we will be soon."

"Agreed," Adana said. "Shana, how much time do you think we have?"

The woman shook her head. "I do not know."

Adana fought the urge to lash out at Shana for not knowing the limits of her skills. Her troops were close to the rise, a position she needed to gain before the attack. "Montee, we must make the hill."

As the First Vision gave the command, Adana sent an image to Kiffen of their position. She signaled for her Watchers to follow. Spurring her horse forward, she kept a close watch on the five Watchers she had sent ahead with Veana. Am'brosia's keen vision gave her a more distinct view, revealing the five Watchers reaching the rise and beginning to fire arrows down the hill.

"We're under attack," Adana shouted to Montee and kicked her horse into a gallop.

Watchers streamed up the rise around her, readying their bows. Veana stood at the summit, arm raised. She dropped it in command to loose the arrows. Battle cries roared from the other side of the hill.

Adana gasped at the sight as she crested the top and reined in. Maligon's men rushed toward them with determined purpose.

She drew her bow and fired into the soldiers with no hesitation between shots.

Her troops, many of them farmers equipped with the tools of war, streamed past her and down the slope toward Maligon's men. Adana stayed her bow as they ran into her shot range. Frustration roared in her head. Unskilled, the troops should have waited for the command to attack. She'd hoped the training her soldiers had given them was enough. She signaled to Montee and kicked her horse forward.

"Yahhhh," she shouted as her horse thundered toward the mass of fighting men.

As if it possessed its own will, Adana's sword arm slashed at her attackers. Muddy ground churned under her horse's hooves. The animal lost traction. She yanked on the reins, trying to pull back. The horse lost its battle with the mud and slid down the hill, taking Adana with him. Men shouted in alarm as her bulky mount plowed them down. Mud and blood splattered over her as the horse dug in to stop the slide. Adana clung to the reins, horrified as her own men fell under her wild advance.

The horse gained footing deep within Maligon's men. They surged around her.

Adana swung at the soldiers. Her arm reverberated from the solid contact of sword with shield and sword. Hands grasped for her. She kicked and shoved. Determined, she rode sideways up the slope, one agonizing step at a time. She swung her sword left and right. It sliced into men and glanced off blades.

An ululating war cry rang in her ears. Montee, Joannu, and Veana converged on her position. Fire raged in Montee's eyes. Her sword knocked down any man who blocked their path.

They formed a tight circle around Adana and fought the grasping foot soldiers. Moniah's army swarmed around them, joining the fray.

Adana's sword drove into a man's shoulder, and his eyes registered shocked pain. She stared into his face, her sword embedded in his armor. His gaze focused on her sword. He grimaced and grabbed it with his other hand. Their eyes met, again. He yanked her from the horse.

Veana flung herself at the man and grappled him to the ground, pushing Adana from his grasp. Montee grabbed the reins of Adana's horse. Adana scrambled back into the saddle.

"To the hill. You must. As planned." Montee dragged Adana's horse up the hill, her soldiers parting around them and swarming into the battle below.

Once they gained the top, Adana turned and stared over the battlefield. Shock numbed her heart. Maligon's warriors swarmed over several small pockets of her soldiers. There were too many. She shivered as farmers fell before the onslaught. Bile rose in her throat. She fought it down.

Helpless, she sent the view to Bai'dish.

* * *

"They've fallen back!" Linus shouted from the walls of Moniah's estate. "Attack!" He turned toward Samantha, a smile on his face. "We've got them n—"

Samantha drove her sword into his belly, taking him from Montee, forever.

Blood spilling from his mouth, Linus stared at her in astonishment. "Why?" His voice gurgled, and he slumped over the sword, grasping at her arm.

"You serve the wrong army." She clenched her teeth and twisted the blade. He fell to his knees before her. She set her foot against his chest and shoved him backward. Her weapon swung wide as it broke free from his body.

"It's the Creator's will," she said. She stared into Linus' eyes as they glazed over.

Samantha wiped her blade on his tunic, feeling the thrill from the act of killing. All her Watchers, the ones loyal to Maligon, stood along the parapet, disloyal Watchers dead at their feet. Samantha studied each woman, gauging the level of shock in the eyes of the younger ones and the excitement in the ones accustomed to the sweat and blood reek of battle. "Open the gates!"

The gates swung inward, and Maligon's men surged toward the fortress.

* * *

The Watcher, Nuala, stared in shock at the walls above Moniah's main gate. Commander Linus stumbled as Samantha's sword thrust into his belly. A cold chill ran down her back in spite of the unrelenting heat of the day. She studied the ramparts. Many of her sister Watchers lay dead at the feet of other Watchers. Traitors within the Watchers? Inside the walls of Adana's View?

From her vantage point in the southern tower, she crouched low, gesturing for the Watchers assigned to help her protect Father Tonch to back down the stairs in stealth. A loud roar echoed through the fortress as the gates opened, and Maligon's army poured into the courtyard like beetles overrunning a dung heap.

"To the aqueducts," Nuala instructed one of the Watchers below her.

The woman narrowed her eyes at Nuala. "It's forbidden." She glanced around at the other Watchers in their squad. "I'm sworn to never reveal the secret entry."

Nuala pushed through the women, her leather tunic swishing in the silence of the stairwell. "It's either that or surrender to Maligon. Which do you choose?"

The alarm on the Watcher's face, followed by her quick movements toward the base of the southern tower, told Nuala what she needed to know. She would lead them to the aqueducts.

* * *

Maligon laughed and surveyed the field of battle. Adana's View welcomed his men as they rushed up the slope. To the east, Adana's troops floundered under his attack. To the west, Kiffen's troops pushed forward, giving the only pressure to his men.

"At least the young brat has some fight in him." He smiled at Kalara. "Pull the west flank back. Send them to rout out the stragglers of Adana's army. The rest, follow me."

He kicked his horse into a gallop, his voice raised in a savage cry as he rode into his new home.

* * *

Adana stared in horror as Maligon's men overtook the First Soldiers and surged through the gates of Adana's View.

Montee galloped up to her. "Adana, we must retreat."

"No." Adana shook her head and stared at the tumult below. "No."

Montee grabbed the bridle of Adana's horse and pulled her away from the battle. "Send the image to Bai'dish. We must retreat toward Kiffen's forces."

Numb with shock, Adana nodded. She sent the image of the catastrophe below while Montee pushed her west toward Kiffen and the Border Keep. Jerold, Joannu, Shana, and Sinti followed close on her heels. Once they cleared the sight of combat, Montee wheeled her horse around and gave a great cry, riding back into battle.

Cold gripped Adana as she replayed the scene of Maligon's men flowing through her gates. The vision of her dying soldiers echoed in her mind. For the first time, she regretted the strength of her Watcher gifts, the ability to recall everything in extreme detail. She wanted to forget all she had seen. She needed to change it. She eased back on her horse's reins. She couldn't flee while they still fought. Wheeling her horse around, she turned back toward the battle.

"Queen Adana, don't!" Joannu charged her horse in front of her. "You can't do anything more. Focus on Am'brosia's link."

Adana shook her head but turned in retreat. She glanced at Shana to her right, noting a greenish tinge to the woman's skin and the horror in her eyes. Shame for her treatment of the woman flooded over her. "Shana, forgive me."

Shana glanced her way with a wild look of fear.

"She's too shocked to understand," Jerold shouted as he rode beside them. "Focus on reaching Kiffen's position."

"He's right," Sinti called over her shoulder. "You said Kiffen's forces are holding."

Adana nodded, too tired to speak. The sounds of battle faded behind them, but she saw Shana's head jerk up in awareness. Am'brosia twisted her neck sideways, her head stretching up to the sky.

"What is it?" Adana searched behind them. Pultarch and three of his men bore down on her small band. She braced for impact, aware her horse couldn't avoid collision with the lead rider.

"Ballene's fire." Shana kicked her horse between Adana and the soldier known as Horace. "Go," she shouted over her shoulder.

Joannu and Jerold wheeled their horses around to join Shana, forming a solid block between the men and Adana. One of the men moved faster than they and leaned in. His sword sliced the rear leg tendons of Adana's horse as Jerold raised his sword to strike the man.

Adana, without thinking, jumped toward Am'brosia's back as her horse screamed and fell beneath her. She grappled for a firm hold, dangling from Am'brosia's side. The giraffe faltered a moment before loping on with Adana clinging to her with all her strength.

* * *

Sword slammed into sword as Kiffen pushed his horse through Maligon's troops. He raised his shield at a blur riding toward him, and blindly thrust his sword up, feeling the impact as the horses collided and his sword sliced into a body. He yanked the sword free. The soldier wore a Watcher's uniform. She tumbled to the ground. Kiffen froze, noticing the purple patch sewn to her shoulder—Maligon's mark of ownership. As Kiffen stared, a man slammed into his horse from the other side, unseating him.

Kiffen threw his arms out to brace his fall. He rolled and missed the downward stroke of an ax. Kiffen grabbed for his sword, struggling to pull it out from under the weight of his body. The man raised his arm to plunge the ax into Kiffen's skull but fell backward, toppled by the weight of his own weapon. An arrow protruded from his chest.

Kiffen scrambled to his feet and turned to meet the eyes of a Watcher. One of the original squad entrusted to guard Bai'dish.

"Adana?" He gasped the name, suddenly aware of sweat streaming down his face and the iron taste of blood in the air.

"She retreats. Am'brosia sends for help."

Kiffen stumbled on unsteady feet, searching for Simeon. He spotted Kassa with Halar rushing toward him. "Quick," he called to them. "Adana retreats. Find her. Bring her to Glume."

* * *

Adana's fingers slid along the armor covering the sloping back of the fleeing giraffe. She tried to grab onto something. Her sweaty hands could not grasp any part of the smooth leather. The giraffe's bristly mane gave her the only handhold. She pulled and twisted the strands, seeking more to grasp. Frustration boiled over her. The giraffe's sloping back stood so much taller than a horse's. Sheer luck had given her the grip to begin with, but it wasn't enough.

"Hold on!" Sinti rode up behind her.

Adana twisted to look down at the Watcher, ready to drop onto the other horse.

Kassa and Halar galloped toward her.

"How?" She panted, registering shock at their presence.

"Hold on." Kassa rode closer. "We'll push you up."

A flash of her riding on Am'brosia's back seeped through the connection, and the next thing Adana knew, hands shoved her body upward. She flung her arms around the stalwart neck and hung on.

Another flash came to her as a warning—a giraffe outrunning horses, leaving them far behind. Adana gasped, and buried her face in Am'brosia's shoulder as the animal surged forward.

One horse sought to catch them.

Am'brosia kicked her hind leg, the contact with their pursuer jolting Adana's whole body. The rider and horse screamed. Adana peeked behind her, aghast at the gore left by Am'brosia's blow.

Keeping a precarious hold on the steep slope of the beast's back, Adana's body rattled with each jarring contact with the ground. Every time she thought she had a solid hold, her body slipped. She struggled to regain her grip, gasping for air. For a brief moment she sensed her dream and recognized the motion of bobbing in the river rapids.

When they reached Glume and Bai'dish, Adana tumbled from Am'brosia's back, grateful for Glume's strong hands as he caught her. She relished the stillness for several breaths, then raised her head, surprised to see only Sinti, Halar, and Kassa behind her. Adana struggled to stand, her hand leaning heavily on the thick hindquarters of her recent mount.

"Where are the others?"

Sinti jumped to the ground and rushed over to Glume and Adana. "Are you hurt, my lady?" She patted the queen's arms and back, checking for injuries.

Adana pushed her away. "I'm fine."

"I've never seen someone ride a giraffe before." Sinti stroked Am'brosia's flank. "I'm thankful it worked."

"The others? Where are they?" Adana repeated her question.

"One of Pultarch's men grabbed Shana. Jerold and Joannu gave chase."

Adana stared at them, surprised at the fear she felt for Shana now that their plan had fallen into place.

* * * * *

Chapter Thirty-Seven

The soldier grabbed Shana. She twisted in shock and confusion. Moments after protecting the queen from attack, the former tavern maid found herself in the tight grip of one of Pultarch's men. They wheeled their horses in the opposite direction as the queen.

Horses' hooves pounded behind her. She heard the cries of Joannu and Jerold, the clang of swords and grunts of impact. They thought to save her. Had they forgotten the plan? Her heart pounded with fear for their safety. Joannu remained true to her. Even after Brother Honest revealed her real identity. Gratitude mixed with fear for the Watcher.

Her captors' horses galloped along the edge of the battle. Before her, the precipice housing Adana's View loomed into sight, and before she knew it, the soldiers pounded up the steep slope and through the gates. Her captor slowed his horse to a canter and rode up to an older man.

The man's arm hung by his side, useless. When he spotted her, the gleam in his eyes crawled over her skin. Was this Maligon? Lord Sarx was evil, but this man resonated with such malevolence, she wished for Sarx's presence, instead.

The soldier reined his horse to a halt before the man and shoved her from the saddle. She tumbled off the horse but maintained her footing, chin held high.

"My Lord, this chit is the royal highness, Adana." The soldier shoved his foot into her back, and she stumbled to the ground. "Bow before the Lord, m'lady."

Shana studied the sandy dirt inches from her nose, worry crowding her mind. This was not the plan. Pultarch knew who she was, but he had yet to see her. How long would this Lord let her live if he thought she was Adana? She listened, holding her breath. The sounds of recovery after the battle came to her. The wounded moaned. The victors shouted of grandeur and slapped each other's backs. Horses stomped their hooves.

Steeling herself to look up, she took a deep breath and gagged on the reek of sweat, blood, and offal. The stench took her back to The Sleeping Dog. She closed her eyes and prayed for a miracle from the Creator.

"Tch, tch," Maligon said. "That's no way to treat a queen, Horace." He reached down to Shana. "Please, Your Majesty, let me assist you."

Shana breathed in through her mouth and allowed the man to help her stand. Surprise filled her as she realized he stood just a little taller than she. But when he smiled at her, she shivered.

"Adana, Adana, are you not happy to return to your home?" He spread his arms wide and gestured around him. "Moniah awaits your coronation, my lady."

Shana surveyed her surroundings. Fallen soldiers and Watchers littered the ground, their eyes staring into nothing. How many had Maligon killed to take the fortress? Her heart dropped at the thought. Would any Watchers or First Soldiers remain who supported Adana? She needed their presence for survival.

She wished she knew more about the layout of the fortress, but there had been little time for Adana or the Watchers to educate her. How long did she have until Maligon learned he did not have the Monian Queen? Exhaustion and fear overcame her. She decided her best option might be to fake a swoon. So she did.

"Horace!"

She heard Maligon yell, and the sound of someone being slapped.

"I told you not to harm her."

"Lord, she suffers from battle fatigue, I'm sure."

"She's not Adana!" Pultarch's voice shouted across the courtyard, and she heard him stumble forward. She felt his warm breath as he bent over to look at her prostrate body.

His leathers creaked as he stood. Another loud slap resounded to her right. A man groaned.

"This fool grabbed the wrong one."

"Pultarch, so glad you decided to return." The Lord's voice drifted away as if he'd left her side. He snapped his fingers. "Bring her. Pultarch, follow me."

Shana let her body go limp as the soldier hefted her over his shoulder. She strained to listen to Maligon and Pultarch as her head flopped against the man's back.

"Where is Am'brosia?" The man they called Lord spoke to Pultarch as if they were relaxing over a glass of wine. So calm, so reserved, as if they sat in a garden, not a courtyard littered with the bodies of loyal Monians.

"We don't have the giraffe, Lord, nor Adana. That is not her."

The conviction and anger in Pultarch's voice alarmed Shana.

332 | BARBARA V. EVERS

They had counted on him accepting her as Adana to save embarrassment. It appeared his loyalty to this Lord ran deeper than anticipated.

"Then who is this?" Shana felt someone grip her braid and haul her face upward.

"Lord Sarx's spy, the Lady Elayne of Glenhaven," Pultarch said.

The soldier dropped her to the ground. She fought the urge to cry out in pain and focused on the knowledge that Pultarch did not recognize her as the woman from the tavern. He did not know.

Her heart gave a small leap of hope.

Could she return to the pretense of Elayne?

"Really?" Maligon's voice held amusement. "This is the tavern maid Sarx found? The one who looks like Adana?"

"Tavern maid?" Pultarch sounded confused. "No, Lord, this is the Lady Elayne, one of Lord Sarx's nieces."

Laughter rumbled from the depths of Maligon's chest. "She fooled even you! No Pultarch. Look closely. I understand you helped Sarx find her at The Sleeping Dog."

All grew quiet.

Shana forced her body to remain limp. How long would they let her live? A finger trailed along her chin and up to her hair. Hot breath washed over her face.

"Blazes! It is the wench. I led him to her?" There was no escaping the pride that rang in Pultarch's voice.

"You found her." A woman's surprised voice echoed across the courtyard. Shana fought the urge to turn her head in the woman's direction. She didn't know this voice.

"Kalara, look what these animals brought us. An imposter for the Seat."

Someone ran across the flagstones toward them. When the woman spoke again, her voice was close, as if she peered into Shana's face. "What's wrong with her?"

"She fainted, my daughter. Do you have any smelling salts?"

Laughter rumbled around her, but Shana focused on the sounds of the woman.

Footsteps retreated, there was a sound of water sloshing, the footsteps returned, and then...

Shana shrieked at the cold splash of water. She sat up, blinking the water out of her eyes.

A woman dressed in Watcher leathers stood close by, her hand on her knife. She took a step toward Shana and leaned in close, her mouth a thin line. "Where is Adana?"

Shana looked from the woman they called Kalara to Pultarch to the Lord. She shook her head.

Silence, louder than the noise of battle, roared in Shana's ears as she waited for the killing stroke. She sensed Maligon's laughter before it rippled forth.

"This is perfect. We'll put her on the throne and marry her to Pultarch. No one has seen Adana for three years. No one will know the difference."

This time Shana did not fake fainting.

* * * * *

Chapter Thirty-Eight

Adana looked up, searching the extensive tunnel. Torches burned in wall sconces along the length of the corridors that led back to the battlefields. Along the walls of the enlarged room, at a crossroad within the tunnels, the battle-weary and wounded waited for help or water or the energy to rise and tend to their fellow soldiers and Watchers. Moans underscored the quiet murmuring of the Border Keep's staff as they tended to the wounded. Adana searched the distance and strained to hear if any new troops arrived. How much longer would Kiffen remain on the battlefield? Reports said he was uninjured, but still he hadn't returned. She couldn't understand why. The secret entrance to the tunnels opened up on a slope near the expanse of ground where Kiffen's forces stood against Maligon's. The distance was short. No need for his delay.

Adana fought frustration. Would he come to her? Stand beside her and cope with the shock of their failure? Or did he lie dead or injured on the battlefield?

Her gaze traveled along the pallets of injured in the larger sections of the tunnel, lingering on the faces grimacing in pain. Some lay still. Too still. She approached one such Watcher, her arm wrapped in whatever cloth had been available to those who carried her into the tunnels. Blood stained through the many layers. Adana knelt beside the prone body. The young woman's eyes fluttered open, and she turned to face Adana. The stamping feet of returning soldiers resounded in the corridor, but Adana didn't turn away from the Watcher. "I'm going to unwrap this cloth and check your wounds. OK?"

The woman nodded.

With painstaking care, Adana began to unwrap the bandages, trying to watch the young woman's face and the pull of the fabric on the wound. Each time Adana passed the strip of cloth under the woman's arm, she winced but didn't cry out.

"You did well today," Adana said in an effort to create a distraction. She glanced at the torn tunic, realizing the Watcher's badge of rank must have been lost during the injury or makeshift bandaging. "What rank are you?"

The woman swallowed and licked dry lips. Adana stopped unwrapping the bandages and unhooked her flask from her belt. She tipped it toward the Watcher's mouth, so a small trickle spilled forth.

The woman swallowed, then whispered, "Archery Trainee." She began to cough, and Adana eased her arm under the woman's back and lifted her shoulders from the makeshift pallet.

After the coughing ceased, she eased her back down, mindful of the injury to the Watcher's left shoulder and arm. Then, she began to rewrap the arm with cleaner bandages.

Archery Trainees knew simple sword and archery techniques. The next rank, Archers, learned true combat skills, but fighting in battle was left to full rank Watchers and Leaders. Adana remembered Honest's story about how his mother earned her rank in battle. She thought of Montee's admonitions. Many Watchers gained promotions on the battlefield during war. She studied the Watcher again, noting the plumpness of youth in her cheeks. "What is your name?"

"Romadona."

"Romadona, you earned your full Watcher status today." The promotion skipped three levels of rank but felt accurate.

The smile that greeted her brought a lump to Adana's throat. "Rest." She smoothed the soldier's dark hair back from her forehead before rising and walking away.

Although there were no sounds of new arrivals, she glanced up the tunnels, looking for Kiffen. Returning troops reported his refusal to leave the battlefield until all his soldiers, Elwarian and Monian, were accounted for. She admired his loyalty to them, but the mounting number of injured and dying pressed down on her. She needed reassurance of his safety.

She brushed her hand through her hair and sighed before returning to the throngs of men and women stretched along the tunnel walls. She moved toward a Watcher who rose from tending to a soldier. This woman had been with Kiffen when they departed Elwar. She touched her arm. "Any news of the king?"

The woman pulled up sharply, staring down at Adana's hand. Her eyes widened with recognition when she looked into Adana's face. She bowed her head in respect. "My Queen."

"Any news?" She glanced at the woman's left arm patch, a runner with a knife, a Tracker. She took in the woman's green eyes and the dusky skin of the people from the southern region of her kingdom.

"Everyone hears of the king, Your Majesty. He comes. Others?" The woman paused and licked her lips.

"What others?" A chill ran along Adana's arms, and her shoulder burned.

The Watcher's gaze searched their surroundings for a moment. She gestured away from the makeshift hospital. "If I may, my lady, let's move over here, out of the crowd."

Adana followed, her arms icing over with dread. What news did this woman bear? So many of her Watchers had not returned. Jerold was missing, too. She focused on her shoulder. So much of her body ached after the battle and jolting ride on Am'brosia's back, she hadn't paid attention to its throbbing. Had it throbbed earlier or just begun because she was about to learn something distressing?

The tunnels held several chambers. The one the Watcher chose held stores of food supplies. It was quiet.

The Watcher closed the door behind them and faced Adana, compassion visible in her gaze. She chose to reveal her compassion, a point that made Adana's stomach churn.

"The king should arrive soon. He found Sir Jerold and the Watcher Joannu and seeks to bring them with him."

"Go on." Adana's ears roared, but she steeled herself for the news.

"Sir Jerold is severely injured. His wounds are bad, so they must move him slowly. Joannu…" The woman's eyes misted over, but she blinked and looked her queen square in the eye. "Joannu's injuries were worse. He brings her body."

Adana fought the urge to slump against the wall. Instead, she forced a Watcher's mask of composure over her face.

The Watcher studied her, concern and compassion still evident in her face. "Your Majesty, may I find you a place to wait? A place to rest?"

Adana shook her head and thanked the Watcher. She waved her away when the woman offered to stay. Alone in the chamber, she slid down the wall until she sat huddled on the floor. The cool stone on her back reminded her of her dream, how she had wandered the darkness, her fingers trailing the cool damp earth. She thought of

Veana's body lying in a makeshift morgue in the outer circle of the keep. Hundreds of bodies lay there, each one painful for her to consider, and Joannu would join them. The two women most involved in her early training were gone.

"Child, you must rest." A cool hand brushed her cheek, and she turned to meet Kassa's concerned gaze.

"I will not rest when soldiers who fought for me are still out there. Kiffen—" Her voice caught. She straightened, clearing her throat.

The old Watcher squatted next to Adana. "He is well. We know that." Her mouth quirked into a reassuring smile. "He did well for his first true battle. We can be proud of him."

Adana pressed her palms against her eyes until she saw white lights. She dropped her hands and searched Kassa's face. "I failed."

Kassa shook her head. "All is not lost. Your plan for Shana went differently, but she is in Maligon's hands. You and Kiffen are alive. This battle may be lost, but you will prevail."

A tumult rang in the hallway, cheers and shouting, exhausted men and women now animated in celebration.

Adana jumped up, heart racing, and ran into the tunnel. She halted at the sight of Kiffen. So many gathered around and rose to meet him that she only saw glimpses, but he was there. His hair hung in limp, sweaty strings, blood smudged his face and leather armor, but he walked with confidence, a look of regal honor on his face.

Kassa came up beside her. "See his power? You have it, too. Together, you will defeat Maligon."

Adana swallowed her response to Kassa as Kiffen spotted her. The noise in the tunnel faded in her ears as the two of them stared at each other.

She rushed to him, and he caught her in his arms. The smell of battle filled her nostrils, but she did not care.

Kiffen had returned alive.

* * * * *

Chapter Thirty-Nine

The next day, Adana stood in the Central Tower of the Border Keep. Tendrils of smoke snaked toward the sky, reminding her of their losses. Her enhanced Watcher vision identified each funeral pyre's smoke and ash wisping upward from the distant battlefield until the tendrils drew together in a haze on the horizon. Any other observer would notice the dark cloud of smoke gathering but would not see the ash-filled smoke so well. So many, led into battle by her forces, to be slaughtered by Maligon. The traitor held her home, her royal fortress, access to the Seat of Authority. How had this happened? Who opened the gates, giving that monster her ancestral ground?

The thought of Maligon striding those halls, possessing all that should be hers, rubbed Adana's soul raw. She turned her gaze to the courtyard below. Refugees continued to stream in from outlying areas, seeking shelter from Maligon's rampage across the plains of Moniah. Her people fled to her for protection, but what could she do for them? She didn't sit in the Seat of Authority.

A knock sounded at the chamber door, and Montee entered. The tall Watcher stood straight. Her braid hung halfway down her back, not a dark hair out of place. Adana paused a moment to admire her First Vision's constant composure. The last day had taken its toll on everyone, but Montee never revealed any signs of the weight of loss pressing down on them.

"They are ready for us, Your Majesty," Montee said.

One pyre remained. One that Adana must preside over. One that represented her own personal losses. The smoke in the distance announced the deaths of those not carried back from the battlefield, but this pyre held the wounded who hadn't survived the night and the ones most dear to her—Joannu and Veana.

Two of her honor guard gone. Dead. And one, Samantha, missing. The two who remained, Montee and Sinti, waited to escort her.

Adana drew in a deep breath, seeking a focused center. The cleansing air spread through her chest and body, extending her mind and ability. She let it inflate her abdomen before releasing it until her belly sank toward her backbone. She repeated the exercise, seeking cleansing and focus with each inhalation. In the back of her mind, she felt a nudge from Am'brosia. With each breath, with the giraffe's coaxing, ashes, despair, and death faded. A Watcher's calm sought to gentle the pummeling of her heart and rushing of her thoughts.

She managed to extend a slight smile toward the First Vision. "Thank you, Montee."

Sinti, Adana's ever-present shadow, fell in step behind them. The three women began the long descent from the tower. With each step, each turn of the tower stairs, Adana's concerns crept back into her heart. She descended to perform her duty, to honor the fallen of her closest companions, yet Maligon had risen to power while she, and her allies, weren't looking. He inhabited her home. He had killed loyal followers. He had ravaged her kingdom and taken away her father and Kiffen's father. With the memory of each of Maligon's crimes, Adana's calm evaporated. She walked faster, her steps catching up to her fury. Servants on the next floor jumped out of her way as she flew around the corner and swept past them, hitting the next flight of stairs with determination.

"Your Majesty," Montee said in a quiet, but urgent, voice. The First Vision rushed to catch up to her. "Your Majesty, wait."

Adana halted.

A wrinkle creased Montee's brow. The Watcher's consternation confused Adana, but she shook her head and continued down the stairs. "This must be done and over with. I mustn't make them wait any longer."

Once they honored the dead, she could move forward, attack Maligon, and take back what was rightfully hers.

"Adana." Montee blocked her path. "They will wait."

She stopped. Her breathing came in short, ragged gasps. What had happened to the calm from her focused breathing? She drew in another breath and closed her eyes to focus inward. As she released the air, she opened her eyes and regarded Montee with annoyance. "Why do you delay me? Has something changed since we left the Tower Room?"

"Yes." Montee held up her hand, gesturing for Adana to wait. She strode down a few steps and checked below them, then turned and cocked an eyebrow toward Sinti who stood behind Adana on the stairs.

The young Watcher did the same, checking the stairwell above them. "Clear."

Montee turned back to Adana, her face calm. "Did you not see those servants you barreled past? You rush to do your duty below, but you have duty before you now. This is not your estate. These servants don't know that you approach on silent feet. You startle them enough by appearing out of nowhere, but rushing, Adana? What gossip will you have them spread?"

"I—" Adana began to object but knew her advisor spoke the truth. Nothing in her training had prepared her to assume leadership without the familiar objects of her royalty—the Seat, her home, and her crown. It was bad enough that she and Kiffen must find a way to unite their kingdoms while exploring their own relationship, but how could they succeed in exile? With so much against them?

Montee's tone softened a little, but only a little. It still carried the import of her words. "You must show decorum. You are a queen and a Watcher. Before all people, you must appear calm. You must give them hope. Nod at those we pass. Talk with me, so they hear us approach. Today is not the day to frighten them more."

Adana nodded, ashamed that she needed to be told this. "You are, of course, correct, Montee. I fear I let my concerns overtake my behavior. Thank you for the reminder."

Montee nodded and whispered, "I regret the need. You still have me. I will guide you as Moniah expects."

Adana tilted her head to the side, studying the remarkable woman selected to stand beside her. Adana's mother had chosen well when her departing spirit appeared to Montee, making her the First Vision. She provided the calm in storms and understood how Adana's training suffered from her extended time in Elwar. Her mother had sought to protect her from a prophecy, but the trials she faced hadn't changed. Her exile gave her maturity and time, little more.

They started down the stairs at a more regal pace, and Adana forced her voice to a pleasant tone. "Have you spoken to Glume about Am'brosia and Bai'dish? Are they recovered from the battle?"

Montee answered, her voice brisk, but with efficiency, not concern. Adana continued to discuss the condition of the two giraffes even though she didn't need Montee's report. Through her link with

Am'brosia she knew the giraffes reveled in their participation in the battle. It struck her that they didn't feel agitation over this loss. Did they know something she didn't? Were giraffes capable of seeing the future without sharing it through the bond?

In the back of her mind, she felt amusement from Am'brosia. The animal's odd humor displayed approval of her thoughts. Adana welcomed Am'brosia's state of mind and allowed the bond to solidify. The connection became stronger, and Adana relaxed, allowing the giraffe to share her sight with her. She expected to see the inside of the stable on the ground level of the keep, its dimensions designed for the two giraffes. Instead, Am'brosia gave her a glimpse of a pond in Elwar, the place where Adana used to seek refuge during her time in Kiffen's kingdom. A place the giraffe had never seen. She recalled the calm of floating in a small rowboat, rocked by a gentle breeze.

Surprised, Adana sent a question to the giraffe. How had Am'brosia found that memory? Once again, the capabilities of their telepathic link astounded her, but she was thankful for this new element. The vision provided the tranquility she needed to get through this day.

They rounded another corner and met two maids, carrying folded linens. Adana nodded, earning a hint of a smile from Montee, as the servants curtsied and backed out of her way. The rest of her descent continued in peace, the calmness so complete, Adana almost forgot her destination. Almost.

At the entrance to the courtyard, Adana paused and drew in several slow, focused breaths while trying to ignore the tang of smoke and reek of many people gathered in one place. She must appear strong and vigilant. She refused to let anyone, including Montee and Kiffen, see her falter again.

The pyre stood in the broad expanse outside the gates of the keep. The constant stream of refugees seeking aid hesitated before the large structure of wood supporting the wrapped bodies of the fallen. They gawked as Adana's procession approached.

Kiffen and the gathered mourners waited for her to begin the ceremony.

He turned toward her, his brown hair ruffled by the breeze. Adana felt her soul sink into the depths of his brown eyes for a moment. They reflected the same worries she felt. She knew this to be true from her Watcher's ability to pick up minute details in the way he held his shoulders and tilted his head, but she also knew this from his link to Bai'dish. The bond created an intriguing circle between the four of them—Kiffen to Bai'dish, Bai'dish to Am'brosia, Am'brosia to Adana, and back again.

"We are ready," Kiffen said as she approached. He extended his arm for her to grasp as he escorted her to the front of the mourners. Adana felt harmony radiate from the puncture in her shoulder. In Kiffen's presence, so far, her shoulder felt calm.

Adana turned toward the wood piled below the stand. The air still smoldered with the faint odor of burning flesh, wood, and glimmer fire from the distant battle fields. Most of the mourners couldn't sense those fires, not with such a gentle breeze, but she and her Watchers knew. Their enhanced vision let them see the smoke, and the awareness heightened their ability to detect the stench in the air.

Several of her Watchers, clad in their leather tunics and leggings, formed rank behind her. She, dressed in the same way, had not grasped her kingdom, yet, but she did have their loyalty. Adana reached up and unwound her Watcher's braid, her thoughts momentarily recalling the young girl she had been at her mother's deathbed. She had refused to undo her braid until ordered to do so by her mother.

The other Watchers followed suit, their hair lifting in the breeze.

She accepted a burning torch from a soldier and held it above the kindling. Those dearest to her, Veana and Joannu, Watchers who died protecting her from capture, awaited their release from this world. She studied the mound of bodies, wondering which wrappings disguised her loyal Watchers. As she hesitated, Kiffen laid his fingers over hers, gently pressing downward. Together, they lit the last pyre. Flames licked upward, hungry for their feast.

Adana coughed as the smoke surged around them, stinging her eyes. As the sticks and brambles burned, aiding the departure of the fallen, she murmured to Kiffen, "How many more must die?" A cluster of young Watchers stood guard to her right, battle-scarred, but far too young to have to know the horror of war. "Will they?"

Kiffen took her hand and drew her closer to his side. She allowed herself the brief luxury, eyes watering from her sorrow and the fires that released the bodies of those who had fought for her right to stand with Kiffen.

"Come," he said to her and nodded toward the departing mourners. Around her, people trailed toward the Border Keep, their faces covered with cloths that did little to protect them from the oppressive black breath of loss. "We must join the mourners in the temple."

Together, they walked through the gates of the keep. Watchers stood at the gates alongside Kiffen's soldiers, keeping a vigilant watch on the hills beyond. So far, Maligon appeared to be satisfied with his triumph of the previous day and had settled into Adana's View. His hold on her kingdom and many of her Watchers, whether in thrall or bondage, burned in her stomach. She should be there, preparing for her coronation. Instead, she and Kiffen must find a way to defeat Maligon and save the four kingdoms and their people who had been scattered to the winds by this malevolent beast.

Prince Jerold of Belwyn, his brown hair sticking up at odd angles above the bandage across his forehead, met them in the inner courtyard. Adana pushed the despair from her mind, aware that Jerold suffered from a similar fate. His mother, Empress Gabriella of Belwyn, remained in her own dungeons, a prisoner to Maligon. That Jerold was the prince and heir to the tiny kingdom to the northeast remained an important secret.

"We will rescue the empress," she said, voicing the one promise no one had been able to offer her or Kiffen about their own parents.

Kiffen grasped Jerold's arm in a gesture of camaraderie. "I pray Ariff's men have already done so."

It seemed eons ago that Teletia's King Ariff had led a small band of Watchers and soldiers into Belwyn, but only a little over a week had passed. The soldiers had probably arrived in Belwyn's ruling city on the same day Adana marched from the village of Roshar. Again, the Creator had chosen to laugh at her wishes. Did he laugh at King Ariff's and Empress Gabriella's?

Prince Jerold grimaced. "I'm more concerned with your thrones at this time. The Empress is strong. Maligon can't crush her."

The two of them inclined their heads, humbled by Jerold's loyalty. The trio turned toward the temple.

When they passed into the cool recesses of the holy place, Adana's shoulder began to throb. The ache spread into the joint and down her arm. Adana leaned toward Kiffen, but this time, his presence didn't ease the pain. Adana tried to ignore the pain and acknowledged those who knelt or bowed as she and Kiffen walked to the front of the sanctuary and took their seats in the front row of benches.

If her people didn't need to witness her seeking the Creator's presence, she'd never cross this threshold. Too many times, the Creator had punished her for allowing Maligon to strike while she accepted the Watchers' and then Elwar's protection. Would she ever please the Creator? She doubted it.

A Teacher of the Faith stood before the altar, facing a large tapestry of the Creator hanging on the wall. This one displayed the Creator looming in the sky, protecting his people from a storm that raged around them. Those gathered under his shadow stood in his protection, safe from the tempest.

The Teacher of the Faith turned, his green robes swaying with the movement, and gazed across the assemblage. "Sad times befall us as they did our ancestors of old." He turned toward the tapestry, gesturing with a long-fingered hand. "See how the Creator sheltered them from the storm? He shelters us, and we must trust in him."

Adana sighed and let her mind wander. The Creator gave people hope, so she wouldn't take that from them. Even Kiffen seemed taken in by the promises as once she had been. Had it only been three years since she beseeched the Creator for her mother's and Serrin's lives? Denied the chance to stop Maligon then, she let others steer her from a better destiny. Serrin and her mother had died. From that point on, the Creator had punished her for her failure. Except for Kiffen. For some reason, the Creator gave her the one man she wanted. As these thoughts tumbled in her head, Kiffen took her hand, and the assemblage knelt in prayer. His sword-callused fingers enveloped hers in warmth and comfort.

The Creator did grant her Kiffen's love and betrothal but at a price. An exorbitant cost that all around them paid. Her shoulder thrummed in accordance.

Following the Ceremony of Remembrance and Release, Adana and Kiffen strolled through the courtyard and into the camps outside the gate, speaking to and comforting those who came to them for protection. The refugee camp grew larger outside the walls.

With the Border Keep situated on an island, it was protected from attack, but the keep took up most of the land. The limited space caused concern over how to house and protect everyone. She glanced around, trying to envision the location of the tunnels and chambers running under the ground where she stood and the lake. They provided quick access to landmarks inside Elwar and Moniah, something she hoped to use for victory in the war against Maligon. But Adana feared they may have to retreat to those tunnels if Maligon continued to overtake their lands.

As they returned to the keep, she studied the villagers and soldiers crowding the courtyard and worried about how to feed all of them. It was a noisy scene—the rumble of wheels on stone, the chatter among people, an occasional laugh or cry. Even during a disaster, people couldn't remain tense and somber all the time. As she watched, she noticed the crowd shift its attention toward the Center Gate, awestruck and hopeful looks on their faces.

She followed their gazes. Montee strode toward her, eyes shining with so much enthusiasm that the people she passed recognized the difference.

"Queen Adana, King Kiffen, Sir Jerold, we have unexpected arrivals," Montee said as she drew close. Delight played across her features. "Please come with me to the tower." Montee turned and marched away at a brisk stride without checking to see if they followed. The ache in Adana's shoulder disappeared. She hurried to catch up, anxious to experience good news.

Montee led them to the planning room of the central tower. Adana loved its circular space with the map table at its center. Through the north window, she could see the edge of the forest with Elwar's mountains rising behind it. To the south, she could watch huge herds of animals roam the plains of Moniah. To the east, refugees streamed in through the main gate. To the west, the plains that flooded from Elwar's mountain snowmelt in the spring provided the sustenance that nourished Moniah's lands.

A group of Watchers and soldiers gathered around the table, their attention on an older man. He sat in a chair, his voluminous white robes travel-stained and wrinkled.

"Father Tonch!" Adana rushed to his side.

The Keeper of the Faith had disappeared when Maligon attacked Adana's caravan in the forest, scattering Watchers and soldiers across Elwar and Moniah. Adana might not honor or respect the Creator anymore, but she loved and respected the Keeper of the Faith as well as his partner, the Protector of the Faith. His safety relieved her more than anything else could on this day.

"Queen Adana," he said, rising to bow to her. "It warms my heart to see you."

"I've been so concerned for you," Adana said, gesturing for him to sit. "Where have you been?"

The man smiled. "I've been at your fortress, Queen Adana. Exactly where I told you I would be."

Adana stared at him. To give herself time to register this revelation, she waited until she took her seat at the head of the table before speaking again. "With Maligon camped outside? Laying siege for days? How did you get in?"

"Or out?" Kiffen said as he settled into the chair beside Adana.

"We hid in the south tower during the battle," Father Tonch said. "When Maligon's troops broke through the gate, we hid in the canals. The secrets of your water source still remain concealed, though the traitor has devoted much time to finding them."

"The aqueducts!" Adana had spared little thought to the deep passages that provided fresh water to the fortress. The canals ran through the cliff below the fortress, feeding water into Adana's View through intricate channels built into the stone structure. The Watchers tasked with their protection guarded the access with their lives.

"Yes. I brought several Watchers and Soldiers of the First Sight with me." The man shook his head. "At least those I managed to convince to leave."

Adana shivered. Had Father Tonch pulled her soldiers away from protecting the estate? Was that why Maligon had succeeded?

"How did you manage to draw others to you if you hid?" Kiffen glanced around the room. "And where are they?"

Father Tonch's face reflected satisfaction, a strange emotion for the representative of the Creator. "I waited until Maligon overtook Adana's View and our loss confirmed. Then we entered the waterways."

"You risked discovery." Adana said, concern for the man's safety returning to her thoughts. "You came out of hiding to gather our soldiers?"

"No, Your Majesty." A stern-looking Watcher stepped forward. "I did."

This Watcher wore an insignia with a giraffe standing on a field of green, the designation of a Strategist Unit Leader. She went down on one knee and bowed her head toward Adana. "Queen Adana, I'm pleased you are here and not in Maligon's grip as we first believed."

Adana felt overcome by the devotion evident in this strong soldier but hid it behind a royal demeanor. "It is I who am pleased, Watcher. Your help comes at a difficult time. I thank you for your protection of Father Tonch. Your name?"

The Watcher rose but bowed her head as she said, "Nuala, Your Majesty."

"Nuala, you are to be commended for your efforts. You mention the rumor that I stand with Maligon, so that must mean Maligon has found the imposter." Adana exchanged a glance with Montee. "It appears our plan worked."

The pain of Joannu's and Veana's deaths eased a little now that Adana had confirmation that their sacrifice stood for something. Whether Shana was loyal to Adana or to Maligon still worried Adana, but either way, Nuala's words confirmed some success in their plan. What might have happened if Shana, Jerold, and Joannu hadn't intervened when Pultarch's soldiers tried to capture her during the battle? Shana now faced whatever fate Adana might have met.

Nuala said, "I heard of a woman rescued during the battle. They claimed to have saved you from your despicable betrothal." Nuala turned gray eyes on Kiffen. "My apologies for the sentiment, King Kiffen. I merely repeat the words as overheard."

"No need, Nuala. We are aware of the lies spread by Maligon."

Montee inclined her head in agreement and turned a commander's face toward Nuala. "What do you know of conditions inside the walls? Do the Watchers inside support him, or do they remain to protect the kingdom?"

A sad look crossed Nuala's face, but she did not hesitate to answer Montee. "First Vision, I did my best to learn what I could before coming to the queen. Inside the walls is chaos. The soldiers and Watchers who stood for Queen Adana are dead."

Montee opened her mouth to speak, but no words came out.

Adana clenched her fists. Her shoulder burned in agreement.

Kassa stepped forward and stood shoulder-to-shoulder with her successor. Though demoted from the rank of First Vision at Queen Chiora's death, Kassa, more than anyone present, understood Montee's loss.

Adana wished she could reach out to give and take comfort from the two of them, but neither one could appear to need or accept compassion in front of her soldiers.

"What of Commander Linus?" Kassa asked.

Montee's gaze reflected a light of hope. To anyone but a Watcher, the emotion was unnoticeable. Adana suspected Montee and Linus loved each other, but their positions as commanders of the two branches of Moniah's armies forbade a relationship.

"Commander Linus is dead." Nuala spit out the words in anger, a rare exposure of emotion for a Watcher. "Murdered by a Watcher just before Maligon breached our gates." The woman's gray eyes burned a strange shade of umber for a moment.

Montee's stoicism failed in the face of this news. She looked like a candidate, lost on her first day of Watcher training. Adana laid a hand on Kiffen's arm, seeking the comfort of his presence, unable to imagine the horror of losing him to Maligon.

"A Watcher?" Montee jerked, as if the sound of her own voice had slapped her in the face. When she spoke again, her words radiated vengeance. "Did you see who killed him?"

Nuala paled before her commander's angry gaze.

Adana held her breath, aware that the woman's body language, subtle as it might be, foretold a horrible treason. Her shoulder burned with a fire more unbearable than any pain she'd felt before. She could only think of one name that might cause this strong soldier-turned-messenger to hesitate.

"Go on, Nuala," Adana said. "We know of several traitors already."

Still, Nuala waited a moment longer, her eyes softening in compassion. "I apologize for this ill news. I did verify it because I could not believe my own senses. The Watcher Samantha killed Linus." She took a deep breath and added one more devastating blow. "And Samantha opened the gates to let Maligon inside the walls."

Montee reached out a firm arm to hold up Kassa, as the strongest woman Adana had ever known sank to the floor, her mouth opened in an unheard cry.

Rage burned from Adana's shoulder into her belly. How had Maligon brought this strange sight to those gathered in the room? Two of the most formidable women in Moniah shattered by one betrayal. Samantha had betrayed them all. Halar stood stiffly behind both women, his hand gripped in his wife's, a tear sliding down his face.

Adana turned to Kiffen to share her shock and found Kiffen's face contorted in pain.

"Kiffen?"

He did not meet her eyes but turned to stare out the window to the east. "I trusted her. She taught me how to link with Bai'dish. She was, was..."

The atmosphere in the room pressed down on Adana. She breathed in and out, seeking Am'brosia's comforting presence and tamping down the emotions at war in her gut. Maligon would pay dearly for this. Her shoulder still stung, but her desire for retaliation felt like a cool compress over the puncture.

Desperate to release the tension in the room, Adana rose, approached Nuala, and took her hands in her own. The Watcher's face registered surprise as Adana bestowed a formal acknowledgement on the woman. "Nuala, you show great courage and loyalty in bringing this terrible news. We beg your forgiveness if we must retire and discuss your findings later."

"Of course." Nuala bowed her head and backed toward the door.

"No." Montee's voice echoed against the stone walls. She straightened and brushed her hands down her uniform, smoothing unseen wrinkles. Kassa rose beside her.

Montee glanced at the older woman who nodded slightly, her lips compressed in a thin, white line. The First Vision said, "We do not have time to mourn during war. We will deal with these tidings on our own time, not the queen's. Nuala, continue."

Nuala paused, but when it became obvious that Montee meant her words, she gestured toward a box on the table. "Father Tonch, may I?"

In the subdued silence, Adana heard a collective intake of air.

"Of course." The man pushed the box toward her. "You're the one who risked exposure to bring it."

Nuala held the box out to Adana.

Its wooden sides felt smooth, the result of a carpenter's dedicated sanding. Etched into the lid was the image of a regal giraffe. Adana lifted the lid and peered inside. Her heart pounded at the sight, and she stared up at Nuala in surprise. "How did you?"

"She refused to leave without it, Your Majesty." A second Watcher stepped forward.

Adana studied the Watcher. The young woman had light brown hair, woven in an intricate form of the tight Watcher's braid. Her insignia depicted a herd of five giraffes indicating the rank of a Unit Leader. Something in her face and stance seemed familiar to Adana even though she didn't know the woman's name.

"Do I know you?" Adana said.

The Watcher nodded. "Not by name, your majesty. I am Suru. I was there when Glume stopped you from leaving the fortress on the day of Queen Chiora's passing."

Adana blinked at the woman, her memory racing back to that painful day. How young she had been, thinking she might slip away unnoticed. How could the Creator hold her accountable to such an idiotic notion?

"You're the one?" She recalled the young Watcher who took the horse's reins from Glume.

Suru met her with a steady, brown-eyed gaze. "Yes."

Adana grimaced at the memory of her youthful exuberance. "You were just raised to Watcher at the time, weren't you?"

"I was."

"I see you're a Unit Leader. You've done well."

Adana turned her attention back to the box. She laid it on the table and lifted the lid for all to see. Kiffen leaned forward.

The box held several small vials. The last time Adana had seen a vial like these was the day her mother died. The giraffe keeper had used it to collect Am'brosia's tears. She picked up a bottle and peered at its contents through the hazy, blue glass. The key to her bond with Am'brosia washed against the sides.

Kiffen peered at the small vial. "What is that?"

"Giraffe tears." She turned to Nuala and Suru. "You've proven yourselves resourceful and valuable. I apologize for my lapse in form earlier. We will discuss a proper reward for your dedication this afternoon when I hear your full report and review the reinforcements you've brought us."

* * * * *

Chapter Forty

Dust motes floated in the thin line of sunlight filtering through the small windows of Gerguld's store on the perimeter of Elwar City. Leera wielded a broom with awkward strokes, a frown of concentration on her face, as she stabbed at the floor more than sweeping it.

Gerguld walked out of the back storeroom and shook his head at her efforts. "Not like that, mistress." He took the broom and demonstrated how to sweep the wooden plank flooring. "Imagine yourself running a brush through those golden curls of yours. That's how you do it."

Leera blew air between her lips and pushed a strand of hair out of her face. "I don't see why we bother. No sooner do I sweep it, then more blows in from the street."

Gerguld sat down on a wooden carton situated at the end of the aisle of dry goods. "Missy, you don't know how much work goes on up there at the palace do you? All the time, everything was clean and taken care of, wasn't it?" He stared at her pointedly. "Someone did the work you're doing, so you wouldn't notice."

The shop hadn't opened yet, so the man's words didn't expose her, but the missing princess flinched when he referred to her home. She bent forward and spoke between clenched teeth. "It's bad enough I had to leave my lovely dresses behind. Do you have to remind me how wonderful the castle was?"

Alarm crossed the man's face. "Oh, pardon, missy. I didn't mean to." He rubbed his hand over his face. "I just thought you might appreciate it more if you understood the value of what you're doing. My wife didn't want me to put you out here, working, but I told her it would do you some good. Helmyra and Mother Sariah agreed."

Leera bristled, but in matters of Helmyra and Sariah, she knew to hold her tongue. She leaned on the broom and surveyed the dimly lit store. The few shops along the outer walls of the city did not compare to Gerguld's. This one was much cleaner, but it still looked primitive compared to any other place she'd been. "I suppose you're right, Gerguld. But how much longer must I remain here? When will you take me to Kiffen?"

Footsteps echoed on the wooden floor, coming from the back of the store. Gerguld jumped up to stand between Leera and the arrival, his shoulders tense. Leera shrank behind him and dropped her head down, pulling a scarf out of her apron pocket and tucking her hair up under it.

Both relaxed at the sound of Sariah's voice. "I believe I can respond to your question, Lily."

The name, although similar to hers, still made Leera want to look over her shoulder for someone else. The Protector of the Faith wore a simple, brown cloak wrapped around her matronly bulk. White hair peeked out from the bonnet tied under her chin. Sariah removed the bonnet and straightened her hair before speaking again.

"I had hoped to hear from your brother by now, but I've received no message from him or the queen." She plopped down on one of the crates and looked up at Leera. "News reached the castle this morning, though. Maligon has taken Adana's View."

Leera's heart plummeted in alarm. Her brother never failed at anything. Had he survived? If he had, how had he and Adana lost Moniah to Maligon?

"Quilla's supporters slant the reports, I'm sure, but we must assume the core of the message is true. I only hope Kiffen and Adana are safe." The woman's voice trembled on the last part. "Those who fought for Moniah shelter within the Border Keep. I plan to depart for the keep tomorrow. If you wish to join me, Lily, I will welcome your company."

That was different. "What?" She couldn't hold back the sarcasm in her voice. "I have a choice?"

Ever since Helmyra and Catch had helped her escape her mother's clutches, Leera had felt vulnerable. The need to hide from Queen Quilla made it impossible for Leera to make any decisions about her welfare. Now, Sariah offered her a choice.

"Of course. War is dangerous. I can't tell you whether to remain in the safety of the city or leave and venture across enemy territory. You have the option, but, in this situation, you must decide."

"And if I choose not to go? What then?"

The woman shook her head. "None of us know what tomorrow brings, my child. We have people who will try to protect you if you choose to stay."

Dust motes floated around her head, and Leera sneezed. She laughed and wiped her nose with a muslin handkerchief, its texture rough on her nose. For the first time in her life, she really had a choice. "I suppose it will be a difficult journey?"

"We will have to travel light. No servants to tend to your needs and no special provisions."

Leera sighed. She wanted to do it, but her fears cautioned her. Life outside the palace was harder than she had imagined. "I wish I had the Watcher's uniform Adana had specially made for me."

Sariah smiled. "You do. Catch found it in the refuse heap, waiting to be burned. Helmyra's making a change of clothes for you, too. And a traveling cloak. That's if you wish to come with us."

The broom clattered to the floor as Leera dove toward Sariah, wrapping her arms around the woman's soft middle. "Yes! Find me Catch. I need to apologize for that kick to his shins."

Sariah pulled back from Leera, arching an eyebrow in surprise.

"Oh, pardon, Mother Sariah." Leera jumped to her feet, hands twisted in her apron. "I'm so accustomed to ordering people to fetch things for me. I'll go find the boy."

Leera forgot the humiliation of asking forgiveness as she rushed headlong into the back of the store. She was going to see her brother and Adana. Her feet screeched to a halt.

If they were still alive.

* * * * *

Chapter Forty-One

Shana laid her hand on Maligon's arm, assumed a regal posture, and let him escort her before the assembly in the Great Hall. An ululating chant rose from the Watchers gathered to greet their queen. Her heart pounded, increasing the heat that radiated from every stone in the structure of Adana's View. The royal fortress astounded her with its wide-open spaces, large fountains bubbling day and night, and the understated elegance of its furnishings. Unlike the castle in Elwar, which she had only seen a small part of, this estate did not overwhelm the senses with opulence. Even the air smelled fresh, not stale from smoldering fireplaces as in Elwar.

Except for the unbearable heat, Shana liked Moniah. When she seized the opportunity to serve the young lord and the nobleman who appeared in The Sleeping Dog, she had thought it might lead to a better life, maybe as a kept woman. She never suspected her sights would fall on people with such high connections. The connection she had hoped for would have placed her in a nice apartment or country estate in Elwar, not as a spy for the queen of Moniah. She chuckled at the thought, causing Maligon to arch a curious eyebrow at her.

Returning to the part she played as Maligon's ally, she whispered, "I'm enjoying this."

The delighted expression on the man's face told her she had said the right thing. Shana's role as imposter for Adana would only work if Maligon genuinely believed she wanted to serve him, not Queen Adana.

Maligon escorted Shana to the Seat of Authority which sat on a raised platform in the Great Hall. Watchers, Teachers of the Faith, and Soldiers of the First Sight lined their path, bowing in succession as she passed. Shana nodded her head occasionally to a few people, wondering if she should know any of them. The two people she did know stood by the throne, waiting. Their own desire for power relied on her ability to become Queen Adana and accept the crown and rulership of Moniah.

Pultarch stood to the left of the throne. He desired Adana's hand in marriage, but Maligon had managed to convince him that Shana would suffice. Her heart pounded at his presence, but it was bittersweet. He wasn't the man she imagined him to be. The truth of that hurt, but her body still desired him, weak as he was. Yet, he longed for Adana, not Shana.

The Watcher Samantha stood to the right of the throne. She claimed entitlement to the position her mother and grandmother once held, the queen's most trusted advisor, the First Vision. Just from listening to these three traitors plot, Shana had discovered the depth of Samantha's anger and feelings of betrayal when Adana's mother, Queen Chiora, selected Montee as the next First Vision. Behind Samantha stood Kalara, the Watcher raised by Maligon. Shana suspected Kalara would make the decisions Samantha sought to make as First Vision.

Today, Maligon would announce Queen Adana's safe return and betrothal to Pultarch. To add to his vices, he would raise Samantha to the post of First Vision. With Adana and Kiffen exiled, Montee along with them, Maligon could do whatever he liked. Shana breathed a prayer to the Creator for protection as she played yet another role.

Maligon's sleek voice rang out over the crowd, and the cheers quieted as he raised his good hand before him. "Loyal subjects of Moniah, your queen attends you. Welcome Queen Adana of Moniah to the Seat of Authority and to her right as heir."

The crowd shouted their approval, unbridled enthusiasm on their faces.

Shana stood beside Maligon, amazed at the adulation. She scanned the crowd, looking for any signs of discontent but saw none. She was not a Watcher. How would she recognize the signs without the proper skills or training?

She strained to use her Listener's ability, but the crowd's noise drowned out any possibility of recognizing concern in someone's voice. She had hoped her gift might help her uncover those in the fortress who remained loyal to the real Queen Adana. They had to be here. She felt sure not everyone loyal to Adana managed to flee when Maligon stormed the gates.

Shana took the Seat, flinching from the heat absorbed by the wooden chair as it sat exposed to the morning sun. In the sky above, a bird flew over. The crowd's noise drowned out the whistle of the wind through the bird's feathers, a sound that would have given Shana a moment of peace.

The crowd hushed as Samantha came forward and took a knee before her. Shana tensed, aware her behavior must fool the remaining Watchers.

"Queen Adana," Samantha said, "I offer my sight and bow and sword to you as protector of Moniah and the crown. Do you wish it?"

Acceptance of Samantha's statement would place the woman in the second highest position in the land. Aware that she had no choice and that her words held no true authority, Shana said, "We do wish it, Watcher Samantha. Arise and be known as First Vision of Moniah from this day forth."

Samantha unleashed a ferocious grin of triumph before she masked it in appropriate humility and turned to accept the crowd's praise. Ululating chants rang through the air, and the people bowed to Samantha.

Samantha accepted a ceremonial knife from Maligon, a makeshift symbol of her office, since Montee held the true symbols of bow, knife, and sling. A flash of irritation crossed the umber-skinned woman's face before she strapped the knife to her belt and saluted the crowd. Cheers echoed off the sandstone walls, deafening to Shana's acute hearing. She shifted on her throne, seeking relief from the scorched wood, as heat soaked through the leather leggings of her Watcher uniform. She'd worn the uniform for some time now, even though she held no Watcher powers, but at times like this, she missed the many layers of cloth in a proper Elwarian dress.

If Pultarch would hurry up and play his part in this charade, she could return to the quiet and solace of the royal chambers.

The young lord wavered a moment before coming forward. He stood tall and strong before her, his brown hair flowing to his shoulders, his full mouth trembling in hesitation. She longed to pull him to her as she had done in the tavern when, in a drunken stupor, he mistook her for Adana. He loved Adana, not Shana. She didn't understand why his presence still drew her, but it did. Pultarch was a boy in many ways, easily manipulated. His behavior over the last few days made her question the wisdom of her attraction to him as he closed eyes in response to her stare. The attraction, real or imagined, did not matter in Maligon's plans, though.

Maligon cleared his throat and darted a menacing glare at Pultarch.

Pultarch dropped his head, a tumble of hair falling across his forehead as he stepped closer.

Fingers itching to brush the cowlick aside, Shana sat up straight and delivered the appropriate prompt drilled into her by Samantha earlier in the day. "Sir Pultarch, do you pledge to the Seat of Authority?"

Pultarch dropped to both knees and choked out in a loud anguished voice, "Queen Adana, I will not go forward unless by your side, as helper and mate. I will serve you and thus serve Moniah."

The passion in his voice surprised her. Pultarch wore his feelings on the outside unlike most of the nobility Shana had met, but she knew he spoke the words to Adana, not her. They might be playing this game of imposters, but Pultarch still hoped to win Adana back.

How would Pultarch react if he knew Adana had sent Shana to play this ruse, to infiltrate Maligon's followers? Would he betray her by his face and body, or would he thank her for supporting the woman he loved?

People muttered and fidgeted when she didn't respond, the ripple of murmurs warning Shana of her lapse. Maligon drew in several short breaths, a signal she had already learned to interpret as building anger.

"Arise, Sir Pultarch," she said. "Moniah accepts your allegiance and hand as helper. We will marry in one year and produce an heir to this throne and kingdom as the Creator wishes and blesses us to do so." Shana felt her face flush at the statement. Pultarch's soft brown eyes widened at the pointed phrasing in the response, but she kept her gaze steady on his, not giving into the embarrassment any further. Maligon and Samantha insisted this was the proper statement to make at the time, and she complied.

The expected roar of approval did not come, and Shana looked up at the crowd in surprise. A discussion near the rear entrance to the hall had drawn attention away from their act.

Three distinct voices shouted in protest, one startling in its familiarity.

"Let me through," the familiar voice said. "These vows must be witnessed by a Teacher of the Faith who holds close confidence with the queen."

Shana stood and strained to see over the heads of those blocking the man. "Let him through. Give the teacher access."

The crowd parted, glancing between Shana and the man in curiosity. Shana didn't miss the look of surprise on Maligon's and Samantha's faces. If they expected her to play queen, they had better get used to her using the authority that came with it.

Happiness spread through Shana's being when her sight confirmed what she had heard. Brother Honest's light brown hair stood out in the sea of dark-haired Monians. She never thought to ask him why a Monian might have light hair; after all, Queen Adana's hair was a lighter shade, just like her own. Adana's father came from a kingdom far north, bringing his paler coloring with him. Maybe one of Honest's parents did too. Or maybe his ancestors had descended from the lighter-skinned Elwarians like hers.

All thought of the deceit Maligon forced on her fled as the one man who had stood by her side during the worst days of her life approached. She felt her breath quicken in relief and concern for the brother.

Honest's green robes, designating him as a Teacher of the Faith, hung in limp folds around his legs. Dust clung to the hem, and sweat stained his front. Shana had never seen him look so disheveled.

Across his shoulders, Honest wore a bulging, leather pack. He carried a walking staff, and it click, click, clicked against the sandstone floor as he approached the queen.

His gaze never faltered from Shana's, an act acceptable only due to his position as teacher. Then he stood before her, knelt, and bowed his head, disrupting the charged connection between them.

"Arise, Brother Honest," Shana said.

With the teacher standing before her, Shana wondered how to proceed. Queen Adana would know what to say, but Shana floundered. Maligon took a territorial step toward Honest, but the teacher never turned away from Shana. He gave a slight nod, encouraging her.

Shana found the words, one at a time, until they flowed freely. "We are pleased to greet you, Brother Honest. You wish to witness for the Faith?"

"My lady, I do wish to lend the Faith's witness to your proceedings." He turned sideways in order to address Shana, but include the gathering, too. This stance kept Honest's back toward Maligon. "With the Keeper and the Protector of the Faith missing from this occasion, Queen Adana needs a Teacher of the Faith known to her to witness this triumphant day."

Heads nodded as a murmur of agreement spread throughout the crowd.

Only then did Honest look toward Maligon. "I'm sure the Lord could not find an appropriate ally so soon. I came as quickly as I could."

The Lord. A name less infamous or inflammatory than Maligon. Honest's use of Maligon's self-imposed title appeared to mollify him.

"Indeed," Maligon said. "We mourned the absence of a true confidante among the remaining faithful teachers. You are welcome here, Brother Honest."

A glint appeared in Honest's eyes that disquieted Shana. He had many reasons to hate Maligon.

Rather than reply to Maligon, Honest turned his attention back to Shana, including Samantha in his address. "I heard the crown for your coronation is missing, probably stolen by those who fled the fortress during battle."

Shana cocked her head to the side, wondering where Honest might be leading them.

The teacher laid his staff on the floor, knelt to dig through his leather pack, and produced an object wrapped in a piece of yellow glimmer cloth. He stood, and with the flourish of an entertainer, tugged on the cloth. The fabric shimmered and glowed in the sun's light as it fell to the ground, revealing a simple crown of gold in the brother's outstretched hand.

"It's not as elaborate as the original crown of Moniah, my queen, but I had little time to make it. I hope it pleases your majesty."

She stared at the golden circlet. A spire rose in the front of the crown, with a single emerald blinking back at Shana, a third eye, an awareness given by the Creator to all monarchs. She stared at Brother Honest in awe. Her presence here had been his idea. What else would the man do? "We are pleased with your offering, Brother Honest," Shana said.

The Teacher of the Faith turned, his green robes swaying with the motion, and faced the crowd. "The circumstances today are unusual. Your queen has languished under the stigma of battle and treasonous betrothals. Today is a celebration of her success in spite of her foes in Elwar."

Honest glanced back at Shana and gave her an apologetic smile before turning back to the crowd. He raised the crown high. "We must seek the Creator's blessing and crown her today, before any other event interrupts us."

Shana heard Maligon's sharp intake of breath and knew that Honest pushed his luck. The man's charm, as well as his empathic gifts for reading people's emotions, would tell him if he overplayed his part today, but still, she worried.

Honest turned to Maligon and said, "Shall we crown our queen today? Do away with these concerns and move this kingdom forward? We still have a battle to fight against those cowards holed up with Kiffen at the Border Keep."

The traitor, the man known as the Lord, the warrior, Maligon, flashed a triumphant smile and shouted, "Long live Queen Adana! Long live Queen Adana!"

The crowd took up the chant as Honest bowed over her and laid the crown on her forehead. "I crown you as the Giver of Sight and Health, the Queen of Moniah, Commander of the Watchers, and Blessed of the Creator."

Before he stepped aside, Honest whispered, "Forgive me. It's the best way to protect you."

One by one, Moniah's landowners came before her, kneeling in supplication. After the landowners, the Soldiers of the First Sight marched forward and saluted her as one. At last, as the sun passed its zenith in the sky, the Watchers stood before her. The women knelt, their bows on their backs thrusting upward like a tiny mountain range.

Under the weight of the crown, the chanting of the gathered soldiers, and the heat of the day, Shana stood on shaking limbs and summoned Pultarch to her side. Gripping his arm, she gave a slight nod to the crowd, trying to keep the crown from slipping off, then gestured for Brother Honest to follow her.

She leaned into Pultarch, her need for his immediate support wavering in her voice. "You must escort me back to my chamber, Sir Pultarch. This day must end on this high note. I feel quite faint."

For once, the look the young noble gave her registered concern, instead of disappointment. It appeared Pultarch could care, could show compassion. Or, she realized, it might be fear that she would faint again.

Pultarch gestured to Samantha, who parted the crowd like a wave. Watchers formed a pathway to the doors. The cheers continued long after they left the Great Hall. Heavy breathing behind her confirmed her fear that Maligon followed her small troop. She had hoped for a moment alone with Brother Honest.

Would Maligon find this turn of events useful? If not, Ballene's fire might rain down on them before dinner.

Maligon stormed into the room behind Shana and her retinue. She shivered at the crackle of fury that surrounded the man.

"What in blazes was that?" He turned on Brother Honest, his mouth snarled in anger, his eyes heated like the fires of Ballene. "How dare you come in and crown the queen like that?"

Honest didn't waver. He stood in his travel-stained clothes and faced down the irate traitor. Nor did he speak.

"You had plenty to say out there," Maligon said. "Speak to me now, or—"

"Or what?" Honest said, lifting his walking staff at an angle. The gesture could be innocent, but in the face of Maligon's attack, it looked retaliatory.

Maligon held his tongue, his shoulders heaving with each indignant breath. Shana listened to his raspy breath, aware that something sounded wrong in his chest. She glanced around. Did no one else hear it?

Laying down his staff, Honest approached Maligon, a look of contrition on his face. "Lord, you knew it had to be done. We had to crown her. Too much time has passed since the queen's birthday. You promised Moniah their queen. What else would you have me do?"

Shana blinked in surprise at the statements. Of course, Honest didn't know that Maligon no longer thought she was Adana. Would his words betray him? He had claimed in the Great Hall to be a close confidante of the queen.

The man Shana feared most in the world took a calculated step toward Honest, coming closer than most found acceptable. Honest still did not waver. He just smiled at the Lord and laid a hand on Maligon's robed arm. "You do want what's best for Moniah don't you?"

Maligon nodded. "Of course. I made a promise to Queen Chiora many years ago. I will always protect Moniah."

The brief contact with Maligon's robe would give Honest a glimpse into the man's honesty. She suspected Maligon spoke the truth, but Shana was only a Listener. Brother Honest was a Seer and an Empath. The Seer part of him would know if Maligon believed what he said.

"What is your next move?" Honest still addressed Maligon.

Maligon's teeth gleamed in cruel glee. "We will attack the Border Keep. Soon. Others don't know the truth, so we must eliminate the true Adana if our ploy with this tavern maid is to work."

Honest didn't blink, and Shana knew he passed Maligon's test with his next statement. "Yes, the stupid princess refuses to be captured or killed, doesn't she?"

Pultarch rose from the chair he had dropped into and slammed his fist into Honest's face.

Shana settled into her chair as Maligon raged at Pultarch and Honest pressed his sleeve to his bleeding nose.

Life was going to get interesting.

# # # # #

Cast of Characters

Name

Adana	Heir to the throne of Moniah, trained as a Watcher
Am'brosia	Giraffe bonded to Adana
Ariff	King of Teletia
Bai'dish	Giraffe bonded to Serrin
Catch	Page in Elwar
Chiora	Queen of Moniah, Adana's mother
Conrad	Earl of Brom, Pultarch's father
Donel	King of Elwar
Father Tonch	Keeper of the Faith, married to Sariah
Gabriella	Empress of Belwyn
Gerguld	Merchant in Elwar
Glume	Giraffe Keeper
Halar	Kassa's husband, 2nd in Command of the Soldiers of the First Sight
Hanna	Leera's maid
Helmyra	Seamstress in Elwar
Honest	A Teacher of the Faith in Roshar
Jerold	First knight of Belwyn
Joannu	Watcher
Ju'latti	Queen Chiora's bonded giraffe
Kalara	Watcher
Karyah	Watcher envoy to Belwyn

Kassa	Watcher and Former First Vision during Chiora's reign
Kiffen	Heir to the throne of Elwar, son of King Donel and Queen Roassa
Lady Elayne	Actual name is Shana, gifted to Adana by Sarx and the Earl of Brom under this noble title
Leera	Kiffen's half-sister, daughter of King Donel and Queen Quilla
Linus	Commander of the Soldiers of the First Sight
Maligon	Traitor exiled by Chiora 20 years ago, believed dead until his return 3 years earlier
Markel	Sergeant in Elwar's castle guard
Memory Keeper	Storyteller
Micah	Husband King of Chiora, Father of Adana
Montee	Adana's First Vision
Morana	Queen of Teletia
Mother Sariah	Protector of the Faith, married to Peter Tonch
Navon	Prince in Teletia
Nuala	Watcher
Ostreia	Watcher Envoy to Teletia
Pultarch	Son of the Earl of Brom
Quilla	Queen in Elwar, 2nd wife to King Donel, mother to Leera
Roassa	Queen in Elwar, 1st wife to King Donel, mother to Kiffen and Serrin
Samantha	High-ranking Watcher
Sarx	Elwarian noble
Serrin	2nd son of King Donel and Queen Roassa
Shana	Tavern maid, known to most as Lady Elayne of

	Glenhaven
Simeon	Advisior to King Donel
Sinti	Watcher
Suru	Watcher
Talia	Innkeeper in Roshar
Taren	Sarx's nephew from Lisseme
Veana	Watcher

* * * * *

Watcher Qualifications

Watcher Rank	Must be able to:
Candidate	Build fire, accurately throw a knife, use focused breathing
Archery Trainee	Display simple archery & sword fighting skills
Archer	Display advanced archery accuracy and sword control
Tracker	Able to track a quarry over rough terrain, can run 4 hours without becoming winded, skilled in knife fighting
Phantom	Evade trackers, able to fire arrow into crowd or at target w/o looking and still hit their mark; must complete the 10 arrow interval
Watcher (Full rank, basic troops)	Can identify specific but minor changes in a crowd or busy landscape, use vision for perception of danger in unfamiliar surroundings, might experience prophetic visions
Unit Leader	Leads a unit of 5 Watchers, must have prophetic visions
Squad Leader	Leads 4 Units (20 Watchers, 4 Unit leaders)
Strategist	Trained in hazardous espionage and military strategy
Troop Leader	Leads 5 squads (100 Watchers, 5 Squad Leaders, 20 Unit leaders)
Strategist Unit Leader	Commands 5 Strategists
Regiment Leader	Commands 10 troops
Tactical Command	Commands 3 Special Forces Units

* * * * *

Watcher Badges

Watcher Rank	Badge
Candidate	Flame
Archery Trainee	Sword crossed over a bow
Archer	Bullseye target in yellow & brown
Tracker	Runner with a knife
Phantom	A closed eye/An open eye
Watcher (Full rank, basic troops)	A single giraffe
Unit Leader	A herd of giraffes
Squad Leader	Brown giraffe under a tree
Strategist	Brown giraffe surrounded by bushes
Troop Leader	Giraffe on a yellow background
Strategists Unit Leader	Giraffe on a field of green
Regiment Leader	Giraffe head in profile on brown glimmer background
Tactical Command	Giraffe head in profile on black glimmer background

* * * * *

Author's Note

While the giraffes in this story are fictional and exist in my imagination, and hopefully in yours now, I hope you'll take the time to find out more about the plight of real giraffes and the efforts the Giraffe Conservation Foundation (GCF) is taking to save them. Giraffes suffer from a silent extinction because they do not receive the publicity other endangered animals receive. According to GCF's website, giraffe numbers have declined by almost 30% in the last three decades to approximately 111,000 in the wild. It is likely that giraffe numbered ten times as many only a century ago. Please check out https://giraffeconservation.org and help if you can. By purchasing this book, you've already helped because I will donate 5% of the book's profits to GCF each quarter.

* * * * *

About the Author

Barbara V. Evers began storytelling at the age of four. She couldn't read, yet, so she roped her Aunt Vivian into taking dictation for her. She is an award-winning author and Pushcart Prize nominee with short stories and essays appearing in several anthologies.

When she's not writing, Barbara is a professional trainer, speaker, and freelance writer/editor. Outside of work, Barbara loves reading, photography, and exploring wildlife and the great outdoors.

Barbara lives in Greer, SC, with two of her grandchildren, her husband, Bruce, and a rescue dog named Roxy.

You can find out more about Barbara's upcoming books and sign up for her newsletter at www.BarbaraVEvers.com. Also, you can follow her on Facebook @BarbaraVEversAuthor.

* * * * *

The following is an

Excerpt from Book One of The Balance of Kerr:

Burnt

Kevin Steverson &
Tyler Ackerman

Available Now from New Mythology Press

eBook and Paperback

Excerpt from "Burnt:"

Tog shrugged. "I like chicken," he said as he pulled out his dagger. Standing nearly seven feet tall and weighing nearly three hundred and twenty pounds, a dagger for him was a short sword to most men. He cut a piece off. He didn't bother blowing on it and poked it into his mouth. There was instant regret on his face. He began breathing through his teeth with the piece of meat between them, the sharpness of his incisors giving away that he was half Orc, if his size didn't already reveal it. He grabbed his mug and drained it.

Kryder shook his head, cut another piece for himself, and blew on it. Before he took a bite, he said, "If I had a copper for every time I've seen you do that, I could exchange them for a piece of gold. I'm talking about a whole coin and not a quarter piece."

Tog wiped his mouth with the back of his hand, ignoring the remark, and said, "So when are we going to be contacted? Besides the cost of mugs, this place isn't cheap. It's not like we have coin to spare. We should think about an inn more in line with our coin purses."

"I don't know," Kryder answered. "The old man said someone would contact us here. If we go across town, whoever it is may not find us."

"Well I…" Tog started to say when he was interrupted by a loud voice two tables away.

"Look here, halfbreed," a man dressed similarly to them, in leather armor covered with a travel cloak and a sword on his hip, said loudly. One side of his face had a scar stretching from eyebrow to lips. He was speaking to them. "I don't eat with such as your kind."

The three men sitting with him laughed. One wearing a half-helmet with leather flaps hanging on each side added his own loud insult, "Since the rape didn't kill his mother, surely bearing an Orc bastard did the deed." The group laughed even louder.

Kryder reached down to his side and drew another smaller, more ornate dagger with his free hand. He laid them both on the table. He stood, turned around, and looked at the four men. Tog, on his feet nearly as quickly, reached over his shoulder and grabbed the axe strapped to his back with one hand. It was dual-headed and meant for two hands when used by a normal-sized man. He placed it on the table beside his own large dagger. A hand's length of the worn leather-covered handle hung over the edge.

The four men realized the object of their harassment and his companion didn't intend to leave. They meant to fight. They scrambled to their feet, knocking over chairs. Several groups stood and moved away from the center of the room, while others left the tavern completely.

The owner's sons looked toward their father. He shook his head. Fights happened, even in his establishment in the better part of town. Usually he had his boys put a stop to it. This time, the insult thrown at the large patron was more than he could tolerate. He decided to let the man demand his apology, even if it meant he had to beat it out of the four. It was an easy decision.

* * * * *

Get "Burnt" now at:
https://www.amazon.com/dp/B0861FRWFH/.

Find out more about Kevin Steverson & Tyler Ackerman and "Burnt" at:
https://chriskennedypublishing.com/imprints-authors/kevin-steverson/burnt/

* * *

The following is an

Excerpt from Book One of Forge and Sword:

Keep of Glass

Steven G. Johnson

Available Now from New Mythology Press

eBook, Paperback, and (soon) Audio Book

Excerpt from "Keep of Glass:"

Trinadan peered at the spot Forge was examining. She thought she saw a bit of movement.

A second later, the wildlife burst into squawking, scrambling motion all around them. A family of rabbits rushed across the trail in a close grouping, making for the distance with great, stammering hops. Birds exploded from every tree and bush in the vicinity, fleeing upward like ashes from a drenched fire. She heard the bleat of red deer and saw a bluish-green lizard leap from tree to tree on fans of skin under its arms.

Forge was off his horse and on the ground in one step, as smoothly as if his horse were still. In another instant, he unslung and strung his bow, nocking an arrow as he knelt behind a blackberry tangle along the trailside. His gray eyes had not left the bend in the trail behind them.

"Forge, what—"

But then she heard it, the thunder of hoofbeats. Several horses, driven hard, had panicked the animals as they crashed toward the spot on the trail where Trinadan's little convoy stood idle. She barely had time to turn her charger around.

And they were upon her. Three horses, swathed in yellow and blue, rounded the bend at speed, weapons held high. They saw her and pointed, the leader in half-plate and a high bucket helm as he spurred into a full-tilt gallop, taking the lead from his two companions. She saw his lance drop to fighting trim, its head growing enormously as it arrowed toward her at the speed of a maddened horse. The head was not the basket-cup of a jousting lance, but real iron, forged and worked to a cruel point.

* * * * *

Get "Keep of Glass" now at:
https://www.amazon.com/dp/B08RMVLWXV.

Find out more about Steven G. Johnson and "Keep of Glass" at:
https://chriskennedypublishing.com

* * * *

The following is an

Excerpt from Book One of The Milesian Accords:

A Reluctant Druid

Jon R. Osborne

Available Now from Blood Moon Press

eBook, Audio, and Paperback

Excerpt from "A Reluctant Druid:"

"Don't crank on it; you'll strip it."

Liam paused from trying to loosen the stubborn bolt holding the oil filter housing on his Yamaha motorcycle, looking for the source of the unsolicited advice. The voice was gruff, with an accent and cadence that made Liam think of the Swedish Chef from the Muppets. The garage door was open for air circulation, and two figures were standing in the driveway, illuminated by the setting sun. As they approached and stepped into the shadows of the house, Liam could see they were Pixel and a short, stout man with a greying beard that would do ZZ Top proud. The breeze blowing into the garage carried a hint of flowers.

Liam experienced a moment of double vision as he looked at the pair. Pixel's eyes took on the violet glow he thought he'd seen before, while her companion lost six inches in height, until he was only as tall as Pixel. What the short man lacked in height, he made up for in physique; he was built like a fireplug. He was packed into blue jeans and a biker's leather jacket, and goggles were perched over the bandana covering his salt and pepper hair. Leather biker boots crunched the gravel as he walked toward the garage. Pixel followed him, having traded her workout clothes for black jeans and a pink t-shirt that left her midriff exposed. A pair of sunglasses dangled from the neckline of her t-shirt.

"He's seeing through the glamour," the short, bearded man grumbled to Pixel, his bushy eyebrows furrowing.

"Well duh. We're on his home turf, and this is his place of power" Pixel replied nonchalantly. "He was pushing back against my glamour yesterday, and I'm not adding two hands to my height."

Liam set down the socket wrench and ran through the mental inventory of items in the garage that were weapons or could be used as them. The back half of the garage was a workshop, which included the results of his dabbling with blacksmithing and sword-crafting, so the list was considerable. But the most suitable were also the farthest away.

"Can I help you?" Liam stood and brushed off his jeans; a crowbar was three steps away. Where had they come from? Liam hadn't heard a car or motorcycle outside, and the house was a mile and a half outside of town.

"Ja, you can." The stout man stopped at the threshold of the garage. His steel-grey eyes flicked from Liam to the workbench and back. He held his hands out, palms down. The hands were larger than his and weren't strangers to hard work and possibly violence. "And there's no need to be unhospitable; we come as friends. My name is Einar, and you've already met Pixel."

"Hi, Liam." Pixel was as bubbly as yesterday. While she didn't seem to be making the same connection as Einar regarding the workbench, her eyes darted about the cluttered garage and the dim workshop behind it. "Wow, you have a lot of junk."

"What's this about?" Liam sidled a half step toward the workbench, regretting he hadn't kept up on his martial arts. He had three brown belts, a year of kendo, and some miscellaneous weapons training scattered over two decades but not much experience in the way of real fighting. He could probably hold his own in a brawl as long as his opponent didn't have serious skills. He suspected Einar was more than a Friday night brawler in the local watering hole. "Is she your daughter?"

Einar turned to the purple-haired girl, his caterpillar-like eyebrows gathering. "What did you do?"

"What? I only asked him a few questions and checked him out," Pixel protested, her hands going to her hips as she squared off with

Einar. "It's not as if I tried to jump his bones right there in the store or something."

"Look mister, if you think something untoward happened between me and your daughter –" Liam began.

"She's not my pocking daughter, and I don't give a troll's ass if you diddled her," Einar interrupted, his accent thickening with his agitation. He took a deep breath, his barrel chest heaving. "Now, will you hear me out without you trying to brain me with that tire iron you've been eyeing?"

"You said diddle." Pixel giggled.

"Can you be serious for five minutes, you pocking faerie?" Einar glowered, his leather jacket creaking as he crossed his arms.

"Remember 'dwarf,' you're here as an 'advisor.'" Pixel included air quotes with the last word, her eyes turning magenta. "The Nine Realms are only involved out of politeness."

"Politeness! If you pocking Tuatha and Tylwyth Teg hadn't folded up when the Milesians came at you, maybe we wouldn't be here to begin with!" Spittle accompanied Einar's protest. "Tylwyth? More like Toothless!"

"Like your jarls didn't roll over and show their bellies when the Avramites showed up with their One God and their gold!" Pixel rose up on her toes. "Your people took their god and took their gold and then attacked our ancestral lands!"

"Guys!" Liam had stepped over to the workbench but hadn't picked up the crowbar. "Are you playing one of those live-action role playing games or something? Because if you are, I'm calling my garage out of bounds. Take your LARP somewhere else."

"We've come a long way to speak to you," Einar replied, looking away from Pixel. "I'm from Asgard."

"Asgard? You mean like Thor and Odin? What kind of game are you playing?" Liam hadn't moved from the workbench, but he'd mapped in his mind the steps he'd need to take to reach a stout pole which would serve as a staff while he back-pedaled to his workshop, where a half-dozen half-finished sword prototypes rested. From where he stood, though, he didn't feel as threatened. He knew a bit about gamers because there were a fair number of them among the pagan community, and he'd absorbed bits and pieces of it. Maybe someone had pointed Liam out to Pixel as research about druids for one of these games—an over-enthusiastic player who wanted to more convincingly roleplay one.

"Gods I hate those pocking things," Einar grumbled, rubbing his forehead while Pixel stifled another giggle. "Look, can we sit down and talk to you? This is much more serious than some pocking games you folk play with your costumes and your toy weapons."

"This isn't a game, and we aren't hippies with New Age books and a need for self-validation." Pixel added. Her eyes had faded to a lavender color. "Liam, we need your help."

* * * * *

Get "A Reluctant Druid" at
https://www.amazon.com/dp/B07716V2RN.

Find out more about Jon R. Osborne and "A Reluctant Druid" at:
https://chriskennedypublishing.com/imprints-authors/jon-r-osborne/

* * * * *

Made in the USA
Columbia, SC
30 November 2021

50070157R00220